CHINA CONUNDRUM

Virginia Fortner

 FriesenPress

One Printers Way
Altona, MB R0G 0B0
Canada

www.friesenpress.com

ISBN
978-1-03-832622-5 (Hardcover)
978-1-03-832621-8 (Paperback)
978-1-03-832623-2 (eBook)

1. FICTION, DIVERSITY & MULTICULTURAL

Distributed to the trade by The Ingram Book Company

AUTHOR'S NOTES

While *China Conundrum* relied on my personal experience while teaching across China, it remains a work of fiction and does not depict persons or happenings encountered there. No character on either side of the earth represents a single living person. Places represent geography met between 2004–2009, which is when I spent my time there. China has developed since then: Today's XiAn has subways, unimaginable then, when only crude stone foundations had marked the first city's ancestral site. Also, I chose the spelling "XiAn," as it was, at that time, the most-often used of multiple spellings on English brochures and student writings for the university-city setting. Google, in present day, suggests "Xi'An" as the Western translation. Back then, English apostrophes and spaces were either used indiscriminately or ignored by most of my students.

Much has changed since the book's 2004–2006 setting. China has developed quickly, and the US has undergone many changes as well. I suspect that values, aspirations, and human feelings (discussed by Regina, Matt, and Joe) have evolved also, though more slowly. Imagination still thrives on both sides of the globe to enlarge individual horizons.

I offer a hearty *shei shei* for all persons I met in China. They taught me many life lessons. Particular US thanks goes to the patient, encouraging people here: the FriesenPress staff, Beta readers, computer guru children, and Hawaii writing groups. Any errors remain mine.

Virginia Fortner

CHINA 1 - NI HAO

Riding a crowded escalator toward baggage claim, I knew the reason I'd retired and flown to China. The teaching adventure of my life awaited.

A seething sea of black heads rolled, bucked, and parted as I stepped into XiAn airport's main floor. The air was filled with strange syllables. Were those two suit-and-tie types arguing, with their hands batting at the air like that? Then why were they laughing? It baffled me.

I stood there, suddenly struck by the idea that I was entirely alone. If Dad were still living, he would've watched intently and probably reproduced some of the foreign sounds whenever he told the story. Mom wouldn't have come in the first place. My ex wouldn't have either, even for an all-inclusive tour. And yet I'd said yes to a six-months' teaching contract with expectations of high adventure into the unknown. As I stood there in a jostling crowd, the adventure didn't exactly feel welcoming.

I waited for my bags on the outskirts of passengers from several flights, with many nationalities speaking languages I couldn't identify. Someone erupted from the tight crowd and bumped into me. A *Time* magazine fell from under his arm. I recognized the cover as countless feet trampled George W. Bush in his Uncle Sam suit.

I called out, "Sir!" The man didn't slow down, and I lost him among the other dark heads. No Eastern eyes met mine as they headed steadfastly toward boxes and bags on the conveyer.

I knew that, if not for my wanderlust, I could've been home, breathing clean Montana air, or at least, the cool air in my Kansas mother's air-conditioned apartment. That thought conjured up my last visit to Mom's, leaning out of her doorway with one last goodbye. I knew she'd thrilled at my chance to visit China and expected I'd be a good teacher. Yet she'd still shaken her finger at me and said, "Just don't bring home a Chinaman!" I'd swallowed my reprimand, as she usually ignored them anyway after she'd spoken some thoughtless remark that she didn't see as offensive. Mom giggled then as we exchanged a rare second hug. There were no hugs at XiAn's baggage claim, just folks hoisting luggage.

My neatly tagged bags didn't appear. I stifled a crazy impulse to laugh, wondering how my one cotton skirt and blouse would look when worn day after day in front of a college English-Second-Language class. I told myself, "Get a grip, Regina, and patience."

A couple of yogic breaths calmed me down. After all, I'd already weathered five continents, moved from Kansas to Montana, earned my PhD, and raised two great kids during thirty years of marriage. Now on the other side of divorce, I'd come to view it as a launching pad—when I thought of it at all anymore. Everything had always worked out for the best. So far anyway.

The suitcase-grabbing and box-dragging around me lost momentum. Most of the crowd exited. I stood next to an empty baggage carousel.

I saw no indication of how to report my missing bags. The Chinese symbols were impossible to decipher. In the US, I'd expect the airline to deliver my bags. In XiAn, I didn't yet know my address. Frustrated tears welled. Mom's words came to me as clearly as if she stood right next to me: *"Snap out of it, Regina!"*

Of course, crying did no good; I blinked twice, determined to think it through. I might not ever see my clothes and books again. No one among China's 1.3 billion people even acted friendly, let alone helpful. Why had I accepted this job? I could be home, cooking stew in my Montana cabin. My stomach growled an Amen.

So much for thinking through what I needed to do. I swallowed twice and refocused.

Another herd of escalator passengers split between my direction and a roped-off area. Behind that, folks held up calligraphy and printed names. A cardboard sign with a computer-generated "REJEENYA" caught my eye.

It resembled my name. I swiped my eyes with the back of my hand to look again. A girl held the sign in front of a clingy tee. I hurried over and ventured my memorized hello, *"Ni hao?"*

Her smile exposed her front teeth. "Welcome from Pei Hua University!" She offered a manicured hand, and we shook. Relief flooded my entire body. Loneliness fled.

"I'm Qian." She pointed to her nametag. Her name was pronounced "SHE-on" and sounded the same as this city's handle to my ears. How could a girl's name duplicate the huge Chinese city's? A city where they'd discovered the Terra Cotta Warriors? I made a mental note to inquire later and followed Qian in her stylish boots, designer jeans, and highlighted black hair.

A male with equally long black hair appeared with both my bags. We made for a black sedan, and my bags disappeared into the trunk. The young man didn't introduce himself. He just opened the back door and gestured me toward a faux-leather seat. I had no language to bargain, even if he'd been the Chinese mafia, so I just climbed in.

Seated in front, the young man drove skillfully to the highway, then down narrow streets with people and storefronts just about everywhere. He and Qian conversed nonstop in their baffling language.

I noticed that Qian actually smiled as she spoke her harsh syllables. Maybe how you said something was most of its meaning. I'd read that there were four different tones, but nothing remotely sounded like the few recorded phrases I'd memorized.

Our shortcut scattered squawking chickens, Mahjong-playing grandparents, and laughing children. Next came a ring road, resembling a Montana interstate, past cement-box buildings punctuated by an occasional steel spire. Trees shaded the six-lane boulevards. An earthy, human-waste odor came in through my open window, reminding me of the Kansas outhouse from my youth. A pump truck approached, spraying the trees. The smell increased. Rolling up my window didn't help, so I lowered it, determined to fully meet this introduction to China.

Forty-five minutes later, Qian pointed out Chinese characters atop a compound of sorts. "First Pei Hua campus!"

I exhaled the breath that I'd partially held since leaving the airport. A guard waved us through to the yellowing dormitory apartments.

Qian's "We go up now" introduced me to a dusty entryway with old mattresses and abandoned bike frames leaning against stairways. Our driver grabbed my bags, sprinted up cement stairs, double-timed it back down empty-handed, and sped away.

Two flights up, Qian unlocked two heavy metal doors. A small blue electric washer greeted me, placed next to a tiny bathroom. Faint fried-food smells hung in the air as we walked through a living room with a light blue fridge still on its packing base to the right. A galley kitchen waited beyond an open door. I told my inner self, *"No judgments, Regina, just keep your mind open."*

The fridge was color-coordinated with a baby-blue couch. Rusty metal legs held up cartoon-printed upholstery with Mickey and Minnie Mouse cavorting across the cushions. The couch was flanked by one dusty chair with a split seat.

We retraced our steps and entered a large bedroom. A desk blocked the doorway to a sunny drying room crisscrossed by clotheslines. The linoleum-tile floor sported a shadowed pattern, probably from a damp mop dragged through dust. I asked about cleaning supplies.

"Supermarket! I show you in three hours. Too hot now."

Hot? I looked down at my comfortable sweater and kept my thoughts to myself.

Qian exited. Both locks clicked behind her, and I collapsed under a child-sized blanket on my queen-sized bed. It was harder than firm, feeling more like a box spring. Pillow-topped mattresses back home had fit me perfectly. Regrets raced around in my brain and banished the idea of rest.

In impossible situations, activity usually proved a better option than tears, so I hopped up from the bed. Another inventory of my apartment found layers of grease in one skillet, a spattered hotplate, a meat cleaver, chopsticks in a jar, a rice cooker still in its box, a huge ceramic spoon, and exactly one plate, bowl, and cup. Detergent, sponges, and rubber gloves awaited on the dirty counter.

I opened a suitcase, sacrificed my National Parks tee, and baptized it in the sink with soapy water. After an hour on my hands and knees, the walking path from the kitchen to the bed shone with a predictable tile pattern. Nothing like a little elbow grease to regain enough control to feel better.

My doorbell chimed. Then a female voice shouted, "LuhJeenYa, we go now?"

CHINA 2 - SUPERMARKET VISIT

Luhgeenya? Luh-what?

Oh, it was that Chinese "L-for-R" thing I'd heard about. As Qian entered for the promised supermarket visit, my black-plastic phone rang.

The English I heard on the land line then made no sense to me: "Dr. Blakely, my name is Matt. I work for Homeland Security, and I've been trying to get hold of you."

Confused, I dropped the receiver and turned to Qian. "Someone just called."

She strode to my desk and picked up the phone. *"Wei?"* After a moment, she shrugged and returned the receiver to its cradle without another word.

"Maybe I will need my passport for the supermarket?" I suggested to her. She had taken it at the airport and had yet to return it.

"No need in China!" she announced, as she linked our arms and pulled me out the doors. We quickstepped the thirty minutes to a three-story supermarket, her stilettos clicking on the cement walkways. I felt like an addled grandmother who couldn't keep up on my own steam.

We checked her knock-off designer bag and my fanny pack and took escalators to different floors, grabbing hand soap, snacks, and boxed drinks. We went up for household items and down for pungent fish, dried fruits, and vegetables still clinging to soil from the fields. This was more like it. Immersion in a foreign country with titillating items to buy. I felt a smile forming.

Qian paid seventy yuan for her purchases, which I figured was around ten dollars in US currency. And as for my haul, I bought a stepstool, silverware for two, twin glasses, rice, blueberry jelly, washcloths, noodles, chicken, onions, unidentified greens, and a fish. Then she hailed a cab to carry our loot the mile home.

Thrusting packages inside the apartment, she then dragged me across the street past two empty tour-sized buses sporting gigantic yellow bows across their grills. "New buses! Tomorrow, you go this one to meet students, fifteen-to-seven a.m." I thought *Oh, she meant 6:45 in the morning,* as she added a breezy, "No need to worry. No lesson."

I was too tired and hungry to do anything but nod. We entered the cafeteria and ordered chicken, rice, and vegetables from three different areas.

Qian paid. "We get you ID card tomorrow. Maybe computer work in English tomorrow also. Now only in Chinese."

Just go with the flow, I told my weary self and took a bite.

Retracing our steps after lunch, we entered my apartment even as the telephone rang. Qian grabbed it, listened for a moment, and then smacked it down. I asked her who had called.

"Wrong number," she said.

Too tired to question this, I ushered her out the doors and turned both locks. I turned toward the bed, lay down, and fell asleep like a child clutching my blanket in an oversized crib.

Qian's "Tomorrow" indeed came quickly, with me barely functioning in my heavy, jetlagged fog. At first light, I stumbled to the bus's honored front seat.

CHINA 3 - SCHOOL VISIT

Early next morning, I clung to one flimsy rail between me and the driver in front as the Pei Hua bus barreled toward oncoming traffic, its horn blaring. A quick thought came as I gripped the metal rail, sans seatbelt: *This is certainly an adventure.* We passed three-wheeled blue flatbeds, rusty tractors, and bungy-corded bicycles. All these transported animals and furniture between darting pedestrians and roaring motorcycles. We met governmental limos and sedans of every make and model. On high alert, my foggy brain cleared as we covered the first block. Seated behind me, teachers conversed in lively Chinese. Most had given me an initial smile and returned my "Ni hao" as they'd entered the bus. I had only shrugged weakly, smiling at each one in turn.

We exited at the grassless Pei Hua campus, which was not a welcoming workplace, with its several three-story cement rectangles and semi-finished tile areas fringed by a cluster of make-shift shops.

Up two flights, in the New Campus English Office, I dispensed Rocky Mountain Bank pens to silent, smiling women and ventured greetings: "Ni hao!" I wondered if secretaries or instructors sat at each industrial-sized desk. They soon returned to chattering in Chinese and left me on my own. Next door, beyond an odorless dried tropical arrangement on a pedestal, I met the Education Dean. He breathed between each word and shook my hand. I thought that English certainly wasn't his first language, and maybe not even his second.

I found Classroom 216. It held church-pew rows of empty desks, and a raised podium below a dusty chalkboard, though there was no instructor's chair or desk. So far, there was no "meet your students" reception atmosphere. *Maybe no one will show up anyway.*

As if in answer to this thought, a few girls trickled in, covering giggling mouths and seating themselves in a clump near the door. I walked over and tried making some small talk. They turned in unison to a spokeswoman among them, who stood up. "Yes, Boss. We are English majors. Do you like China?"

"I like it very much. May I show you pictures of my country?"

They nodded eager heads. *They understand me!* I opened an album that I'd brought with me on this "You don't have to teach a lesson" day, just in case my introduction lagged. Then I turned to address the mostly blank faces before me. "In the United States—"

"Oh!" exclaimed one girl, jumping up with sudden understanding. "America! We like very much! John Denver, Michael Jackson, Madonna! Do you like Chinese food, Boss?"

It continued this way for some time as I answered their conversation-starter questions. I found myself doing an impromptu lesson on the use of "Boss" being a relic from the US past. I explained it as language once used by immigrants who'd sought to ingratiate themselves to the giver of a job. The room swelled to approximately seventy students, all attractive and long-haired late teens, each of them regarding me as a font of wisdom.

"We are so solly, bos— Dr. Luhjeenya… Solly, B—."

I silenced profuse apologies after five minutes. This "meet your students" wasn't what I'd envisioned, but it was certainly interesting. I made a mental note to do a pronunciation lesson and suggested we introduce ourselves using the letters in our names. Leo tried and failed to get Bill to read his, then spent more time saying "It's not very good" than he did reading his acrostic.

"Leo: L - Listener in English; E - entertaining fellow; O - Oldest in the class, twenty already."

Why didn't he call himself "Rio"? Doesn't the L/R thing work both ways? I had a lot to learn.

Applause followed. Leo was clearly class leader. LiPing covered her mouth with a shy hand when invited to share. Like Leo, she walked to the front, then read it out in a near-audible voice: "LiPing: L - lovely; I - interested in many things; P - Pretty; I - I spend lots of time with friends; N - nice, also naughty; G - Glad to meet my American teacher." She ducked her head to thunderous applause, and then a discordant bell shrilled.

Can I go home and rest now?

The students just sat there like polite statues.

CHINA 4 - UNINVITED VISITOR

Students remained, unmoving. I questioned them and found out that the first fifty-minute period ended with a fitness break. Strident female-voiced syllables punched the intercom airwaves then, but no one moved even a digit toward exercise. Girls chatted as boys exited to smoke. Students sought windows for cellphone reception. Leo erased the Chinese symbols and English acrostics on the board, telling me that he was the class monitor, which I welcomed.

Waiting for the tinny recorded commands to end was worse than trying to interact with my non-class students, so I escaped toward the odorous women's bathroom. The outhouse on my childhood KS farm hadn't smelled as bad, yet this one at least had blue-tiled floors. A bank of open, squat toilets featured one door latch and a pull string that activated a vigorous flushing flow. I exited as quickly as possible.

Upon my return, a swollen crowd sat expectantly. What to do? Another "getting to know you" exercise outlined itself in my head. Before I opened my mouth though, a vigorous man in a dark suit beamed his way up the aisle, offering me a handshake. "I am Joe. You teach in the pink! Make new friends but keep the old. One is silver and the other gold!"

I thought he must have listened at the door when I'd introduced myself earlier with an old Girl Scout song. Who was this man who spouted the same cliches my mother used to use? He reminded me of roosters back on the KS farm, demanding attention.

He swept a swath of black hair across his thinning pate. "All students want to meet you. You meet English majors twelve hours each week, lecture two hours in auditorium. All topics about America. A piece of cake!"

"What? We'll see about that. Right after I deal with the next fifty minutes!" Surely, I hadn't said that aloud, I thought, and turned toward the silent class.

He didn't react to my words. He just seated himself in back. Students shifted and made room, but their attention was on me. Momentary fear seized my divided thoughts. While one part of my brain outlined another activity to fill time until the next bell, the other part wondered if that man was only there to make note of any subversive statements against the Chinese government. I surely hadn't said anything politically offensive. But given my tendency to speak first and think later, I knew that the paranoid folks back home half-believed I'd end up in a Chinese prison.

There was no use going over what had already happened, so I focused on the class and ignored the slim man's piercing eyes from the back row. I asked Leo to serve as scribe while students brainstormed. He filled the board with creatively spelled topics that I promised to consider: "fashun, love in America, weddings, Elvis Presly, moovy stars, NBA." I offered "National Parks" or "a day in the life of an average family," but both ideas met mostly blank faces.

With thirty minutes remaining, my thoughts clutched desperately for any meaningful activity with which to engage them. I had students number off and move to conversation groups. That filled ten minutes with shuffling and giggling alone.

When it quieted down, I instructed them to "speak English only and come up with a group spokesperson to ask questions about me or my country." Chinese chatter followed. I reached in a pocket for my lucky bell, carried with me to every continent, and rang it. The din diminished.

"Remember to speak English. If you use Chinese, you get to sing us an English song." Nervous chatter picked up again. I wrote "Chinese" on the board, circled it, and then slashed it like a no-smoking symbol. All chatter stopped. Questions came then, and I did my best to answer.

"How old are you?" they asked.

I told them that my father would have answered "Old enough to know better." And they turned baffled faces to each other. Did this reflect their lack of humor, or was it some cultural difference about double meanings? I made another mental note to research this.

"Is it true that the Chinaman is lower than a Black man in America?"

I told them that I didn't see it that way and left it at that.

"How many people live with you?"

"I live alone."

This was met with expressions of amazement. Only the dark-suited man's expression showed no surprise as he listened intently, making me wonder again who he was.

"What is your favorite food/movie/song?" They added another fifteen "favorites." Then they began a round of "Do you like ___ in China?" Over and over, they filled in the blank and awaited my response. Eventually, I was saved by the university bell. Most students filed out, except for a cluster that formed around the podium to offer ideas. I wondered why they hadn't spoken up in their groups.

I focused on each differing speaker's comment:

"I want to learn about freedom in your country."

"My granny is a lot like you. I like you already."

"Is it true that people can own guns in America?"

"How do Americans view Chinese?"

I thanked each one and promised to answer their question when next we met. A few still lingered though, as did the cliché-spouting fellow from the back of the room.

I leaned closer to Leo and whispered, "Who was that man who visited today?"

"He's Dean Zhou of English Department. Important man, Dr. Blakely."

The dean, whose name was pronounced "Joe," strode forward then, flashed another smile, and thrust a crumpled list into my hand. Then he hurried out, still grinning, with several of my more attractive female students following close behind. As I ran for the teachers' bus, I wondered if I'd see him again.

While riding alone in the front seat across town to the old campus, I ignored the close calls in traffic and read Joe's crumpled note.

> *Dr. Blakely, Lecture 3-4:30 Tuesdays to all English majors. "American Social Life, Sports, American Problems, American Politics." Piece of cake for you. Begin next week, Room 315. Dr. Zhou*

Who did this man think I was? Wonder Woman? I had come to teach Spoken English, not political science. So far, Pei Hua wasn't anything like what had been promised in my contract. Then I remembered that my contract had been mostly written in Chinese, and that Qian had dismissed my questions about signing upon arrival. Instead, she had recited, in a sing-song voice,

"Contracts are to be broken," and placed it under a pile of papers, giving me a last glimpse of what looked to be my navy-blue passport, which had been taken from me at the airport.

CHINA 5 - ALREADY TIRED

I seethed silently for the rest of the week. *That English dean has his nerve. No one at home would assign anything like that list of topics!* I had no friends to ask what I should do. Could I outright refuse? My English credentials and teaching reputation were both impeccable, but sports? Politics? Who did he think he was dealing with? Some polymath? I could hold my own at a cocktail party on most subjects, but that was because I knew how to listen, not hold forth on facts and opinions. The more I thought of Joe's arrogance, the madder I got.

I approached Qian. "Dean Zhou gave me a list of lectures that were not part of my contract."

She gave her toothy smile and assured me that it would be a "piece of cake," and that I'd do "in the pink." She also said that Dr. Zhou had made an excellent request!

I bit my tongue and returned to my apartment. The phone rang then, breaking into my resentful thoughts. The plastic receiver felt light in my hand. "Hello? I mean, *Wei?*"

The voice that answered spoke in English without any trace of an accent. "Dr. Blakely? Do you have time to answer a few questions?" It sounded like some kid who spoke good English. I had no time for practical jokes, so I reacted with leftover frustration and slammed the thing back into its cradle. I'd had enough!

Scrubbing floors again brought me a little inner control. I was becoming used to Pei Hua University. I could adjust. I'd gotten the hang of turning in lesson plans for Spoken English sans textbook, buying produce at open-air markets, and halfway relaxing as the teachers' bus barreled across XiAn's traffic to the new campus. And the three teaching days weekly left me with unanticipated free time to search the internet for material for my mini lectures, whether I wanted to give them or not.

My attempt at Joe's commanded topic, American Sports, got students talking in halting English the next class period. Maybe it actually *was* a piece of cake, as per his clichéd prophesy. In twosomes, one student would role-play a superstar, like Ya Min, in present tense while a partner interviewed them in past tense.

LiPing's interview led things off: "What was the happiest moment of your life?"

"I am happy when I shoot baskets," Leo answered.

As interviews were presented, the class commented only on the use of tenses, not content. No one suspected that they knew more about basketball star Ya Min than their English professor did. Present tense won hands down, but they all began noticing different verb uses. By the last role-play of the class, more of them would raise confident hands to evaluate the verb tenses. It was an effective lesson.

Back in my apartment, Beijing TV aired a 9/11 piece. Homesickness niggled as I recognized only *"ni hao"* and numbers in the Mandarin commentary. It looked like NY's Ground Zero site, a clip from the Nicolas Cage movie about the Twin Towers, and a survey. English Graphs reported that American "anger" and "vengeance" had lessened, though it would "never return to normal," dropping from 70 percent to 30 percent.

The next day, I vegetated with *Gentle Ben* on TV. His grunts sounded the same in both languages and were somehow comforting. After writing in 120 student journals, I muted the sound and watched *Bridges of Madison County*. Good acting did not require words. I told myself that I was okay, just hungry for English on both the tube and the street.

Going to a deeper level, I admitted to feeling homesick after the 9/11 documentary. My mind conjured up sweat-stained President Bush in Sarasota, after a morning run with Secret Service, winking at school kids during a story-hour visit, then blinking in disbelief as a dark-suited man whispered in his ear. They'd hustled him onto a plane then. After asking, "Is Cheney alive?" he'd firmly insisted, "I'm coming back to Washington." I'd thought he'd showed decisive personal strength—unlike what TV clips had suggested during the Abu Ghraib tortures.

I had left the US disappointed in my country's political leadership. Trying to be fair, I credited my president with personable social skills, a nice wife, and a desire to prove himself to his father. I saw my country's saving grace as the opportunity to vote regularly for new leaders. That was what I told Chinese students when they asked about democracy. I felt proud to be an American, a feeling left unvoiced in my classrooms. I prided myself in keeping an objective exterior. I knew how to set boundaries and not get caught up in fads and fervor.

Musing, I moved toward my hotplate to heat water. Green tea could soothe my thoughts. My black plastic phone shrilled for the third time since I'd moved in. Maybe a Mandarin jabberer? Or a Chinese jokester with copy-cat English? Whomever it was would call again if it was important. There was no sign of answering machines at Pei Hua. I stretched out on my board-like mattress, feeling worn out, with little idea of what the next day might bring.

CHINA 6 - HOMELAND CALL

Sleep didn't come, so I relived a bedtime story, considering my previous weekend. SunYan Bo (commonly called Bobo) had called Friday night and commanded that I visit her home the next day and accompany her someplace after that. I'd scanned handwritten lists to match her number with any name I'd noted. Was she a teacher or student? Embarrassed because she obviously knew me, I'd said yes to an unknown adventure.

Saturday, I'd dressed for a weekend outing with jeans-clad teachers. Bobo had arrived in a party dress, and I'd recognized her as Pei Hua's English Office's youngest secretary. Her desk was next to an often-vacant one marked "Dean Zhou." I'd seen her take Chinese dictation from Joe. Bobo had surely heard the exchange when I'd asked if we could discuss his assignment to begin lectures on Everything American. She'd lowered her eyes as he'd told me matter-of-factly, "Already decided. One hundred and fifty students plan to hear your lecture. For you, a piece of cake!"

I'd left his office to spend every spare moment preparing lessons that I hoped would have some substance, and I had forgotten having met Joe's stenographer.

That Saturday, I'd left my apartment early to join her at the old campus gate. Then with Bobo in three-inch heels, she and I double-timed twenty blocks to her apartment to meet Xie, her husband of four months, warning me in advance that "He speaks poorly."

We unlocked doors flanked by lucky red wedding banners. Bobo sat me for a little rest on an orange couch with Donald Duck and Goofy dancing on the printed cushions. Their living room also held a small bookcase, a low square table, and four chairs. I stifled a smile at the cartoon characters under my thighs as a man entered from a back room and offered me a Western handshake.

"Tell Dr. Regina about your job, Xie," Bobo commanded.

"Sell tours," he boomed, then sat to await my next conversation starter.

I thought that, perhaps, he could help me with travel on October's week-off for National Day. So, Xie went and fetched me a catalog of tools his company offered, along with personal photo albums. It took me a moment to realize that he'd said that the he sold *Tools,* with an "L," not *tours,* with an "R." *So much for having Xie get me a tour to see the Terra Cotta Warriors.*

Xie and Bobo had pictures of travels from all around China, mostly by bus. I thought of telling them of my tenth childhood year, when our family had pulled a trailer house around twenty-six states, but decided it was too complicated for good conversation fare. They'd never believe I had read my textbooks and skipped a whole school year while we'd visited family and acquaintances and followed my parents' travel dreams. We had even crossed the Mexican and Canadian borders. I barely understood it myself, but my diary, written in my fourth-grade cursive, complete with wrong verb tenses, recorded every new destination with "Today, we seen The Grand Canyon" or "We seen a bear in Yellowstone Park."

In second-language English, Bobo asked if I'd visit her mountains-and-lakes hometown with them. Why not? And yet no time or plans were discussed. Maybe that was simple politeness?

I followed her to her tiny kitchen's sink and said, "Bobo, your husband is very nice."

"He's short."

Xie was stocky, obviously relished life, adored Bobo, and repeatedly said "Chinese people want love, not war." But short? At 5'2," I was a half-foot shorter than Xie. When no response to this came to mind, I asked if she could use some help.

Bobo rolled circles of dough, and I filled them with mince and chopped vegetables. We soon tore into them with chopsticks. Xie pulled his pantlegs up well above his plump, hairy knees as he finished off the platter of dumplings.

Another couple arrived. Bobo's pregnant friend took a little rest before we hailed a cab to Dayan Temple. We arrived with thousands of families, walking nature trails, climbing on metal folk art, and buying trinkets. Cameras clicked, and lines waited to flash Nixon's two-fingered victory sign beside Tang Dynasty bronzes.

Nicolai Rimsky-Korsakov's "Scheherazade" blared as fountains spouted the length of a football field. Black heads posed under umbrellas and lined the perimeter a dozen deep. Afterward came another little rest. I counted foreigners and found only four other non-Chinese persons in sight.

Bobo's friend patted her belly. "I want a girl, but my husband hopes for a boy. With One Child Policy, this is very important event." I asked about baby showers and learned that they occurred a month after the birth, usually at the family's home.

Xie asked me, "What do you have for supper?" He ignored my protest that I wasn't hungry, and we crowded onto a bus, paying the driver one yuan each, or around 12 cents US. Back at home, Bobo prepared pork and green beans, tofu and vegetables, and spicy pork and peppers. The meal started with porridge. They added sugar and a plastic spoon for me, and I noisily slurped down rice soup. It was delicious. Bobo explained why it was all cleaned up. "We have no refrigerator. Like your apartment." Xie pushed some scraps off the table in one motion, and then swept the floor.

Then Bobo brought dough and stuffing—chopped beef, salt, and leeks— for more dumplings. We all pitched in, pinching shell-shaped half-circles of dough for either steaming or boiling. Bobo gave us several dozen to freeze, plus leeks, soy sauce, and red vinegar for dipping. It had a mild flavor like rice-wine varieties I'd known only in fancy bottles.

Bobo remarked about dessert. "No apples. Maybe rice? It doesn't matter." Her pregnant friend stirred from the couch, then stretched as she announced, "We take you home now."

Heading back to the university gate by cab, I received Bobo's benediction, "A good day!" I overcame an urge to hug them both then, knowing that this would be seen as strange American excess.

With dumplings stashed in my fridge, I'd fallen asleep before I could relive all portions of the weekend. Sleep fled at the telephone's jangle. I fought my way upright and reached toward the phone, unwinding myself from the covers.

"This is the Office of Homeland Security. Regina Blakley?" The voice sounded like it belonged to the same native-English-speaking one I'd hung up on earlier. He had the best American accent I'd ever heard in China.

If this call was some sort of late-night prank, I didn't appreciate it. Someone was "lying as hard as glass," a phrase I'd heard in English when

Chinese people gossiped. It fit. This lie was as transparent as glass, albeit smoky glass, set up between the caller and me. I put the receiver down, and none too quietly either. Five minutes later, the phone shrilled again.

"Ni hao?" I almost barked this greeting. *Maybe I meant "Wei"?*

"Please don't hang up. This really is the Office of Homeland Security, Dr. Blakely. Would be so kind as to talk with me?" The kid did sound like a well-bred American, and he certainly knew how to plead.

CHINA 7 - SNITCH PROPOSITION

"Please don't hang up. I work for the Homeland Security Office, Dr. Blakely. Would you be so kind as to talk with me?"

"From where are you calling? I mean what city?" I asked, deciding to quiz him, half-expecting to hear him say *"Beijing."*

"Washington, DC."

Now, I had the prankster. I asked, "What country?" Chinese people never identified my country as "the United States," only as "America."

"Why, the United States, of course!" His answer was emphatic.

There arose in me then the same feeling of awe that I'd known as a new bride on my first visit to Washington, DC. I'd also felt it a second time on an historic vacation we'd taken when the kids were elementary school age. Senator Larry Winn himself had given us a tour and posed with our family on the steps of the Capitol. His assistant, Dick Bond, had snapped the picture, and we'd spoken about his parents, whom we knew from church back in Kansas. Some photo albums at home in the US held proof of that visit. In recent years, I'd returned to walk the Capitol's hallowed halls and stand in awe amidst the busts of history's icons whenever I attended educational conferences anywhere in the northeast.

Back in XiAn, I felt my breath speeding up as suspicion overtook my thoughts once again, and I started babbling. "I apologize. Perhaps you realize why I thought this was some kind of trick. It's not often I get calls like this." And then, like an afterthought, I said, "You said your name was Mike?"

His answer was immediate and emphatic. "I'm Matt, short for Matthew, Dr. Blakely! And I assure you this is no prank call. Could I send you an encrypted email to convince you?"

He'd passed the second test. I knew he'd said Matt earlier. Unfortunately, I didn't know how or even if encryption worked in China. "I'm sure that won't be necessary, Matt. Just indulge me this one request: Hang up and walk into the Hall of Columns and call me back."

In less than a quarter of an hour, my phone rang again. "Dr. Blakely? I'm in the Hall of Columns." Matt's tone was polite. I asked him to find Father Damien's statue.

After a few silent moments, Matt exclaimed, "Here he is! The dude in bronze, wearing a kind of cloak. Damien is next to a huge Hawaiian guy with a colorful cape. He has one hand held out. King Kam-may-a-ha?" Matt was clearly struggling to pronounce Kamehameha's name, but he was right on!

After having visited Molokai, where Father Damien had served lepers, and Hawaii's Big Island during Kamehameha I's birthday celebration, I could picture easily both statues. In my mind, I could see the painted yellow-and-red feathered cape over the shoulders of the fierce statue, which was draped with numerous thirty-foot leis each June. I'd been told that Hawaii had installed both statues in honor of its 1969 statehood.

"More proof needed, Matt. Can you find Jeanette Rankin and Dwight Eisenhower?" *Maybe he knows Hawaii history. We'll see how he does with Montana and Kansas.*

Matt said, "Dr. Blakely, this scavenger hunt is turning out to be fun! Here we go: Jeanette Rankin. She's been here a long time: It says 1985. I was only born in 1980."

I filled him in as his footsteps rang out on marble. "That was the year the statue was installed, Matt. Rankin was born in 1880; she was the first female congress person and the only lawmaker to vote against entering WWI in 1917. I played the role of Rankin in a community theatre drama just last year. Montanans are quite proud of her."

"Interesting, Dr. Blakely. But I can't seem to find Dwight Eisenhower. I swear I've walked past all one hundred columns." The sound of his footsteps paused then.

He's right so far! Preposterous as it sounds, this has to be my own government calling. I tried to reassure him. "We can stop this proof game now. You won't find Eisenhower there because he's under the rotunda, presented by Kansas just this last year. You passed my tests with flying colors. I can't tell you, Matt, what it means to me to revisit my country's capitol today. And I'm sure I'll remember your name now."

He dismissed this and continued as if my earlier silly requests had never even happened. "Not at all, Dr. Blakely. You were selected by the Advisor for Homeland Security, from the profiles of many expats, to enlighten us on cultural practices. Your identity will be kept confidential, as will whatever you might share. This could be important to foreign relations. It may help present and future Secretary of States prepare to meet with Chinese officials." He sounded like he had just read this from a script.

I shook my head. "Matt, I'm adjusting to an entirely new culture! Mostly living on overload as I set up an apartment, find my way around a huge city, and teach English. There's no time to gather research on foreign affairs. Besides, I have very little knowledge of the culture here."

"Why don't you let us judge that? You're in XiAn, right? At Pei Hua University? We're hoping to understand China's grass roots, to get a feel for what's below their official story. Your life experience there will be of help. Believe me."

"What is it that you want to know? Isn't there some kind of protocol?" *Is this even a legal request?*

Ignoring my second question, he asked, "Why don't we begin by your impressions upon first arriving in China?"

I told Matt about the airport's undulating sea of jet-black hair and the feeling that most Chinese people were arguing even while smiling at one another. I explained that I was only beginning to get used to the harsh tones that were a huge part of Chinese vocabulary.

I wondered if he was taking notes, as he wasn't asking any questions as I chattered on nervously, knowing that he'd called me from Washington.

On a chatter roll to Matt, I covered my limited TV news—all in unfathomable Chinese—and inability to Google many subjects, as well as the infuriating "Unable to access this webpage" notice I got when I tried to pull up information. I told Matt that I was e-mailing blogs in text format to my computer-guru daughter in Kansas to post for me. No blogs were allowed in China, a fact that my students did not seem to question. Never would they say that a site was blocked. I'd recommend an English website, and they would simply answer, "I cannot pull up that site, Regina."

Matt broke in. "They call you by your first name?"

"Being a Westerner, I gave them that option the first day. Some call me 'Blakely,' and I momentarily clench . . . the same way I would before reprimanding a disrespectful teen at home. Here, though, calling you by your last name is a sign of respect, not familiarity. And another thing: the last name is presented first, with no comma between it and the given name. It would be handy for phone books if XiAn had such things. They don't use addresses the way I expected either. People meet me at the campus gate to take me places. Destinations are found by landmarks—behind public garden, next to Dico, and the like. Of course, I can't read the few tile street signs beyond knowing a few number symbols."

"What's Dico?" Matt interrupted.

"It's sort of a Chinese version of Kentucky Fried Chicken with passable ice-cream sundaes; I'm told that downtown XiAn actually has KFC, but my students can't afford to eat there. One English major told the class his dream last week: to be able to afford a beautiful wife, a son, and a wonderful fried chicken meal at the Colonel's. The class nodded in affirmation as he spoke."

I prattled on, which brought an increasing flood of relief, simply in speaking English with someone who understood more than "How are you?" or whatever my students had memorized from their last lesson.

Then I remembered the questions I'd had on my first day at Pei Hua. "Matt, I've been asked by students if most Americans own guns. I answered that a few people I know own guns for hunting. Students kept asking the same question though. Last week, I told them that President Clinton signed the Violent Crime Control and Law Enforcement Act in 1994, banning assault weapons. Is that ban still in effect, Matt? I'm uncomfortable expressing personal views or opening that topic for discussion here. I sense it's not a settled issue in our democracy, a conflict that may even make international news someday. Do you have any words of wisdom for me?"

"Dr. Blakely, it sounds like your short answers are truthful. Leave it there."

I persisted. "It's been ten years since that law was passed. I heard it being debated again before I left for China. Can you enlighten me?"

"As I said, let's leave it there for now, Dr. Blakely."

I dropped it, too tired for discussion anyway. Before hanging up, I felt a need to clarify something else. "I've still got no idea how our talking on the phone will be helpful; surely Homeland Security and the Secretary of

State's Offices have volumes on cultural customs that outline far more than I'll encounter firsthand. Is a trip to China being planned soon?"

Matt came back with a diplomatic answer. "I'm sorry I can't answer that, but I know the Offices are grateful for your personal impressions. May I call you again?"

"Sure, I guess so. Anything for my country," I half-joked. This guy was a master of saying nothing. He'd make a good politician someday.

"Oh, Dr. Blakely, there is one more thing if you would be so kind?"

When he hesitated, I answered with a non-committal "Yes?"

"If you can attend a church, we'd be interested in your experiences."

"It so happens that I have plans for that this Sunday. It might not be appropriate to take notes though."

He kept his formal tone. "Thank you, Dr. Blakley. Good morn — Goodnight."

I hung up, knowing that Matt had momentarily forgotten that his morning was passing during my very present nighttime. What was I agreeing to do? To snitch on a church or on the entire country? Could I get in trouble if Pei Hua find out about either?

Too late to worry now, I thought. I had plans to get up early to go to church with Fu Lin. The week before, I'd asked English teachers if XiAn had any churches. They did, and they met on Sundays. But no one I asked had visited one. Finding an English-speaker willing to accompany me hadn't been easy either. I didn't want to miss the opportunity to experience something I hadn't expected to find in China. Would church be Protestant or Catholic? I decided to let the surreal phone experience rest and just "sleep on it" as my Kansas father used to tell me whenever my mind whirled.

CHINA 8 - CHURCH VISIT

Morning sunlight streamed in the drying room windows. Last night's strange exchange with Matt seemed far removed. I considered putting his phone call to rest by simply refusing to become a snitch. I had enough of a challenge already in adjusting to my Pei Hua job. On the other hand, I wasn't exactly sure how you said no to the State Department. And I'd kind of liked the polite young man who'd taken apparent delight in playing my game of proving himself.

I refocused on my bathroom-cum-shower, removing toothbrush and drying nylons, then firmly closing the rusty door. No chance this time of getting in trouble because of water going into the wrong places. My first shower had cascaded down on the closed commode, sending a river out the open door and flooding the entire living room.

Done right, it was an efficient system, cleaning the entire area with a quick brush of walls, sink, and toilet even while showering. Drying the mirror after I dried myself left us both spiffy.

I donned a modest blouse and skirt and dashed out to catch the morning bus west. Few people waited at the bus stop on Sunday, but workmen pushed carts and speared pieces of gutter trash just like they did on weekdays. A curious woman guessed where I was going, held up her Bible, and chattered rapid-fire Chinese as she clutched my arm the rest of the way. I recognized not a single word. Finally, she dropped my arm to point at a cross, perched high atop a white building, and then ran ahead to join her friends.

The church rocked with music while folks with Bibles and hymnbooks under their arms muscled into pews. Red ceiling banners, lanterns, balloons, and flowers made it a visual feast. It smelled of bodies, not incense.

Fu Lin, Business and English teacher, slipped into the entry beside me. All smiles, Fu Lin announced that she had found this place after I'd asked teachers on the bus if attending a church was possible. "This is first time I am inside," she whispered.

We squeezed into a back pew. No one even looked up.

I recognized "Rock of Ages" and sang along lustily, enjoying the twist of a minor key. The congregation underlined scripture as the minister mentioned Adam, Noah, Abraham, and down the Biblical line of heroes.

After two hours, Fu Lin finally whispered, "David's son! Let's go!" We slipped out, before the minister (speaking mostly in Chinese) could mention other Old Testament sinners who'd missed the mark.

A dark-suited man on the aisle glanced up, then quickly hunched over his Bible to resume his underlining. Something about his haircut reminded me of Dean Joe's comb-over. I dismissed the idea as silly though, knowing that Joe would have given me his usual wide grin, even in church.

I was not sorry to go, but I wondered if we'd acted impolitely. I asked Fu Lin why she'd wished to leave.

"I didn't like it," she said. "It wasn't organized!"

It had seemed quite organized to me. What I'd missed were any of the feelings I usually experienced in church back home. No candle lighting, no standing and sitting, no responses to prayers, and no suppressed giggles or cries of young children. My grandmother, who'd knelt at a Kansas altar every Sunday, would have felt like she was among heathens.

Fu Lin said, "Come to my home and eat moon cake," as we quickstepped several blocks, introducing me to a popular festival sweet that was filled with ground nuts and beans. A guard waved us through a gate, and we climbed to the top floor of a high-rise, where I met eight-year-old Anna and looked at photos with Fu Lin's engineer husband. He spoke no English, but he vigorously pointed out landmarks he'd visited all over the US. The language gap was stressful.

I narrowly escaped having lunch with them. And as I left, I realized that I needed to learn the polite way of refusing something that means "yes," and the other one that means "no." I'd already learned to refuse three times before accepting anything. But how did you refuse something for real? Walking home, I made a mental note to share this custom with Matt when (or if) he called again. I also rethought my babbling from the previous evening, which was not customary for me. I wished I'd asked him more about how

I'd been chosen and if there was some protocol for whatever he was asking me to do. As I hurried home twenty long blocks on busy streets, I decided that I'd simply gotten carried away upon hearing American English being spoken again. And that I wasn't quite ready to dismiss my interactions with him just yet.

Matt didn't call back that day, nor the next. Emailing my kids, I decided not to mention anything about his phone call, although I'd seen no evidence, so far, of anyone monitoring (or even caring about) what I wrote. Settling in, I started bang aingway at the plastic keyboard:

To: AtHomeGroup@ox.net

Friends and family,

The adventure continues. A Chinese teacher who'd never been to church took me to one today. Then she fed me mooncakes in her upper-floor abode, the second home I've visited in XiAn. Monday's classes seemed interminable—40 sophomores, stomachs growling before lunch, reading journal entries in halting English.

Last Tuesday, 38 voices greeted me in unison:

"Teacher's Day is fine because of you. The sky is blue because of you.

Look! Flowers are lovely because of you. And we bloom because of you.

My teacher, diligent gardener. Your bounty is beyond my speaking, but though my mouth be dumb, my heart shall thank you."

Wang Rui, the author, conducted as the class stood and recited those flowery words. He handed me a carved Buddha bracelet with calligraphy on each bead. Quite a moment!

Freshmen arrived this week to do 10-day mandatory military training on the new campus. Unison voices drifted up from fatigue-clad companies below our classroom windows. Rain or shine, trainees marched in step or sat on self-carried camp stools to listen.

I'm told that next August, Peace Mission 2005 starts China-Russia military exercises in Shandong.

I did my Jr-Sr lecture on American Geography. 200 students showed up, and I stood with a chalkboard and microphone. Rather than telling me no, the dean says he'll take the idea of an overhead projector to his faculty.

I'm still waiting for my library card, but a secretary checked out nine books for me. Madame Bovary seemed the best of the English lot. I'd already finished (and loaned to English faculty) the books I brought from the US. It's my greatest hunger: good recreational reading. I'm well fed otherwise: lovely cuisine of fish, rice, noodles, meat, tofu, veggies, and milk bought on the street. Papaya and watermelon wait in my fridge.

Let me know if you get one copy of this or many; the bugs aren't all out of my computer. I long to hear about the happenings in your lives and in my country, especially about Hurricane Katrina's devastation. Limited English info here. Can't read Chinese.

Love, Regina

The next day, I lugged book satchels from the university bus across the freshman-campus street under a rare blue sky with little smog. That grateful moment propelled me up my dingy cement stairs. As I dug for my keys on their wadded string, I heard my phone being muffled behind both steel doors. I caught it on the fourth ring, thinking that the relic was probably a lonely survivor of China's cellphone age. Out of breath, I shouted into the receiver, *"Ni hao?"*

"Dr. Blakely? I hope this isn't an inconvenient time. This is Matt, from the Homeland Security Advisor's Office. How are you?"

"I'm fine, Matt," I panted, trying to catch my breath. "Just home from teaching. "And you should know that no one here uses 'How are you?' So, your American greeting almost sounds strange. I'm used to something more along the lines of 'Have you eaten rice yet?'"

CHINA 9 - DEPARTMENT HEAD

Matt sounded like he was reading from a list of points he needed to touch upon: "I wanted to thank you for our phone conversation; the Director hopes that your observations will help prepare his successor for the job in Asia. Next, I'm to ask what Chinese young people think about the US. Do you mind sharing?"

Their thoughts about the US? Forgetting about my tussle with the many refusals I'd received since arriving in Asia, I quickly decided that my Chinese contemporaries were not spying on me, any more than they were spying on me in the states, but that if either government *was* spying, honesty would probably be the best policy. And who knows? Perhaps one teacher's curiosity about this culture really could help improve understanding between our two countries in some way. I took up the challenge.

"Matt, I already told you about their gun questions. But ones about Black people also often arise here."

I could hear Matt's swelling excitement in his response: "My favorite Advisor to Homeland Security Office is a person of color. She's director of Stanford Institute. Feel free to tell them about Dr. Rice. She's the real deal in Washington, I think!"

"Thank you, Matt. That may silence any further questions." I felt unexpected gratitude.

Warmed up now, I told Matt how I'd organized my United States Geography lecture around "This Land Is Your Land" and a chalk-drawn map. "Pei Hua's juniors and seniors heard a large dose of information about the ecology of the Dust Bowl and the importance of trees in developing landscapes. The young people relayed to me details of huge clearcut areas and some replanting here. They'd never heard of Woody Guthrie and were amazed when I said that his music is remembered just as Michael Jackson's was."

Matt broke in then, seemingly still focused on his list: "What about the administrators? What supervision do they give you?"

"I frequently see faces above black jackets at my classroom door's window. When I motion them to come in, they quickly duck out of sight. I don't recognize them; they may be supervisors."

I didn't mention Joe, Dr. Zhou. Is he a supervisor? I remembered Miss Zhang then. "Oh, I have an English department head. I'd conveniently blocked her from my mind."

"Blocked her from your mind?" He sounded puzzled.

"Yes, I'd noticed her in my first hour-long class, sitting mid-room, and thought little of it. Non-students frequently drop in to learn my foreign methods. As a PR move, I welcome them, although their presence is sometimes distracting."

I sighed, then continued. "The morning she visited, the lesson was about Time zones. I did an English mini-lecture involving having the lights-off, with a basketball Earth marked with a chalked Universal Date Line, and a flashlight for the sun. It was fifth grade science, at best. We taped a cut-out figure at approximately where Beijing would be and wrote the date on the chalkboard, agreeing after a half-twirl that it was now night in Beijing, while it was full sun in New York, a place most recognized by most Chinese. Students giggled, thinking of it being night in the Motherland while America had daytime."

I smiled as I remembered the lesson. "Matt, picture this: I assigned English discussion and floated around the room to get enough feedback to ensure that the groups were with me, if only vaguely, except for Miss Zhang's group, who were preparing for a vote."

"Supervisor Zhang's an influential character, isn't she? What happened next?"

"She shouted, 'A vote: The Chinese way or the American way?' I listened. Consensus was unanimous that the Motherland's vast expanse, without time zones, was definitely the better way for the world to go. While I waited with my mouth open, Leo, who had twirled our basketball-Earth, stood up to ask a question. Miss Zhang interrupted him, commanding a girl to be the next participant!"

I heard Matt's intake of breath, so I plunged ahead. "Another boy stood up, but Miss Zhang pushed a blushing coed to her feet and yelled at her to speak English! The girl mumbled something, sat back down, and put her head down. Then the bell saved us."

Matt almost cackled. "Some supervision! What else?"

"Oh there's lots more. Miss Zhang walked me to her office for a little rest, telling me, 'Your topic isn't of interest. Students want to learn about how to make friends, love, and life in America.' I told her the topics had been suggested by Dean Zhou for Dean Liu. She whipped out her cellphone and called Dean Zhou, and a shouting match ensued, after which she instantly dropped that criticism."

"It sounds like some of my college professors. They'd lecture, and I'd challenge. If I cited a source, they would just change the subject."

He sounds like those bright students whom I enjoy most. "From the sound of your voice, Matt, I'm guessing Miss Zhang's a little past your age."

"I'll be twenty-six next week!" he said defiantly.

His age declaration took me out of Miss Zhang's reflections for a moment, as Hazy questions began to form. "Matt, I'm wondering why you chose a sixty-something like me to report on life in China. And shouldn't there be some sort of document I have to swear to? Or something like that?"

"I didn't choose you, Dr. Blakely, but I'm glad you are the one that was chosen. Nothing needs to be signed. Now, let's get back to Miss Zhang. What happened after she called the dean?"

I sighed loudly so that he could hear it on his end. "She stuck with me like glue until we got to the bus, pointing out an Advanced-English girl and insisting, 'He is an excellent speaker!' As this was referring to a girl, this was a bit confusing, but then I remembered that Chinese uses no gender pronouns, so her confusion wasn't surprising. It's a common mistake among my students."

"That's helpful information, Dr. Blakely. I'm writing it down."

"Oh, and here's another supervisory technique, Matt. Miss Zhang took me to dinner, changed tables three times amidst smokers and floor-moppers, and ordered vegetarian dishes when I told her that I avoided pork. I would have preferred placing my own tofu, mushrooms, and ginger on my rice, rather than her depositing choice morsels on my plate with her used chopsticks, but such is common too."

Matt groaned. And I went on.

"Miss Zhang offered me a Chinese lesson and told me I was a natural. I managed to mimic her tones, but I didn't understand any of it. When the soup arrived, I choked down a spoonful, and she told me that this was 'traditional Chinese flavor. You must get used to it!'"

"Oh Dr. Blakely, that's too funny!" Matt said, seemingly amused by my mimicry as he pictured the scene.

I smiled and continued. "As I downed my soup, Miss Zhang told me, 'XiAn walls date from 1568. Fourteen kilometers of it is set to be repaired in 2010.' I noticed that she used the same singsong cadence that I encouraged my Spoken English students to abandon. I did wonder about how Xian's past, or her own, related to her rise to the position of English supervisor. Luckily, my mouth was too full of what I was trying valiantly to swallow to ask because I remembered then that asking such questions is not part of Chinese culture. So, I just closed my mouth and left the rest of my soup uneaten."

"Go on, Doctor." Matt was still chuckling.

"Maybe you'd like to hear about diplomacy with superiors, Matt? During our last meeting, Miss Zhang asked me, 'What do you think of 'Rainkid' as a name?'"

"Surely, that wasn't her English name, Dr. Blakely!"

"I'm afraid it was! I quickly remarked about the misty nature of a mural on the restaurant wall. We agreed that people need water, mountains, and some quiet time to think. Somehow, that seemed to satisfy my department head's question about her chosen English name."

This account was getting long, but I was on a roll and enjoying his amusement. "Miss Zhang walked me back to my apartment, inspected it, and pronounced each room to be 'Simple!' Then she told me that she had a roommate two dorms over, and that she took laundry home to her sister and widowed mother on weekends. Then she said that she hoped to cook for me soon at her boyfriend's place. I began thinking how unfair my two rooms-plus-washer, for one person, must seem to a department head like her. Then she surprised me."

I shook my head in fond recollection. "Matt, she said, 'The teachers and I talk about how young you are for your age and how kind and gentle you are. We admire you very much. Could I continue to observe you teach?"

CHINA 10 - HOME CONNECTIONS

My telephone line crackled as Matt exclaimed, "I didn't expect that, Dr. Blakely!"

"Neither did I, but Miss Zhang seemed genuine in her request to observe my teaching. And so, I had to say, 'Of course.'"

"Of course," Matt echoed. "Go on."

I nodded and continued. "Still, I couldn't resist asking about her telling me to change my lecture topics. And she gave me a tightlipped reply: 'Dean Zhou said he's satisfied with your work.'"

"Score one for your team, Dr. Blakely!" Matt shouted triumphantly, and I pictured him pumping a fist in the air.

Rather than celebrating that point, I continued my phone story. "You probably can guess, but I continued hearing from her that 'students want to know about love and making friends in America.'"

Matt giggled. "You sure know how to bring a guy down, Dr. Blakely. What's next?"

I thought for a long moment before I could come up with anything more to add. "Okay, well, I knew that Chinese express their regret three times before letting guests go, but I demurred only slightly as I walked Miss Zhang back to my door. Outside, mist was diffusing the streetlight, and my sinuses blocked almost immediately, making my head ache as she walked away."

"Oh man, I couldn't deal with that woman, Dr. Blakely, even in perfect weather."

I had more information for him. "Speaking of weather, one thing more, Matt, about pollution, at least in XiAn. Overnight, it can change from street cleaners' carts being filled under sunny skies to air so bad that one only has a single block of visibility. I cover my nose with a handkerchief when a bus driver lights up under his No Smoking sign or a truck spews out black exhaust. Chinese wear gauze masks on the street. Tell visiting diplomats to stock up on white hankies for XiAn."

"I'll do that."

I still didn't feel finished with the conversation. "Matt, I'm wondering why you asked me about the churches here in our last conversation. I actually did visit a church, but you haven't mentioned it today."

There was sudden silence on his end. Finally, he said, "Not right now. Maybe another time. We've had other things happening on our side of the globe."

Is he trying to be mysterious? I pushed on. Two could play the mystery game.

"I'm missing news from home, Matt, wondering how the Hurricane Katrina cleanup is going. I'm sad over the passing of Chief Justice Renquist and Rosa Parks. I've heard nothing here about the new Department of Homeland Security. Can you tell me if coordinating intelligence between that department and the Secretary of State's office is working out?"

Matt cleared his throat. If he'd been riding a bicycle, I would have sworn that he was back-pedaling, even as he swerved: "Oh, I almost forgot! One thing I wanted to know, Dr. Blakely, was if you'd heard of the discovery of a tenth planet?"

"No!" I said, curiosity sweeping me past our previous discussion. "What's it called? Where is it located?"

"It's called Eris! And it's beyond Pluto, whose status has been downgraded now to a dwarf planet." Almost without giving me a chance to let this news settle in, he pressed on. "Dr. Blakely, I'm glad we talked today, and that I had something that *I* could tell *you!* But I must run now." With that, the line went abruptly dead.

What?

Too bad I'd resolved not to tell anybody about Matt's mysterious calls. With another sigh, I decided to email my kids, who could recognize when their mom was close to losing patience better than anyone. Maybe I'd even tell them further stories about Miss Zhang:

kids@global.net

Your mom seems to have hit her stride. My roller-coaster sinus blockage evened out as Yoshiko (downstairs teacher from Kyoto) and I went to XiAn History Museum Saturday. Two floors of anthropological exhibits from thirteen dynasties moved us toward bartering over visiting art exhibits. Yoshiko offered 2/3 his price. They agreed on ½ her first amount. I now have a traditional style, ceiling-high, rearing horse in rice paper and silk on my wall.

Sunday, we ventured into a third sunshiny day to XingQingJong Park, thinking it was the zoo stop. The park was a lucky find with its green area canals, children steering cars away from fountain sprays, trails, willows, bridges, and stepping-stones. Who needed a zoo? We watched a lively ping-pong match. A Chinese man, teeth flashing as he practiced his English, informed us that we were "on the palace grounds of an emperor's mistress—like Napoleon and Josephine."

Last Wednesday at work, department head Miss Zhang gave me Jr-Sr lecture handouts. She insisted I "have a little rest," while she lowered a screen over my posted map, unplugged the CD player (pre-set to play the fourth song), gathered up maps already placed on the student desks, and introduced my English class in Chinese. The class never got going—only polite student-participation using memorized phrases. At break time, Zhang hustled me off for another little rest. I drank hot water and breathed deeply behind closed doors. You can guess that there won't be any co-teaching with her in my classes.

Dean Zhou (Joe) saved me by dropping by with an invitation to go for dumplings after my lecture. We walked past a colorful market to a quiet street shop. I got my first taste of baijiu and plan to make it my last. It's a cross between kerosene and firewater. Joe happily finished mine. He suggested we meet next week to try XiAn's various widths of noodles. He's my boss, and his wife doesn't like dinners out. Our next meeting will discuss the merits of "CommUnism" (they emphasize the "u" syllable) vs. Democracy, a popular topic here.

Back to last Wednesday's happy ending: Miss Zhang walked me back to the lecture hall, gave another lengthy Chinese introduction, and walked out. My handpicked students sat ready. One read a paragraph as Sacagawea. Another was Martin Luther King as we worked through America's timeline. The rest of the hour zipped past. Groups discussed historical figures, whose names had been taped under random chairs. The microphone got a workout as we heard at least three sentences on each of them from George Washington on down to Nixon. Never a predictable moment here in XiAn! I miss KS skies, MT mountains, and CA flowers. Love, Mom

I signed off with a satisfied feeling that allowed even thoughts of Miss Zhang to do no more than make me smile. Maybe tomorrow's "body check" wouldn't get under my skin either.

CHINA 11 - BODY CHECK

Heading for an early morning walk in less-than-usual smog, I locked my apartment. Few people walked in XiAn; they seemed to prefer group exercise in parks. I could meander and think. I knew I'd have something to share about China's medical world the next time Matt called. My natural curiosity and restless mind seldom took a vacation from analysis, and with him, I had someone willing to listen, or maybe even enter a discussion in English.

I had begun considering East-West medicine, and along with that, genetic codes and human suffering. Surely, Matt had thoughts about scientists editing embryos on both sides of the globe. Maybe my ESL classes had thoughts on that issue. I thought that topic could probably even get them into preparation for English debate by the semester's end.

My footsteps ticked off the pros: curing genetic diseases, making us smarter, protecting against viruses. I whirled around and stepped backwards for the cons: how to oversee it, whether gene-editing is warranted, and accidental deletions of DNA sections. My thoughts hadn't even leaned toward funding and political implications yet.

That reminded me of politics back home. Apologizing for being busy and cutting off some of our conversations abruptly due to office busyness, Matt had confirmed that Condoleezza Rice was the nominee for the new Secretary of State. Because I knew she was interested in AIDS relief, I found hope in the appointment.

My thoughts returned closer to XiAn and my walk with the topic of DNA. I knew that the Chinese government's 2003 regulation prohibited changing human genomes. Yet I suspected that, given my students' desire for innovation, one might become a doctor who treated embryos one day. Perhaps it would happen to avoid HIV infection, something not yet officially recognized as even existing in China.

I turned my feet toward home as my imagination ran rampant: What if my precocious student-cum-future doctor split an embryo, producing twins? One might be immune to HIV while the other became disabled through improper gene splicing. I corralled my racing thoughts, deciding to plan a mini lecture about the need for ongoing debate about health issues.

Walking inside my apartment and relocking my doors, my own recent health experience played out like a movie in my head. The day before, I had returned from my "Body Check," which was mandatory for all people (except tourists) entering China. If not for my Pei Hua office angel, Qian, taking me by cab, I'd have not made it through the International Health Center maze.

The open-air lobby had felt cold after two days of rain. Fresh air helped dispel the men's cigarettes. Qian disappeared, carrying copies of my complete US physical. I waited. An emaciated woman and a white-jacketed doctor exchanged words in Chinese. The doctor turned away as Qian returned. He slung a loud statement over his shoulder to the sick woman, and her head dropped lower with each word he spoke. I turned to my companion. "Qian, what did he tell her?"

"He told her, 'Prepare to die. Diarrhea and severe dehydration. No cure! Even the Dowager Empress Tzu Hsi died from it.'"

Qian departed again, and I was left to contemplate my fate. I decided I'd cooperate and hope to remain a healthy specimen.

Fifteen minutes later, Qian said, "The US physical was refused because they were copies. I must pay for Body Check." Returning, she also produced my navy-blue passport without explanation and pasted passport pictures to some Chinese forms that she also mysteriously pulled from her bag. She asked if I'd had a page list of diseases. I truthfully answered, "No, no…" I kept telling my culture-shocked self to answer only what was asked. *Don't even hint at an ache or pain.* It seemed very strange. Beyond foreign. *Has my passport simply remained on her desk all this time? I'll quiz her about it all when the physical exam is over.*

I looked around at four young Turks who were struggling with forms at our long table. They discussed their hopes to study Chinese in XiAn and teach English to children on the side. I remembered that my contract forbade teaching anywhere but at Pei Hua. A tall Moroccan professor had a Chinese translator in tow. Soon, we all arrived at the first room in a clump without lines.

A white-coated attendant said, "Have a little rest." I told him he needed the chair more than I did. He laughed. "Many peoples today!"

A woman beckoned, drew blood with a clean needle, and waved me upstairs. I turned the soiled pillow over and lay down for some sort of X-ray. How much radiation would I absorb? Scooting off the bed afterwards, while pulling down my sweater, I dodged the Turks and Moroccan as a crowd flocked in. Across the hall, I lay down behind a low screen. A nurse pushed my sweater up around my neck and my slacks down to my naval, attached electrodes, and read her machine. My eyes met the Moroccan's dark ones above the screen before he quickly looked away. Taking "a little rest" left me to observe his identical table experience, except he had no bra pushed up to his throat.

I told myself to just breathe as I walked toward the hall, wondering if people like Joe and other Pei Hua personnel had to undergo this treatment yearly, whenever they travelled, or never.

Two doors down, a nurse conducted a color-blindness test with a chart remembered from elementary school. I stepped on some scales, and she immediately stamped my papers six times before sending me downstairs for more X-rays. Evidently, my first X-ray hadn't done the trick.

I'd read horror stories of Chinese X-ray machines. Could I refuse? Perhaps for religious reasons? Then I remembered Qian's saying, "Maybe ten stops in all." Perhaps I'd need to reserve a religion-based refusal for a gynecology check.

The X-ray attendant had all of his extremities and spoke English, which was a small comfort. I stripped to the waist behind a half curtain and faced a competent-looking machine. Men crowded at the door, so I set a record for getting dressed again once it was done.

"All done!" Qian announced. My new best Moroccan friend asked for my e-mail address while waiting for our caretakers to retrieve passports outside the Visa Office. He was obsessing about his visa expiring in a week when it dawned on me that no one would be working the following week because of National Day.

Qian came out empty-handed. "You get your passport back in one week."

Small chance, I thought, too tired to manipulate an ESL inquiry as to where it had been for the last several weeks.

CHINA 12 - NOODLE WIDTHS

Rather than fume about my passport still being out of my hands, I willed my thoughts to turn to the noodle shop Joe had chosen for our second scheduled meeting. He and I walked straight to the eatery after exiting the Pei Hua bus in drizzly weather, his open four-buckle boots sloshing water on my Tevas. I shook off rain while Joe ordered four widths of noodles from racks near the kitchen.

We hung raincoats on the back of our plastic chairs as steamy bowls of broth arrived. All four kinds of noodles swam up to tantalize my taste buds.

"The slimmer ones are tastiest," I told Joe, as I maneuvered one toward my mouth with my chopsticks.

"I favor the wide ones," Joe announced, getting half a four-incher in his mouth. I told him about my mom's pride in being able to read a newspaper through her thin noodles, which she dried overnight on the kitchen table before holiday meals. I'd never dreamed that story would delight anyone from another culture when I'd rolled my eyes at it back on the Kansas farm.

I found myself slurping in unison with the tables of diners on both sides of us. Making noise to show appreciation was a lot more fun than chewing like a prim American. The rain made a cozy curtain across the shop's open street front, and I felt my shoulders relax.

From discussing noodles, Joe moved on to ask why I boiled water, even when it came in sealed bottles. His eyes judged and questioned this choice as he told me, "China water is good. I'm never sick. I drank it all my life."

I could have mentioned that I had seen the water shops use garden hoses to fill bottles that were delivered by muscled men to hot/cold drink machines like the ones in Education Building. Not wanting to argue, I pled a delicate stomach.

"I'm not used to the minerals in China's water, Joe. My stomach gets upset."

Joe gallantly promised, "I will let you boil the water a second time for your tea. I now understand, Luh— Regina."

You would have thought Joe was a knight fighting to lessen his damsel's distress. I found myself amused, no longer feeling quite so alone in XiAn. It felt good to know he was providing safe hot tea on morning breaks. As a half-curly renegade lock of black hair fell over one of his eyes, he grinned while I ordered another bowl of his choice: wide noodles. It was a good meal in welcome company.

Memories of Joe and noodles drifted away once I was sitting safely at home in my apartment, and my thoughts wandered back to Qian herding me toward a taxi back home after the Body Check. Behind my locked doors, I drank twice-boiled water and thought that, if I knew I had Matt's secure e-mail, I would send him details of my hospital experience. It would be helpful if the proposed Secretary of State, or any traveler, were to fall ill in China. I might start a dialog with Matt about US healthcare costs and/or my vague feelings that pharmaceutical companies would one day go bust from too much greedy control. Time would tell, and my intuitive opinions surely were not what Matt wanted anyway. Having no e-mail address for him, I wrote family instead, leaving out both noodle widths and the Body Check doctor's account of the Dowager Empress's diarrhea and dehydration:

kids@global.net

Dear Kids,

Quite a week! Mary (teaching in Kunming) has a birthday next weekend. I've no pay, plane ticket, or passport to go celebrate. Caregiver Qian's excuses vary from her having a headache to the fact that "Police will have it until Saturday." She mysteriously got it back for a Chinese medical checkup (I passed!), and then immediately relinquished it again. Don't be worried; it seems that's the way they do things here. As it is, I'll soon have a week off and no place to go beyond returning to Wild Goose Pagoda.

Spring, a worker in the art gallery at Wild Goose, said that his boss would "teach me traditional Chinese painting." We're bartering. I taught his young daughter an English lesson. Their Mercedes brought me home, sitting on heated leather seats. We passed one wrecked taxi and another crumpled bicycle-fender confrontation. My finished bamboo painting now hangs on the wall. (It's simple-looking but difficult to do—no focal point, and exacting techniques, especially hard when your teacher repeats his one English word: "No! NO!")

Weekly lectures continue, surprising fun. While making an American History timeline, I realized that our most significant events all equal wars. Is that true of every country? I hope not.

Next week features "Will you go out with me?" dialogues with Oral English students acting out conversations between George and Martha Washington, John and Abigail Adams, Jack and Jackie Kennedy, Charles and Anne Lindberg, Bill and Hillary Clinton, Ronnie and Nancy Reagan, and John Wayne and his horse. The duos sign in on a paper heart, complete with an arrow. Discussions will include China's "Lovers Day." It's not on February 14th. Department head Miss Zhang wanted dating and love? Well, she's getting it in Soap Opera 101, with a historical twist. I'm in good spirits, but with little certainty as to what happens next here.

Love, Mom

CHINA 13 - BOMBS, BREASTS, AND BEAUTY

Feeling I still had more to say, I wrote a second email to everyone who'd asked to be included in XiAn catch-ups:

AtHomeGroup@ox.net

Dear US Friends and Family,

Several of your emails wanted to know what Chinese people thought about rumors of North Korea and missile testing. Nothing recognizable about North Korea on Beijing TV, so I visited both XiAn municipal and college libraries. English rooms were closed, though their Chinese portions buzzed with language I can't speak.

Will, a Chinese English teacher who talks with me on van rides across XiAn, was quite vocal on the topic: "Government doesn't like it, but friends with Korea. Won't take away food or money. Very dangerous for China and America. Need to take a strong stand!"

He glanced at our driver, who kept his eyes straight ahead. We discussed, in English, North Korea's mushroom clouds, seen as evidence of testing missiles.

Other teachers knew about Korea, but they preferred discussing the need for hot tea water, asking about my National Day plans, offering moon cakes, or getting my opinion about grammar examples. Here, it's extremely important to expound on only one right answer.

Oral English sophomores hadn't a clue that anything had or might happen in North Korea. A sprinkling of upperclassmen knew about the rumor of expected testing. One boy boomed, "Strongly disapprove!"

So that's your answer, friends and family. Enjoy your newspaper and TV coverage, even the talking-head debates about official pronouncements.

Zai jian (Bye, Until later), Regina

Exiting email, I again wondered what kind of flurry this international development had stirred in the Secretary of State and Homeland Securities Advisor's offices. As if summoned, the phone rang. Matt's voice was clear on the line:

"Dr. Blakely, you are aware that North Korea has been testing missiles for some time now? It began in the seventies, and ramped up in the nineties, and is expected to do so soon again."

"Hello to you too, Matt. In answer to your question, I'm aware, mostly because of e-mails from home. I was able to access only one article from a US friend's email link; my online attempts to find information here respond with 'site no longer available' messages."

I read him my email to folks back home, adding, "I found an old English *China Daily*, regarding Korea's withdrawal from the 2003 Non-Proliferation Treaty. It stated that the government disapproves of Korea's testing and will not withdraw friendship or support. They believed the UN should take a strong part in negotiations about possible bombing and suggested Six Talks as the best solution. Aren't we coming off the Fifth Talk now, Matt?"

He ignored my question. "What else was published?"

I decided to also ignore his rudeness, but I wondered if he'd get it if I joked about whether he, too, was 'taking the Fifth?' I chose to simply answer his question instead: "One paragraph strongly criticized the US for applying sanctions in the past. Other US articles covered Barbra Streisand's losing it when a heckler objected to an old 2001 skit about the president and Robin Williams' nomination for a Golden Globe Award."

I couldn't help but offer an observation as well: "What a conflicting picture of America we are giving Asia!"

"I understand."

What else could he say?

"And also, Matt, I wonder if our government has a handle on North Korea's missile testing possibilities. Nuclear testing seems just around the corner. What kind of negotiations are in place between our leaders?" I knew I was going out on a limb with that question, but it seemed to me that both sides were doing a lot of non-communicating.

"Thank you for your opinion, Dr. Blakely. Perhaps I'll pass it on. Now, I'm sorry, but I must go." I noticed that this was the second time he'd left what I sensed were uncomfortable conversations for him, but I bid him goodbye anyway before his noncommittal voice could thank me again. This business of being a snitch without getting any feedback or dialogue was getting to me. What possible good was I doing by reporting my perceptions of life in China? I decided to either ask for proof of the usefulness of our talks next time he called, or else to simply bow out. He and I were both from a free country, weren't we? I surely had a choice.

Another phone call cut into my decision-making, and I snatched up the receiver. *"Nie hau?"*

"This is Massage Salon. Go to gate in five minutes!" commanded a female voice.

I snatched up a pink card and headed out the door, remembering that I'd gotten a deal on "back washes and face washes" at the salon. These involved massage, cleansing, and relaxing attention by skilled fingers. I'd barely glanced at an additional pink card as I'd paid 800 yuan for a ten-visit punch card. Was the pink card, written in Chinese, some rider agreement on top of the $112 US I'd already paid? Rather than call Qian to interpret, I ventured out into the sunshine alone.

Then I spotted a woman who'd chattered English at me from the cot next to mine during my entire previous massage. I had gently told her that I preferred to talk with her after we'd finished. She silenced immediately and soon left. I worried that she had thought me rude, but there she stood at my gate with a big smile.

"Luhgina, I am oldest salon customer. I meet you in massage room. I am English teacher. We go now to salon."

Well, okay, since she put it that way.

We walked down the street with our arms locked, and I didn't even try to correct her on the pronunciation of my name. She'd probably pronounce it the same as the young lovelies who worked at the salon did. They lifted tongues in front instead of back on that difficult "R" sound.

Fresh-faced girls with pink ribbons low on their youthful chests welcomed us with dates, cherry tomatoes, sunflower and watermelon seeds, peanuts, and tangerines, plus glasses of hot water. A woman, also with a pink ribbon, gave a Chinese power-point presentation. Was she selling bras? Mastectomy aids? The roomful of Chinese women exited an inner door in threes until I was left alone with more food and water.

When the English teacher returned, I asked, "What was the presentation about?"

After a moment of thought, she said, "Information to be more beautiful."

I tried again: "What are they selling?"

She looked blank. Then she asked why she didn't find my surname in her Chinese dictionary. We discussed how, in China, women keep their own surname. I had followed the American custom, taking my husband's name, and had kept it for professional reasons even after the divorce.

Out of the blue, she said, "Cancer is increasing problem for women in China. America?"

I started to tell her about walking for breast cancer in KS and MT, but it was too complicated. Returning women filled the room wearing pink ribbons, so I surmised that they'd been to a Breast Cancer Prevention presentation. I could only guess what the groups did in the adjoining rooms—surely not mammograms.

I was presented a pink bag containing a facial cleansing kit and a "Happy Teachers Day" CD. The room filled with "Thank you! *Shei shei!*" Then the sweet workers, in identical white blouses with pink ribbons, dragged us out onto the sidewalk. Although just as fresh and beautiful as the Pei Hua beauties I'd noticed clustered around Joe, these girls seemed like carefree children. They acted thrilled as I stumbled through the stylized movements. Maybe the experience wasn't as relaxing as a massage, but my smile matched theirs as they waved me down the block with their oldest salon customer. She covered me in a crazy quilt of English words, her heels clicking over the six blocks to my gate.

Back inside my apartment, I switched on my TV to a miraculous English news clip. As I put the kettle on, I heard the Secretary of State calmly telling CNN that, while China disapproved of North Korea's possible missile testing, they did not hint at any action that they might take to back up their disapproval. I also heard, without detecting a trace of humor, that Chinese people avoided discussion of North Korea. Their attention was more on the political fiction movies and movie-star controversies than on nuclear-testing concerns. Had the Homelands Securities Office talked with Chinese officials? Or was what the woman said on CNN based solely on what I'd told Matt? Surely, I'd have seen her picture on Beijing TV or in a Chinese newspaper if Condoleezza Rice had been on this continent; the Chinese government loved to show themselves with visiting diplomats. I'd not heard her name mentioned in discussions with my few informed and outspoken teacher friends either. One thing was certain: Word managed to quickly get around the world. Somehow.

CHINA 14 - NO CONTROL

Although I had slept well after the interesting salon visit, I awoke with questions floating behind my smog-gritty eyes. What did US foreign relations experts use for resources? I was pretty sure that I'd played a part in what I'd heard in the English news bite on Beijing TV.

Finding no answers, I stumbled into my bathroom cubicle, turned on the hot-water heater, and washed away the coal-dust grit. Unanswered questions washed down the room's central drain, along with my uncertainty about how I'd spend the upcoming National Day and Mid-Autumn Festival. Prospects of a week in XiAn with reading rooms closed and most Chinese connections gone left me with apartment walls closing in. I felt myself on a surreal roller-coaster ride to no destination.

On the other hand, if I line-graphed the aspects of my life in China, my social lifeline had curved sharply upward. I hoped that Joe had noticed how many friends I'd made. Solitude and the possibility of boredom had curved downward until it had nearly vanished. A fourth line, however, depicted the return of nagging uncertainty. I ignored that feeling as I left to take a street bus to teach an Aero Technology College sophomore Tourism class, where I'd taken a moonlight job out of curiosity and as a favor to Pei Hua's bookkeeper. She'd plunked herself down beside me on the bus and confided softly that she, without Pei Hua's knowledge, was also keeping track of AeroTech's accounts. They needed a travel teacher, and she thought I could use the extra yuan the job would pay. Convinced, I'd quietly agreed to try it.

Prepared and ready to teach the first class meeting that day, I found the listening lab doors locked. A passing student approached and informed me that it was Sports Meeting Day. I stood there, disgusted that the unnecessary bus ride had killed an hour of my afternoon, when the student opened his briefcase, pulled out a picture, threw his shoulders back, and began to speak in a sing-songy voice:

"I am Li, your friendly, English-speaking guide, giving you a tour of the American Embassy history in China." *What is this?* I was only half-interested. He held up a picture that looked much like I remembered when visiting Eisenhower's Kansas boyhood home. It showed a white, 1940s style wooden structure with an American flag in front. I was hooked!

He kept on speaking. "The Motherland's only American Embassy was first built in Beijing in 1935. It was called the Chancery Building. An ambassador lived there. It housed less than a hundred workers. It closed for a time and opened again in 1979. It has moved four times."

He had my attention. *Is he some kind of street mime, or what?* His memorized facts kept coming at full volume: "It expanded into four compounds that each held 125 apartments. America's new Embassy design was approved in 2003. It will add diplomatic facilities, housing, and offices for thousands of workers. The building covers four hectares. It has a giant lollipop sculpture near the entrance. President George W. Bush, of America, is expected to dedicate it before 2010."

I'd heard nothing of that back home. He proudly announced the amounts of excessive American expenditures, providing Chinese jobs totaling over a hundred-million American dollars, expected to be spent in Beijing over the next fifteen years.

With a flourish, he rattled off a long phone number where the embassy could be reached once it opened, whenever that might be. Then he added, "When it is finished, the embassy location will be between Third and Fourth Ring Roads." *Well, remind me never to try to find the office if I'm in Beijing!*

After his bizarre performance, he quickly turned, clicked his briefcase shut, and walked away. I called out to him and asked why he had shared this with me. He called back over his shoulder, "I will take your Tourism class. Welcome. You will make us excellent guides for tours across the Motherland. I hope to be your assistant next week!"

Chuckling, I detoured back by the salon for a heavenly facial and massage. A more relaxed week later, during Pei Hua's Sports Games, the mystery of National Day started to clear up for me.

Weeks back, Pei Hua's secretary, Bobo, had invited me to go to her hometown, but—no matter how tactfully I'd tried each time I saw her in the office—no mention came as to where that was, when we'd go, or how we'd get there. At Pei Hua, teachers chattered about going to their hometown on trains, buses, or—for the lucky ones with rich husbands—automobiles. Dozens of times each day, they asked, "What will you do National Day, Luhgina?"

I knew there was a general philosophy here against making plans, "because you then have to change them," yet that didn't prevent them from asking me curious questions. Each time, I answered, "I'm not sure yet," having given up on going anywhere beyond a long bus ride across Xian, while hoping to find the municipal library open so I could check out a rare book in English. Golden Week—peak travel time since 1948, with most Chinese returning home to family—stretched ahead of me like endless boredom within my four walls.

I gave attention to my few remaining classes, thinking, *This or something better.* After the last class, Bobo caught me in the drafty Education building. "We go Zhan An tomorrow. My father welcomes you. Too many people get train tickets, so we go by bus. Take thick 'clotheses' for cold."

"Zhen bang!" (great) I found myself answering in Chinese. *Will dreaming in Chinese come next?* My thoughts swerved in another direction then, and I asked Bobo, "Won't I need my passport to travel to Zhan An with you? Qian will need to get it from the police."

She patted my arm. "It doesn't matter, Regina." Rather than argue, I decided to gratefully trust in a promising weekend and hurried home to pack a duffel with a week's worth of layers for warm, cool, and even downright-cold days.

Bobo met me by the guard gate the next morning, at seven a.m. sharp, and grabbed my duffel, which contained three changes of clothing plus boots, water-purifying pills, and warm socks.

"So many clotheses!" she exclaimed.

We walked to her apartment then, where the duffel and I sat in front of their TV while Xie and Bobo spent an hour getting ready. "We go now," they announced finally, carrying only his-and-hers shoulder purses and the clothes on their backs.

"Bobo, I think I brought too much clothing. Should we leave some at your house?" She removed my down jacket and other wintry items. Then we double-locked doors and walked to breakfast, with Xie toting my duffel.

"National Day is Chinese Fourth of July!" Xie exclaimed, even as he pointed out a "very lucky wedding car!" It was decorated with orchids and roses on mirror-polished black surfaces. We walked onward to our street breakfast of "very famous soybean milk," optional sugar, thick ropy twists of fried bread, and boiled eggs. No salt. Xie pronounced each one "delicious!" I admitted that the long walk had also whetted my appetite.

We stopped at a shoeshine shop. Bobo stepped up in calf-length, high-heeled boots. I protested that my throw-away Reeboks didn't need shining and was told "Do not worry!" The vigorous rag-slapping and fist-beating felt surprisingly relaxing. Xie paid seven yuan with his membership card for all three shoeshines, only a dollar in US currency.

On the street for an hour, cabs sped by us. There were just "too many peoples" holding moon cakes and flowers, so we took a jam-packed bus "to brother-in-law's car." That was when I realized I would enter a government official's Mitsubishi for a two-hour mountain ride. Was I finally meeting a Communist? If so, Joe would be so happy! My inner voice had some advice for me: *"Just relax and pretend you're in a foreign movie where you don't know the plot. No expectations, no assumptions, and no control. Enjoy the moment."*

I quickly came back to the present as Bobo climbed in the back, and I followed. Another surprise then manifested: Xie waved goodbye, and we were off without him. Two quiet Chinese men, Bobo, and I more than filled the leather seat; the smiling brother-in-law and chain-smoking driver sat up front. We wound alongside rushing water, past Buddhist shrines, through villages, under superhighway construction, and around two wrecks. One truck's wheel hung off a precipice; the other one was buried in a deep ditch on a hairpin curve. I kept my window open to dispel the sinus-clogging tobacco smell and watched green mountains turning toward fall colors. Thankfully, my childhood carsickness didn't return as we curved and dipped through shadows and sunlight.

The need for understanding tugged at me. I hoped Bobo would unravel the mystery I'd encountered about our vacation. Miss Zhang and three teachers had explained that "government used to give three days, then they gave four to make it a week," but "we have to work Saturday and Sunday to give back two days because it is too long." Bobo recited these exact but unfathomable words as I inwardly shook my bewildered head once again.

Another question formed: "Bobo, why did you not work today like the others?" This brought only a mysterious smile. I gave up and slipped into silence like the rest of the passengers.

We pulled into a lunch stop, and Bobo happily said, "Brother-in-law's treat!" First came a tureen of delectable broth, with fish balls like fresh clouds set around a whole fish, its open eyes on us. Then came silky tofu with vegetables, beef with green chilies, rice, and tea.

We crammed back into the car, and most passengers snoozed, leaving the driver and me awake for the remaining hour to ZhanAn. It finally appeared, a small town in the cleft of a gorge with sharp "hills" on both sides. Bobo, awake and enlivened now, said that we would visit pagodas on the top of two of them. She also told me that *shan* translated to both "hill" and "mountain."

On the main street, Bobo's silent brother-in-law carried my bag up to a well-used hotel room and quickly departed. Bobo plopped down on the bed's snowy duvet then and said, "We take a little rest, then go to my home."

"Will we return to the hotel afterward?" I asked.

"It doesn't matter." *I hear that so often in China. But to me, the answer matters!*

"Should I take my bag to your family home?" I asked, trying another approach.

"It doesn't matter," she again replied.

So, we took a nap under white duvets. When refreshed, we co-carried my duffel along a river where people washed clothes. We peered into a few clothing shops, stepped over butchered-pig remains, and soon returned to Bobo's father's wide smile atop five flights of steps. Bobo's mother, in her Sunday best, made tea. Wai Po, her blind grandmother, wasn't so sure they'd shouted Chinese truth in her ears about my having come from America. She touched my hands and arms as I sang "Happy birthday, Wai Po," and rewarded me with a big smile.

Either to rescue me from the never-ending parade of shy, adoring relatives or to relieve her own boredom, Bobo proposed a walk along the river. A clump of shouting and thumping people, with their backs to us, filled the sidewalk.

"Bobo, should we call someone to help?" What had begun as a riverside stroll had fast deteriorated. My senses alerting to what smacked of potential danger.

CHINA 15 - ZHAN AN

We skirted a thick circle of onlookers who were watching a young boy cry as a man screamed and slapped him. My heart felt each blow as I started toward them.

Bobo grabbed my arm. "No, Regina. Maybe the child make some bad mistake. We go quickly!" Her grip on my arm was as firm as the riverside sidewalk beneath our feet. "In China, some say important to beat children when naughty. To be frank, many do. My parents did not hit. One child policy, so people want child to act perfect. If I make mistake, parents give advice and suggestion. I think this way better."

After that, there wasn't much to say on the river walk. Children trooped after us when they weren't throwing rocks in the river. Older ones tried skipping rocks, but no one cheered. We turned for home and climbed five flights up.

With no stomach for dinner, I toyed with one dumpling and began noticing the hardness of the couch where I sat alongside five others. Where would we all sleep? I knew at least seven people lived there, and Bobo and I made nine. Bobo's younger brother—whose family of four lived in those same three cement rooms—had cooked, smoked, and roasted nuts, and repeatedly questioned me through Bobo, asking questions like how expensive my plane ticket had been and how old I was.

My listless one-word answers seemed to satisfy him. Children ran around. With effort, my mood lifted. I played "Which hand is it in?" with the youngsters. I taught teens Kings on the Corner with knock-off Bicycle cards. They beat me on the second card game, and as their parents beamed, they shyly ventured some junior high English phrases: "I am ___. Your name is _____?"

Darkness fell. People had been periodically slipping away in pairs, and then returning as others left. My eyes drooped as communication pantomimes gave way to watching TV characters pummeling each other. Then finally,

Bobo said, "We go hotel now," and handed her departing parents the key. It took a while to pantomime our goodbyes.

Upon arriving at the hotel, Bobo's parents met us. They'd shampooed and bathed in our bathroom, a luxury compared to the plastic foot basin and towel I'd observed beside their squat toilet. Finally alone with Bobo, I dropped thankfully into my clean bed and awoke to sunshine and a warm shower the next morning.

Bobo turned in our key and announced, "We go to breakfast." Then she grabbed my duffel to return to her family home. I soon sat for two hours having tea as her parents' kitchen buzzed with chopping, pounding, and laughter. I tried to shake off the gloom that hovered around our second glowing day. Bobo's father proposed that we visit a Nature Art Carving Show nearby.

I admired the bonsai arrangements, rock formations on pedestals, and polished root sculptures. The owner and his wife, while snapping photos, suggested tea and mooncakes. She poured out the first cupful to heat the cup. He then presented me with a natural stone dancer on a carved pedestal and announced, "Worth five hundred yuan to show Chinese American friendship!" I politely refused three times before accepting. They examined my photo album. We took yet another picture and shook hands before we went home to prepare food yet again.

The families of Bobo's five sisters dropped in at mealtimes to feast from their low table. Bobo elaborated on the "rustic food," which I'd found delicious: flat tofu-skin noodles and plump braised soybeans with *nong*, a dark, concentrated flavor bath of soy and vinegar. Father brought a wicker basket of two-inch dough squares and chopped-vegetable filling. He told Bobo that I was "much better with dumplings than a beginner" as we fashioned about a thousand of the bow-tie morsels. They soon began to disappear as still more family members dropped in to meet me. Bobo's brother-in-law dropped by, still smiling. I recognized only one word in their rapid-fire Chinese exchanges: "CommUnist!" He ate and left, an important man with important things to do.

As our second night approached, Bobo abruptly gathered my bag as soon as my eyes started to droop. We walked to her sister's modern cement apartment. There was a big-screen TV along one wall, decorator touches, and separate duvets on our bed in a daughter's room. On their huge flatscreen, Yo-Yo Ma played flawlessly before a large orchestra. I heard "Taiwan" and a barrage of Mandarin before it was turned off. Remembering that he (a child-prodigy) had been born in Paris and graduated from Julliard, and had only performed in China since 1989, I didn't ask questions.

Brother-in-law had either left early or hadn't come home. I didn't know if that was a Communist pattern, but I was glad for his home's generous hospitality. I wondered what Matt might ask about being a guest of a Communist bigwig. Maybe I'd not mention that detail.

On overload, as a guest in a nice Zhan An home, I suffered a long night of mind-circling images filled with the circle of onlookers, as well as a child's screams. I determined to tell Matt what I'd seen and heard the next time he called. I also wondered if Joe had been disciplined with slaps and screams as a child. As I drifted off to troubled sleep, pigs squealed piteously before slaughter, seemingly just below our upstairs window. My mind detoured back to the earlier walk to Bobo's family home. We'd simply walked around that circle of frenzied people, even while my brain questioned this avoidance. *Maybe we need to help?*

When morning finally arrived, I left an American thank-you card on my nightstand, and my *"Shei shei"* to my hostess was sincere. Bobo and I walked to an internet shop, and I paid ten yuan to let folks back home know that I was having a safe, interesting vacation.

kids@global.net

Dear Kids,

I wish I could have taken you up the endless cement steps to a Zhan An mountaintop pagoda, fed you exquisite bow-tie dumplings, and hugged your first-and-second-born this weeklong National holiday. I've had my Reeboks shined, my questions avoided, and my every need eventually met with amazing Chinese hospitality at Pei Hua secretary Bobo's humble home in the mountains north of XiAn. My host (Bobo's sister—in coat and high heels) left her daughter showing me her copy book's Chinese symbols and went "to get breakfast." Fried bread, boiled eggs, and hot soy milk are evidently national street fare in countryside towns.

One incident stands out to share: We saw colorful woven paper-cuttings, like gigantic lollipops, stuck in the ground on the way up a mountain. Bobo said, "Burial place" and hurried me onward. I asked to take a picture, heard "Okay," and aimed the camera toward her father in the foreground. She grabbed my camera and said, "To be honest, Regina, that is bad!" I learned then that death is not mentioned, recorded, or noticed in connection with living persons here. I apologized as we continued uphill toward mournful keening and crying. Bobo and her father studiously ignored a family gathered at a gravesite. Such a contrast to the memorial celebration of life for a friend whose funeral I would've attended if I were in Kansas today.

P.s. I seldom get international news here. Send me your latest take on our national scene and which dignitaries are traveling where. Still learning,

Mom

CHINA 16 - PROJECT APPROVAL

Thanks to Bobo's send-off with a friendly couple who took me under their wing, I returned home safely by train from Zhan An. College students stood so I could sit, took off with my duffel, and hailed a taxi in XiAn's thick air. They could've been government spies kidnapping me for all I knew, but it seemed out of my hands as we sped along unfamiliar XiAn streets. Suddenly I recognized the turn toward Pei Hua's campus. I tried to pay the fare, but they accepted only my profound *"shei shei."* Still thankful, I slept through a very satisfying night in my own bed on an empty, quiet campus.

With vacation time left and the promise of three sunshiny days lifting XiAn's smog, the only problem was booking a tour. I walked to the campus lunchroom, hoping to find Qian for English translation. Instead, I found Joe slurping noodles as fast as smiling coeds brought them. He reminded me of an eager puppy, as he motioned me over with a grand gesture.

"Dr. Blakely! Eat with us." Then he said to the coeds, "Get her the wide noodles. And another platter of beef dumplings."

Needing a tour booking more than I resented his presumption of what I wanted to eat, I sat. The noodles were good; so were the dumplings. He sent one of his lovely lackeys to get me milk from the street market, saying, "China always wants milk. Maybe someday, enough cows."

I told him I'd used soy or oat milk and mostly avoided dairy products before coming to China. A plastic bag arrived with a straw sticking out of one corner. It felt warm, as there was no refrigeration on the street. To this point, I'd only had boiled milk on congee for breakfast. There was no way to put down the plastic bag, so I sipped away. It tasted better than I wanted to admit; surely it was laced with some preservative, along with sugar. I felt Joe's eyes on me. "Very good idea—soy milk, maybe oat milk. Call it Oata!"

I quipped, "How about Oatica—oat milk in America?" He flashed a great smile.

We talked of development in China: a Laos-China Railway. I questioned the environmental impact of a three-thousand-mile project. "It's not like a Belt Road around XiAn," I told him.

Joe said that, since 2001, his country had expanded its energy technology program. "We've put millions into it." His chest actually swelled as he spoke. "China adds over two thousand cars a day on roads now. Our attention has turned from space and biotech industries. Here in China, we soon must use much of the oil we've been exporting." I didn't remind him that he rode a bicycle, another incongruence with his pronouncements.

He kept talking. "China must develop. Then it can turn attention to environment. One thing at a time! Your country did that with tobacco in the south, industries along rivers, and coal mines."

I didn't respond, and in fact, I couldn't think of many arguments against his sweep of America's sins. Instead, I told him I hoped to challenge my students with an Earth Day lesson that might make them aware of environmental impacts during China's development. "I'll give students examples of tree-planting in African countries. Seedlings eventually provide clean air, as well as jobs. I'll tell them about clear-cutting in Montana and pass around a picture of denuded forests. Do you know how long cigarette butts take to disintegrate? Their filters never do, and neither do the plastic bags caught on fences here."

Joe's attendees' eyes began glazing over. I didn't care as I went on. "Each class will hold a contest with a prize. They'll vote for an Earth Day winner after hearing project reports in English. Maybe we'll clean up a little piece of Pei Hua's environment in XiAn!" I felt my voice rising.

I'd read an in-flight shopping magazine somewhere about tech companies coming out with sensor cans for waste. "We might, someday, do away with plastic-bag liners and tell waste cans to compost trash. Some of my American friends just clap their hands to turn on lamps in their homes!" I had the table's attention now.

Before I could go on, Joe turned to his assistants, whose lips had not yet touched their noodles. "*Shei shei,* my dears. You may go back to the office." They left him with adoring looks. Then he regarded me solemnly. "Luh— Regina, I will consider your project."

What? I thought, as it had never occurred to me to run it by him.

"Joe, surely you approve! It will bring excitement and personal involvement to my English class. I only want to give students reasons to speak English and make China a better place in which to live."

He persevered. "Will Earth Day ideas bring students some kind of revolutionary thoughts? We have no such festival in China."

"I assure you that Earth Day has no revolutionary ideas behind it."

"Then I guess your students won't become Tree Huggers. Go ahead with your plans."

I didn't thank him. I could change subjects immediately too. "Joe, my plans for Saturday depend on getting some help. I want to visit nearby sites, but I'll need a tour in English. I'd hoped Qian would help me book it, but perhaps you would be so kind?"

Joe grinned. "A piece of cake! Watch me and see the sun shining on water!" Gleefully mixing Chinese and American metaphors, he took me downtown in a school van, tipped the driver with a cigarette, and rattled off rapid-fire syllables. I signed an itinerary, written in Chinese. He paid a fee and dismissed my offer of yuan to cover it by saying, "You go, my friend! Learn Motherland's history. Very ancient. Very interesting."

We had more noodles, thin ones this time, in XiAn's Muslim section. "Everything coming up roses," he pronounced as his forecast for my upcoming tour. We ate in companionable silence, in spite of my stomach's slightly unsettled feeling.

CHINA 17 - HISTORY TOUR

A car and driver appeared at the campus gate for me next morning. I reached for the seatbelt, but it was inoperable, as they were in most Chinese vehicles. I took a deep breath and hoped for the best.

My thoughts went to the hybrid I'd driven last time I was home, an eerie contrast to the roar of the campus car. Joe and I had discussed automobile industry that added two thousand of them daily to fill his country's highways. Joe hadn't been able to fathom what I was talking about when I first explained that cars made with partial-electric engines were used to save fossil fuels in my country. Then he'd warmed to an idea: China might make them cheaper.

"We don't need to care about the quality of the car," he'd said. "Worry later when we catch up."

Twenty minutes of remembered conversation passed; then the driver shooed me into a fifteen-passenger tour bus at Xian's Bell Tower. People filled the aisle, listening to a guide bark Chinese through a bull horn. I shook my head when asked for 280 yuan. *Not to stand all day!*

Abruptly, half the passengers exited. The guide motioned me to a seat, and we departed.

An English-major coed regaled me with questions, practicing her English: "Feefty?" This greeting was better than "How old are you?" Even though it had sounded more like "feefTEEN," not my age by any stretch of the imagination, I decided we'd get along fine.

The first stop was Tang dynasty's Gao Zong and his consort's tomb. Sculpted winged steeds, stone lions, and ancient guards flanked our underground walk. My interpreter "couldn't understand because guide from other province." I soon realized that she hadn't correctly understood the sites she'd interpreted earlier either.

A Beijing publisher and wife took me in tow and brought the next stop alive: Mao Ling Mausoleum, Wu Di's tomb from the Western Han reign, which displayed life-size dioramas of feudal life. We patted a "Lying Down Horse" worn shiny from thousands of touches.

The next stop lauded Yi Di, first son of a Ming king. The "Warriors of the Kind" display rivaled the Terra Cotta Warriors, but with half-size figures. Horses in full color, with their mouths open and lips curled back, stood ready for battle. Outside this 2300-year-old site sat a Buddha "for getting rid of illness," preparation for our growling stomachs. I patted him for enduring luck.

During Xiangyang City's lunch of flat noodles with slivered vegetables and tea, an Indiana businessman pointed out "dog" on the menu. For tourists? I diverted his attention to Confucius's words: "With coarse grain to eat, water to drink, and my bended arm for a pillow, I still have joy in the midst of these things." Heads nodded my way, and I quieted, like a timid rabbit (my zodiac sign), glad I wasn't born in the Year of the Dog.

I decided I'd choose this vacation trip over any journeys Confucius had ever taken. Thanks to Joe! I drank the end of my noodle broth, lifting my bowl like everyone else.

On the bus, the guide gave background for ZhaoLing Mausoleum, a benchmark for Tang emperors. My Beijing friends snored until we jolted to a stop.

We'd paid extra for a "village visit" and drove washed-out dirt roads. Then it appeared, reminding me of elaborate Kansas displays by elementary kids with its rambling tunnel strung with Christmas lights; depictions of Han weddings, funerals, and harvests; and even a caged bear, pig pen, rabbit hutches, and chicken nests.

Seeing no artful rabbits in the gift shop, I bought intricate butterfly paper cuttings, a craft originating in Shaanxi province. The day stretched on, promising too much Chinese history.

Returning over the rutted dirt road at a higher speed, the sound of screeching brakes and a line of cars halted us. In a field to the right, a battered Volvo tilted toward a ditch. No policeman appeared. Our line of cars headed over the field on the left. A man in a rumpled blue suit lay still on the roadway, leg jutted at a strange angle. My Chinese companions studiously looked away.

Was the man dead? Could it have been a hit and run? There had to be something we could do to help. The silent bus ignored my frantic questions. The Indiana man slept soundly. A woman across the aisle made sweeping motions in the air, muttering in Chinese.

The Beijing publisher whispered, "Frankly speaking, it is not our business. Let me tell you about the next tomb visit." I closed my eyes and tried to calm my drumming heart.

Parked later, we opened umbrellas for a rainy tomb visit. My hands still shook. The publisher explained that Lady Yang, buried there, had outdone other emperors, setting her three-meter memorial between two hills. He told me she had killed all Tang claimants to the throne, including her nephew— "because he said things about her." I tried to focus on the empress, but I kept remembering the poor man lying so still in my memory while people strolled the broad, statue-filled walkways. They resembled Mexico City's pyramid paths, except these valleys and hills rivaled Tuscany views in France. What a strange culture I'd entered! My thoughts ricocheted.

Back on the bus, the publisher smiled as though all I had on my mind was the upcoming "best temple." Fa Men proved a dazzling enclave in the afternoon sun. I kept trying to focus on its clean grounds, stylized rooflines, and golden statues, but the poor man loomed large in my mind still.

We walked past ancient buddhas, smiling monks, and bubbling butter candles. Sakyamuni's revered finger rested in a jade case. *Does the finger remind any of my companions of the man left on the highway?*

The publisher started a full rundown of Fa Men temple's history. He put his fingers to his lips, shaking his head when I asked again about the wreck on the way there. I gave up. I knew talk of death was not accepted in China, but ignoring an accident that had obviously just happened? It didn't compute with the curiosity Chinese people displayed about my age or how much I weighed. Maybe I could share this cultural difference the next time Matt called. The ancient tombs didn't seem worth recounting for political enlightenment. I brooded in silence, eyes closed for the remaining miles to XiAn, hoping to remain upright without a seatbelt.

CHINA 18 - JUST ENOUGH

Exiting the tour bus, I found Joe waiting. My emotions tumbled into a burst of embarrassing tears then, and he hurried me into a Pei Hua car.

"Now, tell me what troubles you."

"Never have I been so relieved to see a friendly face." I wiped my eyes.

He listened, then shook his head. "Stay quiet, and don't worry."

I tried to do that all the way home and up the stairs with Joe. He planted a kiss on my forehead. Then he instructed me to lock both doors behind him.

I tumbled into bed at nine p.m. Was that the phone? I didn't care, already into sleepy escape. It kept ringing, stopped, then started again. I managed to pick it up.

"Hello, Dr. Blakely? I don't want to alarm you, but I need to know how things are going. Do you ever notice anyone following you?"

My nerves jangled me awake and alert. This kid certainly didn't waste any time on polite exchanges. "Whoa! Slow down, Matt." I took a deep breath. "I've been here so long that the 'Chinese relationship thing' is becoming a part of me. Here, if I come barging into conversations with questions, Chinese people strongly disapprove. Matt, can we try their mode and ease into our conversation? I'm not feeling any *guan xi* here, and it feels offensive."

Inwardly, I wondered at my chutzpah, lecturing a White House worker. Matt retreated to a subdued tone and asked, "How are you?"

I forgot his safety questions, which somehow felt like accusations, as he actually listened to my National Day trip to Bobo's. When I started recounting the tour of tombs, he cycled into questions again.

"Dr. Blakely, I must know: Has anything strange happened lately for you?"

Is this persistent kid psychic or what? I told Matt about the body on the highway near the wrecked Volvo. "It will long haunt me, Matt, that man out there alone with everyone but me looking the other way." He listened as silently as my bus-mates had.

"I must ask again. Have you had the feeling someone was following you?"
Why ask again?

"No, I haven't felt like that at all." *That's an honest answer, Matt.*

I remembered my Jackson Hole friend Mardy Murie telling me that, like a flashlight in darkness, we could rely on just enough light for our next step. Perhaps I was learning to live that way. It had made life much easier, even that day's harrowing trip.

I recapped it all for Matt: the Zhan An visit, the cultural-difference revelations, and the historic tomb tour experience. Then I emphasized the gift of Bobo's Communist brother-in-law's accommodations, the Beijing interpreter on the bus, and my embarrassment when tour-bus standees exited to give me a seat. "If anything, I felt pampered."

"Nothing uncertain or suspicious?" Matt persisted.

"Plenty is uncertain, except for the poor man in the accident, but nothing suspicious. Why do you ask?"

The line went dead. Eyes open in darkness, I waited for him to call back. It didn't happen. I checked the locked doors, closed all the windows, and lay back down, still in the dark about Matt's questions.

CHINA 19 - AWL RIDE

My half-thought was that I'd been sleeping a lot since coming to China. When things got hard to sort out, that seemed to be my default approach: Just sleep on it. My next conscious thought was of the phone's jangle awakening me once more. I opened one eye to a shaft of sunlight.

"Luh— Regina, I am Lucy. We bike the city awl this morning?"

Awl? I momentarily pictured a sharp object used for boring holes; then I remembered another pronunciation omission noticed among my students: all initial "w" sounds.

"Oh, Lucy! I'd love to bike the city *wall.*"

I pictured Lucy observing from the back of my classroom, wondering if she was also one of the flock of beauties fluttering around Joe. Had I actually seen her buttering up the dean? If so, it didn't matter. It'd be good to get out of the apartment.

Wearing high-heeled boots that clicked as she walked me to the bus, Lucy reminded me to wear my fanny pack in front to protect against theft. She explained Pei Hua's scheduling, grading, political correctness, and teaching practices on the way to rent bikes. Mine was reasonably new and felt comfortable on old cobblestones. I soaked up the history she shared.

We rode a bumpy fourteen kilometers on earthen bricks made as early as 212 BC. Lucy recited some information for me: "A hermit believed he would be emperor if he built a fortress for protection. The wall began. Repaired in 582 A.D.; it enclosed upscale shops, KFC, McDonald's, and commerce. During Tang and numerous other earlier dynasties, it was ChangAn, XiAn City's pulse area."

We paused to peer through slits in crenelated walls. Peeling her boiled egg snack, Lucy said, "Big celebration tonight!" I drank my bottled water. Gigantic pink peonies and ancient writing on paper-mâché above silk-covered tables awaited XiAn's rich and famous. They'd gather under an auspicious full moon.

We bounced over more cobbles. "Look over awls. Below are ninety-eight buildings and corner towers!" Lucy was proving a good tour guide.

I responded honestly: "Lucy, this wall bike ride is most exciting!" She beamed, and it occurred to me that I had honored her as my companion.

Another stop looked down at a grassy moat. Folks exercised with graceful fans to flute music. After ninety minutes, we recovered our fifty-yuan bike deposit and had spicy BBQ and fried rice at the nearby thirteen thousand-square-meter Great Mosque. Women stood, quiet and distant from a lengthy prayer ritual done by hundreds of prostrate males, their white caps touching the floor.

As we exited, Lucy asked me, "Luh— Regina, do you believe in a superpower?" She told me that she "didn't know for sure," but that she "liked to believe." Her Buddhist family had converted when her father was quite ill, and that he'd recovered after they had prayed to Buddha. Then she asked how I felt about the way "Americans must pay their churches."

I avoided the theological question and skipped to telling her that many Christians supported churches with offerings. I guessed Matt might be interested in this perception when he called next. Then I recalled his earlier, paranoid questions and glanced over my shoulder.

No one seemed to be watching. Mostly men hurried past with their cellphones to their ears, their too-long belts looped halfway-again around their slim waists, and their shoes as shiny as Joe's when his feet were under his Pei Hua desk.

Lucy switched topics. "May I pick your brain about foreign methods you use?" She had passed her master's thesis written on an obscure line in a Chinese poem, and she wondered how it applied to her eventual teaching of English. I had no ready answer as we walked Muslim shop-lined mazes just inside the old gate. Incense burned, fabrics dazzled, and decaying trash and strong perfumes assaulted our nostrils. I spoke honestly about the immense fun she'd brought me.

I didn't mention it to Lucy, but the day's XiAn experience had been as strange an assault on my senses as had the four days in Zhan An. Would I ever get used to the roller-coaster ride through happenings in China? A piece of this, a piece of that, with no way to fit them together.

CHINA 20 - TOO FAST

Grabbing my arm on the street, Lucy abruptly pointed out a XiAn movie poster for *The Banquet,* saying, "It has in English subtitles. We discuss it sometime!"

Before I could inquire further, she began an impromptu query about Terra Cotta Army tours with a downtown booth worker, and then told me that I could go see the warriors on my free day.

I half-agreed. *Too much too fast! I was getting whiplash, just maneuvering between our conversations.* I concentrated until I could tell her goodbye.

Knowing the Chinese custom of taking guests back to their homes, I returned with Lucy, thanked her again, and then turned right back around and went back out, hoping to see *The Banquet* alone. Was I losing my old efficiency-attitude and becoming wishy-washy to avoid offending people? It made no sense to make this extra trip, but somehow, I found myself happily doing it.

I had no problem retracing my steps from the bus stop. It took a lot of fractured Chinese and pantomime to make my way to the movie. Beautiful costumes and Daniel Wu's artful directing made me wish for immediate discussion, though I guessed that teachers here would have few analytical skills to see the contrasts and comparisons of this film—set in the time of a short-lived dynasty—with Shakespear's *Hamlet.* I thrust my last hundred-yuan at the ticket-taker and put the handful of change deep in a pocket. Payday would surely replenish my supply soon. Regardless, it was my first movie in China, with artful scenes, subtitles, and a velvet front-row recliner.

When Pei Hua resumed classes, I told Lucy I had enjoyed the movie, and she asked, "Did you see a parallel to *Hamlet,* Luhgina?"

I started to draw comparisons, but Lucy quickly excused herself and moved to the back of my classroom. Too much English information, I surmised.

Classes went well with only half the students back from vacation. I started with their chosen saying, translated to English: "If you wish to eat honey, you must suffer the sting of bees." I used chalk, sketched a side-view tongue and vocal cords, and explained how English-speakers easily open mouths and lift tongues for "La la la," which I knew felt impolite and awkward to them.

Faces lit up when I told how them that they'd wow those who'd missed this lesson with their impressive English pronunciation. With mirrors, they reluctantly stuck out tongues for "I think..." instead of "I sink..." and "Thank you" instead of "Sank you." They giggled and bit bottom lips to say "five, fifteen."

We set up shop with CD covers and "sold" only to shoppers who correctly pronounced prices: "$1.50, $1.15, $1.75, and $7.13." Giggles continued. Many spoke, showing their teeth for the first time. Lucy gave a thumbs-up as she exited the room. We'd tackle her "city awl" in another lesson.

Then came Monday, with dawn slanting in my window even as Lucy telephoned. "Luhgina, you go to Terra Cotta Arriors today." The tour bus picked me up: Chinese guide, driver, and eleven native passengers plus me. No Lucy.

Forty kilometers east, we examined Qin vaults of pottery figurines: soldiers, chariots, and horses in terra cotta. I'd seen extensive warriors displayed at Shaanxi History Museum and suspected that the limited display had been dispersed for wider coverage and income.

I got lost in a dark room full of shouted Chinese, found my group a half-hour later, and returned to view what I'd missed when given a free hour. There were gilded bridle bits, steel chariot whips, and two completed chariots with four horses and drivers. Watching hummingbirds while I waited brought another nice memory to store. Without English to enlighten me, I wasn't sure if I'd seen the Warriors most tourists saw or simply some knock-off display. No one offered to translate, but all treated me with silent respect. *Just go with the flow*, I told myself.

We stopped at Hauquin Hot Springs' waterways, where Wang Yu Han's voluptuous white form graced one green pool. An English interpreter echoed the guide's words: "One of Asia's four beauties." I didn't tell them that, to me, all the figures looked alike. My stomach growled as I'd bought only a bun at a lunch stop, rationing my few remaining yuan.

Chaing Kai Chek and Madame Chaing's lavishly appointed cement rooms sported a few bullet holes, proudly pointed out for tourists. Chaing had hunted gorillas in the mountains beyond Hauquin. I vowed to reread Seagrave's *The Soong Dynasty* after seeing this spot, as I lumped FDR, Churchill, and Clare Booth Luce into the Generalissimo's era. I doubted any of them had to endure gnawing hunger pains while living there. My stomach growled repeatedly.

Back at Pei Hua's freshman campus, home in time to insert my key without digging for my penlight, I diverted hunger to another thought. Most of my vacation would never have happened if I'd insisted on knowing "what would happen when." I heard again Mardy Murie's twentieth-century words about "just enough light for the next step." That wisdom had prepared me, years ago, for China's twenty-first century experiences far from my friend's Jackson Hole home. It all felt wonderful, since leftover chicken and rice waited in my blue fridge. The "awl" still between me and my passport and salary could be tackled after I ate.

CHINA 21 - LOSING IT

On the English teachers' bus, I heard no post-vacation answers to my questions about world news. They chattered about the emperor's doll-sized terra cotta warriors and the foot coverings that preserved that ancient site they thought I'd visited. Not one teacher had seen, read, or heard of an injured man or a wrecked Volvo outside the village road near JingDi's tomb. I decided that maybe I was making too much of a mere broken leg and minor accident. I still wondered if those were the real Terra Cotta Warriors I'd visited. It was unsettling. I felt lost in Chinese syllables and chatter I didn't understand.

Between classes, I'd found nothing helpful to settling my nerves in an edition of *China Today,* in the Pei Hua library's reading room. So, I stewed beside an empty seat on the homebound bus across XiAn, with no seatbelt mooring me, of course.

My phone rang even as I unlocked my inner door with the key. I dashed inside to grab it.

"Dr. Blakely, how are you today?"

"A little ashamed, Matt. What I learned might help the Secretary if she reaches the end of her rope, but otherwise, I don't know that it comes close to diplomacy."

"I don't understand."

"Let me begin by saying that I'm tempted to skip talking today for fear of giving you a wrong impression of Chinese people, or of me."

"Tell me more." Even his patient responses irritated me today. *This guy either learns fast, or he's humoring me.*

Matt let me yammer on about Mary, a Kansas teacher, now in Kunming, far south of XiAn. She'd emailed me to visit for her birthday. I wanted to go, as I was desperate for English conversation. I told him that I'd gotten as far as her saying, "I presume you have your passport by now," when the power had gone out. I also told him that I knew she'd been paid twice since her semester began, and I had yet to see a single yuan. Discouraged and broke in the dark, I'd slept, but not well.

Matt broke into this sad story. "Why don't you ask your Chinese caregiver? Qian, isn't it?"

"I did called Qian! There was no answer. She was also out of the office the last three times I went by. Hoping for my salary, I wrote her a note that said I had almost no yuan left. I asked her to help me get paid, and I told her my computer had also quit working."

Turning dramatic, I recounted our dialog word-for-word for Matt, just like a bad script:

"Maybe I come this morning," she offered.

Since two could play the Maybe Game, I replied, "Maybe you can bring my passport with my pay?"

"Pay? Oh, you mean salary." She finally came to my room, tried the computer, and made her pronouncement: "Maybe it is broken."

"Qian, I need to finish tomorrow's lecture. The technician must come today," I insisted.

"Maybe I telephone someone," she replied.

Then she showed me a Chinese document, stamped in red. "There is problem with passport. Police keep it to fix."

Finally, I told Matt that this had been the last straw, and that I'd started crying, even as Qian had fled through the open doors. "And Matt, the drama continues. I stood in the doorway until my sobbing gave way to angry shouts about my helplessness in this foreign land."

"Dr. Blakely, uh... What happened next?" I could tell he was feeling uncomfortable hearing about a grown woman's breakdown.

"Well, Matt, Dean Zhou came to my rescue, but it's a long story that's not worth your time. How about we talk again when I have something to report?"

I could hear his relief as he replied, "No problem, Dr. Blakely, another time." Then he hung up.

My thoughts were anything but finished. I was instantly back to my multi-frustration raging as I stood in my doorway. Really steamed up, I heard footsteps on my cement stairs.

Joe appeared then, his brows almost knitted together, though he was using his normal quiet voice when he spoke. "Regina, you are like a leaf, fluttering downward. What is it?"

"Where did you come from?" I blustered, angry to find myself as one of his similes. As I wiped my eyes, I knew they were as red as my face. I clamped my mouth shut to keep from saying my thoughts aloud: *I can't deal with this man right now. I don't want to think! Just vent!*

To my surprise, Joe silently took my hand and pulled me toward my couch. Then he put an arm loosely around my still-shaking shoulders. "Tell me what makes you cry."

I swiped at my nose with the back of my hand. "I need my passport to fly to Kunming. It's my friend's birthday."

"As I thought, you are but a leaf, fluttering to return to the roots of its own tree. You, little leaf, are withering from homesickness?"

I simply cried harder at this question, which seemed like another pronouncement.

"Don't cry," he said then. "Reveal your soul burdens, Regina. It doesn't matter."

Even in my stormy state, it registered that he'd said my name correctly this time, without the "Luh" false start that I was used to hearing.

"Joe, you said my name like an American!" I sniffled. "But I feel like it *does* matter!"

I knew that oft-repeated phrase was used to help one approach everything without attachment, but it always felt like a cop-out meant to placate me. Momentum gathered as words tumbled out of me

"It *does* matter!" I repeated. "And crying might make me feel better! I'm down to two hundred yuan! I don't know when I'll get paid; my computer won't work; the plastic pipe they fixed in the bathroom is leaking again; the hall light still hasn't been fixed, and I have no passport!"

Joe was close to sniffling too by then. "Don't cry. I feel like you are a friend of mine. We will soon be in a landscape of tears if you don't stop."

I sniffed. "Qian may be doing the best she can, but nothing works for me in China."

Then we both cried, with Joe quickly out-wailing me. There was no more of his metallic, expressionless voice.

I stopped crying first. "I'm told Chinese women buy cheap dishes to throw when frustrated. What about Chinese men, Joe?" I looked around for something to throw. No luck, but the comic relief brought a hiccough, quickly followed by a shared giggle.

Joe surprised me further by pulling another clean handkerchief from his pocket. He wiped at my eyes, then his own. "All will be okay, Regina. We must not open the book too far. Your bone weight is heavy now. Good fortune will come. Now I take you for baijiu to answer all your questions." Gratefulness flooded over me.

As I washed my face in the bathroom, I thought about how good it felt to hear passable English and feel someone treating me kindly. I had felt lonely, as well as vulnerable and powerless. Joe's listening to my ranting had offered an unexpected gift, showing me that the authoritative clown had a soft underside—an underside that had emerged just when I needed it.

CHINA 22 - TURN AROUND

Managing a smile, I rode side-saddle on the back of Joe's bicycle. It felt good to let someone else be in charge and just leave the uncertain future out there. The stress of being broke without my passport receded in the street-dust that our tires kicked up. I could almost go along with his "It doesn't matter" attitude. Joe reached back and pressed my arm to his slim waist.

"Like ginger dipped in sugar, Regina!" he shouted into the wind. "Sweet and explosive at the same time!" As we arrived, I found myself wondering at this clown poet and his hidden personalities.

He chose an inside corner table and ordered a bottle of baijiu, along with a plate of beef dumplings. "Moutai's brand of ancient sorghum-based liquor went global in 1915 at a San Francisco exhibition," he told me. "A Chinese delegate had smashed one earthenware jar. The aroma attracted the judges, and it won first prize."

Joe poured the clear alcohol into my small glass as he continued. "This is the most-drunk spirit on earth. Twice vodka or tequila sales. Someday, it overtakes famous British brand. Already outsells wine and beer worldwide. *Ganbei!* Bottoms up!"

I tipped my glass, preparing for a repeated assault on my senses. My introductory taste, weeks back, had seemed a mixture of mushrooms, licorice, and old sox. This time, I detected a sweetness, along with a rice flavor that was still pungent.

"Mutai compliments the dumplings," I managed to say. "Thank you, Joe."

I scooped up a beef/onion triangle. No sooner did I maneuver one dumpling up for a bite than Joe would order another plate. He fed me tastes with his chopsticks, and I quit caring about germs. *Ah, Chinese hospitality!* I ate pork-cabbage, chicken liver-greens, and even donkey's ear and herbs dumplings. Each bite tasted better, with each swig from the diminishing bottle. "Mmm. I'll bet people buy a lot of *baijiu* around Chinese New Year. Isn't that in February this year?"

Joe positively glowed. "It is most-given gift to family and friends to celebrate. We are friends, Regina!"

We kind of stumbled out of the noodle shop and wobbled home on his bike. The earlier gloom completely lifted. I felt like I was over my snit. I knew I'd survive whatever happened today or tomorrow. I decided I'd buy Joe's family as expensive a bottle of Montai as I could afford when Lunar New Year came, maybe one with a dragon on it to mark a hopeful coming year.

When we returned, I thanked Joe again and went carefully upstairs, steadying my spirit-filled body by holding the railing.

Qian waited at my door with a surprise for me: "Computer repairman say he come in half hour. Maybe I get your salary today. What about go to Kunming by train? I telephone." She clattered down the stairs before I could find my tongue to answer.

I floated over to the couch, patted Minnie Mouse's hair bow, and kind of collapsed without thinking much of anything. Time and thoughts receded until Qian brought the technician and told me I could travel thirty-six hours one way by bus. She had called Pei Hua to cancel Friday's classes so I could get to Kunming by the weekend. Not a happy prospect, but at least she was trying. Qian pressed a fresh package of dates into my hands. "Do you feel better?"

"Yes, but I cannot travel seventy-two hours just for eighteen hours in Kunming. I really thank you, but there is surely something else you can do." I'd found my old assertive self under the fumes I was sure must still be rising from my liquid experience at the noodle shop.

Qian then said I had 4500 yuan "salary advance" and that she'd "borrowed back my passport" from the police. She would order an airline ticket for Friday afternoon. Then she promised a Pei Hua car to the airport and a return ride on Monday. She reached into her gigantic handbag and produced my first package. An ex-student in the states had sent candy corn for Halloween. I gave Qian the first taste, and she smiled her way out.

The phone ringing halted this happy ending, with Matt's youthful voice inquiring, "Do you feel like catching me up now, Dr. Blakely?"

"Okay, Matt, but I'm a little ashamed to tell you that I lost it with Dean Zhou and my caregiver. Maybe their cavalier attitude about paying salaries and getting the seemingly impossible accomplished will help your office understand some tense situation with China."

"You lost it?"

I half-joked, "I can better sympathize with people who cross from Mexico or Canada without proper papers now. It's no fun being an 'illegal alien,' even if you thought you were doing the best thing when the authorities took over."

Matt sighed. "So, you're not worried about anything now?"

"Maybe one more thing, Matt. Tell the National Security Advisor that— when all else fails—tears work wonders, but only if they're shed with someone who feels like you're a friend."

Did he actually chuckle before he hung up? And if so, what did that mean?

CHINA 23 - KUNMING BIRTHDAY

I packed to visit Mary's southern aggie-university city, just in time for a Pei Hua driver to deposit me at the airport. Shortly after China Air's beef-vegetable and rice, I exited in Kunming, waving toward Mary's familiar face. Her student carried my bag, practicing his English.

Mary's detergent-scented apartment differed from mine, having overstuffed furniture, a black-tiled bathroom, and windows cleaned weekly by a maid. It twinned mine with its cement walls, water purifier, hot plate, rice cooker, thin mattress, and low table. A vase of zinnias sat near the computer that was playing KUFM from our KS alma mater.

We were off down memory lane when a Chinese teacher knocked, then carried in a cake in an ornate box. Mary held it on the crowded bus ride to dinner with colleagues. I quickly gave up on learning names.

Around the room-sized table, toasts increased in length and hilarity as *pi jiu* was raised and drained with cheers of *"Ganbei!"* This literally meant "dry cup." I surmised that this tasted the same as the *baijiu* I'd been introduced to with Joe. *Perhaps China confuses "p" and "b" sounds, since our mouths produce them identically, except one is sounded and one is not.* I told myself to focus on the party, not to think like a teacher, and quickly began to enjoy the noisy fun. During contests to see which cup went dry first, I drank tea like a wimp, toasting only when it was the group's turn.

The cake sat atop a chest of drawers while Mary matched eight toasts. On the seventh, she yelled, "Down the hatch!" Then she sang an acapella torch song to a great cheering response.

I figured we'd eat cake and go home. No. Mary grabbed the cake box. We gathered to get cabs for a karaoke hotel. The cake slid onto the sidewalk. We left it. Mary hummed all the way up to a room furnished with a big screen and sofas, and ashtrays on the coffee tables. As soon as the first person uploaded a song, Mary danced. Five male teachers were willing partners. Evidently, Chinese men didn't sit home evenings with their wives.

We took turns at the microphones, doing rock and roll, Madonna, and Tibetan music. Someone whispered, "I think she's having a good birthday."

The next morning, Mary groaned and had a talk with herself about being a year older before we went to Green Lake for a group dance lesson. I bought her a caricature drawn on the spot by a street artist. I didn't even mind when we both thought he'd said, "Three yuan," and he'd charged me thirty. I made a mental note to add syllables and accents to my XiAn Oral English classes.

We got *bao zi*—sweet-filled, steamed buns—for a hostess gift and rang a doorbell in Mary's neighborhood. She placed the gift nonchalantly on a corner table. The hostess took no notice. I made another mental note to never arrive empty-handed at Chinese homes, yet not to proffer gifts like Americans do.

We made small talk with another guest, who told us of an upcoming trip with college students to identify plant species. Two hours of listening to chopping and sizzling in the nearby kitchen was worth the wait. A music teacher dropped by to sing as she helped cook. That filled the rooms with melodies and aromas. We finally ate it all.

The throng boarding the Kunming bus home was scary. We waited in what I assumed to be a line. Mary pushed us onto the next bus. In XiAn, young people had stood and given me their seat; not so in Kunming. Mary and I, backpacks clutched to chests to avoid thievery, chattered in English. Exiting gladly together, we stopped for on-the-street massages, sitting on stools, to finish off the evening.

Mary told me how small Kunming, bordered by Vietnam, spoke over fifty dialects. Many of its subcultures could not understand each other, conversing in old ways, rather than Mandarin. That accounted for the distinctive crafts sold near temples and lakes. The flower shops had unique bouquets too, grown and arranged in the same ways parents and grandparents had always displayed them. Kunming was a fascinating change for me.

By the time morning light crept in Mary's windows, we had dreamed up a proposal for sharing a semester apiece in Kunming. That would allow her to teach in Mongolia while I taught in Kunming. We'd expose students to two English-speakers, instead of the usual one.

We then envisioned a week's train vacation to travel the length of Vietnam. Her Vietnamese students could put us on overnight buses to the border and help buy tickets. I fell asleep imagining bombers taking off from China for Vietnam, determined to learn more about those countries' cooperation, or lack of it, during the controversial war. I'd only paid minimal attention to Vietnam War news while raising children in the United States.

When you've not talked with a native English speaker for a while, especially a friend from home, it's amazing how quickly you slip back into the vernacular, assumptions, and familiarity of shared experience. We shared our university experiences. She told me that she had one able assistant whom she could call at any time, and he'd be there, speaking perfect British English. She'd already invited him to visit her Kansas home after her return. I thought of Qian's vague responses and frequent absences when I'd sought her out at my old campus office. Mary reminded me, "We work for them; they can keep us here or send us back the minute they're not happy with us. It's not like we have any rights here."

That sounded harsh to me. I dropped some noncommittal remark about not having felt that way and redirected our thoughts to what we'd take with us to Vietnam. Mary and I agreed that my birthday trip was just what we both needed and vowed that we'd make the next visit longer. I borrowed her computer to write a quick note to my kids:

kids@global.net

Dear kids, I'm visiting Mary, who had a typical birthday dinner and karaoke singing in Kunming. I've learned that Chinese airlines leave when the plane is full, feeding you almost the moment you take off. That's a nice reward for all the pushing and shoving where no one stands in line. I finally got paid—in the nick of time, before I was forced to figure out how to use my credit card where all writing is in Chinese. I threw all 450 of the 100-yuan bills over my bed and played in them like leaves under fall trees! Rich now,

Mom

CHINA 24 - EXPLORING CONTRASTS

Home from Kunming, I found myself genuinely glad when Matt called. I thought I had gained some insights to help East-West people understand one another. To avoid repetition and save time for myself, I asked for his email to blind-copy him my next update to family and friends. I heard "Thank you, Dr. Blakely, but I'd have to get cleared for that communication."

"What kind of clearing would you need, Matt?" The line was silent, so I persisted. "It's as if you assumed the role I would have expected a Chinese official to play, not an answer from Capitol Hill."

"Dr. Blakely, I look forward to reading your email as soon as communication is cleared." Something had clearly flustered him, and just when I'd been starting to enjoy our talks.

"Matt, is there something you want to share with me? Or something I should know about the situation at home?"

"No, all is good, Dr. Blakely."

Hmmm. There wasn't much to talk about after that, so we ended our phone conversation. I was soon hammering away at my plastic keyboard:

kids@global.net; AtHomeGroup@ox.net

These days, thoughts keep rumbling around like bowling balls, homing in for a sure strike, then leaving two pins standing far apart. Some thoughts gutter halfway down the lane. Yet the strike's possibility remains: a clear enough picture of Eastern and Western philosophy, showing people communicating on a level beyond prejudice's expectations.

Your emails repeatedly ask about cultural likenesses and differences. I imagine cubby holes for each contrasting category. "This is

Chinese. This is American." It keeps eluding me, just out of reach, yet somehow present.

Here's an example of Americans living in XiAn: Idaho folks setting up a Micron-related company here invited me for Sunday's dinner. We played Scrabble with rules made and agreed upon on the spot. Diet Coke with ice, then Great Wall cabernet almost put my feet back on American soil for a few hours. Forty-five minutes from Chinese community housing warrens, their 11th floor apartment looked beyond gardens toward developing Xi'An. It had a full kitchen, maid service, new appliances, and adjustable light. I sat on a spacious sectional near an entertainment center and handy treadmill above heated tile floors. My eyes rested on art objects and plants. Table settings looked like matches for a New York penthouse.

Yet, as I lifted the just-purchased china and silverware, it weighed almost nothing. Filling dinner glasses with water from their purifier, I was clearly back in China. I thought of my galley kitchen with its hot plate, couch covered with Disney characters, and free-standing TV on a dingy tile.

Curious Chinese also want to label contrasts. They ask, "How is the living condition different in America?" I'm imagining your answers, friends and family. Given my first two months here, mine probably sounded like a fairy tale. When you've always burned coal distributed through radiators from November 15 to March 15, you can't fathom owning central heating. When you've not seen an oven, the idea of standing rib roast or apple pie is beyond understanding, especially if topped by cheese or ice cream. That would require a refrigerator, absent in Chinese homes. Forget about coffee. Here, it's tea. (Although a Starbucks is rumored to be opening downtown soon.)

When with Westerners, I hear complaints about the quality of goods and services: Pipes leak, break, flip out of the hole in the wall, and flood the room. Shoes come unglued. Appliances quit working after a few days.

My Chinese friends respond, "Not a problem." They tell me who to call for a few yuan's repair—less than $1 US. No "stitch in time saves nine" idea here; they're proud that they can help.

When I return a defective CD player, or shoes with a tack poking my sock or threatening my sole, I'm met with congenial acceptance. After inspecting it thoroughly, consulting at least one other person, and getting a supervisor to fill out triple copies to sign separately, I'm taken across town for an afternoon's bus/walk search to find a repairman. His assistant has me fill out more papers and wait until my turn comes up. Actual repair takes about five minutes; these guys have met that nail or wire's problem before.

All the while, the parent inside my head keeps preaching, "Anything worth doing is worth doing right!" Then I wonder, "Why do shop owners take such pride in their gleaming goods yet show no chagrin when I return it a day later, pointing out its defect?"

The answer springs from a different set of values. My Chinese companions proudly sum it up. "We help many people have jobs today."

(Maybe you're ready to hit Delete by now?)

To be continued, if you wish,

Regina

I stood up and stretched, feeling like I was on a seesaw. How long could I teeter from one end to the other without falling off?

CHINA 25 - MORE CONTRASTS

I abandoned my computer to boil water for green tea. Aromatic leaves floated, eventually sinking to the bottom of my glass. Fortified, I returned to typing:

(This email's becoming a tome. If still interested, read on, friends and family.) What of East-West contrasting service ideas? Three examples: 1) Airline tickets are delivered to my door, with all Chinese symbols and no airline noted on the receipt. "Ask at airport." 2) Two costumed lovelies bow my guests through an ornate restaurant door and direct us to a bare table. The waitress notices me wiping up grease, brings a once-white cloth, and we cover it. 3) A co-teacher says that she "learned to drive last weekend" and is "still afraid." Practice was in a parking lot. She hasn't driven on a street, but she passed the course with honors.

I asked a Pei Hua secretary for a darker room to show a class movie last week. The English Dean called a summit meeting about "my problem." I invited the Foreign Language Dean to a class presentation as a courtesy, and three days later, I heard from them: "About your teaching plan, you may go ahead with it." An official representative attended because "Dean is busy." Yet the dean takes time every day to invite me to use his water purifier and "have a rest" on his mock-leather couch. There is a different standard, not disrespectful or lower here, unless measured by my Western plumbline. (I hear Mom's "That's too deep for me!")

(I'll push on about Contrasts.) From my experience, it seems Americans expect quality first and foremost. I must ask students how quality is translated in a Chinese dictionary. They wish for "an excellent school" or "a developed country," like tourists wanting

to fly rather than drive. Here, thinking has more to do with pressing steadily ahead while keeping an eye on "a happy life"—the expected destination.

(Here's a Chinese illustration to make Mom shake her head again.) Build a twelve-story building—actually eleven, skipping an unlucky fourth floor—for Perfect Gardens. Top it with an eye-catching spire. Move lucky folks in, firecrackers popping to ensure safety and happiness. If the elevator breaks or cement crumbles, families move out. Bring in sufficient men with sledgehammers to tear down twelve stories and build eighteen—actually seventeen, with the digits adding up to a lucky "8."

I ask, "Why not repair the elevator or mix better cement?"

"More jobs!" is the proud Chinese explanation. And if someone takes too long or changes the status quo too much, fifteen people wait to willingly do that job in the same manner as before. They explain the process as "keeping balance." I'm still trying to understand what that means. I do know it's not what I used to think it meant. (How I'd enjoy discussing this at my son's table!)

If my teacher-daughter were here, we'd compare these classroom behaviors. What I read before coming here is true—as far as it goes. Chinese custom avoids standing out from the group. Students want everyone to succeed to the point of unapologetic plagiarism. They share answers in Chinese, even when penalized for doing so. Great shame is professed over and over at scoring poorly, along with promises to "do my best," with not much idea of how to approach "best." Students tenaciously fight me for higher scores, even offering gifts bought at great sacrifice, apologizing when I politely refuse the fourth and final time. Most announce test scores immediately. Explanation? They want to know who's on top so they can emulate them. It spurs me to set fair, spelled-out objectives that they can achieve in my classes.

(Play this contrast like a movie in your head if you're still having fun.) Picture a man dressed as every other Chinese man on the

street: black purse over his shoulder, just-shined shoes, dark pants belted half-again around his waist. He gesticulates with his lighted cigarette and screams into a cell phone while walking a long block among thirty people who ignore his rantings. Above him, a telephone number containing five eights hangs from the top of a soon-to-open high rise. "Eight" resembles "prosperity" in Mandarin. I've yet to see a 4 in an advertised number. I surmise that the man in black just demanded an investment trade ending in 8 and found an unwanted 4, a Chinese "death word" that represents misfortune. Has someone done a study on the cost of this number bias as rich Chinese invest?

I'm repeatedly told "I'm sorry you are lonely" by Chinese friends who refuse to believe otherwise. They cite their happy childhood home with "many people per room" as evidence of my misery. Lately, however, several Chinese women have lamented the "no time for myself" theme and said, "In my opinion, Blakely, you enjoy your life." Using surnames is a traditional sign of respect, something I'm getting used to. No "Call me Regina" here!

Here's one for the grandkids: In a theme park, adrenalin-surging passion rises as flashlights wave to a nationalistic pop song. Dancers move in unison. Pride and unity are almost palpable. Is the great desire for oneness the reason that even the Chinese word for "no" (bu) becomes "no yes," (bu shi) when translated? Perhaps it's more like "Surely not!" Every one of my students says, "Yes, you cannot find the answer." Are they hedging their bets for True-False tests?

For whatever reasons, I know that I cannot bring Western ideas of efficiency or "the shortest point from A to B" to the Chinese process for following maps, making schedules, or expecting answers. Four people, united in a genuine wish to help, give me four different versions of the way to visit a temple via map. If I don't get there by Bus 40 (because it's empty, containing the number 4), then someone puts me on the right bus. If an office is closed today, it may open tomorrow. If the map is upside down, "Maybe we make a mistake." If told, "Will call you Monday to meet," but no call comes, there's plenty of time. If I call, I hear "You wish to meet? I am very busy today." If the dean calls, that cancels all appointments. He's the highest "Com-U-nist" in command.

I stretched high overhead. Too much sitting at the computer had tightened up my back. I eyed the bed, considering a power nap, when the phone rang. It was Matt.

"Dr. Blakely, I must apologize for cutting off our last visit. I can tell you now that a lot is happening here; President Bush has appointed a new Homeland Security head, and I like my boss so far. Change isn't always easy for me. Let's see. You know about skirmishes in the Middle East? Hurricane Ivan's damage is about cleaned up. You probably also know that Willie Nelson was part of a Fall Farm Concert back in September. As I said, it's busy here."

"Wow, Matt! I understand now why you seemed distracted last call. I've been busy with understanding this culture and didn't know any of that news. Thank you for the catch-up; it means a lot. I'm out of touch and missing home."

I told him memories of a farm concert done at K-State years back, when Willie and friends had sung from a tractor-pulled wagon on the football field after a close game with KU. The crowd had loved it. Matt listened politely, but I cut the story short.

"Is anything else happening of interest at home, Matt?"

"I'll let you in on a little secret, Dr. B; Tom Brokaw is stepping down as news anchor on December first. We just found out."

"He'll be missed, Matt. Again, I love hearing about home."

"I should probably let you go and pack for my Thanksgiving Break trip. I, uh, guess you don't have that holiday in China, do you?"

"No, Matt, but that doesn't keep me from being thankful for your catch-up call. Until next time!"

As I stretched the receiver toward its cradle, my back-ache disappeared.

CHINA 26 - DIFFERING VIEWPOINTS

I'd explored a lot of contrast examples in my email home, yet wide awake, I found my thoughts still clamoring. So, I resumed banging away on my plastic keyboard, taking up where my email had left off.

Here in China, I've learned that Confucius said, "Never make friends with others not equal to you." Coming from singing, "Give me your tired, your poor..." and a practiced Christian eye for seeing worth in every living soul, I'd like to sit down with Confucius and chew on that for a while. Lucy, a Master's-level student doing her thesis on the great teacher's works, explained, "To have a successful society, you must always move upward into relationships that increase your status." She saw nothing to be gained by befriending those below you in the pecking order. It's a sort of "pick yourself up by others' bootstraps" approach. That sort of explained why many here ask if we can "be friends," yet blatantly ignore me as a person.

I asked, "What about lessons learned from people different from ourselves?"

Lucy replied, "There is nothing to be learned from the poor. The government takes care of them."

It reminded me of conversations back home about government and a less-regarded minority, migrant worker, or addicted street person who "deserves that station in life." I often left those discussions stimulated but disappointed that critical thinking simply underlined my already-held prejudices, clashing with arguments from the other side. Not much changed within or without. It was easy to focus on my logical solutions, and hard to see someone else's. Here, I long for vantage points from which to see both.

Scratching below the surface, one finds thinkers, doers, dalliers, and dreamers in societies on both sides of the globe. Most Westerners bring to the present moment what's experienced, thinking it the best approach to life, perhaps straightening out a few kinks based on past happenings. We explain the behavior of others in light of our own prior knowledge. This kind of one-upmanship doesn't work here. Is it possible to set aside ingrained ideas of quality products/time/ relationships for a group cliché that "It doesn't matter" and "take a little rest"? I suspect that, if we find workable ways to believe that all will truly be well, we may find that it already is.

Enough of this teeter-totter, yin-yang thinking! It may discourage any questions from coming in your next emails. Give someone nearby a hug or kind word, and thanks for keeping in touch.

Your Observing Wanderer in China,

Regina

I reread the near-essay written home, rather pleased at my conjured-up contrasts. I hit "send" and grabbed my pajamas. An eerie wail pulled me up short. It sounded like an animal in pain. My first impulse was to rush out and down the stairs. It came again, urgent and deep. I turned off all the lights and crept to my dark kitchen window.

Below, on the curb, sat a boy with his arm around a girl. She shouted and beat at him with her fists, then wailed again, sobbing into his chest like her heart was broken. In the streetlight, I saw his eyes turn up toward my second story, as if to find some answer. I crept back toward my bed, wearily remembering that I had to rise early for class.

One more conscious thought came before I fell asleep. I wished for a surveillance camera trained on my entrance. China's cellphone glut surely placed them miles ahead of the US in technology. I'd heard that cellphones here could also take pictures. Probably in ten years, China would have a CCTV camera for every two people, keeping track of everything from who visited Tiananmen Square to dramatic scenes below my window.

Through my earplugs, I heard the outside girl's wail crescendo, punctuated by the boy's deeper bass. Crazy plots passed through my hazy movie-screen mind. They were breaking up. They'd just found out that they were actually half-brother and sister and not permitted to marry. She was pregnant. He was returning home at Christmas. She had failed a test and planned to kill herself. . .

They stood and walked away.

CHINA 27 - XIAN CHRISTMAS

I was awakened, leisurely remembering the second verse of "Jingle Bells," when the ringing phone interrupted the melody.

"Ho Ho Ho!" Matt said in a hearty voice.

"Merry Christmas, Matt," I said with forced merriment. "I must get ready for a Christmas party here."

"Merry Christmas to you, Dr. B. Tell me about celebrating that holiday in China?"

I sang a Buddhist-flavored Christmas tune into the phone:

> *"Chestnuts roasting free of all desire*
> *Jack Frost sitting in repose*
> *Yuletide sutras intoned by the fire*
> *By monks adorned in Santa's clothes.*
> *And so, I offer you this fond lampoon*
> *With tongue in cheek, but reverence too*
> *Although it is meant in a nondual way*
> *Merry Christmas, empty Christmas, merry emptiness to you."*

Matt was silent a moment more, then said, "I don't know what to say."

"I thought maybe, since China's more Buddhist than anything else, you might enjoy a little levity while roasting this season's chestnuts."

"If you're becoming Buddhist, that may be a little hard to explain to the office. We're a Christian country, and the secretary's a lady from the south—"

"Don't worry, Matt. Look at it as my crazy sense of humor on top of a little homesickness. How will you celebrate Christmas, Matt?"

"Shopping's done and calendar's filling with parties. I'll visit the big city for Mom's turkey dinner. I dread nieces and nephews running around, but it makes my parents happy on holidays."

"Enjoy yourself, Matt."

I hung up, satisfied that Matt's response was a Western-thinking one. He seemed to have no idea of the Buddhist/Taoist/Communist foundation I'd come to expect in XiAn. I went to my keyboard to compose the nearest thing I could manage to a Christmas letter:

ChristmasAtHomeGroup@global.net

Dear Ones, Old and New,

Nearly Christmas

Last September, I taught Pei Hua sophomores a Girl Scout song, "Make new friends, but keep the old. One is silver and the other gold." This week, I told classes I had chosen Kai Jin Lu as my adopted Chinese name. After two hundred student suggestions, one girl said that "Open Golden Road" was like my first lecture's "old friends." I'll celebrate Christmas with an American Open House for Chinese friends.

I'm trying to do holiday goodies with no oven—just a hotplate, rice cooker, and microwave. It'll be tuna salad, no-bake cookies, and candy canes found at the market. We'll sing "Jingle Bells," rewritten for Thanksgiving, and "Silent Night" with a borrowed guitar. I'll conduct gift-giving of American mementos wearing a Santa hat found for a yuan (twelve cents). It tops my Qin Opera mask, a festive touch above my entryway washing machine.

Every day in China holds surprising, rich experiences. I'm learning much about myself and how wide our world can be.

My Kansas kids' Christmas letter was a hoot. One grandson's karate chop on a milk carton didn't turn out well. The other boy set traps for the tooth fairy.

I hope to visit them and Mom soon. Her quilted potholder graces my tiny kitchen. I remember past Thanksgiving tables set by my sister, our family cook extraordinaire.

Letters keep binding ties. Kansas Citians write of snowy, icy streets. None yet in XiAn, but there's bone-biting cold while wearing three layers in unheated classrooms. My apartment's warm from government-distributed coal that hammers allergies and expels acrid odors.

For Chinese New Year, I want to fly to California to celebrate that grandson's birthday and see my son's new family house. Those hopes stay alive when homesickness threatens. I send season's greetings from a very different perspective: No holiday stress and anxiety here. It's just another workday. No worry about menus or decorations. It's another meal of fresh vegetables, rice, dumplings or noodles. Plenty of fresh market fruit with toilet-paper roll/napkins on the table, the same touch of red on the walls all year. I'll seek a church for a "Jesus party" Christmas Eve and remember the reason for the season. Grateful for all your thoughts, cards, letters, and packages,

Regina

As I hit Send, I thought I'd better get my mind off of home if I wanted to keep the self-sufficient attitude of my newest email. Had I overdone the acceptance and brotherhood bit?

I turned to preparing for the Sophomore Christmas party, just a few hours away. A yellow cake mix found in a lone aisle of Western foods was rising nicely in the microwave, turning an unappetizing gray. I'd found one can of chocolate frosting on the same shelf. Pulling my velour robe around me, I grabbed the rag mop to give the apartment a little shine before twenty-eight pairs of shoes scuffed it up again. Then a knock rang through both doors. *Who on earth?*

"*Wei?*" I yelled.

Joe's unmistakable voice answered: "Regina, Merry Christmas!"

I pulled buttons through buttonholes and opened the doors, leaning on my mop handle.

"Joe, I didn't expect you for a couple more hours."

He entered, flanked by two pretty coeds who lowered themselves to my Mickey and Minnie couch only seconds after Joe sat. He thrust a brown bag of oranges my way. "I cannot come to your party, but I wish you a Happy Holiday, Regina." His grin reached from ear to ear.

He looked around. I tried to keep my mouth from flying open to say how much I had to do to get ready. I managed to let it go at *"shei shei."*

"I like the wreath above the TV. Your students will have a happy Christmas party. We must go now."

I reopened the doors and let them out, not having learned the young lovelies' names and feeling resentful for the intrusion, yet happy Joe had remembered the party. Maybe, down the party-giving timeline here, I'd learn that people came at all hours. I made a mental note to tactfully bring the party to a close so that students would exit before the neighbors beat on the walls. Then I realized that I was feeling angry with Joe for parading his office harem into my apartment. What was he trying to do? Make me jealous?

I mopped furiously through the living room into the bedroom, deciding that this was no way to think during a season meant to be merry. I frosted the cake, arranged Joe's gifted oranges in a blue bowl, and put on a green blouse with black slacks, just in time for my first guests, Min and Lina, who brought crack seed to share.

Soon, three dozen young people were elbow-to-elbow as they checked out my living quarters, exclaimed at the calendar pictures on my walls, asked, "Do you live here alone?" and helped themselves to the lemonade punch atop my washer. No one commented that the punchbowl looked like the plastic basin they used nightly to wash their feet at home.

I slipped through the press of chattering students, hearing a mixture of Chinese and English. Five girls clustered around my computer screen, giggling at the English wording. There were no Chinese symbols like they saw on their screens.

Leo, always up for a good time, orchestrated a game involving each person getting a card: Hearts sang a song, spades told a secret, diamonds recited something, and clubs chose what to share.

It was time to go, but the ubiquitous picture had to happen first. All three dozen young people perched, crouched, stood, and sat in a happy composition; I took turns with Leo, standing on a chair to snap photos. When they trooped out the door, I felt like hostess of the year.

As I picked up party remains, the previous night's heartbroken wail reached my ears. There was still no Christmas cheer between the couple sitting on the curb below my darkened window.

CHINA 28 - SANYA INTRODUCTION

Tired of disappearing dramas recurring below my freshman campus window, I greeted Spring Festival vacation with anticipation and energy that matched my students. I would fly to meet Mary in "China's Hawaii" on Hainan Island. While boarding China Air, I pictured her striding toward me, a signature scarf around her neck.

When I landed near the southern tip of the island, we hugged in Sanya's teeming airport, together by almost a miracle. Spring Festival travelers alighted elbow to elbow, heading for tropical vacations. We followed them to where Mary's Kunming bags had arrived. My XiAn soft-cover rollers finally circled around, along with cardboard boxes taped by Chinese mainlanders.

We haggled with a cab driver—shaking our heads negatively and showing him a small number of yuan bills—to find our weeklong home away from home. We'd both learned the hard way to determine the cost of a ride before getting into a cab. Mary chattered up front to the taciturn driver, who was puffing on his cigarette. I tried to breathe, with my back window wide open.

Sanya's jungle growth gave way to canopied deciduous trees, white pine, and coconut palms near busy sunset beaches. I'd already heard that lovely Sanya Bay was so polluted that few swam there, but the waters farther south were safely swimmable. We'd landed at the sunny, northeastern edge of a South China Sea harbor city.

Maria, our XiAn headhunter friend, had offered a deal on her vacation high-rise apartment. She would be nearby. That was fine with us, though I secretly wished Maria's English name was farther from Mary's given one. Mary's natural wholesome beauty was nothing like Maria's perfect makeup, salon coif, and designer clothes. Both had hearty laughs and seldom reverted to negative thoughts or complaints. It promised to be a carefree holiday.

We sped past palm trees as Mary warned me that our gated community was holding an all-night funeral below our window. That marked three deaths in the housing complex during the past year. Mary didn't know if the wake was for the old guy with a tippy-toe Alzheimer's shuffle, the man who sat all day on a board raised by a sawhorse and a tar bucket, or the bow-legged woman who leaned on her cane to make her morning circuit. We'd have to wait through a night's celebration to find out.

First stop, though, was a bicycle shop. We rented two reliable ones, which the cabbie piled on the back of his station wagon and delivered to our third-floor apartment. Sure enough, a red-white-blue awning, red banners, round tables, and plastic seats filled a flood-lit garden just below my bedroom window. Fragrances of ginger and Chinese Five Spices bubbled in cast-iron cauldrons. Mahjong tiles clicked at a few tables.

I splashed water on my face and caught Mary on the way out to Maria's other condo. We took the elevator up, left our shoes outside her door, and entered to quietly put thank-you gifts on a corner table. Maria's father and Helen (age four) beamed welcomes. He boomed, "You eat!"

And eat we did: dumplings, beef and broccoli, pork, and cabbage, which we washed down with Tsingtao 4.7 percent alcohol pale ale. I managed only a couple of swallows and returned to my purified water.

Conversation stretched far into the evening. Exhausted and sated, we returned home, where I fell asleep to the rattle of drums, firecrackers, voices, and Mahjong tiles. The last thing I heard was Maria's voice saying, "Funerals usually last three days here."

The next morning, after Maria's father's noodle-soup breakfast, Mary and I rode our bikes to explore suburban Sanya. We passed preschools every few blocks. At attractive Golden Sun Kindergarten, a stylishly dressed woman was closing its gate. I introduced myself and asked what ages attended. "Up through kindergarten. I'm Helen, and I'm looking for a teacher."

Mary politely rode away. Helen, the owner and principal, kept talking. I found myself considering teaching kindergartners English and helping Helen's teachers. We toured, and I met Filipino and Chinese Early Childhood graduates eating in the break area. Other workers diapered toddlers, closed doors so three-year-olds didn't escape into the courtyard, circled four-year-olds to hold up numerals and yell call-and-response numbers, and tiptoed around mats during the five-year-olds' naptime. The kids were adorable, and the need for good pedagogy seemed great. I decided on the spot. I'd report

Monday with a morning plan for Helen to consider. I could go to beaches and play tourist with Mary in the afternoons.

Helen soon suggested that I "hold a weekly English corner." Mary had explained how Chinese gather in parks and practice English. I envisioned Hyde Park. Mary laughed and said it was more like "Hello! How are you? Do you like China?" over and over. I was determined to have the young teachers pick a theme, plan a couple of related questions, and prepare at least two bits of information to share with whomever showed up from the school's residential neighborhood. I found myself becoming even more excited about this Chinese Paradise vacation.

CHINA 29 - FACING DADONGHAI

Mary encouraged the idea of my teaching half days. Afternoons, we pedaled and brainstormed how I'd help five-year-olds make Xin Nian Kuai Le Happy New Year's cards for their parents. The kids would learn to count to ten in English while the glue dried on firecrackers made of red construction-paper rolled around toilet-paper tubes. Firecrackers were part of house-warmings, business openings, and festivals, so the kids understood that experience.

Monday's lesson went well. Eight children sat on three-legged stools semi-circled in front of my low chair. With pantomime and a little call-and-response, they caught on to simple English commands. They counted to ten by rote, but identifying one item versus three baffled them until we used objects, fingers, and toes. We pushed understanding one-through-four number concepts, using simulated firecrackers, toys, and children to count in groups.

I looked up. Teachers filled all four courtyard windows, watching "Western methods."

A maid watched children eat noodles, tomato-egg soup, and rice before they stretched out on small mats for rest. Ella and June said, "Dr. Blakely, the children like it very much." High praise. We dined on rice, wilted greens, and shrimp. Ella walked me toward my bike at the gate.

"We go in the morning to watch Dadonghai sunrise, remember?"

I wondered how they'd see sunrise on a beach facing southwest but realized that their limited use of English couldn't fathom the complexity of what I'd already tried once to explain. "We can try, Ella. Meet me at the gate?"

Sure enough, a half dozen young women biked behind Mary and me down Phoenix Road at daybreak the next morning. They asked at empty intersections, "Which way we go?" and I'd take off in the general direction, carefully waiting for stoplights. After thirty minutes, we got to Dadonghai's stretch of venders' stalls, overlooking a gray sea. We locked our bikes to posts and shed our shoes to walk in the morning surf.

June led us to the top of a flight of cement stairs. I sat and twisted east as far as I could turn. Low mountains obscured any rising sun, but the clouds were turning pink on their undersides. Xiao Jin and June found newspapers to sit upon, facing the sea to the west, as did their friends who remained standing.

"Where is the sun?" Xiao Jin asked.

"It will come over the mountain soon," I assured her, pointing back.

"I dreamed of seeing it rise from the sea," she dreamily informed us.

Not one young teacher had an understanding of directions in Sanya, where they had lived for at least a half-year. We did an impromptu N-E-W-S lesson to give them an acronym to memorize, along with the fact that the sun rises in the east and sets in the west. Mary watched, amused.

While we waited for the sun to come over the greenery behind us, I was surprised to find myself wondering how Joe would have handled this outing. Did he understand the cardinal directions and his earth-location in the universe, or was he tossing about with only fragmented knowledge like these young teachers? He'd been wonderfully understanding with my hysteria over the missing passport and lack of pay before it had miraculously fallen into place for this trip. A wave of gratitude swept over me. I hoped Joe got to enjoy a sunrise—facing the east—once in a while.

Mary looked at me. "A penny for your thoughts?"

"Oh, they're probably not worth that. 'Peaceful here, isn't it?'"

She whispered, "Yes, I hear there's a males-only nude beach at the far end of Dadonghai. They're nude because they want to heal psoriasis."

I thought of the young teachers, eyes turned toward the China Sea behind us. "I think we'll stay on this expanse of white sand. The sun's making the water glisten now."

"Spoil sport!" Mary giggled, grabbed her camera, and took off alone.

CHINA 30 - GOLDEN SUN

Back at Golden Sun, Helen conducted a faculty meeting about red carpets for an upcoming New Year's program. As tactfully as possible, I told her why I preferred natural classroom themes to memorizing a "festival drama" required of each preschool class. She said she understood, then reminded me we must finish the Smart Kids curricula, with five seatwork books, by the end of my week there. A dozen heads nodded in unison before teachers, aides, and I all lowered our eyes.

I plunged ahead, making a case for developmental pedagogy, rather than having small hands tracing letters with adult-sized pencils. Again, Helen said that she understood, and then suggested that we might pursue a space theme.

I conceded. Kids probably knew "alien, spaceship, and planet" because of cartoons. Maybe I could sneak in concepts like "this/that, next to, behind, over" and a few pronouns here and there. It might work to meaningfully teach English.

There was a different story to tell Mary and Maria over our drink each evening. In only three days, my class had their presentation memorized. They circled their paper-mâché sun, singing a space song to a Beatles tune, and bowed on cue during rehearsal.

Helen said, "Wonderful!" Ella thought it too short. Her four-year-old's presentation took thirty minutes, with other kids unable to stay quiet during rehearsal. Teachers' tempers flared into "ATTENTION!" to which kids screamed "ONE TWO!" and quieted momentarily. Maybe, in the future, we could laugh about the anxiety-related fisticuffs between an overworked nursery teacher and the male cook. She hit first, then fled when he hit back, leaving thirty-three three-year-olds with their mouths agape.

Some evenings felt sad, like times when I could only listen and hug a tearful lead teacher, who struggled to do twenty minutes of English a day with twice-too-many kids. I wished I could speak Chinese to better help them. Mary, college teacher extraordinaire, had no suggestions for me. My modeling of frequently changed activities, cueing, and making repetition a game continued each day before a window-packed gallery of onlookers as I taught. It was too big a stretch from the yell-and-response method they'd always known.

Stories about teachers smacking kids came out, along with shame, as inexperienced teachers reverted to how they'd been brought up, instead of using the Western idea of responsible discipline. I'd usually go to that class the next day, divide the class, and do whatever captivating lesson I could dream up to involve the smaller group. Then I'd switch groups. It was part pantomime, part participation, part rewarding behaviors you wanted, and part hanging on with patience. I didn't dare invest any ego in the mix; preschool egos were out in full force.

On my last day at Golden Sun, loudspeakers blared as parents arrived. Jerry, the prickly class porcupine who worked at being disliked, planted an unexpected kiss on my cheek.

Co-teachers Ella and Shirley gave them a rest from lessons without consulting me. After fifteen minutes of looking at books, the kids were karate-kicking, screaming, and fighting.

I suggested giving them choices. And so, balloons, dot-to-dots, color-keyed pictures, and paper cutting claimed the next fifteen minutes. Ella arrived with noisy clackers that immediately became guns, and they went wild again.

Defeated, I swept up crayons and escaped to an early lunch, then biked to a massage while Golden Sun took its usual two-hour nap. I returned to see that Tom had the beginning of a shiner. Ella told Helen, "Somehow, when he played…"

Carefully-applied make up transformed kids into superstars who marched onstage at exactly three p.m. "ATTENTION—ONE! TWO!" They greeted parents with English New Year wishes, circled Ella's cardboard sun, and sang lustily.

Back in the room, we rolled sweet dumpling dough around bean curd. I told parents how much I liked teaching their children, gave each child a lucky red candy, and bade them farewell in time to get to Yalong Bay's Hilton. Mary and I had volunteered to sing Christmas carols with a choir in English/

Chinese/Russian/Filipino/Mongolian. The choir's first big gig was another chance for a rise in our cultural learning curve.

Unforgettable Sanya's Golden Sun Kindergarten imprinted on my memory as I grabbed a white robe with a red stole and turned my focus to entertaining four hundred Russians in the hotel ballroom. Some were preening about, showing off their multicolored rooster tails for the old year. One fellow, whose mask sported a red comb, cavorted around the tables during "Deck the Halls" saying, "Cock-a-doodle-doo!" We moved on to "Silent Night" in Chinese. The same guy returned, this time in a full dog costume.

Disneyland's Goofy joined our choir, ears flopping as he grabbed a microphone. My ears tingled with recognition. That was Joe's voice, or did he have a twin in Sanya? The accented English sounded all too familiar, as the guy behind the mask cracked a joke about "having to wait another four years to say Happy Niu Year." I recalled one day in Pei Hua's office, when Joe had explained that "Niu" meant "ox," a year not due until 2009. Then he'd let out that same humorous cackle. At the hotel, few of our choir members got the joke; Russians sat in puzzled silence. Goofy gaily left the stage, spouting platitudes about man's best friend, and disappeared.

CHINA 31 - CONSIDERING DEMISES

Safely home from my Sanya vacation, I walked through silent falling snow past where I'd heard nightly cries from the young couple sitting on the curb. No sign that they'd been there. Had I imagined the wailing?

I opened my doors to find a letter hanging from some duct tape. My daughter's familiar running print had sent news of her father-in-law's death. It wasn't unexpected, and I was not expected at the funeral, but I found myself coming into a new awareness of passings. Like a butterfly flitting from flower to fading flower, I began noticing demises all around me.

I pondered *China Daily*'s English announcement that West African rhinos had just become extinct as I hopped on the fast weekend bus downtown. An Italian woman sat next to me, chattering about falling in love with XiAn six years earlier. She'd stayed, and never looked back. Her lovely accent and musical English made it a needed exchange. My days of hearing only Chinese seemed to have met a demise also.

Some demises turn out well. I got off the bus, feeling very hungry, and entered a promising restaurant. My request for beef brought a barrage of unrecognizable words. A Caucasian couple from St. Louis walked in and ordered three vegetable dishes in Chinese. We shared their pork and my beef soup. That brought hunger's demise! We then walked beautiful QingLing Gong Park together.

That couple put me in touch with Amanda, a single foster-mom I soon helped on non-teaching weekdays. Holding the liveliest spina bifida baby at the foster home, I heard Amanda tell Baby Sarah, "We're going to Hangzhou and get that ugly thing off your back!" Sarah and five others could then grow up with only slight scars, and perhaps, subconscious memories of the sacs on their spines or their cleft palates preventing them from babbling into perfect speech.

There are also demises of expectations. English teacher Liu Rong and I visited ruins where a Han Emperor and wives were buried. As we viewed small figures of horses, warriors, people, and pots, Liu Rong told me that her archeologist brother-in-law had dug them up. We returned via XiAn's Museum of Steeles (stone tablets with lovely Chinese symbols). She promised to soon interpret poetry in Confucius's wisdom at a villa atop Qing Ling Mountain near the new campus. One hour later, she cancelled because her friend said it was too cold up there. We perspired in XiAn instead. This kind of demise happens a lot here.

The Pei Hua dean, whose stressful exchanges about everything from whether to boil water to what subjects I should teach, also taught me something about good deaths. Joe seemingly held no recall of our differences of opinion after we'd dropped a subject; they were, like he said, forgotten.

Recently, he'd been in the Education Office almost daily, reading required papers from seniors on everything from "The Religious Rite in America" to "The Influence of UK on China's Education." I'd heard Joe and his pretty assistants discuss the fine points of English grammar, although I avoided going there whenever I could; those girls were gorgeous, and they seemed to adore Joe. He ate it up. Even the back of his head seemed to carry a continuous grin. However, determined to get on with my ESL life, I needed to discuss with my boss my parting of ways with Pei Hua.

Determined, I approached his desk and heard, "Doctor! Sit down and rest. Have Chinese bread." He'd made it himself. I ate the flat and saltless bread and drank tea made with boiling water with the kettle's green light blazing. Joe announced, "Now it is Internationally Famous Bread!"

I asked him, "Can we talk about a matter of importance, Dean Zhou?"

He dismissed his assistants, indicated a quiet corner of the English office-cum-lounge, and waited for me to sit.

I did so, taking a deep breath. "Are you the person to tell that I will not return to Pei Hua next year?"

Joe nodded, then loudly said, "The Education Dean will decide what you teach."

My thoughts surfaced. *What happened to the compassionate man who wiped my tears and set things in motion for my returned passport after I fell apart with homesick frustration?*

"I have enjoyed my students," I said, "and like China very much, but I miss my grandchildren." I'd thought I said this quite firmly, but he didn't get the message.

"Then a half year," he said just as loudly as before.

Pei Hua hadn't offered that option when I first came here. I doubted Joe had the power for such a compromise.

I lowered my voice and looked him in the eyes. "I think it better that you get someone else. I will not teach again here."

Joe countered with "You let us know in May. A half year."

A demise of listening on his part? Perhaps. Either way, on my part, it was the end of "needing to communicate." Just when I'd begun to like the man, he was acting like an arrogant prig. I left him without another word. I was seething . . . for some reason I couldn't explain right then.

CHINA 32 - TWISTY TURNS

Within days of my pondering these XiAn demises, offers to teach started coming out of the cement-work—there was very little woodwork in this city. I met a man from Guangdong, a tropical southern province, as I sipped tea near the old city wall. He convinced me that the universities there merited a visit. Mary e-mailed me to say that her department head liked our proposed half-year each in Kunming and promised an answer soon. Students and teachers from XiAn International nudged me to re-apply there for the short-term assignment that had not been open last year. On a bus across town, the hire-and-fire guy from Nanjing's Kansas-State equivalency gave me his number and suggested I call Kansas residents teaching at Nanjing Forestry University. I did so, and they told me about how they often biked around a nearby lake, saw bird shows on the islands, and climbed amidst flowering trees to a pagoda-view up on Purple Mountain in clear air and great weather. All of these sounded like possibly good trades for XiAn's smog.

Some friendships, like Maria's, didn't feel like demises. She frequently dropped by to offer impromptu adventures. We'd just finished a Chinese lesson when someone knocked.

I opened the door to see two policemen, rocking on their toes like they were nervous. One said, "You are safe" to me in English. Then he told Maria in Chinese that they were trying to "catch a thief in a white coat," or at least, that was Maria's non-emotional translation to me. At least fifty curious onlookers stood below in the street, peering up at my kitchen window.

Maria closed the door on the uniformed men. Then in a soft voice, she said, "Regina, I take you now to a temple meal for dinner, then a foot bath. No more Chinese lesson today."

I locked all windows and doors and climbed into Maria's white Jeep. The only answer I got about the exchange with the police throughout dinner and the subsequent foot-washing and massage was "Never mind." It was as if such exchanges about campus thieves happened every day. I gave up and relaxed into the strong female hands that were massaging my calves, ankles, and the reflexology points on my feet. Maria came to life then to show me the "difference in "footbath." One small foot, painted near the last line on signs or price sheets, signified what we got as women versus what was offered to businessmen entertaining associates, who expected more than just foot massages. "My husband often uses those," Maria reported.

"So your husband is a businessman?" I ventured.

"Yes." The subject seemed closed with that.

She pulled up on the dorm sidewalk—where she usually parked—and watched me climb the stairs. I unlocked my double steel doors to peace and quiet. It was as if the earlier drama with the police visit had never happened.

Everything was just as I'd left it in my apartment. Doors and windows remained locked. I stayed up late and graded 150 exams from my Tuesday-Thursday class, deciphering butchered English and chuckling over a note that had been left on one: "The answer is behind this paper." Sure enough, it was written on the back.

The next day, I gave a lesson on how to take notes and quiz yourself for details pertaining to big ideas for essays, rather than memorizing what the book says to prove points. I doubted that I made enough impression on them to get them to kill off such an old practice and try a new one. I did glimpse small increments of thought each week though. Students shed their reticence and started shouting syllable markings to team-representatives like little kids after Friday's pronunciation lesson. Nobody's perfect though. I still longed to hear "PROTestant" instead of "ProTESTant" and "COMmunist" rather than "CommUnist."

The phone rang. I was sure Matt wouldn't call at midnight. It scared me. The ringing persisted. I detoured past the kitchen and grabbed a heavy skillet—although I knew I couldn't defend myself with a skillet over the phone. Holding on for dear life, I breath in and picked up the receiver.

"*Wei?*"

It was an Italian woman, another ESL teacher whom I'd met on the street. She apologized for such a late invitation to Scrabble the next evening. I returned the skillet to the kitchen, half-laughing at myself, and memorized the landmarks near her apartment to guide the cab driver. What a treat it would be to lose myself in an English word game.

CHINA 33 - CLOSER GLIMPSES

The phoned Scrabble invitation reminded me that my Italian friend had offered *"Shei shei"* after our first brief English exchange on a bus. I had responded, "You are welcome!" We'd laughed at the mix of languages from our three cultures. I'd told her that bumping into her was just what I'd needed on a day when I'd felt isolated. She'd promised a game in our near future. "Ciao until then!" Her call had given me a glimpse of how her culture's vocabulary intersected with this one.

In class, my throat began to feel scratchy, and a cough threatened. I persevered, tried to use my voice less, and gained personal glimpses and new understandings almost daily. Students were considering a piece I'd written for them: "Miss Regina Comes to Teach in China."

XuSiSi asked what it meant when "Miss Regina chuckled about 'today in China was yesterday in Kansas'." Bill explained time zones to her, quoting my earlier lecture's information verbatim.

XuSiSi asked, "Does it refer to development?" She saw China's lack of time zones as a sign of development toward a bright future, while Kansas continued to live in the past. I secretly wondered if she might find that the rewriting of science texts by Kansans confirmed her premise. There was no need to muddy political waters with that bit of Americana.

HauBeiBei, often late or absent, wrote a note: "Dr. Blakely, I ask for leave because my family must do something important." Soon, her best friend asked for leave as well. I asked her what was more important than attending class. HauBeiebei looked stricken, then whispered, "My father died." I expressed sympathy and excused both girls, knowing they immediately faced a cold, seventy-two-hour train ride for the burial.

The remaining two dozen students sat quietly, raising expectant faces toward my on-the-spot mini-lecture about whether American "mom" or English "mum" was "correct." I told them that, actually, it's okay to say "mom" in England's Middle Highlands; it just came to America and stayed, leaving "mum" behind in other parts of England.

One boy confided that he had marked "mum" on his seatmates' paper when we traded. He apologized for his "MEEStake." I commended him for listening and speaking up, then gave both students full credit.

Other miscommunications came to mind. I excused students when they asked to "answer the call of nature" until I found them in the hallway, unapologetically on their cellphones. I sent them back to class. No one asked again.

Another twisty turn came some time earlier in class. Hoping to spark creativity in my classes, I'd requested suggestions for my Chinese name. They had offered the names of revered poets, philosophers, and even a beauty's name, but nothing creative. So, I had combined Kai Jin Lu, explaining that it was my maiden name's first syllable, the second syllable of "ReGINa," and then half of my spoken middle name.

One courageous girl raised her hand. "I don't mean to criticize, but Kai is not a surname in Chinese." Was there an approved surname list somewhere? They told me of a complete book of surnames in English, along with translations into traits and behaviors. Parents used them religiously.

My creativity had fallen flat. First name, Lu, meant "open golden road," a nice shining image for East-West, teacher-student, and past-present-future. Consider also: two tones for Lu represented stubbornness and nature. And Jin meant "Victory, kingly, and closer in relationship."

Then they asked why I hadn't chosen one of the two hundred names they'd submitted. My explanation, that I didn't want to choose one over the others, was met with blank faces. I guess it came straight out of my Western thinking, which was not close to theirs. After lots of discussion, they decided that I didn't have to take a sanctioned surname. I could be their "adopted Chinese teacher." I sent that explanation to Matt, and also to my Kansas child to post on my blog, which could not be opened in China.

CHINA CONUNDRUM

AtHomeGroup@Global.net

Friends and family,

At Pei Hua Spoken English class, we're five down, two to go, debating the worth of TV. I challenge any English teacher in America to have better debates. Students now come armed with research data, bull their way through opinions, and speak forcefully with direct eye contact. Twelve got to waive half their later oral final. Judges—the other 25 students—were severe in their ratings. I heard an impassioned plea for watching TV because it stimulates the economy. One girl painted a verbal picture where Chinese families need five TVs to meet their children's Play Station needs, Dad's sports, Mom's cooking shows, and grandparents' movies. Thus, China would see economic growth where everybody lived a happy life. Her opponent shot this down by discussing TV's contribution to materialism. Judges were so swept away by the vision of a happy life that few noted the rebuttal. East swept West. End of debate.

We're celebrating our English progress with the old Alabama-set Big Fish *movie and popcorn. One hitch came with Tuesday's first class: Seating was sparse with two debating groups absent. Volunteers forged ahead. At break, in trooped the missing dozen. "We're sorry. We were late, and our headmaster punished us." I recalled wondering why seven students from last Thursday's class had stood sheepishly against the wall when I'd gone to the office; then I realized what had happened on Tuesday. What tardy US college student would stand fifty minutes against a frigid cement wall?*

CHINA 34 - HAPPY LIFE

After writing emails, I wished for a yoga mat on which to relax my tight shoulders. Instead, I scrambled under covers to stay warm, intentionally relaxing my toes, ankles, and calves. The phone caught me before I got remotely close to relaxing my upper back.

"Nihau?" I knew my now-customary *Wei?* would bring a barrage of embarrassed apologies, still in Chinese, when the caller realized I was an ignorant American.

"Dr. Blakely, excuse my calling back, but the Secretary of State, my new boss, just listened to your rundown of students' lives and made a comment I'd like you to clarify. Do you mind?"

"I guess I'd better watch my grammar, Matt, if you're recording."

"I hope you don't mind; I knew I couldn't take notes fast enough, and I didn't want any misunderstandings because of my dyslexia."

He sounded stressed. I let go of the tightness in my own neck and tried to use a soothing tone when I responded. "I guess it's fine, Matt. I worked with a lot of students considered dyslexic in the US. I'm guessing you're actually very bright and just learn differently. Taping is a good coping practice." I paused for emphasis. "But you've made me wonder if there is anything else that will surprise me about our phone conversations?"

His laugh sounded nervous. "Nothing comes to mind. Here's why I called: The Secretary remarked that Chinese people don't consider 'the pursuit of happiness' as a right. She wondered if Jefferson's 'life, liberty, and the pursuit of happiness' was something they understood."

I reached for random thoughts to tie together into a response. "I get notes from students often wishing me a happy life and see wonder in retirees' eyes when they ask about my travels. They say I must have 'a happy life,' an oft-used Chinese phrase. I don't know if they've any idea of what Jefferson meant when writing the Declaration of Independence."

"What do you think he meant, Doctor?"

"I doubt Jefferson had personal bliss in mind, Matt. His new scheme of pride in the governed, rather than the governors, was based on Aristotle's idea of happiness being the whole point of life. Kind of an end point. Not happy faces or immediate bliss, like I see pursued across America—or in China, for that matter, where I hear 'I feel so happy' when someone's karaoke song rates a 90 percent." I wondered if I sounded pedantic, like a boring teacher.

"I'm trying to help this office understand Chinese idiosyncrasies and minimize conflict with their country, Dr. Blakely. Not critique my own country."

He paused to read the next words from his notes: "It involves trade policy, currency manipulation, theft of intellectual property, and restrictions put on US businesses operating in China."

Matt's papers rustled, and I wished for time to think. I knew that, since 1972, with Kissinger in that office, China-US relations had been led by the White House.

"Well, Matt, it seems to me that our countries have a mix of combustible cooperation and competition. Your boss surely wants to come down on the right side of history as it shapes up. I don't feel qualified to give advice."

"No advice asked for." Matt sounded miffed. "I thank you for your time." He hung up abruptly then, leaving me open-mouthed. A half-formed sentence that I wished I hadn't started fled my mind. I wondered if it had been recorded back home by this young upstart. It was too bad. I had only just started to enjoy challenging him.

CHINA 35 - PERSONAL HAPPINESS

I'd no number to call Matt and apologize for sounding like a teacher, assuming that was what had twanged a sore nerve with him. Wondering if I'd ever learn to park my opinions elsewhere, even when asked for them, I went into my rusty bathroom. I figured that I might as well relax my tight shoulders under a warm shower.

The phone rang just as I removed my pajamas. It was Matt again, and he quickly began apologizing. "I got overwhelmed, Dr. Blakely. Too much information, but I'm ready for another stab at this 'pursuit of happiness' thing if you are."

"I can go on and on, Matt. That's how I work through my own thoughts. So, it's my bad, not yours." I was just standing there, naked as the day I was born, but I was glad he'd called back.

He was quiet a moment. Then he said, "You make me smile. It's the history that snows me in this job. It was never my best subject."

"Mine either, Matt. I don't have much of a mind for it. Yet I pick up on feelings, sights, and sounds from experiences and remember them forever."

"I just thought I was hopeless, but come to think of it, I *would* be able to tell you some incidents that shaped my personal history." He sounded excited at the prospect.

"Speaking of history shaping us, Matt," I said, holding tight to our earlier thread. "Remember that America enforced Chinese-exclusion laws until 1943. Then China became our ally against Japan. Immigrants' grandchildren survived late nineteenth-century bigotry and violence. And those stories pass down to what are now fifth-generation Chinese Americans, maybe *your* generation."

"Got it." Perhaps I'd made sense to him. Matt was bright, I was sure, despite his dyslexia.

I couldn't stop there. "I see China well on the road to economic, political, and military power. In the US, the Chinese Question never went away; I suspect that Chinese Americans feel like its 'Us versus Them,' just as much as in any other culture. But the US welcomes Chinese intellectuals and their skilled contributions. That looks like a success story to me, Matt. Future events will determine whether Asian Americans feel they belong or not. At the moment though, I don't see equal 'happiness' on both sides of the globe."

"Why not?"

"What a great question, Matt! What I see is this: Chinese culture emphasizes form over critical thinking. Hours of traditional dances and practices come before they feel it's right to focus on problems. Americans usually 'get right to the point.' Looking at substance, in choosing topics to discuss and agree upon, seems rude and yields little results here. Remember *guan shi?* If there's patience and trust, shared thinking comes."

"What else, then?"

Fearing those last thoughts had gone right over his head, I elaborated. "I'm not sure I've heard anything that furthered US-Chinese relations at home or here. Maybe they feel they don't matter to the present administration. Certainly, their four thousand years of contributions to the world doesn't matter. They're warm, generous people, proud of their accomplishments."

"Have you examples, Dr. Blakely?" He was hooked now, asking for practical applications.

"I get asked about the US presence in the South China Sea, especially around Hong Kong. I'm told repeatedly that they'll clean up the environment once the Chinese economy develops. Students ask me if I see that 'Communism is a better, faster system than Democracy,' and it's not an invitation to debate. It's their core belief that the Motherland's 'happy life' is felt moment by moment, rather than being as goal oriented as it is in the States."

I'd lost myself in words again, so Matt broke in. "That might be well and good, but we've countries in Africa, South America, as well as the Middle East to worry about."

"And to learn from what's happened so far," I countered. "Khartoum's genocide, rightly named by Colin Powell, might've saved many of those 300,000 lives if the US had reacted quickly in Sudan." Now I was meddling.

115

Matt broke in again. "I can't discuss how Russia, China, and Libya shielded Sudan from censure."

"Sorry, Matt. Forgive me for getting politically specific. My opinions are just that. Opinions."

"Let's get back to the 'happiness' question."

"Fair enough. Perhaps the founding fathers saw happiness in long-term good conduct and generous citizenship. Maybe happiness was the pursuit of individual excellence that shaped a better community? We Americans define ourselves by our exceptionalism and entitlement to whatever defines our personal happiness. Chinese people are shaped by ancient history. Both sides seem out of balance. Remember there's no promise of catching happiness, just pursuing it."

"Interesting. I'm hearing happiness is more of a process, not an end."

"Wise words, Matt. Tell the Secretary that. Another interesting thing is that Jefferson's early texts all included the 'pursuit of happiness,' even when he had to make room for that phrase by taking out the term 'property'."

"I didn't know that."

What fun it was to exchange ideas with this bright young man! I pressed on. "Now, I see property and prosperity closely tied to political and social liberty. Most Americans hope owning things will make their lives better. It's probably seen as a right. In China, it's more of an increasingly realized hope."

"You've got me thinking, Doctor. Until now, I thought of happiness only as what's inside of me. But maybe it's what's shaping up outside of us."

"It could be, Matt. Or maybe a balance of the two."

"I guess government's about the same kind of balance. Thanks, Dr. B! I thought differently until this phone call. Happiness. . . Who'd have thought?"

I felt a slight shiver and glanced down at my bare toes. "We could go on, Matt, but my shower's running. If my floor gets wet all the way to the living room, my personal happiness will suffer."

That got a belly laugh. Then the phone clicked off, and I slipped under the streaming water, just in time for the hot reservoir to reach empty and tingly cold water to squirt out of the shower head.

CHINA 36 - INTRODUCING LUNA

Coal pollution continued across XiAn. My irritated nose drained to my aggravated throat and plugged ears. I snatched groggy naps. In need of exercise, I padded around my apartment, heard hallway sounds, and peered through the peep hole in my outer door. There stood two unfamiliar men, shadowy under the dim bulb.

"Ni hao?" I called, which brought a barrage of unintelligible Chinese in return. I tried again. "Speak English? I am American."

I heard them exchange more Chinese. Then they abruptly left.

After a sneeze, I returned to snatch up my telephone receiver before another ring increased my already painful headache. Again, I croaked, "'Had to answer my door, but the men left. *"Ni hao?"*

Matt's voice shouted, "Dr. Blakely, those examples you gave last time were helpful. Thanks to you, I'm the office Golden Boy!" He sounded jubilant, like he'd won a sports competition.

"I hoped to help understanding between our countries, Matt, but I'm less eager to help tip the scales in any contests between you and your fellow aides."

"I'm sorry. That was out of line!" He instantly sobered to silence. I waited. Then he continued in a more business-like tone. "The Secretary has asked for more. Are you game to keep sharing?"

"I've a bad cold, but I could share some personalities I've come across. I've kept a diary."

"Hey! Wait! Did you say some men were at your door?"

My patience was growing thin with this abrupt shift in subject.

"Did I?" I sighed in growing frustration. "What exactly did you call to discuss today, Matt?"

"Dr. Blakely, your safety is most important to us!"

I snapped. "I'm fine. They left. It was probably just someone going to the wrong door."

"You did well not to open it. Still, I worry about you, Dr. B."

"Don't worry, Matt. May I share my journal entries about another personality? I'm still coughing from a bad cold, so please forgive any interruptions."

I began to read straight from my diary:

"Luna, senior student transfer from XiAn International U, quotes clichés which end like question: 'Early to bed makes you wise?' She e-mails frequently to wish me a happy day, skips classes to attend my lectures, and seems to do so from a mixture of naïve hero-worship and ambitious self-interest. Luna's stylishly slim skirts, boots, and layered tees display popular phrases: 'Sweet girl.' (No 'hot lips' or 'sex kitten' for her.) Often, she mentions that she must 'exercise herself' because of overeating.

A cough niggled. I cleared my throat and read on.

"After a lecture, Luna asked, 'Dr. Regina, do you hate the Japanese? We are taught that from an early age.' The surprising question had never even occurred to me.

"A day later, she gifted me a piggy bank, explaining her Year of the Pig and my Year of the Rabbit birthdates. She and her roommate Emily then invited me to their former campus. Remembering her question, I asked Junko along so that the girls could interact with a sweet seventy-three-year-old Japanese teacher. Luna immediately took Junko under her wing, offering her arm as if Junko was her grandmother. Childhood hate-training dissolved.

"We strolled bridges, admired fountains, and rode in battered tin boats that the girls rowed in circles, banging into rocks. 'I lose my face!' Luna laughed. I taught them to coordinate oars, and they chorused, 'Teacher Regina is wise.' Explaining that I'd learned naturally because I'd lived near rivers didn't change their minds.

"In traffic, Emily and Junko waited at lights. Luna hooked her elbow through mine and crossed in the middle, dodging oncoming traffic the Chinese way.

"I asked the girls why they had transferred to Pei Hua. 'Not a choice,' Emily explained. XiAn International didn't offer English degrees. After graduation, Emily hoped to teach. Luna didn't know. 'Careers are very difficult in China. I hope for a job. No boyfriend like Emily.'"

I swallowed as a cough persisted, unable to go on reading. "You'll have to excuse me, Matt. This cough won't let me continue until I get a drink." I hacked all the way to the kitchen, poured myself a glass of purified and boiled water, and returned to the diary.

"Last Thursday, they clattered up Pei Hua's stairs, Luna's high heels clicking twice to Emily's flats. Then I heard, 'Regina! We take you to lunch!'

"We chose vegetarian food from Luna's region among the line of campus restaurants. She chatted with the cook and the waitress. All beamed when I ate heartily. Afterward, the girls divided up the bill and tossed one yuan of change back and forth. Emily put it in her big bag, saying, 'Now I owe you one apple and two pear. You always too generous!'

"I asked to visit their dorm. 'It would be our pleasure!' they said. Then Luna started worrying. 'I am messy girl. You will see dirty room.'

"I borrowed the phrase 'It doesn't matter' to reassure her.

"We ate dried fruit while sitting on Emily's bed, one of six in half the space of my bedroom. Luna's upper bunk had a curtain she swept back to reveal an unmade bed, her study light with its toy-car base, and a toss of open books. I made a mental note to shop for cute lights for my grandsons.

"Emily laughed and said, 'Luna is our night bird. She reads all night. Gets up very late.'

"'I'm naughty girl,' Luna said, showing no desire to change her ways. 'Now you know my bad habits. I lose my face. Your home so nice and clean!'

"I told her, 'I pile books and papers all over until I get lessons planned.' Then I asked Luna, 'Does your style work well for you?'

"She replied, *'Emily is always tidy. Her space is neat. She is slim. I am fat. I eat too much.'*

Reading aloud from my diary in my coal-heated apartment, I couldn't hold back coughs any longer. "That's all I can read, Matt. How will Luna define herself when Emily and she go their separate ways? Will she convince an employer to hire her in China's competitive job market?"

"I don't know, Dr. B. I did notice that Luna seems a lot like the women I meet in D.C. They all think they're fat. I'll revisit that when you're better. Your cough sounds bad. You'd better see a doctor."

"It's actually better than it was. It'll go away when they turn off the heat. My radiator pipe spews black coal dust. And I can see a mountain of coal across the back wall of our compound. Thank goodness decongestants are over the counter here."

I didn't tell him about finding bloody discharge on my pillow one morning. "I'm okay now, Matt. More journal?"

Matt sighed. "Enlighten me."

I started reading aloud again:

"Emily asked, 'Regina, when do you teach classes this semester?'

"I told her the schedule, and she said, 'We want to learn from you, but Dean Zhou forbids it.'

"Luna interrupted, saying, 'Do not tell her! It's a secret. Snake!'

"That's how I learned why so few visitors observe my teaching now, after the constant stream of teachers and students last semester. Joe evidently decided it was wrong. Should I confront him? Maybe he was simply lightening my load a bit.

"I told the girls that I didn't mind observers; in fact, I wouldn't be enjoying the lovely outing we were having if Luna hadn't visited my classes. I discretely added that I 'would leave the decision to Dr. Zhou.'"

I closed the journal. "Matt, I could have spotlighted other Chinese personalities. There's soft-spoken Abraham, the junior class monitor from an Inner Mongolia teaching family, for example."

"And?"

"And weekly, I help British Mama Amanda, who instructs nine employees and countless volunteers in the organized chaos of Starfish Foster Home's sixteen babies. And then there's Fu Lin, my bus seatmate, who is always ready to get a discounted fare. She 'taught' me Mahjong, yet she played my tiles before I could even touch them.

"There's also generous Bobo, a newly married Peihua secretary, with her snappy clothes and merry laugh. And what about Minnie? An active kindergartner at Perfect Language School who can't answer in anything below full volume? Then there's Stella, who moonlights at Peihua. She lured me into teaching AeroTech University's Tourism English, where she's a department head and too busy to keep appointments that she herself requested."

I played a movie reel in my head of these Chinese personalities, which filled frame after frame. "They all make my days far from boring. Oh, there's also Bear Lee, who keeps me on my mental tiptoes. And of course, Joe, who teaches me patience. And Luna, who reminds me that, however admired or appreciated I may be here, I remain a Westerner. I have an expected role to play and must not rock the boat too much."

Matt was probably on overload by this point and hurried to wind things up. "Very interesting, Dr. B. Our office can't thank you enough. Please, promise to be very careful when you answer your door, okay?"

"Why?" I asked too late. He was already off the line.

I coughed, my chest hurting so much that I didn't dwell on how he knew enough about my situation to issue such strange warnings.

CHINA 37 - TOPSY TURVEY

I double-checked my doors and windows—mostly to be able to reassure Matt the next time he worried about my safety—and then deposited my briefcase by the door to pick up next morning. My cough didn't seem worse, but I still boiled some ginger root and lemon and downed two cups of pungent tea. I'd save my voice with careful lesson plans. I mentally listed class members to thank for extra effort before I'd have them read exemplary English entries aloud. Students repeatedly told me that they wanted to know who the "A students" were. Those expectations could reward efforts and spur laggards toward better English. I started mulling this over, and instead of drifting off to sleep, pondered these lessons.

My grateful habit of thanking people became a problem from time to time in China. I was repeatedly told that "Your Chinese is good!" when I knew perfectly well that they hardly understood my attempts to speak it. I'd long ago learned to say "thank you" when receiving compliments at home, but such comments, feeling like flattery or droll sarcasm, were another matter.

Curious, I'd started observing compliments and other Chinese communications. I decided that we Westerners had a hard time wrapping our heads around what was good for the listener instead of ourselves. Our rote pleasantry, "Have a nice day" was invariably met with a look of puzzlement on Chinese faces. I tried *"Zai jian"* instead, presuming it meant something like "See you later."

Topsy-turvy examples flooded in. Our "How are you?" got confused answers, even from good students like Luna. She explained that the greeting and response *"Ni hao, ni hao"* was literally "You good" twice, given by both parties in an exchanged acknowledgement. Asking someone how they were made no sense to Luna. What showed interest in my culture was downright weird in China. With so many people seen in a day, it was too much to ask each one how he felt. So, instead, they showed interest by stating the obvious: "You just came from market" or "You've put on weight."

Oft-asked questions kept coming my way: "How old are you?" "How much money do you make?" "Do you live alone?" And of course, my most dreaded: "How much do you weigh?" I got a handle on those broken records by realizing that Chinese conversation started with what's important in their country before they finally got to the individual. People strove to be like the person who got the highest salary or made the highest grade, so that they would know exactly the width of the gap between them. Age was revered and prized, as were extra pounds. Here, many generations occupied the same home. They pitied a lonely person who wasn't surrounded by family. A hefty body showed that you were a healthy person living a happy life. Rudeness in the Western world equaled interest in the Eastern. They stated an obvious observation to get conversation started.

All students had been told to avoid politics, religion, and age, but the culture would come out anytime they met a new foreigner. They'd ask, "How old are you?" They never did catch on to the humor in my late dad's standard answer: "Old enough to know better." Dealing with two twists of language was far too complex for me to explain.

The Motherland was also reflected in XiAn's mail system. I'd prepared an intricate paper-cut birthday card to send to my mother. Qian helped me address the envelope. I already knew that one started with surname, stating the given name second. I learned also that a proper Chinese address started with the country and ended with the person. I addressed it both ways, just to be safe.

Enough of topsy-turvy thinking, I told myself. New examples would surely surface the next day at Pei Hua. I had no idea what the morning might bring and willed myself to be well enough to meet my classes. Instead, I coughed and sputtered, conjuring up blasts of clear air that battled it out with the diminishing coal-dust particles.

CHINA 38 - CRAZY COMMUNICATION

Despite my mind's late ramblings, I slept well and readied myself for the upcoming day's classes. Alone up front on the teachers' bus across XiAn, and willing my attention away from the speed of oncoming traffic, I tried pondering the trickiness of giving compliments in China. But instead, as we made three stops, we added new teachers. All three stood. They probably knew that the kamikaze drive across town was safer if they didn't accept my honored suicide-seat. I saw no one I'd known from the pre-break semester.

At the new campus, I lugged my satchel over boards that had been laid across snow-dusted mud. Inside the building, I stepped my left foot into the gizmo that shined our shoes and pulled the level to brush mud off both sides of my boots. Quick footsteps approached.

"You are cleaning your shoes." It was Joe, beaming this observation from above a starched white shirt that he wore open at the neck. "We have tea in Dean's office when you finish teaching. We discuss some things. Now, you have class."

I swallowed my instinctive response ("Thank you for your thoughtfulness"), knowing I'd hear, once again, that when one is only doing their job, there is no reason to thank them. Maybe I was finally learning.

Soon, in my classroom and in front of my class, I announced, "I'm going to show you everything a squirrel can do with a tree. It's called a preposition." This got their attention.

Rod raised his hand and asked, "What is squirrel?" Angel explained that they were big-tailed animals that ran freely in parks long ago. Her granny had told her how delicious they tasted during Mao's times of hunger.

I then realized that I had not seen any squirrels in XiAn. Oh well. I picked up a piece of chalk and drew a bushy-tailed squirrel and a tall tree to illustrate "up, down, around, over, under, and beside." And by the time class was dismissed, I was pleased with the participation. Most of my students had expanded their grammar usage. My understanding had enlarged to Chinese experience in history.

The rest of classes went well. Students read English essays, and then took bows to thunderous applause. A few took notes. I managed not to cough even once.

Reaching the Foreign Language Dean's office, I noticed that he was nowhere to be found. Joe waited for water to boil, and we luxuriated on an oversized faux-leather couch.

"This is the Life of Riley, isn't it, Regina?" Where had he picked up that cliché? I hadn't heard it since I was a child. But what he said next really amazed me.

"I think I ask you what you want to talk about. I listen. Okay?"

Him listen to me? Maybe he's actually learning from our lack of communication. "Well, Joe," I said, "I've been thinking about how Westerners and Easterners think."

"Maybe I can shed some light on the subject," he said. "We understand each other more in future."

"That would be good." I ignored another urge to say "thank you" and just plunged in: "Superstitions are very different. Like crossing your fingers, avoiding black cats, and walking under ladders. Those are all considered unlucky acts in the West. Yet this puzzles my students."

"That's easy to understand, Regina. Their ancestors, including their grandparents, grew up smearing chicken blood on doors and wearing protective white masks and armbands. They swept brooms in the air, shouting, 'Pig!' or 'Ghost!' to fool the gods so that they wouldn't want to take a newborn child. For protection, especially if it was a healthy boy."

"Really? Well, what about this? Last week, an anxious student told me that her friend's father had 'gone to the fourth floor,' and I found out later that the man had died."

Joe shuddered. "In China, certain numbers are avoided—especially '4'. The number sounds similar to 'death' in Chinese."

"I had noticed that there are no fourth floor in hotels! It sounds like a Western belief that 'Friday the thirteenth is unlucky.'"

Joe gave a hearty thumbs up and turned serious eyes toward me. "Also, Regina, clocks are the worst possible gifts because 'give a clock' sounds like attending someone's funeral. Mandarin language is full of homonyms."

"Like 'pear and pair' in English? My students don't get English puns at all."

"That's because they have a different idea. Here's an example from China. For thousands of years, 'dustpan and broom' has been the pun ideograph for 'wife.' See the difference, Regina? It's how words sound and how they look, bound up in our unbreakable ties to the Motherland."

I was still distracted by the wife ideography. "Joe, that insults me as a woman and is more of a put-down than anything else."

Joe interrupted, on a roll: "Other taboos include ice in water—you don't want to cool down your body because heat is good Chinese medicine. And women never tan. Too much sun. Everyone knows."

I tried a joke. "Maybe it's good that my mainland tan has almost faded," I said, remembering the umbrellas opened from morning to dusk all across campus, even when there were no clouds in sight. "But I like the feel of sunshine on my skin!"

"Regina, you are lovely as you are. No need to copy our Four Beauties. It is wonderful to talk story with you." He stretched an arm toward me on the back of the dean's couch and smiled into my eyes.

It should have felt uncomfortable, but I simply carried on: "Here's another thing I've wondered about, Joe. When we take someone out to eat in the West, we ask what they would like. But here, you ordered for me. People even put their chopsticks right into my mouth, by way of telling me something is delicious."

He shifted away and removed his arm. "We order the best dishes to honor our guests. Did you notice that we shout for the waitress? She won't bring the bill until you do."

"That is considered rude where I come from. Cultural differences, I guess. Another puzzle for me is Chinese friends insisting that I don't need a seat belt in their cars."

Joe looked puzzled at that. "But you're only a few blocks from home!"

I stood firm on this one. "Research shows that most accidents actually happen only a short distance from home!"

That made no difference to Joe, who ignored scientific research in favor of group consensus. He then added, "Another thing you might not know is that Chinese bathe at night, not morning."

"Why?"

"That's the practice," he said simply. Amused, I remembered how many bedheads showed up in my morning classes. "I love it when you smile, Regina. I am but a toad lusting after a swan's flesh."

Joe suddenly clutched my hands and pulled them toward his lips. A jolt of something akin to electricity ran up my arm. I panicked, lost for anything to say, and jerked my hands back. "I should go, Joe," I managed to say.

"You're right, Regina. As the water recedes, the rocks will appear."

"What in the world does that mean?" I gathered up my papers, half afraid of what he would say next.

"We have a saying, Regina: 'Don't be impatient and demand to get hurt for nothing.' It means, 'Wait until you're ready.' Advice for young people. You're a true woman warrior, Regina. And I'm used to women whose grandmother's feet were bound, who still believe that being loved means being a supported woman."

I felt my impatience rising as Joe continued.

"We'll let it walk." Then he frowned at himself, realizing he'd misspoken. "No, you say, 'Let it run,' or maybe 'Let it lie? Two brush strokes can change 'mountain' to 'bird.' 'Two strokes can change 'wings' to 'human'."

"*Zai jian,*" I said, unable to hear any more. "I must go and think about all the information you've given me."

I almost tripped over my own feet as I hurried out the door.

CHINA 39 - THE DONGS

I ignored my mix of emotions by dashing down Pei Hua's four flights. Running for the bus, I promised myself I'd sort out my feelings and proper behavior with my boss when I got home.

To my surprise, a middle-aged woman sat in my normal seat. She patted the side near the window, so I crawled across her ample knees and settled in beside her.

"I am glad to meet you. I am Dong Mai, and you will teach me English. I work in payroll office at Pei Hua on Mondays."

I had seen her name, printed in English, on a document somewhere. Could she be the comptroller for the university? She seemed like a take-charge Chinese woman, not unlike many I'd met. I sat quietly and turned her way.

Dong Mai's English was good. She told me that she'd been a Chinese Psychology professor before going to work farmland under Mao's re-education program. She'd met her husband there. They'd had a son, finished their farming obligations, and been allowed to move to Xian.

"You come to my house tonight and meet my son. My husband cooks special meal for you!"

I started to protest, but quickly cut that short, realizing that all my consternation about my recent encounter with Joe had evaporated as my curiosity about the woman mounted.

"Okay," I said with a smile. "But I must not stay long, and I'll need a ride home."

"We get off here." She tugged at my arm and hefted my briefcase. Together, we walked four busy blocks, weaving among laughing people working on the sidewalks. Two men repaired a stripped-down motorcycle, an aged woman winnowed dusty grain, children ran in and out between the legs of women cleaning fish, and one stoic white-headed sage with his pantlegs pulled up above his knees watched from a three-legged stool.

Up six cement flights in a rectangular high-rise, Dong Mai unlocked double steel doors. She ushered me to a sofa, offered a glass of hot green tea, then disappeared through a curtained doorway. My stomach growled as aromas drifted in from an open door opposite me. I realized suddenly that I'd skipped lunch.

A handsome young adult in bib overalls and a baseball cap entered then, his right hand outstretched to shake mine. "I am pleased to meet you, Dr. Blakely. I am Dong Liu. Mother said you will help with my English."

"Your English seems very good so far, Dong Liu. I thought your mother wanted help."

"She did. Help for me to practice my English." He plopped down on the couch. Then followed a discussion of American government under George W. Bush, the popularity of Michael Jackson, and the availability of Kentucky Fried Chicken. I didn't have to give my views, since Dong Liu was happily expounding on his own. The slim kid was no slouch with English, opinions, or the gestures he made with his tapered fingers.

Didn't I agree that British English was superior to American? He knew about Shakespeare and that a car's trunk and bonnet meant the same thing. He spelled "tire" and "tyre" for me. I gave him some lame answer about understanding a conversation's meaning being the important thing to me, And then he plunged on. Did I know that there were no weapons of mass destruction found? I silently agreed, then asked how he'd arrived at that conclusion. He'd read what he could find in both Chinese and English and discovered a few obscure internet sites that weren't blocked by his government. His voice rose as he asked what I'd learned from CNN and BBC, and whether or not Americans blogged.

I told him that many did. I didn't volunteer that I emailed a blog to my mainland daughter to publish to the English-speaking world, since I couldn't access it myself in China. He turned his baseball cap backward and lowered his voice to say that he was working on a firewall that might break through that barrier. I felt the same awe that my computer-savvy grandson had inspired in me back in Kansas, when he'd programmed fifty headlines to pop up for him to help him decide what news he wanted to read. I told Dong Liu this.

Liu blinked his long lashes, suddenly quiet. Then he looked toward both doors, lowered his voice to a whisper, and asked, "Is it true that gay people can come out of the closet in America without going to jail?"

"We still have prejudice in the United States, but I don't know anyone who has gone to jail for sexual preference, Dong Liu."

It seemed beyond his comprehension when I mentioned that celebrities had helped that segment of the population open up, along with the San Francisco marches. Ellen DeGeneres had come out in 1997. He'd heard of her comedy, but not her sexual preference.

Did I know him well enough to probe a bit?

"Why are you asking me this?" I asked gently.

"My classmates tell me I act gay. They tease me."

"Is there someone you can talk with to sort out your feelings, Dong Liu?"

"I asked Mother what to say. She said to act like they aren't there. It doesn't help much."

Before I could respond, Dong Mai appeared. "Now we eat!"

Dong Liu's conversation turned to a recitation of the dishes his smiling father placed before me: "Salted duck egg, scrambled egg with tomato, pork and bitter melon!"

Mr. Dong ran back to the kitchen for a fork to supplement my chopsticks. When I managed to use the chopsticks right up through the final bowl of rice, his smile was positively beaming.

I asked about the chewy salted duck egg, which was much like a boiled chicken egg with a yolk flavor like a roasted chestnut. Then they passed quail egg delicacies, buried with salt and lye for between forty-five and a hundred days. They proceeded to tell me about pickled eggs, smoked eggs, and "Virgin Boy" eggs, which involved soy, ash, and a young boy's pee as marinades. I didn't reach for seconds.

Dong Liu sensed my discomfort, passed the beef and vegetables, and retold the story of how his parents had met while working the rice fields. There was a rapid Chinese/English exchange as Liu translated how Mao's Red Army had hidden in caves in YuNan after the Long March. He emphasized that eighty thousand men, women, and children had started out, chased by the Nationalist Army, over rugged terrain. Only five thousand finished. At one point, his father had been given a bus ride and ended up in rice fields.

The three-way conversation, told in bits and pieces, was hard to follow. Perhaps, at another time, it would be possible to fill in the gaps or ask questions. For now, I just listened.

The disjointed story skipped and pieced together a little as it continued. It seemed that later, in XiAn, Dong Liu's father had cooked while his mother worked in the college business office. Dong Liu had attended school plus private weekend English school and had gone on to study business at a nearby university. His parents weren't happy when he asked to change to another college that offered courses in Western history.

Dong Mai interjected that "Dong Liu made straight A's, so it was a good decision to support him. He is waiting for a grant to go to Canada for master's degree study."

As long as I kept my rational Western brain turned off, the conversation was interesting and the food delicious. In no time, darkness fell. Giving another round of *"shei shei,"* I asked where I might catch a cab or bus home. "No cabs here at night. Last bus already gone." That dismissed that idea. Dong Liu's father, still silent, exited quickly. Then I heard a motorcycle start below.

"Come, Dr. Regina." Dong Liu took my hand, giggled, and pulled me down four flights. "My father takes you home now." He started saying something in rapid Chinese, even as his dad nodded.

I climbed on the back of the bike, sans helmet, and held on for dear life. We putt-putted through side streets for most of an hour, avoiding main roads. The bike's light cast no more light than a normal flashlight.

At Pei Hua freshman campus, a still-silent Mr. Dong walked me up my two flights, and then clasped his hands to his heart as if I'd done him a favor. I returned his gesture.

Inside, my phone blinked. Someone had called, probably either Matt or Joe. I couldn't face more conversation right then. Another XiAn day had brought totally unexpected events. I still had not had a talk with myself about Joe, and I'd gotten no closer to discussing my hopes of a trip to Kansas for Mom's birthday. I'd traded that intention for the promise of a weekly home-cooked meal after English interaction at the Dong home.

Like Scarlet O'Hara, I decided to *"think about all that tomorrow,"* and then my bedtime thoughts were gone with the wind.

The light on the phone kept blinking.

CHINA 40 - DEEP BREATH

The next non-teaching day found me still procrastinating about any sort of serious thinking, and instead catching a crowded bus to Small Wild Goose Pagoda. I'd be away from the telephone if Matt called. Calm waters near the park structure would give me plenty of green area in which to breathe. Maybe ancient Tang and Han Dynasty energy would settle around me and bring clarity to my thoughts.

When I arrived on site, I exited the bus and wasted no time finding a shady, wooden bench, with a wonderful view of a pond in which lily pads floated and lotus flowers lifted their pink petals to the sun. I took a deep breath. I closed my eyes to see where my thoughts and feelings might go.

Instantly back in Kansas, I heard again my mother's voice, giving her offensive admonition from her apartment doorway behind me. *"Whatever you do, don't you bring back a Chinaman!"* Rather than reprimand her language usage, I'd joined her in laughter.

After the last conversation with Joe in the dean's office, that flashback wasn't the least bit funny to me. I remembered his gallantly lifting my hand to his lips, the unexpected thrill racing my wrist to shoulder, and the undignified way I'd simply bolted from his office. It was not very teacherly, for sure. More like a junior-high girl unsure of how to handle her first boyfriend's advances.

Then a second thought arose: *Joe might've been paying me an honest compliment. If so, how do Chinese women respond?* I knew it wasn't with "Thank you."

I thought about how, for the last several months, I'd been starved to hear spoken English. Gone was the closeness of my own culture that I'd once taken for granted. While I'd loved so many new ways of being in XiAn—the foods, adventures, and even attitudes—I'd grown more and more internalized and lonely. Joe was an almost constant in that panorama. He'd begun as a caricature of the "slim Chinese man with a too-long leather belt wrapped around a belly full of clichés." Often, he made me laugh, both inwardly and out loud.

I'd followed his unbuckled overshoes in sloshing through rain puddles from bus to market for our first lunch, where I'd learned that he was married. He'd dismissed his wife as being "old. She plays flute." End of subject.

Whenever I inquired about his home or marriage, he told me something similar: "She stays home, except she goes to the park to play flute." Soon I stopped asking. He'd not asked about my home or marriage. Although I sometimes told him about my children and grandchildren, he'd shown no interest.

Joe also had an infuriating way of pronouncing what I would do at Pei Hua without any thought of consulting me. I'd gotten used to telling him what I would and wouldn't do in regard to class responsibilities. We'd had stimulating conversations, maybe arguments, about Chinese and Western differences.

So, why had he spoiled it by acting like a lovesick Don Juan?

My next thought was that he'd probably thought nothing of that adoring look while kissing my fingers. After all, I'd only seen him once without a bevy of coeds carrying his books and hanging on his every word. I'd noticed that there wasn't one constant pretty face among the jean-clad beauties whose high-heeled boots followed him around both campuses. He seemed to expect their adoration. Maybe his rung on Confucius's ladder put him just above continually gorgeous attendants. They also hadn't shown any jealousy or posturing for his attention as they clung to his shadow, which was baffling behavior to me.

Was it possible that *I* was jealous? The idea that a middle-aged, cellulite-covered woman might try to compete with fresh-faced college girls was absurd. I quickly tired of stirring that pot!

My attention caught a flash of orange and gold koi beneath the lakeside shade. One old ugly fish, marred by dark areas on its whitening back, chased others away and grabbed a winged insect. Maybe there was something to be said for maturity.

I weighed my thoughts, imagining Justice slipping her blindfold just a bit to give me a stern look. Joe was becoming a good friend at a time when I needed one, and he was making an effort at being flexible. I had to give him that. And that was enough.

The idea of him entering my other-side-of-the-world moved into a comedic realm as I imagined him in Kansas. Mother would be polite, laughing at his cliché jokes. Then she'd take me aside for a heart-to-heart about bluebirds and redbirds never sharing the same nest. I chuckled, remembering college freshman year, when I'd told her that I planned to ask someone out during college "Women Pay All" week. He had been the nicest guy I'd met so far, and by the way, he was Black. She'd given me her redbird-bluebird story. And I found out later that she was right. If we'd have gotten serious, our children would've had a hard time, indeed, against the prejudices in Middle America. I'd long forgotten the guy's name, and I figured he hadn't even considered asking me for a date during any of the other year's 364 days.

Finally, I set my intentions out loud. "Tomorrow, I'll march into the English office and tell Joe I need his approval to go to Kansas for Mom's eighty-sixth." Family was important. He couldn't refuse since there was a short respite—sports game again—and a weekend. That would give me five days and six nights to make the roundtrip flight to Kansas City. I'd even have lesson plans ready. Qian should have no problem getting my reservations since it wasn't a festival time.

What I'd say was the easy part. Next, I envisioned my charming smile, and my friendly, relaxed, arms-length attitude. I'd keep the context of "Remember that you're married, Buster."

That done, I was ready to board a bus home to steam chicken and vegetables in the top tiers of my rice cooker. With all restlessness gone by the time darkness fell, I slept well.

At my first waking moment, Mom was there again. I thought maybe I missed her more than I thought. She'd never been terribly touchy-feely—more of a "make up your mind and do it!" sort of person, and a "Stay out of trouble, and don't make a mistake" kind of parent. I never seemed to please her, no matter what I achieved. The Chinese idea of "doing your job because that's what's expected" fit her thinking. She never congratulated me when something turned out well. I thought I might give up that bit of fun, congratulating my own self, or maybe I wouldn't. We'd see. At any rate, I looked forward to surprising Mom around her birthday and was sure that she'd be pleased to see me.

I showered and dressed for success the next teaching day, walking confidently into the Education Office. Bobo smiled up from her desk, printed cloth cylinders were elasticized at shoulder and wrist to keep newsprint from rubbing off on the sleeves of her knock-off designer blouse. Joe's smile was wider than hers. He stood as I headed toward his desk. "Regina, I have something to discuss. Sit down."

Uh-oh! I sat down opposite him, and he pushed a sheaf of papers in my directions. I saw a plane ticket on the top.

"What is this, Joe?"

"Time to renew your visa. Pei Hua will send you to Hong Kong this Friday. Arrangements are made. A vacation, Regina!"

"How ironic. I came here this morning hoping that Pei Hua would okay my trip to the mainland in February for my mother's eighty-sixth birthday. I never suspected anything like this. Can you explain?"

Joe pushed back his escaping lock of hair like a delighted schoolboy. Then he laughed. "I surprised you. Go to mother's birthday later. This weekend, see Hong Kong!"

"Wait a minute, Joe! Don't I don't have my passport to renew my visa? Qian said the police have it. Don't I need it for this trip?"

"Do not worry, Regina. Arrangements are all made." With that pronouncement, he handed me my passport.

Was this something for which I should say *shei shei?* Was this some gigantic snafu in Pei Hua administration's processing of my visa that I didn't know about, or was it simply another Chinese adventure? I hurried off to teach a lesson on "their/they're/there," hardly able to stand upright in the wake of all these whiplash changes.

CHINA 41- TRAVEL PREPARATION

At my apartment, I gathered lucky red underwear from my drying room and ran a dark load in my egg-shaped washer. As I doublechecked that its hose was down the bathroom drain so it didn't back up into my living room, Matt phoned, sounding agitated.

"Dr. Blakely? I've been worried about you."

"Sorry, Matt. I've been busy, gathering observations about a few more East-West practices to share with you!" I chose to keep another thought to myself: *And busy figuring out how not to act like a stupid, lovesick schoolgirl.* "Also, I'm going to Hong Kong, an expenses-paid vacation to renew my visa. Never a dull moment here!"

Here I was, spouting cliches. Joe would be proud.

Matt asked exactly what my airline tickets said and surprised me with, "Dr. Blakely, you must get a cellphone that works in Hong Kong. Upon arrival, go immediately to the electronics district and buy a Nokia; don't worry about Babaling, 880 capability for 'hug you,' or Qiqiling, 770 for 'kiss you.'" He laughed. "So Chinese, don't you think? Those texting aps probably won't work for you anyway since they're mostly simplified Chinese pinyin characters. Make sure it has time-telling and long-distance capabilities for that area's sim card."

It sounded like a *nerdy* joke in a third language. "Okay, Matt. My Verizon cell phone's no good here. So . . . I suppose I'll need another sim card for a Hong Kong one to work in XiAn, right? I've heard about phones that take pictures. Might I get one of those? That would be handy."

"China's phones may be smarter in some ways, but I doubt you'd be happy with their pictures. I'll tell you a secret, Dr. Blakely. Apple is coming out with a smart phone with a built-in camera in a little over a year."

"My students seem to like Bird, or at least, that's the icon on most of the phones I confiscate when they're being used during my class."

"Do *not* get Bird, whatever you do. We think that Blackberry Pearl, LG Chocolate, and Motorola RAZR won't last here in the states. Samsung may make it."

More foreign language? "I feel like an inside trader, Matt," I joked. "Are you sure I won't go to jail for having advance tips when I return home?" It was my turn to laugh, but I noticed that Matt didn't. Martha Stewart's incarceration was probably still a US controversy.

Matt filled me in on another fact or two: In the mid-1990s, Hong Kong had represented almost a third of China's GDP. That had diminished over the last decade as capital flight put a damper on growth. Laissez-faire capitalism raised its ugly head, along with money launderers, smugglers, North Korean shell companies, and the Chinese mainland's archaic banking system. He further explained that the economy was diminishing in Hong Kong. "We expect their GPD percentage to move to one-digit numbers in another decade. "Mainland China's on the move, on the other hand. It's a tense situation, building toward a confrontation with a government that doesn't tolerate protests. Any insights?"

I shared all I'd recently discussed with Joe of yin/yang and East/West cultural practices, but I left Joe out of it. Then I told Matt the questions of my new friend, Dong Liu, about homosexual practices in the US, leaving out my late-night motorcycle ride across XiAn. Matt relaxed, then had me repeat a series of steps (twice) for calling him the minute I got a new cellphone.

After we hung up, I relaxed. Tomorrow was soon enough to pack for Hong Kong. I'd take my nicer outfits, according to what I'd heard from an AeroTech student's presentation. I wanted to get time on Qian's shared office computer to further research Hong Kong history. Maybe I could also find out who would accompany me on the long weekend journey. If they didn't speak much English, it might be a problem.

Offices were closed the next day, with no explanation being posted in English. I planned a travel wardrobe around my best navy skirt and sensible walking shoes, taught the rest of the week's classes as usual, and met the Pei Hua car at the gate four hours before the time on my plane ticket. Thank goodness numerals were the same in both languages, and I was comfortable with military time.

The hour-and-a-half ride to the airport felt safe and almost familiar. My ticket was processed without a hitch. I rolled my bag toward the gate, scanning female travelers and guessing who might be my Hong Kong companion. People jostled noisily in line for the plane. We walked a long corridor, and I found my aisle seat. Was this placement due to some thoughtful person's effort or benevolent luck? I'd already pointed to beef and noodles, not pork and peas, on the menu handed me when a firm hand tapped my shoulder.

"I sit next to you."

CHINA 42 - KOWLOON COMPANION

It was Joe, standing in the airplane aisle. I was shocked. "Joe! You're going to Hong Kong?"

"You hit the nail on the head, Regina. I sit next to you."

Lost for words, I got up and watched him take the middle seat. Without another word, he pulled out a copy of *Men are From Mars, Women are From Venus* and started reading.

Why that book? And where did he get it? Only the cover title was in English. The characters inside were in undecipherable Chinese. I inched as much toward the aisle as my seatbelt would allow and eyed a screaming baby that was jumping up and down on his mama's lap. She popped a pacifier in his mouth, chosen from the three pinned to his shoulder. His father, nose buried in a book, was mouthing words and ignoring the world. I thought it must be one of those "man things" that we mere women were meant to take in stride.

Our food came soon after lift-off, and Joe became talkative, reciting his knowledge. "You have questions about Hong Kong, I think. Between fifty-seven and sixty-five degrees Fahrenheit and sunny. No danger of typhoons until September. We land at Lantau, biggest of hundreds of islands. We take Express Luxury bus to the visa office. You will see gleaming skyscrapers, gorgeous hotels, and multi-level shopping centers that make you think of Paris or Madrid. No cathedrals though."

He laughed, even while I was still trying to adjust to the idea of his presence. What was coming the next long weekend? I consciously kept my mouth closed.

"Do you know Hong Kong history, Regina? Like our motherland, it goes back to Stone Age inhabitants. Fishing communities and pirate raids. Colonial period around 1800-1930, when British ruled 156 years. Margaret Thatcher visited in 1982. July 1, 1997. The British flag lowered, and the One Country-Two Systems Agreement began giving it back to mainland China.

Most Chinese prefer it become China, not separate. Now, we must be patient to preserve happy life for many, many inhabitants."

An attractive attendant picked up our trays, but Joe turned his full attention toward me. "You tell me interesting facts about your country, Regina."

What on earth did this man have in mind to knock me sideways next? Was he serious, chatting like this as though taking trips together was an everyday occurrence?

Well, two could play his game. I cast about for factoids I'd read, mixing in television, movies, and one Hawaiian vacation. "I'll tell you about the bright-colored aloha shirts men wear in Hawaii, Joe. The first ones were probably made by Japanese wives from kimono material in the 1920s, but it got its name when the King-Smith trademark, launched in 1930. Bing Crosby's shirt had hula dancers and palm trees when he recorded *Sweet Leilani*. Surfer designs began in about 1935. Elvis wore flowered aloha shirts while he played ukulele in several of his movies."

Joe nodded, happy as a child with a brand-new game. I went into my long-term memory for something else to finish my shirt dissertation.

"There's a picture of the US Army's Infantry Division, in aloha wear, a decade after World War II. Most Americans own an aloha shirt if they've visited the islands. Presidents Harry Truman and Richard Nixon wore hibiscus designs. My own children, though, called it 'corny Dad-wear in a closet'."

"So, Regina, the young generation does not like flowers on men. Too feminine!"

"I don't know, Joe. My son got an aloha shirt when he went to Hawaii as a young businessman. Perhaps it's a way to connect. I see many Chinese men wearing pink shirts. Could that be for the same reason? I never saw American ads for men's pink shirts."

"You hit the nail on the head, Regina! I love our history game." Joe was all smiles, while I felt deflated.

"If you'll excuse me, I'm very tired and must close my eyes and nap."

I awoke just as we landed, with green mountains in every direction. Joe herded me onto a bus, pulling my roller-bag along among hordes of people. On the bus, I noted greenery up close, then solid arteries of moving people. Driving and walking was on the left, along with surprising cleanliness and order instilled in the locals by the British long ago. Tall windows displayed Gucci, Cartier, Chanel, and Louis Vuitton. I wondered how long it would be until the diamonds and gold designs would lose some of their glitter. Multi-million-dollar high-rises and high-end shops stood next to hotels catering to wealth and privilege. *Is one of those gleaming entries my home-away-from-home?*

"We go to Dragon Hostel on Kowloon," Joe told me, as the streets narrowed. I looked up several stories, past laundry hung on bamboo poles sticking out of the windows. Occasional buildings in progress were buttressed by lashed bamboo scaffolding. *Do men stand on those flimsy fishing poles to work?*

Where we exited the bus, it looked more like a stark, mainland-China office building, towering over a street buzzing with black-haired people walking every which way. We climbed above the teeming crowds and found an open door.

My visa application went smoothly, except for four wrapped candies taken from my fanny pack and sent through a scanner just inside the entry. The guard scrutinized my passport, looking suspiciously at each visa stamp filling its back pages. Joe quietly handed over his red leather passport, which got a quick glance, and I promptly had back my navy-blue one returned to me.

The candies were returned as we set out for the underground. Then we bought Mass Transit Railway tickets, and Joe took my elbow. Throngs of people both pushed and came toward us. No thrill this time, just a focused concentration to stay on my feet so I wouldn't get trampled. I held onto my roller bag for dear life.

Somehow, the rush of oncoming crowds tore me from Joe's grasp, and as I found myself carried along, I turned and called out to Joe, my voice quickly drowned by the noisy crowd.

Like an unclaimed suitcase at an airline baggage claim, I was spit out beyond the edge of the constantly moving humans. I noticed no smell of urine or debris, something I'd experienced in every nook and cranny in XiAn. Stifling an urge to sit on my roller-bag and cry, I decided that I could figure it all out. Chinese characters on signs were paired with English, both languages jockeying for positions in my sightline and at least two stories up. The solid mass of people kept moving, ignoring me.

I sucked on one ginger candy. An hour and a half later, and with kindness from Chinese English-speakers, I found historic Argyle Street. I passed under Virginia Hotel's sign, which promised "Rent by Hour," and was glad that the other two thousand people on the sidewalk kept moving.

By then, I was a veteran of politely pushing, perhaps even shoving a little, and looking like I knew exactly where I was headed. I almost missed the tiny Dragon Hostel sign a half hour further along. I unwrapped my last ginger candy and maneuvered my bag up toward my hostel cubicle.

The phrase "I am woman. Hear me roar!" alternated in my brain with my urge to kill Joe. I headed for a tiny, rickety elevator. The guy in the iron cage pushed a key through the rectangular opening after a quick look at my passport.

A blond kid a third my age, with dreadlocks half his age, nodded and punched buttons for the seventh floor. The skeleton key in my hand looked identical to the one dangling from his backpack. He opened the door on the right. My key fit the one on the left. No other doors were evident on the seventh floor. My twin bed had worn but clean linens and a pillow. A small TV sat above a shelf for my bag. Two hooks protruded from the hospital-green wall. A chair held wrapped soap, shampoo, paper slippers, and eyeshades atop a thin towel. No washcloth. This was Pei Hua's expenses-paid Hong Kong vacation.

I put on one-size-fits-all slippers, exited, and found that my door only key-locked from the outside. I re-entered, stuffed my HK$, ID, and passport into my pockets and went down two flights to a communal toilet. A large mirror and chest stood outside the shower/toilet, providing a hallway stand-up dressing table. The elevator took me to the entry, but the guy in the cage who'd handed me the key had vanished. I asked for "Zhou?" in my best Mandarin. The new attendant smiled. No English.

I approached the lobby's white plastic water dispenser, pushed the blue button to boil the water twice, then filled my bottle. Nearby stood a haphazard shelf of books, evidently left by travelers from every continent but Antarctica. I picked a John Grisham novel and returned to my rectangle-cage room. Nothing was disturbed. I slid the ladder-backed chair under the doorknob and didn't even try locking it from the inside. The chair didn't have far to slide.

Later, I learned that Dragon was one of a hundred hostels on fifteen floors, established when the Hong Kong economy had caused families to move out of busy Argyle Street. Dragon boasted that each narrow floor had a TV, a fridge, the internet, a shower in a shared toilet, boiled water, and books.

In my pint-sized room, I fell on the bed, too exhausted to organize my thoughts or give vent to my anger. I felt as drained as the shower hole in the fourth floor's bathroom. Rational thought fled, so as I stretched out, I tensed my toes, visualizing them uncurling and letting go, then did the same with my ankles, then my calves. I released my knees as timid taps brought me to full alert.

My doorknob turned slightly, though the chair back held the door firmly closed. Then all was suspiciously silent. If it was Joe out there, I didn't want to talk to him. And if it was someone else, I wasn't about to open the door anyway. I stayed silent, barely breathing. After several long minutes, I could hear footsteps receding.

Wide awake, I listed Joe's unforgivable behaviors in my head. He'd secretly come to Hong Kong, abandoned me near the underground, and had probably booked this miserable hostel.

The door suddenly vibrated with loud pounding; then a male voice shouted, "Regina! Tell me you are okay!"

There was no mistaking the panic in his voice. I shouted, "How nice that you came to call, Joe! I would offer you tea, but there's no teapot in my room."

He couldn't have missed my sarcasm, but he didn't address it. "You came across to Kowloon all alone! How wonderful!"

I tried again. "Joe, I needed a *travel companion*, not *you!* And now I need some rest, a proper shower, and some privacy. I can't tell you how angry I am!"

"You are emotional, Regina."

"How perceptive of you, Joe. Go back to your book, or your cave, or to Mars for all I care. I'm from Venus, and you don't have a clue!"

Joe's patience seeped through the door. "Now you sleep. We meet my friend Steven for University of Hong Kong dinner in one hour. Steven is a graduate-researcher in linguistics, translation, and computers. He hopes to make 172 on LSAT and study law in America."

How dare he act like I care about his Hong Kong friend or him!

"I don't care if your friend is Kubla Khan himself! Go away!" Then my stomach growled.

He was quiet again for a moment, then started speaking again, quietly now. "Steven will take us to Coffee Bay for bar-b-que: roast beef, pork ribs, sardines, chicken wings, and white bread cooked over coals. We eat by the ocean at sunset. I will come to your door at seventeen hundred sharp."

I turned my face into the pillow. The next thing I felt was my gnawing stomach. Surely, I hadn't fallen asleep. A powerful hunger grew as I lay on the hard mattress.

The other side of Joe's ledger sheet filled in to balance the many minuses my head. He'd seemed concerned that I might not be okay, admired how I'd made it to Dragon hostel, and hadn't answered my anger with denial or protests. Instead, he'd arranged an outing to feed me, and we'd have a proper chaperone in his friend. I unpacked my navy skirt and blue blouse, went downstairs to freshen up, and was ready when Joe knocked at the appointed time. I opened the door with a careful smile.

Steven met us at the university gate, hugged Joe, shook my hand, and pressed two $78 Hong Kong tickets into Joe's pocket. He talked incessantly about his American law school acceptance. He said he had "fingers in a number of political pies," and I found myself hoping he'd achieve his dream.

Coffee Bay offered beach sand and turquoise water. Steven excused himself to shake hands with a hundred or so college families quietly conversing around barrels of glowing coals.

Joe and I started with pork balls, gave up tickets for cold sodas with no English name, and went on to enjoy chicken wings and white bread. By the time Joe conversed our way around the fires, we'd sampled the whole protein-and-carbs menu. I felt stuffed. He stopped introducing me to each orderly group. We walked on white sand toward the sun as it sank into the China Sea. As we stood apart in awesome silence, I blessed the British influence on this beautiful island. It felt natural when he reached for my hand. Neither of us said much on the way home to the hostel and much welcome sleep.

The next morning, Joe knocked politely on my door, asking me to walk Kowloon's Nathan Street with him to find Tin Hau Temple with its green tile and nice gardens. We strolled through Jade Market, hearing "Authentic from Burma, Missy!" at each new stall. I declined Joe's offer for a bracelet. At the Night Market, which was open mid-morning, Joe spoke Cantonese and bought whatever they put in his bag. They ignored me as an ignorant foreigner.

In Tsim Sha Tsui district, I saw Sojo Hong Kong and told Joe I'd like to buy a cellphone. In a giant shopping center eighteen stories underground, we entered an electronics store that covered a square block. I wondered how in the world the workers had ever dug out Hung Hom Bay enough to recover and build this place. Electricity blazed, and choices abounded. The salesperson responded to "Nokia," and I soon had a simple phone with long-distance capability. Rapid-fire Cantonese followed, with Joe interpreting for me:

"You get a XiAn sim card when you return."

I waited while he wandered the aisles.

Soon returning, he said, "This is good phone—bare bones, but good." Thanks to Joe and my exchange of cash, we were soon on our way.

The thing jangled almost immediately. "Who could that be? I just got this phone," I wondered out loud. Internally, I wonder if it was Matt calling, and what I would say if it was. I also wondered how I would explain it to Joe. When it rang again, I held it to my ear and said, "Hello?"

"Dr. Blakely, thank goodness you got a phone. Do you like it? Can we talk now?"

"Yes, I got a phone. But no, I do not wish to talk now. Thank you for calling."

I hung up before he could ask another question. Joe hadn't seemed to hear anything, but I knew that he'd been listening.

"Regina, was that the telephone company verifying your phone number?"

"Yes, Joe," I lied and turned off the new purchase.

At Tsim Sha Tsui, the beginning of Kowloon's new territories, which was land built up over many years of development, we took the transit to Central on the north shore and walked the causeway. Star Ferry let us both ride free because they asked only my golden age. Joe raised one quizzical eyebrow at me. We bought Lady Godiva chocolate and lemon gelato. I explained how it felt just like San Francisco and climbed up on a sunny ledge. A security guard tapped me. "No sleeping!"

Back on Star Ferry, Joe handed me a ticket to the Hong Kong Ballet. "It is Shakespeare, Regina, at Cultural Center!"

Where did he get those? I couldn't refuse.

He left me at the door, promising that he'd meet me there after the performance. Had he only enough HK$ for my ticket, or did he not want to attend? It didn't matter. I could almost taste the excitement in my throat.

Romeo and Juliet was presented with near perfection by the orchestra and dancers. The cultural crowd's attire ranged from faded jeans to evening dresses. I felt okay in my navy skirt and sensible shoes. We all left with shining eyes and wonderful memories of Prokofiev's score, which had been mercifully shortened and beautifully danced.

Waiting for me at the gate, Joe's eyes also shone. He told me he'd gone to Starbucks and met his first "Chinese hippie." I'd forgotten that Chinese people drink coffee in the evenings, not the mornings, but I didn't feel like bringing up yet another contrasting way of life. We didn't talk, both of us lost in contentment the rest of the way back to Dragon Hostel.

Joe wanted temples on our last morning in Hong Kong. Our tiny-print map showed Golden Buddha at the tip of Wan Chai's spit. We walked, asked, and were met with blank stares until we found ourselves at a monumental golden flower. Crowds snapped pictures in front of the waterfront Expo Center. This Golden Buddha was Golden Bauhinia, a five-petaled lotus sculpture, symbolizing the reunification of China and Hong Kong beneath two flags, with China's yellow stars on one, and Hong Kong's white *bauhinia* on the other: Buddha confusion.

Still seeking temples, we found a bus to Lantau Island with seat belts, which were needed to avoid sliding off on curves. Mountain views lifted spirits, but the mood was a Disneyland downer. I got into the lockstep climb with Chinese tourists and surged forward whenever there was a slight opening. Joe slogged along doggedly behind me; then he was swallowed by the crowd. The huge Tian Tan Buddha afforded freedom to walk around 223-cubic-feet of a seated figure gazing benevolently toward the mountains. Joe waited by the cement stairs where people went down eight-abreast. He seemed unperturbed that I'd left him.

Descending side-by-side, I remarked that I preferred climbing to the knee-jarring descent. "You are so energetic, Regina."

I laughed. "My students tell me, 'You are like my grandmother, but she is not so energetic.' I take it as a compliment."

"I am younger than you, Regina, yet you have much more energy."

I chose to laugh, but I couldn't help admonishing him. "Joe, in your studies, didn't you learn not to refer to an English-speaking woman's age? It's considered bad manners."

He almost missed a cement step. I reached out to steady him. "It's all right, Joe. I don't think the number of birthdays means much. It's the relationships and experiences that mark life."

Joe persisted. "But in China, men must seek—" He cut off this thought abruptly.

We both concentrated on our footing. I didn't care to hear more anyway, as we moved in lockstep with six other people, down, down, down. . .

At the foot of the mountain, I could almost feel the *feng shui* move through Lantau Square. Children frolicked in the fountain, and myriads of languages passed between sips of cappuccino and bites of Big Macs.

"A good place to retire," Joe said and bought a baguette to share. It was very fresh, crusty outside and delicious inside.

"Could you retire here, Regina? Let the rest of the world go by?"

I couldn't tell if he was joking or not, so I opted for somewhere in between. "It's an interesting place. Actually beautiful. Maybe I could live next to you and your wife. She could play flute in Kowloon Park, and you could retire early."

Joe had nothing to say. He shook his head and changed the subject. "Tonight, we watch the Symphony of Lights from the Kowloon side. Nothing like it!"

After eating street noodles, we got to Kowloon Bay as darkness overtook Hong Kong island's magnificent architecture on the opposite bank. Jugglers and flute-players showed off their talents and passed their hats. Then the Symphony of Lights began. Ships and boats passed through the deep canal, punctuating the music and narration that began at dark. Colors flashed, outlined buildings, crept up arched entryways, and lingered in dark patches across the way. The laser show surpassed any I'd seen—colored lights blinking, zipping up and down, zigzagging and coloring reflections on the harbor waters. We wandered the Avenue of Stars and read the Cultural

Center's schedules. If we stayed one night longer, we could hear the Tuba Throat Singers. *Maybe next time.*

I was so full of sound and light that I didn't mind returning to my concrete rectangle up the rickety elevator. *Hong Kong dreams couldn't be much more beautiful,* I thought, as I wished Joe a firm and heartfelt goodnight. "There is truly nothing like Hong Kong."

CHINA 43 - PATIENCE REQUIRED

Landing in XiAn, Joe ushered me into a plush back seat behind Pei Hua's driver, who tucked the cigarette Joe gave him above his right ear and kept his eyes on the road. As we pulled onto Ring Road, Joe said, "Regina, that vacation was the cat's pajamas. I relaxed myself. You were wonderful each step of the way."

It sounded like he was giving me an American thanks for something I couldn't quite put my finger on. I had to smile. My head was still full of the beach sunset after the barbeque when he'd reached for my hand, the boat ride around Hong Kong harbor, and the long climb to reach the Sitting Buddha. Thirsty after our descent, Joe had bought us delicious bubble tea before fantasizing about twin retirements beneath nearby tropical shade. My fingers were ready for him to, at least, clasp my hand again.

Instead, he turned a serious face toward me. "Let's play our game while we are riding. I'm developing a point system I'll tell you about. I respect your opinion, Regina." He was impersonal and objective once again. *What's with this man? I can't figure him out.*

My curiosity heightened like the unexcavated green humps in the middle of the fields out the car windows. "Okay. Tell me, Joe."

Then the old authoritative Joe I'd first met announced, "I have made a social-credit plan for the government to score the trustworthiness of every adult in the motherland. Each person would start with a thousand points. Ways to get more would be by doing voluntary work, like donating bone marrow, or being a model worker. Points for bad behavior would be deducted: things like late bill payment, breaking rules, or committing crimes. What do you think? Foolproof and easy!"

It sounded like a control-freak politician's dream inside my head.

Joe continued. "Residents could look up their scores on the internet; it's becoming available all over China. If your score is green, you get rewards like discounts on transport passes or entering the hospital without paying a deposit. If your score is red, you need to fix your behavior."

"Joe, this sounds a little like my country's economic credit-ratings. I think it would be much harder to measure social behaviors. I'm wondering how it would work with fraud, plagiarism, shoddy construction, and sales of fake goods."

He'd gulped at the thought, especially when I'd mentioned plagiarism. Many of the students' theses that I'd helped score had contained paragraphs lifted verbatim from textbooks. My students learned the hard way after I wrote "word-for-word web references" and "Do over in YOUR WORDS!" on their papers. Most put on their thinking caps and redid the writings for a passing grade.

"Rule breakers will always be with us, Regina, but social credit would use rewards, not punishment, to help people be more civic-minded. More objective and uniform. Twenty points for blood donation. Minus twenty points for unpaid power bill. High scores borrow more library books, get cheaper sports tickets."

I couldn't resist. "Joe, how about 'not wearing pajamas on the street,' 'not staring at your phone in public,' and 'not encouraging others to drink'? Those were all uncivilized behaviors in the US last time I was there, but I see them a lot here too."

I had shot down his social-credit system by suggesting what to put on the blacklist. And I hadn't even gotten to fairness in the ratings of officials, the difficulty of determining consequences, and how it defines the best-behaving citizens.

He hung his head. "Regina, I even could see officers in Neighborhood Service Centre booths, assessing integrity of shop owners. People could see unsightly sale signs or dirty displays circled in red. Neat shops could earn free ads or parking space."

"Maybe I'm overreacting, Joe, but it reminds me of a book by George Orwell: *1984*. It caused quite a stir when it was published, but my country didn't take to its system."

I felt awful. Joe had spent a lot of time on this idea. I patted his arm. "I know you want to help your country with social management."

He pulled his arm away. "Maybe you can tell me about your country's management, Regina. Your president's management of Hurricane Katrina by flying over the flooded homes? His authorizing United Flight 93 being shot down when it was on the way toward your capital? Torturing prisoners at Abu Ghraib?"

Joe questioned the same things I had found abhorrent. The best I could do to defend my country was this: "Thank heavens those brave passengers stopped Flight 93 before the orders were carried out. Maybe democracy's idea that each person has a say in what happens gave them the strength to act." Then I shut my mouth until we were at Pei Hua's gate.

My goodbye was honest: "Joe, I'm glad you went to Hong Kong with me. It's been interesting."

Then Joe disappeared for the next several days. That surprised me and left a strange, empty feeling. I purposefully put time into lectures, plus mulling over the issues Dong Liu asked about weekly. He knew about the Civil Rights movement, police raiding Greenwich Village's Stonewall Inn in 1969, and the seventy's Gay Pride movement.

I told Dong Liu of attending a P-FLAG meeting in Montana—a very small group of Parents and Friends of Lesbians and Gays, TV coverage of millions demonstrating in Washington DC, and a Kansas Native American friend playing organ for a gay wedding in Iowa back in the nineties. She'd brought me an armful of pink rosebuds from the two grooms, her thanks to me for friendly encouragement. *Where might Dong Liu's questions lead?*

The next morning, my belly still happy from Dong Liu's father's dinner, I marched into Joe's office before class, determined to collect on the promised trip to Mom's birthday gathering. He quickly told a pretty attendant, "That will be all. You may go."

I tried not to feel victorious.

"Joe, my mother's birthday comes in a week. I have arranged it so that my one class has a guest instructor. What else must I do to visit family?"

He frowned. "You will be gone over Valentine's Day, Regina."

"Yes. It's Mom's birthday. You promised me before the Hong Kong trip."

He looked around. No one was listening. "Qian will order your ticket." And that was that. I didn't thank him; after all, he was only doing his job.

CHINA 44 - MOM'S BIRTHDAY

I'd visited markets for gifts that Midwesterners wouldn't consider cheap Chinese goods: Buddha beads, jade bracelets, hard candies, and mechanized toys. Finally on the US-bound flight, I thought about having brought a book of Chairman Mao's sayings for Conservative readers but changed my mind, deciding that it wouldn't be funny to them.

Tired and travel-weary from my twenty-four-hour ride, with plane changes in L.A. and Denver, I landed at Kansas City's Mid-Continent International. My California son, daughter-in-law and two youngest grandkids, also flying United, had arrived a few minutes earlier. I spied Joy's ponytail above her unzipped parka among the KS greeters. Is there a more beautiful sound than "Hi Mom!" chorused by one's children? I wondered. My second grandson grinned at me from below his new glasses and tussled with his big brother over who would grab my carry-on bag until my son-in-aw told them to "Knock it off!". We headed for underground parking and a new-model GM van that was badly in need of washing.

The hair of both my thirty-something kids was longer than I remembered, and my primary-school grandson hadn't lost his taciturn ways. He endured one hug, then answered my questions from the back seat with as few words as possible. My kids broke into a chorus of "Here on Gilligan's Isle," then chattered away in the front. Backseat conversations bounced between whether my grandsons could rent their rooms for five dollars a night as their impressive coin collections now swelled with yuan and ancient Chinese coins.

Biting wind rushed over a crust of snow whenever windows opened. We drove past skylines toward Grandma May's apartment in suburban Bonner Springs. I marveled at my organized, spacious, green old home, Kansas City, while thinking: *I wish I'd greeted them in the familiar "How are you?" form of "Ni hao ma" and explained how Chinese use it for friends and family, rather than "Ni hao." Mom might joke that China had added her to their greeting.*

Out the car window, suburban Bonner Springs awaited like Hometown, USA, with a Dollar Store and Dairy Queen doing brisk business judging from the number of cars in parking lots. We noted chain motels, where family members had reservations.

My crash pad was the couch in Mom's senior apartment. She hugged me for several seconds, and for once, didn't look me up and down and say, *"I see you've put on weight."* My Chinese rice and vegetables had left me thinner than she remembered. My words fled. I hugged her back and noticed her freshly cut white hair and new cane, which she seldom let tap the floor as she carried it.

One left turn down her first floor's hallway, Mom unlocked a door displaying a wreath filled with thread, thimble, and quilt motifs, and a "You are SEW welcome" ribbon. Inside her apartment was neat as a pin and quickly filling with wall-to-wall relatives. We ran out of chairs and lined up on her bed.

My Montana brother and his son arrived in his sleep-in van, still in good humor after the three-day drive. My California niece's family drove in with a sleeper-camper. The California nephew startled Grandma May with news that she would soon, once again, become a great grandmother. She took it in stride, but I knew that I'd eventually hear about it: *"Surely they're getting married soon?"*

Emotion overcame me for a moment. I took refuge in Mom's handicapped-equipped bathroom. My head filled with yards of satin I'd sewn, the wedding cake she'd festooned with icing-roses, and the "happily-ever-after" idea that I'd carried with me since age four. Problem was that the picture had tarnished and ripped into divorce years later. Mom hadn't reconciled herself to my crumpled picture. The dream of a beautiful bride floating down a staircase to her Prince Charming was still the way it should be in her mind.

I knew she'd never understand that my freedom was the best gift my ex had ever given me. My heart knew that all was well now. Yet my head still played old tapes when I least expected it. Having retreated to Mom's tiny bathroom, I ran warm water, ritually washing my hands of the American dream part of my upbringing and then rejoined my noisy family.

"Who is hungry?" one of them asked. "Let's go to the Dairy Queen." Agreement with this plan was unanimous.

My Oklahoma sister's family, including the kids' spouses, joined us as we trooped through roadside slush to the DQ. Mom wanted a hot dog and a Blizzard. The rest chose something from the burger-and-sugar menu. It sounded like foreign food to me. The gum-popping teenager who took our orders and the fry-cook did their best for our eight bills. Joy still ordered her "hamburger with catsup only," which she'd requested ever since she had learned to talk. Vegetarian family members ordered fries. We returned to Mom's communal dining room and ate our take-out. She made sure we left it cleaner than we found it, reminding us that she'd already paid to reserve it. We even wiped down all the tables.

Mom brought out Scrabble and photo albums. I crashed between frequent trips to her bathroom. Perhaps the water I'd drunk most of my life no longer agreed with me. Or maybe it was the well-done burger that had done it.

Then next morning, Mom flipped pancakes and llama sausage to serve those bundled up in the campers. I begged off, hoping I wasn't coming down with the flu. China's Bird Flu epidemic had moved on to Scotland, so I was pretty sure I hadn't brought that to the states. I watched family members snarf down breakfast, play cards, and consult Scrabble dictionaries while I hunkered in a rocking chair under a crocheted coverlet.

My kids picked up Arthur Bryant's BBQ, my sister produced multitudinous salads, and the camping folks brought chips and dips. It was a tantalizing feast, and my plate, with a tablespoon of each, smelled like a memory of past reunions. I managed a bite here and there, glad that everyone was recounting family stories so that I didn't have to answer questions about China. In fact, it was as if where I'd been the past months did not even exist in their memory.

My Missouri cousin (Mom's twin brother's daughter) and her family arrived with a huge cake with a computerized wonder of icing covering the top: a digitized picture of the twins taken at Stephenson's Apple Orchard before my uncle had died. Mom blew out candles. They dug into chocolate and fondant, announcing that it wasn't as good as Mom's chocolate cake with Seven-Minute Frosting.

She beamed, then declared this to be her best birthday yet and that she was going to take a nap. We hugged, made our farewells, and hit the road. It was hard to tell them goodbye, but I remembered Dad's admonition to "Quit when you're ahead" and genuinely felt glad for the time we'd had together.

My daughter's family dropped me off, with hugs all around once more, at my home-away-from-home on Kansas City's Missouri side. They headed three hours south to their Kansas home. To avoid feeling sad at the departures, I walked a nearby museum's sweeping lawn among its statues, made by famous sculptor Henry Moore. The feeling of elegant green space in America washed away images of China's press of teeming storefronts. When the time was right to return home for good, I knew I could get used to this again.

CHINA 45 - UNMOORED OBSERVATIONS

Rockwell-Nelson Art Gallery on Kansas City's Missouri side provided a lovely place to walk. I put one wobbly foot in front of the other and focused on the grassy expanse. Whiplash between recent family time and my pending return to China's demands slowly stopped jerking me around. The US tax deadline descended next, threatening to unmoor me. I'd tackle the paperwork as soon as I settled into my next home-away-from-home. I circumvented Henry Moore's gleaming metal "Sheep Piece," standing placid and solid across the expanse of green, and focused on grounding my thoughts.

My nearby host had stayed with me one night back in XiAn, where I'd shown her the ancient beginning of the Silk Road. Use of her mother-in-law's quarters in the Country Club Plaza here had been her generous thank you. From the Nelson lawn, I went straight to bed and slept until noon.

Then began a whirl of lunches, dinners, and parties. There wasn't enough time with any one person, yet I had opportunity to catch up on my friends' lives. Most had moved on, with one couple selling a home for the painful move to assisted living. Two self-reported their memory problems. All had pictures of their grandchildren handy. Their hair was grayer, and their familiar figures hid beneath extra pounds, but their personalities were the same and greetings were genuine.

One friend, a veteran China teacher from twenty years earlier, drove me to an experience in the Kansas City suburbs. We joined an anti-protest that was gathering in support of Ohev Shalom Synagogue, where a noisy handful of notorious Fred Phelps' folks picketed. A friendly policeman asked us to stay quietly on our side of the street. Protestants, Catholics, Jews, and agnostics quietly sang "We Shall Overcome" in support of the berated synagogue members as "Christ Killers" was displayed on signs across the street. The children of lawyer Phelps held up vile illustrations footnoted with Bible quotes. One man preaching hate for minorities, abortions, and homosexuals.

I thought about China's risking to break sexual taboos with its first gay movie: *Spring Fever*. The Midwest picketers left, rather like automatons, after thirty minutes. I surreptitiously snapped pictures, wondering if I'd show them to Dong Liu, and if I did, what he'd say. It dawned on me that this was the anniversary of a protest in Beijing that had ended in the loss of lives a world away.

In my Kansas City quarters again, I wrote a check with completed forms for Uncle Sam's Internal Revenue Service, glad to contribute. It had been surprisingly easy to complete, with few receipts and little income for the past six months. Moore's "Sheep Piece" remained firmly in place outside my window. Content and satisfied, I turned my attention to an evening with co-teachers, biking buddies, and friends.

My hair got a lick and a promise; then I hurried downstairs and was met with questions about how Chinese viewed Americans and the economic downturn. It felt wonderful to find interested friends asking questions. I hoped I did justice to how hard it is to draw conclusions about so vast a country, with development bringing changes in attitudes and knowledge almost daily. I knew that, with my appetite now restored, I did justice to the gourmet treats disappearing off trays from my host's oven.

CHINA 46 - EARTH FOCUS

Smooth flights and an uneventful return home to China felt good. At Pei Hua, I caught up on lecture material and stored a few activities up my sleeve for the upcoming Earth Day that should generate a lot of spoken English usage. I was wiping down the laminated placemats with pictures of the Grand Canyon, Lake Michigan, New York, and Yellowstone Park, which I had just removed from the bottom of my suitcase, when my telephone shrilled.

"*Wei?*" I said into the receiver, the habitual greeting returning. Then I heard English voices in the background on the other end of the line and realized who it was. "Oh, hello Matt!"

"Dr. Blakely, you're home in XiAn, I take it?" He paused and the background voices receded. Then I heard a door close. "I wish I could send you a movie. I just saw *Star Wars, Episode III*. Are you a fan? Never mind. You'd probably rather know I just finished *Harry Potter and Goblet of Fire*. That's my recreation when things get too heavy here in Homeland Security." Matt finally ran out of breath. He certainly seemed more at ease than usual, talking with me, as compared to when he was stressed. I liked it. We could just chat.

"What's happening on your end, Matt? Though I was in Kansas for a short time, I seldom heard anything beyond snatches of the usual talking heads on the three networks. My family avoids political discussions, unless there's some big breaking news."

"We just got word that Israel's Sharon— Oh, no need to share that! Saddam was— No, that's not ready for publication!"

Just asking what was happening had brought back the old, stressed Matt. I heard papers shuffling as he returned to news I'd already heard: Rosa Parks had died, Chief Justice Renquist had too; and they'd also found a tenth planet, Eris, beyond Pluto. "Both Pluto and Eris are considered dwarf planets," he added.

"Perhaps I can share that in English conversation class, Matt."

"Feel free. Let's talk about computers, Dr. Blakely. What do you know about Huawei, founded in 1987? We're hoping the US can soon launch something new to connect people socially and professionally via the internet. 'Face-to-face' sounds promising."

"It's funny that you should ask about Huawei, Matt. I searched on Google for it."

"You can use Google there?"

I nodded. "I hear Google's been available here since July last year. A former Microsoft person was put in charge of a global China project. There was some talk about skipping censorship."

"That's right. Do your students use Google much?"

"Actually, they seem to favor Qi Hoo 360's SO.com. From what I see here, that tech company's growing."

"Back to Huawei, Dr. Blakely. . ."

"As I was saying, I researched it—in English, of course—for a class-discussion topic teaser. Ren Zhengfei founded the company with $5600. It's growing like hotcakes here, along with Chinese 'smart phones.'"

"It'll probably be like BlackPlanet here; it started tiny, had 2.5 million registered users two years in, and now it seems to be morphing into a dating service."

I haven't even heard of BlackPlanet.

"Perhaps you're right, Matt, but our country should not ignore Huawei technology. The company's tied to the Communist Party, of course, and given the Chinese practice of putting family into positions over other candidates, I'd keep an eye on who's moving up in Zhengfei's company. They attribute their growth to excellent customer service, but I haven't seen examples here that bear out that claim."

"Wow! You found that all out on Google, Dr. B?"

"And also on China's SO.com. If I avoid the three T's—Taiwan, Tiananmen, and Tibet—I can find most anything. My students love to hear about Nobel Prize Winner Richard Feynman's 'quantum computer' idea—using laws that govern nature at a subatomic level. Pass that on to IBM, Intel, and Microsoft. According to my electronic geeks in class, China's Alibaba is already working on it."

"It's technical," he said, excitement in his voice now. "As I understand it, they don't use ordinary 'zeros and ones,' but 'quantum bits' that inhabit multiple states at once. The catch is that they must be kept very cold."

Is he lecturing me or just showing off? This is one smart cookie. "I can barely get my mind wrapped around refrigerated 'quibit' computers. They're supposedly tiny in comparison to the old titans of intelligence."

"Fascinating, isn't it?"

I nodded again, though he couldn't see it, of course. "Surely some of the California-based companies are already trying to build these machines to crunch data faster and faster. Banks? Investment companies?"

"I'm not free to discuss that information," he said primly.

"Okay. How about pandas? I've been researching them."

"President Nixon's successful trip to China was the reason they sent Ling Ling to our zoo," he said. "We've a program to lend them out for annual one-million-dollars donations toward conservation!"

"Good idea, Matt! Let's talk after I do some more research."

"Have a good day or night, or whatever time it is in XiAn, Dr. Blakely." His hung up.

I'd enjoyed our exchange, yet it seemed strange after his dire warnings to keep my doors locked and one eye looking back to see if I was being followed.

My plastic placemats were dry by then. So, I gathered them up and headed for the teacher's bus. Once it was loaded, we barreled past plastic debris blown against fences. The usual garbage-gatherers speared sacks, ads, toilet paper, and cast-off clothing along gutters as we passed through downtown— all signs of China's economy intersecting with its vast population.

Arriving at the new campus, I clutched my coat shut and hurried into the unheated education building. No heat rose to the second floor. Students filed in, wearing fingerless gloves and earmuffs.

I announced that, next month, America would celebrate Earth Day. Curious eyes turned my way as I told them of spring gatherings in Kansas at the Shawnee Mission Park to plant trees, conduct water purification, learn organic gardening, and discuss projects to keep our planet healthy. Then I challenged them:

"Choose a project to help China become more healthy. You have four weeks. Keep a journal, and report to us in one month. One student will win one of these historic American scenes." Most eyes remained glued on the Grand Canyon placemat I held up as I told them some startling facts, like how long it takes for plastic to disintegrate, what a compost pile can accomplish, and that cigarette-butt filters are the biggest pollutants on beaches. Then they chattered in small groups, using excited English phrases and consulting their notes. Occasionally, someone would go to the chalk tray for a closer look at the Grand Canyon or New York. You'd have thought they were dreaming of winning an Academy Award. I wondered if the excitement would stay alive for thirty days.

CHINA 47 - EMPHASIZING MATTERS

I couldn't help but smile. Those placemats had stirred up enthusiasm in my English classes. And my AeroTech class, meeting every-other-week to do in-class presentations on places to visit in China, was proving to be a forum of hardworking English majors. For me, it was a win-win situation that required almost no preparation from me. I got their internet-researched perspectives on The Great Wall, Emperor's Palace, Shang Ra La, and Hua Shan, while they got suggestions from me for better sentence structure, improved pronunciation, and clearer communication.

Remembering that it was tutoring day made me smile too; Dong Liu's English was so good that I did little but discuss topics of interest with him, instead of pronunciation or grammar. It was the highlight of my weeks, sharing stimulating conversation with him hanging on my every word, followed by his father's good cooking.

I'd complimented Dong Liu the previous week on how he never confused number pronunciation. We'd laughed about "ThirTEEN versus THIRteen," and "FourTEEN versus FOURteen." He didn't know how he'd managed to catch onto proper syllable emphasis and avoided the confusion I met in markets or class. I'd even built a lesson around fifTEEN-dollar and FifTY dollar items, using old knock-off CD and movie cases. Dong Liu hadn't seen the humor when I'd explained the lesson. He said I'd wasted my time on it where he was concerned. *Too complex for him? Or arrogance about his gifted learning ability?*

Then I remembered Dong Mai saying that Dong Liu would meet me at XiAn's Bell Tower to practice English and treat me to dinner. Perhaps the parents wanted an evening to themselves. I exited the bus near the old ancient walls. Dong Liu wasn't among the rushing throngs. I hadn't asked on which of the four sides of the Bell Tower he'd arrive.

I climbed up to get a better view of the large square area. Tentacles of traffic streamed in four directions. Pre-Xian, Chang An of the Tang and Han dynasties had probably been one of the world's largest cities. Most of progeny of those million inhabitants seemed to be coming at me or elbowing me aside. My stomach gnawed at me.

Historical views lost their allure as I descended for the sixth time into a huge faux-McDonald's. I knew they had a flush toilet, as well as a sink in one dining corner for washing one's hands. At the counter, I swatted an elderly woman's hand away as she reached into my jacket pocket. Then I paid for my faux-chicken sandwich. The woman moved into another line, nearer the wash basin, and tried to pick another pocket. I retreated to an uncleared table and wolfed down my faux burger. Dong Liu found me there. He'd been doing the same climb-and-look technique, just missing me repeatedly for the past frustrating hour.

"It is rush hour," he said. "I will take you home on the bus." No argument came from me. We queued up with a huge clump of people, half of them squatting as they waited. Suddenly, Dong Liu grabbed my hand and charged forward. We got inside just as the bus door closed. He wrestled my backpack off, saying, "Put it on frontwards!" I did as I was told, feeling rude as I invaded the space of persons on all sides of me.

The bus stopped. A half dozen more people shoved their way on board, pushing us along with the tide. This was repeated at four more stops. I could hardly breathe. Tears welled up. I felt panic rise. What if all this weight on the seats, aisles, and wheel-wells suddenly shifted? We'd have the vehicle on its side in no time. I held on to the aisle strap for dear life.

Then the exiting began, and as people pushed down the aisle, I cowered until the nose of a seated elderly woman practically poked a hole in the side of my hip. Others got on the bus. Where was Dong Liu? He had disappeared again.

For the next two stops, more people exited than entered. I felt eyes on me, but it took a moment to find their source. A Chinese man with a long-braided ponytail stood calmly in the aisle. He carried an artist's portfolio under one arm. He might have been in a Zen garden, surrounded on all sides with peace and beauty. My panic exited with the next rush of people, and I became acutely aware of my tear-streaked, blotchy face turned his way. Dong

Liu's arm snaked around a couple of people and handed me a slightly used handkerchief. I thanked him, feeling ashamed.

At the stop before the freshman campus, the peaceful, handsome stranger came down the aisle. He spoke briefly to Dong Liu in Chinese, gave me a smile, and exited. I felt strangely empty, as if some possibility had gotten off the bus with him.

I asked Dong Liu about their conversation. "He's an artist. He asked if you're one too. He wished he could speak your language to talk with you."

"Here's your handkerchief, Dong Liu. I got scared with so many people pushing on the bus. I'm sorry it's all wet. I could wash it and bring it next week to your home, but let's not meet downtown anymore."

Dong Liu's stoic face gave no clue as to what he was thinking. "Okay, Regina."

I felt I had to know more. "Dong Liu, what did you think when you saw me crying? After I was done feeling scared half to death, I felt embarrassed."

"I thought you were emotional, Regina."

Will I ever get a glimpse of what lies behind these Chinese facades?

When we parted ways, I simply told him goodnight and saved the discussion topics for another time. I'd had enough for one day.

At the apartment, I saw a note taped to my door. "I am in 402 above the Ed office. If you don't wish to climb four floors, I can come to you at seven p.m. We can have dinner."

I knew Joe's scrawl, although the note was unsigned. I also knew that the campus fourth floor across the street was vacant. It was better, though, to meet the boss there than to have him coming to my apartment at that time of evening. What on earth did he have in mind? Since our ride home from Hong Kong, he'd been scarcely in the big campus office and stiffly professional. I made a mental note to have an honest talk with him about his wife and her feelings, as well as the coeds that flocked around him. I'd be honest about the way that rankled me, though perhaps that wasn't entirely out of concern for his wife. It was complicated.

Maybe today's meeting would help me sort out what was normal human feeling and what was a clash of two cultures while one side was lonely. I crossed the street and climbed the four cement flights of stairs.

Room 402 was far down the musty, poorly lighted cement hallway, past several locked doors and grillwork that might have housed a library in times past. I knocked quietly on the open door, seeing Joe at a wooden desk. He stood and indicated a chair at the side of it. "Sit please."

I did as he asked. And when he spoke, Joe was all business. "The dean appreciates the work you have done for Pei Hua. He wants you to teach foreign teachers how to inspire students. Eight weeks, not four. The need for understanding Western problem-solving methods and motivating students is greater than can be met in four weeks. You begin next week."

What on earth is he talking about? Then I remembered mention of an in-service workshop on critical thinking that had been discussed at a recent faculty meeting.

Visions of jealousies flashed across my mind-screen, should a 'how to teach and inspire' class be presented with me as the new teacher, asking other teachers to attend twice their expected number of in-service hours. And how would I handle the Japanese-speaking teachers whose curriculum was written in the same unfathomable symbols they'd used for years? The ESL teachers from Australia, New Zealand, and Britain at least spoke my language. It was impossible to envision eight evenings of interactive discussion on goal-setting, group activities, or individual adaptations that usually got my students involved and interested. I slammed the brakes on my thinking and turned to Joe. "I can try such a class with foreign teachers for four weeks."

"Eight!"

"No. Four weeks. For the other four, I can also do the same with Chinese English teachers."

"Good idea! Their methods need changing. I am sure the dean will agree." Joe breathed a sigh, still shuffling papers. "Oh, Regina, there is another small problem." His feet shuffled slightly beneath the desk, as his hands shuffled his stack of papers. "The number of students in this semester's Oral English class has changed. It will be sixteen." He wrote down "60," even as he repeated, "Sixteen in Oral English."

"Did you say sixteen? Or sixty?" I wrote the respective numbers in the dusty desk's surface, so he would have a visual. "I cannot teach sixty in Oral English; sixteen is as many as can have opportunity to speak. I'll teach sixTEEN . . . as we agreed when I turned in the syllabus."

"No? But you *must!*" He went back to shuffling papers.

"I'm sorry, Dean Zhou. I will *not* accept sixty," I continued, shaking my head.

"How many? I could ask my boss to split the class. Maybe you are free evenings?"

I didn't tell him I had just been asked to moonlight at Babe English School two evenings a week. Other teachers had assured me that everyone did that. "Thank you for offering to split the class. I am free Wednesday and Friday evenings, and the mornings I am not already scheduled." I started to leave, then remembered something: "Oh, is there a class list?"

He shuffled papers furiously now. "Yes, but the list is not finished. Uh, there are a few more than sixTEEN on it."

"How many?"

"A hundred, but we won't know how many signed up until first class meets." I heard that loud and clear. No confusion about emphasized syllables on 'a hundred.' I supposed I could make it a pun . . . as in hunDREAD.

"A hundred? That means fifty per class, even if you split them. I will not do that, Joe."

"Regina, you have your teaching principles, but just teach them a little something. Don't worry about teaching quality."

"Joe, a hundred people won't have a chance to speak for more than a minute each period. I won't do it." My voice was rising. I felt heat flush across my cheeks and into my eyes.

"Regina, I'll talk to my boss. I'll call you."

It was all I could do not to stomp down the stairs. How could Joe coldly change just like that? I went to the cafeteria and ordered a huge platter of dumplings and a Tsing Tao. I simmered as they cooled a bit, then drowned my frustration in tasty morsels filled with chopped beef and greens. Yuko, a neighbor who taught Japanese, brought her dinner to my table.

"Yuko, how would you get an idea of a hundred people's Oral English levels in the first class?"

"Have them write a paragraph about themselves."

Rather than debate how written paragraphs could indicate a speaking level, I turned to my dumplings and talked about the weather. Yuko would probably be one of the reluctant students in the upcoming all-teacher class the dean was trying to double.

The next day, Joe caught me outside my classroom. "Dr. Blakely, I have informed my boss now that I understand the seriousness of your teaching. Maybe we need classes of twenty every day."

"Joe, did you tell him I refuse to teach Oral English classes of more than sixteen?"

We repeated ourselves for about twenty minutes while my students filed in, studiously eavesdropping, and heard me say, "It appears that nothing has changed since we last talked. If I walk into a class of over sixteen, and no one is there to split it, I will simply walk out."

That is how I learned that Pei Hua students signed up for classes, dropped out in droves (often without attending even once), and sorted themselves into classes of about twenty. The university got the tuition either way.

CHINA 48 - TIBET BOUND

I left my class with plastic placemats clutched to my chest, happy with the amount of English spoken. Classes fairly buzzed as small groups discussed how they'd honor Earth Day and win one of the coveted pictures of American landmarks at the month's end. Gao, my jokey student who returned from breaks reeking of tobacco, overtook me. I felt my allergies kick up. "Dr. Zhou wants to see you, Regina."

I approached Joe's office like a divided personality. One part of me wanted to recapture the easy relationship we'd enjoyed after our rocky start in Hong Kong. The other apprehensive part was hiding behind a red flag marked "Beware." There was nothing more to discuss about class size. I was sick of talking about it. I approached his desk, noticing that the other office desks were empty.

Joe stood up. His big smile lit a small flame inside me. He held out both arms, and I blundered right into his chest, or at least, the placemats did. He ignored them. "I am so happy to see you, Regina. Hong Kong seems long ago."

"It felt that way to me too, Joe, but what about the time since Hong Kong?"

"We don't have privacy here for long, Regina. Let me tell you the good news. The dean is pleased with my proposal for you to have travel time. You need to know our motherland, and Pei Hua can help us—you—with time to go. Prepare for four days." He looked around and dropped his voice to a whisper, "In Tibet Autonomous Region."

"Why, Joe? I didn't tell you, but I've wanted to visit Tibet for a long time, ever since I did a trek in Nepal!" I didn't add that a Tourism-student presentation at AeroTech had rekindled that desire.

I felt his firm hand over my mouth then. Somehow, it also felt tender. He looked directly into my eyes. A shiver of pleasure started down my spine from deep inside of my brain. I heard "Shhhh, Regina. I am happy to do this for you. I will be on today's afternoon bus. Please get off on the east side of the square downtown. I will take you to get documentation."

"But what about my classes?"

He took a quick step backward and raised his voice as a secretary entered. "That will be all, Dr. Blakely."

I taught my next class by intentionally thinking of my two feet planted in front of the students. After they filed out, I ate wide noodles, as promised last week, with Luna and Ella in Pei Hua's cafeteria. Tibet moved to the back of my mind as we visited their dorm room: four rows of double bunks flanking a wide aisle. Ella's sheets, in disarray on the top bunk with her tiny lamp atop an insect base, awaited late-night study.

Present with these hospitable girls, I thought about how much my youngest grandchild would enjoy the toy lamp. We went by kiosks until the girls insisted on pooling their yuan and presented the same lamp to me. No amount of protesting or attempts to reimburse them would do. I accepted gratefully, determined not to let this influence me when it came time to distribute final grades. A surprising number of gifts—calligraphy poems on wall hangings, a watermelon, and a carved bracelet—had come at last semester's end as students entered their final's oral conversation. Word was out that I couldn't be bribed. *Guan xi* and Chinese hospitality made a strange mix in my mind.

My afternoon class, becoming more comfortable with an interactive non-lecture format, was as enthusiastic about an Earth Day contest to beautify the motherland as my former three classes. I made a mental note to display the placemats with informative bits about Yellowstone Park in my next class. I'd weave it into whatever theme the syllabus stated. Then I headed to the faculty bus. I didn't see Joe among the forty-five teachers seated behind me, ignoring their seatbelts.

Exiting from the east side of XiAn's square felt like descending to Dante's doorway. People brushed past me as I stepped around a deformed child on a skateboard-like contraption. Her one good arm propelled her toward anyone who might proffer a yuan. Mother watched from a nearby doorway. Students had told me that parents sometimes broke their babies' limbs to arouse sympathy and gain begging income.

Joe appeared at my side. He took my hand, raised his other to his lips to indicate silence, and headed into an off-street market. We picked up beef BBQ on sticks, bit into it as we walked narrow alleys, and then entered a dusty room with a desk and three chairs. I sat. My skirt would likely need washing before I wore it again. Why hadn't I worn a dark outfit that wouldn't show the dust? Joe and the solemn man behind the desk exchanged staccato syllables and head nods, and then one gaze each in my direction. I heard "Tibet" and "Lhasa," but the rest was a blur of mystery.

Joe turned to me finally. "You pay him a hundred yuan, and I return in three days for your permit to travel four days in Tibet. You leave in two weeks. No need to sign." I handed over a hundred-yuan note with hardly any hesitation.

"Joe, is this another trip where you surprise me by coming along? Like Hong Kong?"

"No, Regina. Tibet for only you. I make sure your needs are met with reservations, so you need not worry."

Questions and elation shared space in my heart. I'd long wanted to go to Tibet, though it was closed to travelers. How had Joe known? Had I let slip that impossible wish on that rainy evening when the spirits had flowed too freely while we dined? He'd read my biggest wish while in China, the dear man! And this transaction had seemed so easy that I felt a grin stretch my face as we walked to the bus stop. I was going to see The Potala, the famed palace with its gold glittering above the mile high city, next to the Himalayan peaks. He dropped my hand and spun off toward another bus.

CHINA 49 - TIBET TIDBITS

Two weeks passed more quickly than I had imagined. The Tibet permit came to my door in a sealed envelope, written and stamped on both sides in Chinese. All I recognized were numbers and my printed name. My Pei Hua students in their assigned English groups chattered about their efforts toward Earth Day. Joe made himself scarce, sending an unsigned, sealed note: "You will fly next week. Your classes are covered."

Sure enough, a driver soon knocked on my door and delivered me to the airport. My window seat eventually revealed brown Tibetan mountain ranges, with what looked like powdered sugar dusting their ridges. Those turned red as occasional ice-sculpted heights gave way to Himalayan snowfields sloping to emerald lakes. We set down at an elevation of 11,800 feet, "the highest airport in the world," by diving between non-snowy peaks, along sand-rock valleys and the dark meandering of rivers.

I circumvented insistent cabbies and wedged into an airport shuttle. Bags stacked to the ceiling threatened the passengers who filled every seat, including ones that folded down from the aisle. I showed the driver "Xue Ya," which was the name of my hotel. He shook his head, miming ignorance and pointing me outside, where my bags sat on the curb.

I found myself at the mercy of a double-priced cab to the Potala area with the Dalai Lama's palace. It was as regally impressive as its well-known pictures, sitting atop Red Hill, centering Lhasa. The driver proudly pronounced his first English words: "Land of the Gods!" Then silence reigned for a two-mile backtrack along the route we'd just taken. He stopped at a modest cement structure. "Xue Ya!" He broke into a huge grin. "Tops in the world, Lhasa!"

My mind was still reeling from the sight of passing by pilgrims, who prostrated themselves on roadsides one length at a time. Settling in, I came to believe that Xue Ya was new, despite being flanked by construction, worn-out businesses, and its lived-in appearance. The squat toilet gleamed, and white curtains cut glare and noise from a bus station out an inner-courtyard window. At the desk, a young man wearing a hotel uniform bowed and declined a tip for lugging my bags up three flights. There was no elevator, but my room was clean enough, with a door that seemed to lock.

I used my bedside phone to offer the Chinese syllables for pork sandwich, fried rice, egg, and tomato: *"Jai rou, yu ca le, fan qie ji dan."*

The desk clerk asked, "Deliver?" Then followed a barrage of some sort of Chinese, so I just whispered *shei shei* and replaced the phone in its cradle. It never occurred to me that she might have been telling me meals were included in my prepaid room. The dish arrived, along with two bowls of rice.

Deliciously fortified, I took a walk towards Potala, passing by a park filled with Mahjong foursomes, lively children, tea drinkers, and colorful umbrellas, shading a population whiling away lazy afternoon hours. Altitude tugged at my sinuses as I strolled, and one of my knees was beginning to hurt. Stalls lined a block-long entrance along a mustard-colored wall next door. I peeked behind the wall and saw that it blocked rubble and debris. Was this on the next day's temple tour? I decided to retrace my steps. My body felt heavy, and I needed help placing a call at the desk.

Pu Bu, my guide, answered my call in English and told me to "Meet at Snowland Hotel. Can't miss it." I asked him to spell the name of the nearby temple in Pinyin; later, I realized that he read and wrote only Tibetan and spoke only Chinese. That call wore me out. I repositioned my lone chair beneath the locked doorknob and fell on my bed in my clothes.

The sun was slanting sideways into my western window when I later awakened. I still had time to seek the Snowland Hotel though. A tricycle-cab waited by the curb with a skinny guy with huge calf muscles, who spoke Mandarin's number language. We agreed on a price—five yuan, less than an American dollar, after he'd started at twenty.

He'd nodded and smiled widely at my request: "Snowland?" Then he'd consulted three other pedallers, who didn't know where it was either, though they wanted to steal my guy's fare. We hunted for a half hour. If I'd known how far he would have to pedal, I wouldn't have haggled.

We passed a museum, the entry to a street-carnival fair, and a park where women boxed up Mahjong tiles while clutching their winnings (yuan notes).

Then the glorious Potala spread before me like a heavenly vision lowered to within five hundred-feet of the earth. He didn't stop pedaling as pilgrims slowed our progress past a green expanse, the beginning of small shops and connected dwellings on narrowing streets. He braked at the Jokhang temple, accepted my five yuan, and motioned me onward down a side street.

A man came from the back of what seemed more like a stall than a hotel. "Lee-geen-a, we take a cab." His voice sounded like the man I'd phoned the day before, so I trusted him. Pu Bu frowned when I insisted that he make a copy of my document. Then he hurried inside, returning shortly and thrusting it into my hands. Then he barked at our waiting driver: "Sera!"

On the way north out of Lhasa, he gave me a memorized litany of dates. "Yellowhead sect—not red or white or black—arose in 1419, was destroyed in 1949, protected in historic relics in 1961, secretly practiced until 1979, group-practiced again in 1989."

We passed statues of Buddha—Past, Present, and Future. I practiced Tibetan, *"shi de lai"* (hello) and *"Hali shu"* (goodbye), as he told me that monks did not like hearing Chinese spoken. I thanked him for the one-on-one tour of the area and asked how many would join us tomorrow for the Potala tour.

"Just you."

Before I had time to wonder about that, we approached the wooded and suburban Sera monastery. I turned to Pu Bu, and said, "I've heard that red-robed monks hold heated debates here."

"No."

"No?"

He was already out of the cab and headed toward the nearest building. I needed all my breath to follow Pu Bu's long legs uphill.

First, we peeked into the empty assembly hall as skylights sent three wonderful rays of light toward rugs from which prayers were lifted morning and evening. We walked the grounds. I was told that three colleges and thirty-three houses marched up Sera's mountainside. Lines of people in dark Tibetan garb paid a tenth of a yuan for Children's Blessings, so that their favored darlings could receive black smudges on their noses. Devout adults bowed and left jiao for numerous deities or mumbled as they spun prayer wheels.

In a nearby clearing, red-robed monks sat beneath trees, focusing on a standing pair who were shouting in a vigorous exchange. The two spoke with jabbing gestures, making their points while others gave them their stoic attention. Then those two then quieted, and another pair debated the winner with the same shouts and jabs. It wasn't quite my mental picture of peace-loving monks, and it certainly wasn't meditative.

Then the tour was over, and Pu Bu repeated, "Sera Monastery, famous debating monks." He ignored any further questions. We sped back toward the Potala. I was dismissed with "Tomorrow morning, Potala." Then he disappeared without another word.

I felt ravenous, as if I'd been the one using up calories in those Sera debates. Cuisine in the touristy Old Town was a fine mix of European, Western, Chinese, and Tibetan. The words "Yak burger" caught my eye from a sandwich board, an offering served with American French fries. It was surprisingly tender, with bite-sized pieces of meat complete with ubiquitous mayo, tomato slice, and lettuce. I peeled the tomato slice's skin off and left the lettuce. Greens were a no-no for me here, where human excrement was used as fertilizer, unless they were cooked in a boiling hot pot.

Sated now, I sought out Jokhang, the seventh-century, four-story temple resplendent in golden roof tiles. I knew a copper buddha, brought here by XiAn's Princess Wen Cheng, stood among its relics. In the Bharkor stalls outside the temple, a purchased "Yak, yak, yak" t-shirt found its way into my backpack. An artist painted exquisite Tibetan faces, but I overcame the urge to buy several smiling, apple-cheeked portraits.

It wasn't quite sunset yet, as SUVs, tricycle-cabs, green taxis, and tour buses sped past faithful worshippers, who kowtowed with their dusty foreheads to the pavement near the Potala. A few moved like inchworms all the winding way to the monastery. How long had they been repeating this devout movement? Maybe from the airport highway, ninety meters from Lhasa? I gave them wide berth, then slipped inside Jokhang Temple through a sea of tourist backpacks, dreadlocked Americans, and curvy Chinese women in cropped tees, making my way toward the yellow-orange rail. I saw a one-hundred-dollar bill being handed over the wooden railing to one monk, who interrupted his chant to offer a huge smile.

Red-robed monks sat lotus in rows of enlarging circles, chanting with their eyes half-closed. I felt rather than heard their soul-stirring sounds. Kind visitors outside the saffron-painted rails propelled me forward until I could have touched the outer ring of shaved heads. One pair of dark eyes bored into mine; then his forehead creased as he pointed wordlessly toward the open door. I got the message to go. Now!

I retreated, found a pedicab cycler, and rode back to the more orderly Han section and my hotel. Halfway home, darkness fell, and my heartbeat slowed. Had I done something to offend the monk? I didn't think so, but I might never know for sure.

CHINA 50 - POTALA ESPANOL

The next morning, I walked the Lhasa pedicab route that I had seen the previous afternoon. My stomach was growling for almost an hour before I stopped at a street vender who was boiling congee. I knew my foreigner's request for sugar and milk would get a wry "I knew it" smile in return, so I added a generous dip of the usual pickled greens. It was palatable and hot enough to kill any germs. Chopsticks in hand, I slurped the final cup-or-so from the cleanest lip of the bowl, said *shei shei* to the woman, who plunged my used bowl into a bucket of cold suds, and then brushed curb grime off the seat of my skirt.

Nearing the Potala, I sat on a worn bench circling a lone shade tree and looked for guide Pu Bu to appear. Then I waited another dusty hour, and then another. Groups formed on the packed dirt courtyard and entered through the doorway for the tour. Dreadlocked yogis whirled prayer wheels, weary travelers prostrated themselves, and tourists conversed as they snapped pictures. More dust and body odor drifted toward my nostrils as each visitor moved near for a better view of the revered place. I wondered if devotees would prostrate themselves up the long lines of stone steps as well. Maybe reaching the lower entrance was their goal. No one seemed to go in or out of the darkened doorway.

I consulted my guidebook. The beautiful Dzong Fortress, built with love, had housed the Dali Lama from 1649-1959. High above the skyline, this winter palace had administrated Tibetan government from a thousand rooms. I'd heard that before, in a sing-song tone, during a Tourism presentation.

Pu Bu had taken my permits with him, telling me, "I get you ticket for palace." I wondered why I had trusted him with my documents. Then I rechecked my fanny pack to make sure my passport was still safely inside with my return air ticket. Worst-case scenario would be that I had come to Tibet and only gotten to see the inside of Jokhang and sit in Potala's courtyard.

I people-watched, taking in the wizened faces above whirling prayer wheels, the wise eyes of toddlers peeking over their father's shoulders, and Europeans shouldering backpacks. I began to make up stories about the characters in motion all around me: The dreadlocked Americans with the trekking equipment hanging from his packs that had just climbed that distant peak; dusty street sweepers, busy with straw brooms, were dreaming of their waiting brides; white-collar Chinese men on cellphones were describing curvy women in cropped knit tees and rhinestone jeans atop strappy heels; guards trailing sweaty tourists were hoping to dupe them out of heavy bribes. It was better than an exotic movie.

Pu Bu appeared as casually as if he'd been right on time, saying only, "We walk to entrance." Words ping-ponged between him and the ticket-taker. I learned that individuals now had to have a twenty-four-hour reservation (easily gotten yesterday). He would put me "in a group" if one had a vacancy. While we waited on my tree-bench, I learned that Potala Palace, built on Old Lhasa's northwest corner, had two parts: a white one for government, and a red-brown one for religious sites. The smell of incense wafted off the people descending the steps. Halls, tomb stupas, sutra room, balconies, and courtyards still awaited me—thirteen stories by four hundred meters—just inside the barred entrance.

During another lazy hour of waiting in the shade with Pu Bu, I learned more about The Bodpas, as Tibetans call themselves. "They number 3.4 million and don't have surnames, but their two-to-four syllable names suggest Buddhist meanings. Bodpas love ornaments and striped aprons, practice sky burial, and stage fast festival horse races."

The noon sun beat down as faithful worshippers kowtowed in front of us. SUVs, tricycle-cabs, green taxis, and tour buses sped past their prostrated forms.

Pu Bu introduced me to a friend of his, who arrived with nine Spaniards in tow. Then he abruptly left without another word. There was nothing left for me to do but fume or contemplate the population mix around me. I chose to contemplate.

I had read that, in 1992, there were 96,000 Tibetans and 40,000 Han Chinese in Lhasa. Those figures were turned on their heads as the Chinese had moved in and come as tourists, prompting national phrases like "population invasion" and "urban exclusion." Growth to "help the development of Tibet" continued, as the ratio of Tibetan-to-Han reversed, with Han claiming shops, jobs, and housing in 2005. I made a mental note to find out about growing populations across mainland China to compare the percentage of growth that happened alongside Tibet's changes.

I was getting hot, hungry, bored, and indignant. Was Pu Bu really trying to get me into Potala? Why hadn't he explained the difficulty of getting in alone before?

Suddenly, Pu Bu was back. "Come. You join this group."

He plunked me into a Spanish-speaking tour group from Madrid. Luckily, I remembered quite a bit of high-school Spanish, and the group was very friendly. By the time we walked three stories of gold deities, offerings, altars, chanting areas, and jeweled statues, the Spanish words had brought me adequate understanding.

I marveled at such riches compared with the ragged crowds in pilgrimage covering the ninety-kilometer road from the airport.

"Built in seventh century," I heard, "thanks to Tang lordship over Tibet by Qing Dynasty's administration, this became Winter Palace for many Dalai Lamas."

My map had other details to share: "After 1911 Revolution, the Republic of China exercised management. In May 1951, the Seventeen Point Agreement opened a new historical page over Tibet." There was also a nationalist summary of tumultuous history.

". . . Tibetan King Gampo, a rebuilding by the fifth Dalai Lama in seventeenth century, Princess WenCheng married Tibetan lord, allowing Qing Dynasty's administration to declare it Winter Palace." It was too much opulence and information!

With stomachs growling and sweat pouring, we descended Potala's long stairs. Pu Bu was nowhere in sight. The group invited me to eat with them *"por favor."* They treated me to a yak burger in the old quarter. We'd become a bonded group by then, as they included me, with my limited Espanol, in jokes and rapid-fire comments. We shared email addresses, and discussed the absence of Spanish Buddhists and the growing numbers in America. I was glad of our half-day together.

Starting home, I noticed a sandwich board advertising "Lake Namsto, 200 yuan tomorrow" and "journey to the highest lake in the world."

I reserved a spot for the next morning, with a return time of three p.m."

"English-speaking guide?" I asked.

"Sure. Mostly foreigners, and they speak English." I paid the man, hailed a bicyclist, and headed home.

CHINA 51 - WORLD ABOVE

In the next early morning's darkness, I double-timed my usual Lhasa route again, arriving in time to slide into a van beside Leslie (London TV writer, Australian born) and Dave (London food distributor) just down from Qomolangma. They described Mt. Everest camping life, mostly mentioning how cold they'd found it, and told me of long waits for permission to enter and the reasons why: some westerners had illegally gone sans guide and unfurled a freedom banner where the Olympic torch was to be carried. Persons video-taping the event had disappeared. I finally realized why I had received warnings to say that I'm with a group; it also further explained my long wait at the Potala. Staying mum, I listened and observed.

While driving into the mountains, our group got acquainted: Mexico-city native Jose told us, "The best thing about Mexico is the people! The worst thing about Mexico is the people!" He bonded with two Germans, who headed across the highway to look at yaks when we made a pit stop. Guys went in one direction, and girls went the other. A girl who spoke both Chinese and Tibetan, back from a few years in France, snoozed with her pretty European friend. One German spoke minimal English, but his talkative countryman behind him made up for it. Looking all of seventeen years old, he gave treatises on George Bush and young people at the U of Michigan, convinced that Americans "think what they have is better than anyone else." He pointed out "awesome sights" ad nauseum.

At the pass, and in the snow, we stopped again. Our driver only spoke Tibetan, but we worked things out. He pointed into clouds and said, *"Namtso."* Rain? Snow? Sun? On a clear day, maybe, it didn't matter. The yaks dotting the mountain slopes, the hairpin turns, and the river on one side made the 1100-meter drive to the "Tops in the World" (4,718 meters or 15,479 feet) quite exilarating.

Temperatures dipped as we passed prayer flags draped over piles of stone. It began to snow as we neared the lake. Biting wind made it a cold reception. A dribble of tented eateries and yak rentals lined one side of them, above a lake. The driver showed us two bars on his cell phone before he motioned us out. We exited into a near-blizzard, braved the smelly WCs, and had tea until the restaurant workers pestered us to buy necklaces. It was time to walk toward the lake, a faint blue blur through the storm. We avoided riding yaks, momentarily got some sun to snap pictures, and wondered aloud about the web-footed fowl at the water's edge. Then we returned through the snow toward cliffs and boulders dotted with white scarves, called *chadas*, and prayer flags.

Dave stood sentinel while Leslie and I went al fresco behind a tent for another less smelly yet much needed bathroom stop. We ate scrambled eggs with a few vegetables, drank more tea, and continued the other way along the lake in the sleet. A huge red stone leaned toward the low mountainside fifty cold steps along the sandy lakeshore. A red-clothed monk emerged from the opening. Her shaved head shone as she motioned us into her mountainside abode. She watched Lesley's video of debating monks intently, then pointed out her bed and cooking utensils, stoked her wood fire, and called to another woman, who arrived spinning a prayer wheel. We offered our hostess a few coins. She refused. Dave was the star, with his blond beard and blue eyes. The women even seemed delighted with his English warning to us about the butter tea: "If you drink it, they constantly refill your cup."

We visited a huge Buddha in the cavern, then an un-roofed portion with two small rooms, interacting as much as our language skills allowed. The monk pantomimed that she would long remember Dave's eyes. We took our leave, clasping hands to our hearts. "Namaste" echoed all around. *The buddha in me greets the buddha in you.*

We chose a tent with "Sichuan" scrawled on the side for some well-seasoned rice, eggplant, and fried tofu. We drank more tea, then piled into the van and left Namtso Lake, trying to outdo each other with stories of our experiences on those icy shores. I noticed, though, that the one Chinese fellow was silent, although I urged him to share. The multi-lingual young woman had fallen asleep and was the only one who could ask our driver questions, so when he offered to stop halfway down for us to swim at a huge cement pool, the chilly air and lack of hygiene pushed us to refuse, urging him to continue down to Lhasa.

Two toilet stops and two photo stops later, we pulled off toward a steamy village. Jose insisted that the steam came from cooling tanks, and he was right. The hot springs, wedged between development and debris, was a large modern swimming pool. A swim seemed a poor cap for the magical day though, so we motioned the driver again to descend to Lhasa.

We returned after dark. A Vancouver couple joined me for dinner—pan and dahlbot for them, Indian food for me. I walked slowly past Potola, with a sound-and-light show bouncing off its sun-lit façade. Then I hailed a bicycle-taxi driver to take me back to my hotel.

The front desk and I used sign language to clarify the next day's early departure for the airport; then I fell into exhausted, grateful sleep. I dreamed of flying over ice sculpted by playful giants' then I flew above red terrain, streaked by glaciers, and soared on toward upthrusts of chocolate dusted with powdered sugar.

I awakened craving sweets, heated a leaky hotpot for tea, and hurried down to a taxi that the front desk called for me. The return flight to XiAn felt like déjà vu backwards, as I half-watched the peaks below through sleepy eyes. Had I really been to the "Tops in the World" or had it all been a dream?

CHINA 52 - LINGERING LARYNGITIS

Tibet was already a bittersweet memory as the Pei Hua driver sped toward my apartment. Icy rain pelted down outside as I stumbled into bed, setting my alarm for a seven a.m. departure. My briefcase held Earth Day placemats and outlined English mini lectures. I'd steer clear of mentioning Tibet. That once-in-a-lifetime gift from Joe would probably remain our secret. Someday, I'd ask how he'd persuaded the university to let me visit it. Maybe I'd even ask why he'd risked giving me this opportunity. This gift. The dear man!

Morning streets were slick, but our bus barreled right on to the new campus. Snow gusted. I saw a lovely line of blooming cherry trees out my window just before my eyelids drooped. My nap lasted the entire forty-five-minute ride.

Hurrying into the building with my head down, I went straight to my empty classroom. Chalk squeaked as I wrote our bullet points on the board.

Gao and buddies filed in then, joking in Chinese. They immediately changed to English to greet me. I opened my mouth to speak, but all that came out was a phlegmy croak. My first word of the day was unintelligible. I quickly wrote "Laryngitis" on the board, erased the bullet points, and put simple directions in their place.

> Directions: Use seven minutes each. Each begins when I ring my little bell.
>
> 1. Discuss your Earth Day project with one other person. Choose only one of the two.
>
> 2. Two people join two others to share the chosen report. Listen to it, then choose one of four to report."
>
> 3. Four join four others to share only two chosen reports. Listen. Choose one to report."

4. Eight join eight others to hear four chosen reports.

5. Window side of the room joins door side to hear four reports.

6. Listen, vote for one report from all you hear.

The class puzzled over the directions on the board until I dramatically acted out my lack of voice, complete with Kleenex and nose-blowing. Gao read the first two lines. I rang the bell; he and I manhandled a few twosomes into their first sharing duo, and then they were off. I wandered about and heard students tell of picking up trash, cleaning flowerbeds near the dorms, pulling off plastic bags caught on XiAn's fences, and even one student who had convinced her family to flush only once-a-day to conserve water.

The lively hour passed like a charm. Gao was final winner of the Grand Canyon placemat, with his pledge to stop smoking meaning that he would also stop leaving 4,380 cigarette butts-per-year to pollute the environment. He'd been smoking since he was seven, the age his father had given him his first puff "to relax himself." I left class quite proud of my English-speakers.

The rest of the day was equally lively, with my students rising to the occasion. I remained mute and masked, as both were expected practices across China. Outside, a near-blizzard blew. Inside, my nose dripped. I slept all the way home on the bus and fell asleep without eating. I kept liquids handy through the night.

The next morning, I heard heavy pounding on my door. Bleary-eyed, I opened the inside one and looked through the peephole on the outer one. There stood Joe, looking worried. Feeling too lousy to worry about my bedhead or red nose, I opened my mouth to say, *"Go away,"* but nothing came out. I opened the door to whisper it.

Joe blustered in. "I was worried. Students said you are ill. I brought medicine."

I collapsed on the couch while he heated tea water, spooned some vile liquid into my mouth, and said, "You must eat." He'd brought dim sum. I choked down a bite.

"Now, Regina, let me tell you something important. I do not want to beat around the bush anymore. I love you. I can arrange an apartment for you, or you can stay here. I must be careful, but I must see you more often. It will be heaven on earth."

I put two fingers on his lips to stop his words, hoping the fingers were clean and hadn't touched my nose, pushed him out into the hall and locked both doors. Then I tumbled back into bed, thinking that Joe had never been a master of timing. *I'll think about what he said when I wake up.* Then I went back to fevered sleep. *Maybe it was just a dream anyway.*

Suddenly, I was in a Chinese New Year celebration. Mostly strangers sat in a great ballroom, where a huge meal spread across a two-tiered table in front of me. Joe sat on my left. A woman on his left played a melody on a flute. I knew my place on his right was an honored one. He smiled from ear to ear and whispered how romantic 'this great extravagance' was. He called me "Little Dog," which sounded like an endearment.

I turned to the crone on my right and heard that adultery was a great extravagance. She said that marriage was "taking a daughter-in-law" and asked if I was ready to live with five generations under one roof. She told me that I must slow my walk, soften my voice, put my hair in a bun, and stand up straight without hinting at what was beneath my loose grey tunic.

She pulled me into a small, dark room then and sat me down. Suddenly, she began running a double twisted string across my forehead, yanking out hairs from my eyebrows. I yelled and woke up.

What on earth was that? Fever ravings?

It felt so real that I surprised myself by pulling my earlobes back and forth. Somewhere I'd read that this was a way to drive fear out of your body and mind. Or had my students told me that? I looked out through the drying-room windows and saw the stars—a Chinese source of pardon and love. The dream melted back where it belonged to the language of impossible stories. Someday, I might revisit and journal it.

Half-afraid to go back to sleep, I reached for my lesson plans. Then the telephone rang.

"Dr. Blakey? It's been a while."

"Matt?" I whispered, my throat still not cooperating.

"Yes. First, why are you whispering? Is everything okay? Are you safe?"

"I have laryngitis, Matt," I croaked. "I'm just tired from a trip. I'll catch you up when my voice comes back."

"Then I'm relieved to hear you're okay. News here might interest you. Indonesia had an 8.7 Sumatran earthquake, the biggest since 1960. That country has also been protesting gas prices big time. Here at home, a judge dismissed the Vietnamese case about using Agent Orange. And the Supreme Court found capital punishment charges against persons who commit crimes before age eighteen to be unconstitutional."

He paused, then added, "Don't respond. Save your voice. I just wanted to know you were back and safe."

"Bye, Matt," I whispered, wondering if his concern was genuine or "lies as hard as glass" like the Chinese say. I felt ready for another nap, unbalanced after my dream, which was no longer dipping into my subconscious.

When I woke up the next morning, I was feeling a lot better but still had no voice. I scrambled an egg and fixed a hefty cup of Nescafe for a day of teaching. Mine was a silent bus ride across XiAn. The driver's constant honking wasn't so silent, but he got us through crazy traffic to the new campus without any close calls. I headed to the upper floor, nodding to students marching up and down stairs and shouting whatever portion of English they were memorizing. Gao, my self-appointed assistant, was busily erasing our dusty chalkboard.

I wrote "laryngitis" again, and "Skills you want to improve," listing: Pronunciation, Listening, Vocabulary, Speaking, and Organizing. I gave Gao a sticky note. "They are to pick one and join that skill group."

"Sure thing, Dr. Regina!"

I filled the other board with "Topics to Discuss: Travel, Sports, Films, University Culture, Family, Babies, and Foods."

Gao caught on right away. "First they go to a skills group; then the group chooses one topic for discussion. Right? I make them report to the group the last half-hour, ten minutes each."

He ought to run for village mayor or top Communist official, I thought as I settled down to watch the fruits of my labors with ESL. The morning went even better than if I'd had a voice.

There were a few surprise questions. One group asked if Martha Stewart was still in jail, and Gao diplomatically told them I'd answer that next time. Another group surmised that American college students smoked all the time, and the Travel group decided they would rather go to Ireland because it banned smoking in public places. Incredulous heads shook at that. Gao dismissed them as the bell rang. A recorded voice directed arm exercises as they stomp-marched down the hall in line, counting in Chinese.

Gao stayed behind to whisper, "Tell them about *Goblets of Fire* and *Star Wars* next class. I got a copy in the market, and my friend has *Harry Potter*. Very valuable! I will bring them."

"Thank you, Gao." *This kid's worth his weight in gold,* I thought as I exited to catch the bus.

Halfway down the stairs, he caught up to me. "Would you visit my village, Dr. Blakely? My mother and father will welcome you. I will get us train tickets for this weekend."

"I must get well, Gao," I whispered.

He smiled happily. "Yes, you will be well. I will take you to my village this Friday."

We'll see, I thought, then stumbled to the bus and slept all the way home.

CHINA 53 - VILLAGE VISIT

By Friday, my voice had returned, and Qian got me a morning cab. It idled by the campus gate in semi-darkness and carried me across XiAn's hectic twenty-four-hour traffic to the train station. I knew better than to tip the driver, but I gave him my biggest smile and left a sack of tangerines on my seat with a heartfelt *shei shei*. I thought about the first time I'd left a five-yuan tip on a table and heard *"Meigoyan!"* and the sound of running feet behind me as I'd left the restaurant. My waitress had then thrust the five-paper yuan into my hand, yelling, "Forget yuan!" Then she'd run back the way she'd come. Baffled, I'd told Joe about this, and he'd laughed, "Chinese do not tip, Luh—Ruhgeen-i-a! Americans say thank you and give money for services. That is capitalism. Chinese are only doing their jobs. Workers earn their wages. No need for tips." I found myself smiling at that memory as I scanned the train-station crowd for Gao's wave and kilometer-wide smile.

We stood in line for my ticket. Getting on the train to Wuhan wasn't easy, even with Gao parting crowds like an offensive linebacker. We had to find it first. Then there was the car designation, far down the line of those stopped in front of the station exit. A self-important official looked at our tickets, raised an accusatory pointer finger, and shook his head, barring our entry up his car's two metal steps. Gao asked him a question, which I recognized as such by the *"ma"* he used on the last syllable, in an ascending tone as the last syllable. We learned that we were to go to the very back car with standing room only.

Narrow wooden benches sat about a yard from walls along both sides. Students filled every inch of the benches and floor. Some sat on coats folded like cushions. Four noisy boys rolled dice in front of their crossed legs. Another strummed a ukulele, already in his own world.

Gao pushed me into the throng. All quieted. I felt several dozen eyes on my aging form and smelled varying levels of body odor. Gao announced,

"Dr. Blakely!" in thundering Chinese, and the entire population stood as one, each person gesturing me to their spot. I smiled a *shei shei* and sat down, keeping my backpack on and placing a satchel of gifts between my knees, mostly tangerines and snapshots of US national parks for Gao's family. The other riders resettled, games resumed, and we were off. Age had its privileges, especially in XiAn.

As time rolled by, I became increasingly grateful for the hard wooden bench. It was amazing that the stoic twenty-somethings stood so peaceably as we passed through the farmland. I saw a few villages through the window past elbows and occasional openings between bodies. I was extremely stiff by the time we arrived, having silently endured a painful leg cramp.

Gao announced, "Wuhan!" And we exited, pushed along the aisle with half the train car's population. We exited past vender's cubicles lining a sizable station. Wizened women squatted beside boiling kettles, while grinning up and imploring us to buy bowls of their soups. The clash of syllables and overwhelming smell of spicy broths left me dizzy. Gao ignored it all.

He carried my backpack, as we walked several blocks to a vendor and sat on low, three-legged stools at his tree-stump table for noodles. The aromatic broth, probably pork in Chinese Five Spices, made my mouth water. Gao proudly paid a few yuan, and a toothless crone dipped into her cauldron to fill bowls that she fished out of buckets, where they were soaking in water. I hoped I wasn't catching some kind of swine/bird/cow flu from the previous user. At least her cauldron was bubbling in a good rolling boil. We maneuvered bowls and chopsticks, slurping noodles when they were cool enough, then drinking the broth. I could have finished off another bowl, but Gao stood to go, and I followed.

We walked some more, bought tickets at a bus station, and found the proper queue, which was a surprise to me, since people in XiAn didn't line up. We joined a group with backpacks worn across their chests. Gao gestured for me to reverse mine as well, and I did.

The bus was crowded, but Gao was a pro at pushing on and protecting me from the jostling crowd. He leaned past a seated grandmother and a teenager on her phone to pull the cord for our stop. The bus was approaching a few storefront buildings, most of them with roll-up garage-door frontages open. It stopped then, and we stepped down.

Gao's father pulled up in an ancient Massey Ferguson tractor, pop-popping in front of a creaking wooden wagon with sideboards about a foot high. Whooping children ran alongside and dashed away when he came to a stop.

Smiling his welcome and chattering in Chinese, Gao's father escorted me to a rocking chair on the wagon; Gao scrambled to sit on bare boards at my side. I thought of Granny Clampet rocking on top of the Beverly Hillbilly's wagon. Or maybe they were making me queen for a day. I couldn't help wondering what I would say to Joe if he stepped out of the crowd on the streets below me.

We passed along the main street's packed dirt, turned off on gravel, and then onto a weedy two-track. I hung on and rocked a little while Gao entertained me with a shouted story. His father, the "most important CommUnist" in his village, had been given money to buy permission for his birth, their second despite the "One Child Policy." They had sold the village pig, meant to feed the village over the winter, to pay the government's price. Gao hooted loudly, "So I know I'm worth the price of one pig, Dr. Regina!" I could tell he'd told this story many times before.

We rolled past aromatic fields lined with dark green rows of ripening cabbages on each side of dry irrigation ditches. The stench of human waste assaulted my nostrils. If it had been rainy season, I imagined that the smell would be even worse. We continued into the countryside toward a cluster of gray cement structures, some like boxes standing on their ends, and others like earthen squares topped with rusting tin or dried-limb roofs.

Gao's mother came out of their cement rectangle, all smiles. She welcomed us with chapped hands clasped. Without another word, his father retired to the yard and began hacking at a tree trunk that lay where he had probably felled it right before leaving to pick us up. Gao's mother didn't attempt any English, and I could not decipher anything she and Gao exchanged. *Is that another dialect?*

She hurried back to an outdoor kitchen and poked dried twigs into a kiln-like oven. I discretely put a half-dozen tangerines in a twine-tied sack on a corner table. Smoke billowed and burned my eyes. A huge pot boiled merrily atop the fire.

VIRGINIA FORTNER

Gao excused us (in Mandarin) to both his parents, and we left to walk a worn path through his village. We passed a three-sided outhouse facing away from the house and a pigsty with one dusty boar grunting along its fence. Chickens flocked at our feet. I glimpsed dirt floors through open doorways.

At one such doorway, Gao called out *"Wei, ma?"* instead of the more familiar *Ni hao.* Then a wizened, white-haired couple inside moved to stand within it. "My grandparents, Dr. Blakely. My teacher, *Megoyian.*" The respect he paid them was evident, and their pride in him was almost palpable. I asked him to translate for them the fact that I too was the first of my family to attend college in faraway America. After a brief conversation with them, he abruptly said, *"Zai jian,"* and without touching either of them, he led me away.

We returned there for dumplings and noodles, bitter melon with pork, squash, and hot green tea. I couldn't manage an appreciative burp, but as per *American* custom, I exclaimed over the wonderful shell-shaped dumplings, even while identifying slivered pork and cabbage on the first platter, and chicken and onion on the second. His mother ducked her head; no one else spoke during the meal. My tangerine gifts appeared, peeled and arranged artistically into flowers made of citrus sections. She silently served me first.

Afterward, I made a hurried trip to the open-air outhouse. Gao then escorted me up, up, up to the topmost room of the home, which was adorned with a lone poster of a sad, big-eyed waif and had a large cement crack running from the ceiling to the lone window. "My sister's room," he explained. "She is away this weekend."

That explained the dusty pink quilt bunched up on the hard bed, which I would share with a once-white teddy bear and a kewpie doll that looked like she had stepped right out of a catalog from the WWI-era. Gao handed me a pillow, stuffed with hay and smelling of other heady odors, and said, "Get a good sleep."

I surprised myself and did just that.

CHINA 54 - VILLAGE VACATION

I woke up with daylight barely shadowing the cracked wall. I inched my way down the narrow stairs and outside, well away from the kitchen. No one was out and about, so I pretended I was in the woods, took care of my business, and slipped back upstairs. Snores came from several rooms below.

Next thing I knew, sunlight was warming my closed eyelids as Gao knocked quietly at my door. "Breakfast time, Regina."

His mother gave me a wash basin for my face and hands. She served me, her husband, and then Gao before sitting with us to eat congee. I added pickled greens as they did, and the slurps and burps began. After each bowl, we tipped the last bit of liquid down our throats. Eventually, Gao turned to me. "Father says to take you to a resort today. We'll walk around village property. He told me the way. No need for a map." I followed meekly.

We walked an irrigation dike, past a cow pulling a plough for a man who waved, and then past fields of produce and bearded grain. Egrets landed on cows' backs or pecked at insects on the ground. Gao regaled me with village stories about building their house for his father four years ago. Before that, they had lived in their grandparents' house. He told of leaving, in split pants, to live with a childless aunt and uncle in XiAn, and asked if young children in America wore the open-seamed, crotchless "split pants" worn in China. I told him that my country usually used disposable diapers.

Then he resumed his story of living in XiAn until he could return to the new, larger house where I was now a guest. "I will take you to visit my XiAn mother sometime, Regina." He was enjoying familiarity and being the star of the show. It delighted me too.

We stopped at a three-sided brick wall edging a smelly lagoon; I knew that I should go inside and use the facilities, such as they were, as it might be a long wait before the opportunity arose again. I did so, holding my nose with one hand as much as possible. Inside, feces piled in one corner and tumbled into the urine trench. Bits of Kleenex and rags dotted the hard-packed floor underfoot. I wasted no time. Outside, Gao awaited his turn. I stood on the upwind side of the scummy lagoon, looking at swirls of thick green/brown/orange liquid. Plastic bags clustered on the vertical side, along with blown flip-flops, rusting buckets, old shoes, and half-submerged tree limbs. If you didn't consider the materials, the arrangement of colors and shapes, and rough and blended edges, was almost artistic.

Gao joined me. "Can you stand it, Regina?" That was the only time he acknowledged my need to adjust to difficult experiences in his beloved village.

"Of course, Gao." I exhaled. We made our way to a country bus. A choking, dustbin ride took us to a large utilitarian-looking cement building with a few bushes outside. It was closed. We sat on a bench built around the largest trunk and ate hardboiled eggs his mother had packed, sipped nearly empty water bottles, and talked politics.

"You will soon become CommUnist, Regina. I see America agreeing that it is best."

"What makes you say that, Gao? I've not really considered it until you brought it up."

"It is efficient way of government; in America, you must wait and wait to get a better life. All must vote. With CommUnist leaders making good rules, life becomes better and better."

"What if you want something changed, Gao? Americans know each citizen can change policies and leaders through voting. How does that work here?"

"Change can come quickly through revolution or through good leaders. CommUnism gets things done. No arguments."

I couldn't help but argue with this in my mind, thinking of examples against this. *Tiananmen Square's deaths when troops opened fire on a student uprising, the Dali Lama leaving Tibet in the dark of night, and the majority of Han people taking all the prime business sites in a short time in Lhasa.*

Gao continued. "Young Chinese do not have to worry about times like America's 9/11. All love their Motherland and train to be part of military to defend her. Our Mao and heroes fought for Motherland alongside soldiers. Your president gave okay to shoot down United Flight 93 before it crashed. Passengers were brave heroes and died with the terrorists. Your Vice President was hiding somewhere."

Where did he get that information? "Wouldn't your government want your leaders and vice-leaders to be safe in crisis times also, Gao?"

"You capitalists have a place called Guantanamo, where prisoners were tortured to get information. CommUnists use torture, but it is expected, not called "enhanced information techniques" like in your country."

"I'm very saddened by much that my country has done, Gao, and how information is not always reported truthfully. Sometimes, I take comfort in writing my congressperson or campaigning for a better candidate in the next election. What do you do in China, when you cannot agree with what has happened?"

Gao was thoughtful. "I trust, Regina. I love the Motherland and pledge to help her like a true hero." He launched back into his story of his father being head Communist village leader and the improvement of his family's life. I listened to the youthful idealism, the logic-tight compartments that allowed him to avoid topics like life during the revolution and what had happened to Chaing Kai Chek's backers, and I wished for that ease in curtailing some of my own discontent.

At least I have freedom of speech in my country, I thought argumentatively. Then I thought of the discussions about China's policies in rides shared to and from the English Corner. One man had seemed unafraid to speak up, and to my knowledge, he'd never looked over his shoulder to see who was listening. *Might there be a day coming when I'll wonder if the benefits of messy Capitalism does NOT outshine those of Communism?*

I wisely didn't speak these momentary thoughts out loud.

We wandered back toward where we expected to soon find a return bus. A vender with a yoke across his back, from which hung sacks of oranges and sugar cane, took a yuan for each, and we wet our palates with oranges. The bus arrived. We abandoned politics and watched the countryside, mostly seeing workers dotting the fields with bent backs. An ancient tractor dragged a hand-crafted harrow across one empty field, raising a cloud of dust.

"I noticed that no one said anything at dinner last night, Gao. Might you tell your father about our trip at dinner tonight?"

He was silent for a long time. "But what topic would we discuss, Regina? Who would pick the topic?" It seemed unfathomable to him for families to talk during meals, as we did in America. I gave up, climbed aboard the newly arrived bus, deposited my yuan fare, and smiled a *shei shei* as a young woman, whose hands looked like they'd been pulling weeds all day, got up and indicated for me to take her seat. I knew better than to suggest in pantomime that she keep her hard-earned seat. All good citizens in the Motherland revered their elders and showed it through practiced actions. I felt confused gratitude for my tier in Confucius's hierarchy of age and class, but who was I to upset the system?

CHINA 55 - QI SHAN

My solo return from Gao's village was pleasant. He'd been able to secure only a single ticket back to XiAn in time for Monday's class. He ended up standing in line another half-day in Wuhan to get there by midweek. I had learned not to introduce anything on Monday to save repeating lessons as everyone returned from hometown visits. Spoken English class played the "two truths and a lie" game, struggling with past-tense phrases to "put the tall hat of flattery" on their own heads or tell bald-faced untruths with believable details. Written English attendees wrote a sentence, passed it on to the second person to add another sentence, and then fold it beneath the previous one. This process repeated through hilarious ten-sentence stories. We called it our "Partial Picture Game."

We'd just heard the last ten sentences read aloud when the bell rang. Bobo beckoned to me. "Dr. Zhou asked you to meet in the library after Friday's class, Regina."

What did Joe want this time? For a moment, I felt annoyed at his summons. Then I dismissed it. I'd find out eventually. No need to dwell on how scarce he'd made himself lately. I hadn't seen him since returning from Gao's village. Perhaps this meeting would be for another debate about Communism and Democracy. I mentally listed what I had on my agenda: laundry, a trip to the market, and lesson plans to keep me busy the rest of the week. So, I didn't need to spend much time wondering about whether or not I was eager to see him.

Right on time on Friday, I left my materials at the front desk and wandered past the stacks to the very back, where two chairs sat at a secluded study carrel. Joe's black leather satchel sat across them both. *Should I sit and wait for him?*

Two dusty books moved on the shelves to my right. Then Joe's head popped up between their spines, and he whispered, "I am coming, Regina."

What on earth? I sat down, curious but not the least wary. He tiptoed around the end of the stacks, unlatched his briefcase, and sat down next to me. "Regina, look!"

He dipped his hand into the briefcase and began pulling out necklaces, stickpins, pendants, and bracelets and piling them on the wooden surface. Even in the muted light of the stacks, I could see what looked like twenty-four-carat gold, completely untarnished, unlike my silver earrings in XiAn.

"Are they not beautiful, Regina? They are from an age gone by. Gold has ability to bend. It is soft, helpless in its purity, too yielding to be of this world. Precious . . . like you." He looked closely at me then, his dark eyes shining like a puppy's seeing a bone.

I drew back, suddenly aware that my chair was caught between Joe and the wall, although I felt more curious than frightened. "Where did you get them, Joe? Tell me about them."

He picked up an amethyst pendant surrounded by what appeared to be diamonds. It was all I could do not to reach out and touch the lines of the stonecutter's art.

"This piece and its matching ring are from three generations back. And these…" Joe lifted two jade bracelets in different shades of green, and I heard a slight tinkle as they touched. They seemed almost alive. If I had held them up to a beam of light, as I did with the cheap imitations handed me by market venders, I was sure that I could follow the tiny beams and pierce their secret places.

Joe brushed them past my fingers and over my knuckles. A tingling sensation shot through my arm, past my elbow, and to my shoulder. I didn't draw back. I could almost feel the bracelets' hearts beating in unison with my own.

"But why? How did you get these exquisite pieces, Joe?"

"Never mind, Regina. They are long in my family, waiting for an auspicious moment for a new wearer. It is you! I am honored to have you wear the jade!" He held a finger to my lips. "But one important thing. Wearer must never tell where they came from. Very bad luck to discuss them. It is our secret forever. Promise?"

What should I do? It was a beautiful bracelet pairing, not too different from ones I had seen other women wear, yet there was a feeling of something priceless happening that I couldn't quite put my finger on. "But why, Joe? Surely, they belong with family if they are antiques!"

He brushed that aside. "I said never mind."

Any thought that the tingling arm was due to Joe's touch went away immediately with his brusqueness. It had to be due to the jade's properties, I decided after an easy debate with myself.

I knew that if I returned the bracelets, I would hurt his feelings; besides, I wasn't sure I could tug them off over my large Caucasian hands quite as easily as he had slipped them on. And they were exquisite, quite unlike the marketplace jade my students sometimes brought me. And Joe didn't seem to be attaching any strings to them either. Or was he?

"One more question, Joe: Is there a meaning in this gift that I'm not aware of?"

His smile nearly lit up the cubicle. "Jade is heavenly stone, Regina. We have a saying, 'Gold is of great worth, while jade is priceless.' It brings longevity, renewal, and good luck."

I kept my cool and looked directly into his smile. "That's a tall order. I'm honored, Joe."

"Then you will accept this symbol? You bring all those to us at Pei Hua, Regina. I am renewed because of you. I am young again because of you."

He looked behind me and raised a finger to his lips as someone approached, becoming all business once again. Once the person had passed, Joe looked back at me once again.

"One more thing, Dr. Blakely. Emily will accompany you to Qi Shan's Computer and English School this weekend. Pei Hua sends you there to show them how Americans teach. The dean has permitted also a visit to Famen and Zhougong temples. You return for Monday's classes."

Joe's mood had pivoted, and the case was closed. I seemed to have no say in this matter. I decided then and there to just go with the flow. It had worked with Gao's village visit. Hadn't I come to China with a desire to travel as much of it as possible?

Jade tinkled on my wrist as I walked past the library desk. Emily was waiting for me, as Joe had promised. "We go now by bus," she said. "You teach very noisy children at Qi Shan Computer and English School. Three classes. Teachers watch."

Teach three classes? No toothbrush? No overnight bag? Emily appeared not to have any luggage either. This seemed to be taking "go with the flow" a little too far. I did have *some* limits after all.

"I am pleased to visit your hometown, Emily, but I would like to get a few things before we go. Perhaps we could meet at the bus station early tomorrow?"

"Do you mind staying in my village home?" She described farm families all sleeping in one brick-heated bed. I told her that I was a farm girl and didn't require a daily bath if I showered before leaving but that I preferred not to sleep with her family before teaching three classes at Qi Shan.

Her brow furrowed, though she did not object. She said that she would tell her mother to get the house ready. I realized that, while they all slept together in the same bed, they must still have a telephone. This would be an adventure. I just barely caught the teachers' bus, and got back home, where I was able to pack a change of clothing, take shower, and catch some fitful sleep.

CHINA 56 - ED LEADERS

Saturday morning, Emily and I met at the bus station near my old Pei Hua campus, seventy minutes from her new Pei Hua dorm. She off-handedly introduced me to Zhang Li, vice-chair of Pei Hua's Oral English Organization. He proved to be a electronics major and very bright.

A boyfriend? A spy reporting on this American subversive? There were no outward signs of either option really; he just seemed like a typical all-Chinese guy. He indicated a safe spot away from early morning hawkers and bought tickets on a fifteen-passenger van to Fu Feng. Winter wheat provided green against mountain backgrounds as we sped by sunken fields, old tractors, and trucks piled with hay. Zhang Li shared information about what we were seeing, telling me that Chinese man/woman power had dug incredible amounts of earth to provide huge platforms for village complexes and immediately replanted the mounds to corn or wheat.

The van belched us out. And in the taxi, Zhang sat on a board between my seat and a stranger, with Emily perched on a board behind the driver's seat. After a double U-turn, we went down an alley. The woman nearest the window took a yuan while crouched below the window.

Zhang whispered, "Police check to see that only five passengers ride in this vehicle." We'd crammed in nine passengers. Emily disappeared the instant we exited the taxi, quietly returning a moment later from behind a pile of rocks, where she had vomited.

I breathed a prayer of thanks for our safety at Famen Temple. With Emily's translations, artistic roof lines, Sakyamuni's finger bone, fine pottery, gilded Buddhas, and detailed histories were interesting. I also found them quite photogenic in sunshine. We stayed three hours, then climbed atop a cement buddha's base for photos before running for the bus to Qi Shan.

The villages we passed appeared increasingly poor. Preparation for winter was evident, with ears of corn ringed higher than my head around tree trunks, and ripe persimmons hanging on limbs above reachable levels. The bus stopped by a dirt path. I was asked if I minded walking thirty minutes.

It was sweet relief to stretch my legs. Emily helped me practice Chinese commands to sit/stand/look/listen/say as we walked. I paid careful attention to her tones, not wanting to say something hilariously different from what I intended when I would be attempting to control a roomful of elementary students.

We approached farm buildings. Emily's mother was preparing dinner off a dirt courtyard. It smelled delicious. Emily led me past three sows, two boars, and fourteen squealing piglets penned near the outdoor WC. We washed in a basin in the courtyard and toured the house. Emily pointed out her parents' bedroom. I glimpsed her father's veterinary kit, a half-room of corn, gunny sacks, two motorcycles, and old tools. I did not see Emily's room.

We called *"Ni hao?"* but received no answer as we entered a high-ceilinged room with a couch, a low table, and a chest overflowing with bottles. Emily's brother soon brought us fruit beer, vegetables and pork, flatbread baked on a burner, and local noodles in a delicious, vinegary sauce. More noodle-soup variations followed. Zhang expressed amazement at the large home compared with his in a southern province.

Emily answered her cellphone, then announced that her schoolmaster was coming to take me to a hotel. Another photo was snapped with "first foreign visitor to our family," as Teacher Yang, his wife, and two children arrived in a car. I climbed in, and they each immediately asked if I had eaten. I assured them I would drink tea with them. They carefully repeated my English as we drove to a Qi Shan hotel, where five of us sat together while the TV in my room blared.

The schoolmaster made tea, checked out the bathroom faucets, and interjected Chinese comments; his wife put yellow flowers into a carved vase I'd gotten at Famen Temple. I hopped over the bed, playing a guessing game with bored second-grade Yang, who asked, "How old are you?"

"Old enough to sleep by myself," I said, just as my father used to, and they held a conference in Chinese about that specific meaning. Mrs. Yang fingered my cotton slacks. "Are you cold?"

"No, but I am a little tired," I admitted.

She persisted. "I worry. Can you stay in this hotel by yourself?"

I assured them that I often stayed alone when traveling. The schoolmaster tested the shower's water to make sure it wasn't too hot, told me to be careful, and then sat back down.

Teacher Yang then quizzed me about American education. Following that, he informed me that I would teach three forty-minute classes the next morning. "Only sixty students in each class," and starting with the primary level.

I explained that sixty in a class would not allow me to show them much of my American methods. He listened respectfully, then told me, "Have a good rest. Maybe just talk to students. Do not prepare a lesson. Do not worry."

This time, they left, but before I could sleep, I had visions of sixty kids raising the roof, not understanding a thing I said, with three groups of this going on forever. I revised plans to do small demo groups with group-pantomime responses and drifted off under a white duvet that matched the thin pad beneath me.

CHINA 57 - AMERICAN METHODS

Early the next morning, Emily and her sister came for me. The teenager soon exhausted the vocabulary most Chinese used: "Hello. Pleased to meet you. Not at all."

Emily brought specialty noodles and a thick pancake filled with chopped pork. After we'd eaten, our first stop was the schoolmaster's computer store, where I had green tea while two dozen employees posed around me for pictures.

We walked into the "youngest class" amidst flags and cheers. Learning games, involving linking ordinal and cardinal numbers, went well. I then met Honorary Headmaster Liu, who was "having a little rest." He told me that he was eighty years old and retired, having started this school eight years earlier, after translating for the historical Zhougong Temple nearby.

"Time for second class!" This announcement interrupted our chat. These children seemed much smaller than those I had given the primary school lesson.

"Maybe I make meestake," Emily said. "Do just ABC. Vowels too hard."

I gave it a try anyway, after asking Emily to stop translating in Chinese. We pantomimed our way through vowel pronunciation, reading, and writing lessons with four students at the board each time. All sixty waved their hands, wishing to participate. Emily pronounced it my best lesson, then stopped us early to take pictures and distribute gifts of phrasebooks that these children couldn't read.

After another "little rest," it was a class of teens. We played "Taxi Driver" by reviewing global places, starting with each letter of the alphabet, mixing English and Chinese with two points for English pronunciation. We played three rounds of AJK—"I'm going to America, Japan, and Korea"—with four students writing five words beginning with one of the three letters. Budding adults finished class by lustily singing the ABC song, just as one girl arrived in tears, having missed my lesson completely. She hastily dried her tears as I posed with her for yet another picture.

The restaurant of the computer school's owner's brother's wife was our next stop for pictures taken by the corn, under the sign, under the persimmon tree, in the kitchen, and at the entrance. We were served nicely seasoned and beautifully arranged dishes: several types of noodles, lotus root, chopped spinach with garlic, and sheep's blood. I managed small bites as Teacher Yang told them what he'd learned from my methods. To my surprise, he mentioned using patience, giving cues, moving at a fast pace, and involving everyone's interest. Then he told everyone, again, how I had jumped over the hotel bed the night before.

Two hours later, Emily asked, "Do you want to visit the English School?"
Isn't that where I just taught three classes?
"I thought we were going to the temple, Emily."

We immediately piled into a taxi with the restaurant proprietress and her photographer. At the temple entrance, he took pictures of me for twenty minutes before waving us past ticket-taking monks. I had more than earned my ticket price.

Inside, Headmaster Liu translated signs with explanations of the cement buddhas, historical dioramas, ancient trees, and past miracles. Then we descended a dank tunnel to see more fearsome deities, one winged deity, and the Creatress herself, who looked lovely right down to her long red fingernails. Emily's English wasn't up to telling the backstory on these figures, although I asked for more information on each one. Zigzagging up a steep path, we entered the cave of the white jade buddha.

"I do not believe," Emily said, "but my mother does. We could rub his tummy to cure carsickness."

She opted for rubbing the buddha's shoulder; I touched his index finger with my arthritic ones, and then we helped each other down over stones worn slick by the feet of believers.

Outside, an ancient tree waited, covered with red strings tied by supplicants wishing for good luck. I stifled a chuckle and decided that the next time Matt called, I would ask him if "the Secretary knows that the Creatress wears red nail polish." That should set Conservative America to thinking awhile.

The trip back to Pei Hua took until bedtime. Waiting for taxis and buses, eating juicy oranges after our water ran out, watching a full moon rise, and a try at "Twenty Questions" topped off a wonder-filled weekend. Somewhere along the way, I tapped my fingers and found that they no longer felt arthritic.

CHINA 58 - JOANNA'S VISIT

Between the impromptu teaching weekend and the regular Pei Hua demands, I almost forgot that a Kansas friend of mine was coming for a Yangtze cruise. She'd arrive soon! I spiffed up the apartment and made myself a pallet under my drying Disney-print PJs, so that Jo could have my bed.

Finding her red hair among an airport full of dark heads posed no problem at all. Dodging April raindrops, I boarded the airport shuttle and soon gave her ample frame a welcome hug. We got her two oversized bags into a cab, and I felt pretty good about giving directions in Chinese to reach Baisha Lu, my street, where we turned off.

Everything was different. Blue corrugated tin now made a one-way passage where traffic usually came and went in both directions. What had happened?

I soon learned that, while I was gone, someone had du, two-foot-wide trench across two lanes and closed the college gates. Pulling out more *yuan* convinced the cabbie to brave it to the guard shack, wait until they opened one gate, and wrestle suitcases upstairs to the apartment. Then at last, Jo and I literally fell into bed.

At 7:10 a.m., I waded through the loblolly, recalling Dad's term for our KS barnyard mudhole, to catch the new campus bus while Jo rested. In the afternoon, we waded across again for a delightful Japanese lunch with near-silent Junko and Yoshiko, downstairs language teachers, seemingly tongue-tied by Jo's flame-colored hair. Jo chatted solo, enjoying every bite.

A quick return home, and then we crossed the moat again, our backpacks bulging with eighty-five bottles of Poly-Vi-Sol for Amanda's orphans, who had just returned from Hangzhou with repaired spina bifida and cleft palates. We climbed cement steps, and Jo got a taste of the lively nursery. One toddler lifted his arms to Jo, which was more than enough payment for her donation of vitamins from Kansas. Amanda was overwhelmed that a stranger had brought such a bounty. Jo's generosity also helped my standing as a sporadic volunteer. After the happy visit, Jo returned to sleep off her jetlag, and I read journals.

Wednesday morning, we went to Tai Chi in New Era Park, took pictures in the market, and got facials that expanded to full massages. Qian got Jo a Saturday reservation with an English guide, who would pick her up at our Pei Hua gate.

Thursday, Jo attended my classes. She got a taste of the "I don't have a book/pen/paper, so I'm not participating" logic often tried in the immature ten o'clock class. Becoming a teaching pro by two p.m., she used short sentences to explain healthcare-privacy laws. When I looked up from administering a make-up exam in the back of the room, she was explaining "safe and sound" and other English phrases she'd unintentionally dropped. Bells rang, and freshmen trooped out behind Jo to the sunny courtyard. Luckily, half of XiAn had already asked her to pose for photos, so she handled her celebrity status well. I slipped into the English office, wondering if Joe might notice the jade bracelets tinkling on my arm. His desk was empty.

I had to teach make-up classes on Saturday "to pay back the government's nine-day vacation," so I left Jo at the gate at seven a.m. for her tour departure. When I returned, she was standing in my front entry. It seemed the gate guard either didn't speak English or else she hadn't recognized the driver's pronunciation of "Terra Cotta?" when the van had pulled up and had declined to go with them. We shook our heads, then began using "Terra Cotta" as a catchword each time we misunderstood something. It felt good to laugh.

We went to the Shaanxi Historical Museum. The guide adopted Jo, hoping to practice her English, and ignored her job as explainer of exhibits. Finally exiting, we headed for the downtown square. Pei Hua Sophomore Bear Lee met us at Muslim Quarter so he could practice his "bartering and guiding skills." Jo stayed put, but Bear Lee and I climbed Bell Tower. He wondered why a female tourist ran away when he asked, "Can you use me?" And I told him he might get to do more than guiding if he used that line again. More puzzlement followed.

He bought us local apples as we discussed the pressure of getting jobs in China, how he didn't want to disappoint his parents, and what is most worthwhile in life. He talked. We munched. Bear Lee wondered if Americans "have to be busy and can't enjoy themselves," while we wondered if he was depressed.

Jo proved adept at mime-bargaining for souvenirs. Bear Lee, saying goodbye, observed that he didn't have a chance to barter much. It was interesting to watch the interactions between a Midwestern nurse and this serious student. I mostly listened and thought about what to pack for the Yangtze trip.

Cruise day arrived. Guide Rachel greeted our small plane, pointing at and naming the sharp ridges. Cows walked in front of the cab as we paid the usual "foreigner" double price.

Rachel said that we would be the only Americans travelling with Three Gorges Entertainment. Then she handed us chopsticks and waved us aboard the *President # 5*, an eighty-passenger ship, with eighty crew members at our beck and call, though it was not the one we had paid for. On board, we passed a buffet line on our way to a smaller boat tethered on the other side.

After an adequate buffet, someone brought out a guitar. I tuned it while Jo finished eating. The chef visited our table, beaming at her as he pounded out a few words in Mandarin. I couldn't follow his dialect or recognize much of what he was saying. During the evening talent show, without any rehearsal, I sang "Your Cheatin' Heart' with a lanky cabin boy named Gerald. Jo and I won applause for "Country Roads, Take Me Home," with a large German contingency singing lustily along with us.

Becoming momentarily aware that I'd forgotten about Joe for quite a while, I also forgot that I was no longer seventeen and danced until one of my knees popped. Staying off it most of the next day got me back to walking again.

A clerk at the gift shop asked me to model a glitzy peacock shawl for the Captain's champagne reception. There was an Asian fiftieth birthday party, where Jo and I were toasted as guests of honor. No one slept much during the noisy days and nights of photographing cliffs, sitting on deck, or watching brush-stroke demos.

Jo crashed first, telling me to awaken her for dinner. I sat alone on deck, musing aloud over a brochure's characters: "The partially constructed project expects to flood the gorgeous valley and provide electricity…"

"…maybe for the world," said a familiar male voice in a familiar singsong tone. "Sun Yat Sen's 1919 dream was thwarted by lack of money."

I looked up, and there he was, beaming down at me as he translated the next part of the brochure I'd just been wading through.

"Joe!"

He continued, as if his memory were magic, even as I tried to close my mouth: "1949 liberated the project. It began in 1993. The largest water conservancy project in the world. Yangtze River changed its course with resettled workers working for flood control, navigation improvement, and power generation. It will replace fifty million tons of coal combustion each year."

"Joe, how…?"

"The five-stage locks," he continued, "are interesting, with the usual problems: sedimentation, landslides, and stability of concrete placement. Twenty-six hydro-turbine-generating units discharge 102,500 meters at flood capacity, well ahead of Hoover Dam."

"Now wait a moment, Joe. I didn't read anything in here referring to Hoover Dam! I read 'Grand Coulee,' and that a bigger dam than Hoover."

Joe laughed and parked himself on a nearby deck chair. "My joke. Isn't it wonderful, Regina? I was in the bus behind you and your red-headed friend, so I studied the tour brochure! China's face is changing, and we're seeing that happen."

What a marvelous, delightful mind he has!

We talked for the next hour as dark-skinned dancers pranced by in workers' vests and hard hats. I was thankful they left us alone. Joe's enthusiasm for the project caught fire as he pointed out the south channel's red buoys and the north's green ones, saying that the Yangtze had receded eighteen feet already.

"The moon will be full tonight. We'll see it's as beautiful as Norway fjords. We'll go past two hundred landslides of the past forty-seven years and see Pillar Peak. Don't sleep too much and miss it."

Was he teasing me? I couldn't tell. He began another story: "In 1985, forty-foot waves destroyed a town, already rebuilt with cement pillars and crisscrosses of cement up the steeps. Peasants move farther up or to Shanghai. Government gave them twenty thousand yuan to move."

We moved past crisscrossed cement that was holding our side of the gorge in place. I wondered if Jo might awaken and come find me. What would she make of Joe and his sound-alike name?

I didn't wonder long. Joe pointed upward toward two rock silhouettes with a tall sliver behind them. "That piece of rock is a Wu princess. She liked the beauty and people so much that she stayed. A romantic story, no?"

It was extraordinarily beautiful along the river, with its subtle variations of greens, and workers cutting straw on steep hillsides. I relaxed, listening to Joe's monologue about the Yangtze project. Eventually, he quieted, fingering my jade bracelets almost reverently as we drifted along. We passed hanging coffins in caves with bamboo scaffolding, verdant fingers of granite, and cypress-dotted deciduous growth.

Hawkers called from shore, "Lay-dee! Velly cheep! Hello!" Joe waved them jauntily away and began speaking softly again, describing the sites. It was a tropical dream from which I didn't want to awaken. I closed my eyes and let his words wash over me as we moved slowly with the stream.

A few minutes later, Joe quietly claimed my attention again. "Regina, between Qutang and Wu Gorges, we will visit Fengdu, the temples of the City of Devils. In a yin-yang society, evil is necessary, and often beautiful, as it balances goodness. You cross slippery bridges, climb thirty-three steps, and balance on one foot to pass the test. Leave blue temple walls and escape final judgment. A god catches unrepentant souls with a chain."

I made a mental note to see if Jo could be carried up the mountain or if she'd take her chances with reincarnation-preventing gods with chains.

A full moon rose. Vegetation slid by as Joe quieted and tucked his jacket around my shoulders. I'd missed dinner and didn't even care. Without a word, he produced an orange, expertly peeled it, and fed me its sweetness section-by-section. It was a perfect evening.

CHINA 59 - CHENG DU

Someone touched my shoulder, and I awakened instantly. The deck-chair slats beneath me felt hard, and Joe was nowhere to be seen.

It was Jo, who quickly began chattering. "Regina, you've been sleeping here since yesterday? I ate dinner without you. I figured you'd surely be in the room when I woke up. You weren't You must've been tired to sleep all night in a deckchair."

She went on and on about dinner, then about breakfast. I stretched and yawned, wondering what had become of Joe. Then she noticed his jacket, still around my shoulders.

"Where did you get that?"

Rather than try to come up with a complicated explanation, I simply shrugged. "Maybe someone thought I'd be chilly, falling asleep out here. I'll leave it so they can get it back."

It was as if Joe had vanished. I knew I hadn't dreamt his presence, his teasing voice, or him touching my bracelets. Or had I? They tinkled assent as Jo grabbed my arm and pulled me up and toward a boarding gangplank that crossed to ShenNong Stream, where a pea-pod-shaped boat awaited. We climbed in, and seven men in loin cloths rowed us in unison along the tributary, taking us over narrow streams. Their muscles gleamed, and we figured they had probably only donned the loin cloths for the sake of us tourists. There was not a tan line in sight. I surmised that this remote water-area's population had been introduced to clothing about the same time that the Yangtze River project had begun.

After ShenNong, the rest of the cruise stops were just as Joe had described. I looked for his familiar frame at every stop. His jacket had disappeared from the deckchair. But where had he gone?

At another stop, four men carried Jo's weight up/down thirty-three mountain steps in a wicker basket. She nimbly hopped over the doorframe, laughing, to continue the cycle of reincarnation. We photographed blue walls and visited the once-opulent temples of the White Emperor, who had declared himself emperor for a twelve-year reign. That stop ended up being such a disappointment that I joined Jo in the manpower-carried chairlift down the mountain. Back on board, our table mates exchanged business cards.

After disembarking, we caught a taxi for Chengqing's bus station, where we bought tickets for Chengdu, which was written as "Cheng Du" on the same English page. I suddenly understood that Chinese publications disregarded rules for English capitals, spelling, and separation of syllables because their visual symbols encapsulated visual information and ideas, more than spoken vocabulary. Perhaps Americans were the ones relying on there being only one right answer, making those learning English insist on it.

"Too much information!" mused Jo, then changed the subject.

On the four-hour bus ride, Jo and I lamented how the vertical magnificence we'd just seen would be destroyed when the project was completed. She was surprised when I explained that 175 meters was higher than the width of Qutang, the Wind Gorge we'd recently looked across. The chalky blue paint from Fengdu Hall at City of Devils had since been cleaned from Jo's hands, but our knees still bore the wear and tear of climbing our portion of the 2700-mile Yangtze River. Sated by breakfast bars, sunflower seeds, and packaged crackers, we snoozed our way across mountainous terrain to the suburbs, opening the occasional sleepy eye to glimpse at what we passed.

Once we were in a cab, I was instantly alert, deciding that Chengdu drivers were worse daredevils even than those in XiAn. We arrived, with our hearts in our throats, at our multi-story hotel-shopping complex and had a delicious chicken dinner. Even Sichuan non-spicy cuisine was laced with chili peppers. *Qingcai* green vegetables, corn on the cob, sour cabbage, bread, and rice left me sleepy again, but we pushed on to Su Feng Ya Yun Theatre for "face change" opera.

Tea flowed through long curved spouts. We declined ear cleanings, but I enjoyed a foot massage that helped my dancing/climbing knee to relax. Sichuan opera's high-pitched singers jumped from atop stage-prop buildings, then whirled around to assume another face and character right before our eyes. Neither of us had seen anything like it. I did not understand one word sung in a whining tone that grated on my Western musical sensitivities. Yet we agreed that it was interesting, well done, and had required much talent.

In bed at last, sleep came quickly, and we awoke the next morning with Chengdu's zoo beckoning us. Jo and I wound along bamboo-lined paths to see giant pandas, blue sheep with monstrous horns, monkeys, hippos, giraffes, elephants, one white bear, leopards, and peacocks. Chengdu felt quite wondrous.

It was a jolting come down, though, when crowds cheered each time the feeder extended a huge steak, like a fish on a line, to the tigers, then jerked it away. The angry beast would roar, eliciting another excited cheer from the spectators. We hurried our grim Caucasian faces away from the crowd, while my mind turned thankfully to humane societies and legal actions targeting animal cruelty in my country

At nearby Zhao Jue Temple, lunch was a community affair. Attendants found two clean bowls and chopsticks and led us to the kitchen for rice, potatoes, and cabbage. Bland noodles followed. An emphatic head shake and *"Bu!"* denied us the spicy hot vegetables. Jo sat down in the shade of a thousand-year-old tree grown around a stele that looked like a headstone outside Sakyamuni's temple. We decided to leave, but getting a taxi was a hassle in the hot sun. A laughing policeman sent us to three places. As we reached the first spot, we watched as a man jumped ahead of three grandmothers. I got disgusted and stuck like glue to one of the policemen for what seemed eternity. He finally hailed us a cab that had only one passenger already in its back seat. We climbed in anyway.

CHINA 60 - CHENGDU CHARADE

The passenger scooted over for Jo to join him in the back. I climbed in beside the cab driver, scrutinized the meter, and told him our hotel destination. Joana reached forward and handed him the card she'd picked up from the front desk, and the driver nodded knowingly and hit the accelerator.

Then I heard a familiar voice. *Joe?* I turned around to confirm this, remembered that Jo didn't know about him, and suddenly found myself speechless. Silently, I watched as he introduced himself to Jo: "Dr. Zhou, from Pei Hua University in XiAn."

Jo shifted her sun hat to her left hand and then shook his with her right. "Nice to meet you," she said, offering him her name, and then nodding towards me. "My friend, Dr. Blakely, teaches in XiAn."

I craned my neck toward their back seat, thinking, *What next?*

His eyes met mine. "Hello, Dr. Blakely."

Two can play this game. I called on my Leo personality and asked, "Dr. Zhou, what brings you to Chengdu? Your English office workers must have trouble carrying on without you."

He chuckled. "I was awarded a vacation. It is truly wonderful to meet you two lovely ladies here. Please, let's stop at a tea house." My Chinese Rabbit personality nodded a quiet assent.

The driver stopped. Joe paid him, and then we went inside a shady stall to sit on low stools, surrounded by aromatic tea, some of which was in a cylinder embossed with a rabbit, my sign.

Joe told Joanna, "I am Year of the Rooster! This year!" Then he started speaking rapidly in a local dialect, and the man working here wrapped my rabbit for me. The tea ceremony took a long time—boiling water, choosing dried flowers with just a hint of orange and lavender in the closed petals, and listening to more strange syllables being exchanged as it all steeped in a ceramic pot.

Looking into the murky depths, we saw the colored petals open. Then finally came the pouring and tasting. I was so intrigued that I almost forgot the strange charade Joe and I were still keeping up.

"Do you like it, Dr. Blakely?" he asked, reminding me of a small boy who's just offered a special gift at Christmas.

"Very much."

We left with tins of dried tea flowers for Jo and me. The tea vender kept winking at Joe, shaking his hand, and then bowing to us.

Joe gallantly hailed a cab, and all three of us climbed in. As it headed back to our hotel, I asked, "Where are you staying, Dr. Zhou?" I didn't want him to evaporate into thin air again, nor for Joanna to know the whole story about our escort. He handed me a card written in Chinese, showing me that his room was on our floor of this same hotel.

As American Jo exited the cab, Chinese Joe winked at me and put a finger to his lips before settling back in his seat. Baffled, I thanked him for the tea and left him there, following Jo to our room.

"What a nice man!" Jo said as she bustled around our room.

I felt like we were in a stage play without a script. I felt a headache start to creep around my temples. Jo allowed me a fifteen-minute power nap, reminding me about her "pre-birthday" dinner that evening. "Hot pot is supposed to be the best in Chengdu!" she said as I drifted off to sleep.

An hour later, awake and refreshed, I noticed Jo snoozing in her chair, her mouth hanging wide open. It looked like she had fallen into more than a nap, so I tiptoed out, gently closed our door behind me, and looked for the room number I'd seen on Joe's card.

When I found his room, I knocked quietly, still feeling like a voyeur looking in on a suspenseful scene. Joe opened his door as far as the chain would allow. "Regina!"

"Joanna's asleep, and I had a power nap and slipped out."

"It doesn't matter." He unlocked the chain and pulled me inside, his hand just above the coolness of my jade bracelets and feeling warm against my skin. "I'm so glad you liked my gift. They look beautiful on you. Never take them off."

I found myself in Joe's strong arms then, my face turning upwards almost involuntarily. A thought flitted past my awareness: *I had no idea he was this tall.* Then our lips found one another, drawn together as though by magnets.

Then a timid knock on the door pulled them apart.

"Wei?" Joe called, running a hand through his hair.

I was instantly back in China, returned from Love Land.

The reply must have been the equivalent of "Room Service" in Chinese, because Joe opened the door to find a table set for one with a chilled bottle of *bai jiu.*

Foiled again? Or saved in the nick of time?

"Joe, your dinner is served," I said, then swept out the door and went back to my room. My headache reappeared halfway back to it, but Jo was now awake and ready for her last evening in Chengdu. My thoughts tilt-a-whirled from thoughts of Joe to the presence of Jo, and I tried to focus on fully joining her in the upcoming experience. We were still packed. So, we wouldn't have to rush dinner or hurry before our departure for the airport. My head throbbed, but I soldiered on, buoyed up by her happy chatter.

We walked to Carre Four Department Store for huge aspirin packs—10 cents US—and watched a cake-decorating activity behind a bakery window. My headache retreated. Our conversation ran to how long we'd known each other, baby showers, how her daughter's birthday was also mine, and overnight visits when our sons kept us awake by reciting the entire "Who's on first?" comedy routine. It was good to reconnect and laugh.

At "the best hot pot in Chengdu," we chose fish from a menu that promised to be "very delicious in very famous sauce." They lit a fire under our tabletop hot pot and brought vegetables and mushrooms on a tray. The fire went out, and then there was no "hot" under our pot. Three fish heads eyed us from above the soup-pot rim. Fire relit, we recounted other birthday dinners we'd shared, with thoughts of Tres Hombres, Salty Iguana, and Bryant's Bar-b-que making our mouths water for spicy sauces. This Sichuan cuisine only tasted peppery to me, and we both wanted spicy. I removed the staring fish, but the soup never got hot enough to boil. We finally gave up, rather than chance non-boiled soup and raw vegetables. She was a good sport about it, but I felt like our Sichuan visit had just crashed.

We checked out. I had to hunt for thirty minutes to produce our receipt and the free Chengdu booklet I'd packed to pass on to a friend. They also wanted a free Chengdu map Jo had put in her luggage. A bell boy loaded us in a cab with a businessman until I asked, *"Fei ji, ma?"* Then he awakened a second cabbie, who mumbled, "Forty-two RMB." We reloaded. I turned on the meter to see that it said 42 RMB. At the airport, the driver added ten RMB for the airport toll. I had no Chinese vocabulary to tell him that was the cab's responsibility. This seemed to be Rip-Off City, what with Jo's first dip into the non-hot pot. We shared an airport glass of chrysanthemum tea that came to $4 US, another rip-off, and said reluctant goodbyes.

After she waved from the Beijing-bound exit line, I headed for the XiAn gate, glad for her visit.

CHINA 61 - STRANGE MOVES

I slept off a lingering headache on the return flight from Chengdu and awakened feeling grateful for the good time I'd had with Jo. A Pei Hua driver in a black sedan loaded my luggage while I opened the back door. Again, there sat Joe, smiling like everything was bright and cheerful.

Conflicting feelings battled in my brain. A rush of familiarity and warmth wanted me to scoot across into his outstretched arms, but revulsion at the about-face he'd shown when room service had knocked welled up as well. Was he ashamed of me? My mother certainly would be. Warmth moved from my chest, up my neck, and inflamed my cheeks. "Joe!" I blustered. "You're making a habit of turning up in the back seat of my rides."

"This isn't just your ride, Regina. He's my driver. I wanted to tell you the good news in person. You now get to visit Mongolia for a few days while your students have Sports Game Days." The smug old Joe was back, and his tone was all business.

"What?" Then I recalled the AeroTech's Sports Games. I'd envisioned a China-wide fitness competition, far beyond the blare of recorded hallway exercises between classes, which my students mostly ignored. That vision had lasted until another Pei Hua student told me that he had joined a team for rope-skipping. I'd lost interest in attending as a spectator after learning this.

"Yes, Regina, here is your ticket to Hohot, Inner Mongolia Autonomous Region. You will realize this dream that I have long held for myself, dear Regina. Tell me all about it when you return. Here is two thousand yuan for your hotel and a guide for two days." He thrust a travel packet emblazoned with a Hello Kitty logo toward me.

"Why are you doing this, Joe? I'm just returning from going to Chengdu. Surely the school doesn't send other teachers on trips like this."

He smirked just a little. "I arranged it for you. I cannot go, but you can visit the grasslands, Genghis Kahn's tomb, and Zhao Jun's legendary area. She was one of China's Four Beauties, who found a way to power despite being passed over as a concubine."

He'd done it again, pulling me into a curious story. "Joe, why was she not chosen if she was one of China's Four Beauties?" I held the packet and listened.

"She hadn't bribed the court painter to make her face desirable enough for the emperor to choose her. Not like your face, Regina. If I were emperor, you would be First Beauty. Even a painter could not make you ugly."

I looked at the plane ticket with its Chinese symbols and "Zhao Jun Hotel" written in English. Why not accept this strange windfall? I recalled my Montana brother's lifelong ambition to see wild mustangs, supposedly only found now in Mongolian grasslands. I'd wanted to travel and was being given a great windfall of just that. As my father used to say, *Never look a gift horse in the mouth.*

"Okay, Joe. Thank you." He looked directly into my eyes with such delight that I felt like all the presents under a sparkling Christmas tree. I could feel warmth glowing just behind my own eyes, as I imagined waving grasslands and the armies of Genghis Kahn. The driver unloaded my just-loaded luggage, and Joe directed him toward the airline check-in as I fished my passport out of my fanny pack.

I soon found myself on another plane, with my seatbelt tightened, and eating vegetable-beef and rice as it lifted for Hohot, Mongolia. Another exhilarating, roller coaster of Chinese events!

Upon landing, my first impressions of Hohot were wind and poverty. Abraham, a taciturn man with weathered skin, met me via the ubiquitous "Luh-geen-ee-ah" sign, and helped me find my hotel. The problem was that it was the wrong hotel. I would apparently have to go to the *other* Zhao Jun Hotel. This one wanted two thousand yuan in advance. I told Abraham that I couldn't afford that.

"I will ask for a cheaper price," he said, as though the case was closed.

The second hotel lived up to its promise of a cheaper price. Its neighborhood had no streetlights. Barbed-wire fencing held bits of plastic bags that flapped in the wind. With my limited Chinese and body language, I insisted on checking out the mostly clean room and a workable door lock. Abraham thrust a dog-eared card into my hand and disappeared. I stayed inside as dusk came and ordered beef—the only syllables the person on duty seemed to understand—and tried to make sense out of the travel brochures left on my dresser. Then my cell phone jangled.

"*Wei?*"

"Dr. Regina? It's Matt. Where on earth are you? There's been no service or answer for quite some time. Are you okay? We've been worried."

"Oh! I'm fine, Matt. I'm in Inner Mongolia for the weekend. The university gifted me another cultural adventure to tell you about!"

He sounded relieved. "Ride a mustang for me, Dr. B! In grade four when I figured out how to read, I read about nothing but horses for a long time. I envy you."

"I'll think about it, Matt. Bye for now. It's time to explore Genghis Kahn's old territory!"

It felt nice to know that at least one person in the US, and another in China, were envious of my good fortune.

CHINA 62 - INNER MONGOLIA

Matt didn't hang up. "Hold on, Dr. B. Can't we chat a bit? You've been out of touch!"

For some reason, Matt trying to extend the call began to annoy me. "I thought I already told you that a Kansas friend and I went on a Yangtze cruise. I didn't answer my phone much in either Tibet or Chengdu. And more recently, Pei Hua arranged a trip to Mongolia while my classes have a Sports Games Break."

"We're glad you're seeing new places, Dr. B, just uneasy with being so out of touch. The Secretary of State has her hands full enough at the moment, what with…" He let his voice trail off.

"ISIS?" I ventured, expecting a quick denial. The US repeatedly refused to align its vision of Islamic radicals to how they saw themselves as a state.

To my surprise, I heard a weary sigh on Matt's end of the line. "Frankly, we've been far from feeling 'Mission Accomplished' since long before the president's speech last year. It has our leaders reeling, despite strikes and wins and pushing back borders. It's not like we're actually in a war, and yet we're in a war."

That word "war" triggered something in me. I quit listening and started lecturing.

"Yes. And parts of what you just said might be ripped straight from Mao's 1937 pages. At the beginning of the Second Sino-Japanese War, he argued for a struggle Chinese Communists waged for eight years. It laid out a three-phase model."

To his credit, Matt stayed with me. "Three stages?"

"In phase one, guerrillas earned popular support by distributing propaganda and attacking government. In phase two, it escalated things by attacking military forces and vital institutions. And in the third phase came conventional warfare and fighting, seizing cities, overthrowing government, and controlling the country."

"Phew! That easy, huh?" I could hear sarcasm dripping from his words, but I knew that he was still listening.

"It worked for Mao. I think Ho Chi Minh used the same strategy, as did his successor, until Chinese-made tanks invaded South Vietnam in 1975, along with North Vietnam troops. That eventually led to the fall of Saigon."

"But, Regina, we have the equipment and the intelligence, and yet the terrorists keep on!"

I nodded. "And the US also has the impatience and lack of experience to call human beings 'terrorists.' The terror all seems to be on our side, not knowing how to deal with those we call the 'enemy,' which is a definition that changes over time. They're like gnats buzzing around our heads while we go after them with a surgeon's knife, or even a fly swatter. They persist."

I had mentally mounted my anti-war soapbox. "Wars end with some iconic image, Matt: Lee and Grant at Appomattox, Japanese surrendering aboard the USS Missouri, a helicopter lifting off the CIA station's roof in Saigon. What is the image that our president or your boss have for ending our involvement in the Middle East? Do you know?"

"A good question. I'm not sure we've discussed it quite that way."

I came back at him, offering more observations for him to chew on. "Maybe it's because our impatient, adolescent society focuses on winning any competition. While it seems to me that the goal here in China and in the Middle East is to keep the competitive-ideal alive."

Matt sighed again. "I have to think awhile on that one. Have a good Mongolian vacation, Regina. And ride a wild mustang for me."

I hung up then, not knowing whether I'd spoken wisdom or sedition. I asked myself where my boldness was coming from. Then immediately decided to sleep on it.

After an escape nap, I rang Abraham repeatedly, but he didn't answer. So, I struck out along broken sidewalks, avoiding manhole-covers tilting ajar. A sleepy head with matted hair poked out from under one. The person who emerged readjusted a musty overcoat, quickly crossed the road, and turned into a narrow alley.

I ate fluffy fried bread with hot soy milk at a street table, got advice from a Chinese English student on a bicycle, and found the north bus station. Every man on the bus lit up a cigarette, and my sinuses burned despite my open window. The scenery was rugged upland under the sunshine. After waiting a half hour at a village bus station, a cab driver escorted me to his vehicle and asked for 350 yuan to take me to XiLaMuRen Grasslands. A crowd gathered as we bargained, finger-writing numbers on the dusty cab's hood.

A girl in her late teens came by then. "Can I help you?" she asked, then spoke to the driver to ensure his understanding of what we'd agreed upon: a hundred yuan for a round trip and that he would wait for me while I saw a show. Then she piled into the back, saying, "Okay! Okay!" And then we were off.

The driver immediately asked how old I was. "Seexty?"

I shrugged, thinking I could live with that. Suddenly, we sped off the curved road onto grassland at an English sign that informed us that we would need to "Pay toll ahead" in order to drive overland. A man undid a rope stretched across our path, and we proceeded through a village surrounded by a brick wall. Re-entering the highway beyond the toll booth, the driver pulled a face and winked so that I'd notice his clever bargain.

At very old, locked Wudangzhan Buddhist Lamasary, we took a dusty road into a yurt village. Sun shone on white mushroom tents with striking blue symbols, making for a beautiful landscape against dry grass. I imagined how it must look in June when everything would have greened up. Eventually, I sat inside its circular room, under Genghis Kahn's picture, as the girl working there snapped one of me.

"You stay all night?" she asked, but I declined. She left abruptly, kick-started a motorcycle, roared off, and wheeled around to bring me her tour-guide card. This was either her yurt home or her business office.

We drove another half-mile to a pasture where shaggy, scrawny beasts were tied. Some wore tiny saddles. I took more photos of mustangs and kept declining to ride, even as I snuck several pictures of primitive potato cellars that dotted the hillside. The girl then announced an upcoming show with singers and "famous instruments." She waved a brochure at me, then disappeared. Back in the car, the driver and I silently passed a rock-crushing operation and what appeared to be coal processing, being done by men in hard hats. The strong sun put me to sleep until we stopped thirty minutes later beside a gas station.

"*Wei shenme?*" I asked. (Why wait?)

The driver gestured toward the empty back seat. He was waiting to fill up the cab out in the middle of nowhere. I gestured toward the empty road, and we started back. I pointed the singers on the brochure out to him, silently asking where they were.

He pointed to a pavilion with twins painted on the side. Then he held up his cellphone, with the number "8" on the screen, letting me know the show would start at eight that night. Then he pointed to the steering wheel. "No bus. Hohot 400 yuan." I wondered if "8" was also the bad-luck death number in Mongolia, as it was in China.

We started dueling with our cellphone's calculators, with suggested numbers being offered and rejected, until he finally accepted two hundred as his fee: 150 for me and fifty for the freeloaders in the backseat. He laughed heartily.

We passed flocks of sheep, an old man's buggy behind a horse, and numerous chickens. Rolling terrain that reminded me of the Flint Hills of Kansas stretched out on both sides. The bus awaited at the village station. The driver tried for three hundred yuan again, but he accepted a hundred for the entertaining adventure.

In Hohot, I had to pay 168 yuan before my key would work. After a short nap, I was ready to walk to a good hotpot dinner, featuring mutton. The sidewalks were populated by street venders with animal-antler aphrodisiacs spread out on blankets and women carrying rosy-cheeked children. Later, back in bed, I wondered which of them had been Han, which Mongols, and which Hui, and what other groups might have been represented as well. I fell asleep forming still more questions without any answers.

Exploring Hohot the next day, I found the well-preserved Dazhai Temple. The museum was closed. I got Muslim sweets shaped like donut holes and happened along a street that looked Russian. Five Pagoda Temple lay up ahead as I watched a costumed TV movie being filmed. Returning, I pondered how the lightly populated (24 million people) province next to Russia had played a key role in the Silk Road trade. My mind was already forming my next email home:

Dear Friends and Family,

The Mongolian grasslands are littered with plastic bags, probably from baked potatoes sold to tourists. Hohot is dirty, and winters must be brutally long. Cows, pigs, horses, donkeys, and people mostly look healthy though. They are quick learners when it comes to ways to earn a few more American dollars. I wish you had been here to see if you wanted to ride a mustang; I spared the small, scrawny beast. Perhaps he'll become fat when the grass gets lush and green again. I'm glad I got this opportunity to visit. Love, Regina.

My thoughts turned to Pei Hua's Sports Games then, feeling glad that I'd been given an extended vacation. Jotting down a quick lesson plan, I decided I'd form "What if…?" groups to project future-tense English toward sports arenas and architectural wonders, urging them to invent a future where competitions moved beyond rope-skipping or outdoor basketball to worldwide events. Who knew what might happen if they put their creative minds to work?

CHINA 63 - PHONE CALLS

I'd barely gotten home to my Pei Hua apartment when Matt called. He seemed distracted, listening to my Inner Mongolia account without even questioning why I hadn't ridden a mustang. When I said goodbye and put the receiver back in its cradle, I breathed a sigh of relief.

Half out of my dirty clothes on the way to bed, I heard the phone jingle again. My, my! I'm certainly getting popular among the twelve million people of XiAn!

"How was Mongolia, Regina?" Joe asked the moment I picked up the phone. "Wonderful? I cannot wait to find out!"

I told him of Hohhot's wonders, the ping-ponging between ancient history and hope for the capital's projected future. It felt great to have him cling to my every word, almost like he'd been right there with me. Here was a man who would share my travel itch if he lived in America. He, too, seemed to understand curiosity and the adventure of not knowing what each new day in a new place might bring.

I glanced at the clock and realized that I'd been talking for almost two hours. Joe now knew about my times spent on horseback in Montana, riding until my legs felt bowed, and understood my pity for the half-starved mounts of the Mongolian grasslands.

Joe was full of eager questions. "Regina, what is the procedure to pack a horse for wilderness trips? Do Americans name their horses? How far did you ride in a day in Montana?"

I did my best to answer his questions, then finally told him that I needed to start reviewing lesson plans for next week's classes.

"Wait, Regina! I've more wonderful news. The Dean has approved our trip to Harbin for four days. He allows me to go as reward for suggesting that you bring travel lectures to our students. What you have told classes so far has reached his ears, and he sees a great surge in knowledge of our entire homeland!"

"B-But Joe," I stammered, "I've only discussed the history of places I've visited. Students know little about their country beyond memorized history. They know only life in their own villages."

"Bingo! That's precisely it! You are turning into a valuable Chinese asset. And we reap this harvest next week. It is all arranged, Regina. Trust me?"

For a moment, I thought the old Joe was back with another command to trust him. Then I realized that his tone rising on *"ma"* had made it a Chinese question.

Could I trust him? I didn't promise anything, but I didn't say "no" either.

I taught during the week, answered questions about Inner Mongolia during Q&A periods, and learned which students had excelled at rope-skipping, basketball shoots, and martial arts during the sports games. They all expressed hope that video-game competition would soon become a medal-winning category. Lively spoken English continued throughout the day's classes.

Joe called that evening (and each one that followed), telling me that Ha Er Bin—spelled out as three Chinese characters in English—would have doorways with red banners. He explained Chinese calligraphy as well, announcing that "Like minds have limits. Like-minded communities lack internal methods of self-criticism," among other lofty sayings. He pondered these pundits, somehow related to our trip like clouds floating through a heavenly dream, while I stifled a yawn.

Rather than Western debating or Socratic questioning, I let go of trying to understand. Listening to the poetry of his musings, I almost got some of the elusive "it" he was entrusting me to hear with my heart. Who would've thought this cliché-spouting man, who'd infuriated me little more than a semester ago, had thoughts in his mind like "Service doesn't require like-mindedness;" "history changes by the gift of dissent;" "we can't deny history;" "it's hubris to think my picture includes the Big Picture;" "have respect for the gift of conscience;" "new classes are unopened gifts;" "fireworks make demons and imps run from a benevolent spirit," and so on. It was like Joe was leading me in a meditation, something I was absorbing almost by osmosis. I closed my eyes and let it flow over me like a gossamer coverlet.

When I next opened my eyes, an hour had passed. The distinct feeling of an invisible hand holding mine washed over me. I could feel our caring connection. It didn't matter if it was a future promise, divine connection, Joe himself, or all of the above.

I felt joy.

"Goodnight, Regina," Joe whispered. "See you Friday on the train."

CHINA 64 - HARBIN HAPPINESS

I didn't need to fish out my passport from the outside pocket of my zippered roller bag. My "Ha-Er-Bin" train ticket cost 154 yuan, less than $25 US, for reserved window "soft-seats." My Chinese-made coat, padded and quilted under a water-resistant, layered, sleeping-bag material, wadded easily into a sort of pillow with a wide window view.

Joe silently slid in with a nod as impersonal as he gave to the young people squatting in the aisles, between them, and on purchased seats. I stayed quiet, occasionally lifting eyebrows his way. He ignored my questioning face. Was he afraid of someone recognizing him? I wondered if he had second thoughts about spending a weekend with me. *Surely, he'll speak to me soon.*

We silently observed a young man begin a four-hour flirtation with a pretty girl—sharing tea, playing computer games, and taking pictures. She got off the train. Then he spoke only to Joe, while trying to teach me a card game. Joe finally spoke to me in order to translate.

"Maybe Three-Card Stud, Regina?"

We played for boiled peanuts through a gorgeous sunset and increasing snow next to terra-cotta houses with round pipes extending above chimneys. Even trash in occasional village tenements shone with color. It looked like I'd imagined Russia, tinged with pink.

At Harbin's—no three syllables printed here—station after dark, the only return tickets available to XiAn were hard seats on the late train the following night. Joe secured them, telling me, "We have to do this, Regina."

Is this trip worth it? My dad's saying, "Never look a gift horse in the mouth," reminded me to stay silent. I closed my coat against the breath-grabbing air.

Two cabbies, frosty as the weather, quoted forty yuan to Gloria Hotel. Joe haggled. One accepted thirty up front. So, we climbed in, unwound our scarves, and sped past wonderlands of ice and lights. At the hotel, the desk clerk had us scheduled for one night later, but had "two rooms left, 350 yuan."

My teeth chattered in the cold lobby. Joe gave both of our passports to the concierge, then dropped me at my unheated room, where I slipped into the icy bathroom to put on long underwear, knock-off Sorrel boots, and an adventuresome spirit. From my window, I saw fireworks skyrocketing over Harbin's largest lake.

Joe returned, having added his own extra layers of clothing. Stepping outside, we saw bleachers and sculptures, all covered by ice. *"Bu, shei shei,"* he puffed into ice crystals when Joe told moonlight venders we weren't customers. I could scarcely breathe beneath my face covering, and my feet threatened to turn numb like my fingers inside two pairs of gloves.

We scurried back to our own beds. I took off only my coat and placed it atop the comforters and bedspread before burrowing beneath them both.

I awoke surprisingly refreshed the next morning, thinking that Joe had been a perfect caretaking gentleman the night before, while I'd been too cold to function. He knocked before I had done much but splash icy water on my face and smooth wrinkles out of my slept-in clothing. Six tables of Asian food presented breakfast with a sunny lake view. We met Westerners with children from Beijing, and Serbian women who smoked, not something I'd seen in China.

A friendly New Zealander suggested we hook up later. Speaking English was a treat; Joe remained mostly quiet and watched me with shining eyes. He seemed to be simply listening. It was my first brush with things Russian, and I chattered away about the dazzling sun, the onion domes, and the breakfast of boiled eggs and coarse breads with China's usual rice.

We walked briskly to Zhou Lin Ice Park. Global warming hadn't melted the sculpture contests. I went under an ice arch, ran along a maze, hid behind a dragon, then climbed Great Wall steps to a slide. Joe's feet pounded behind me. We giggled, as he caught me at the bottom of a giant slippery slide. The ice didn't seem cold anymore as we clung onto each other, laughing, before heading toward seven carvings on block-ice walls, holding gloved hands.

No one else was about. Mickey and Minnie Mouse stood in the middle of a happy dance on one panel. Sorrel boots, stiff coat and all, I found myself twirled around to stamp out a kind of jitterbug to match the mouse couple's stance. Joe pulled me close; then I spiraled out to see him break into a loose-jointed Goofy dance. He gruffly sang "Duh duh DUH duh," and I gave him the same syllables in my best Donald Duck voice in front of the next Disney panel.

Between breathless laughs, I heard, "Regina, you are so wonderful!"

"You're wonderful too, Joe! Who would've known you had so much fun in you! My Mickey Mouse watch says we've just enough time to meet the Serbian woman at the French bakery. Come on!"

Our breakfast Serb was smoking and drinking strong coffee. We ordered coffees, talked with her and two Canadian engineers helping the Chinese build a helicopter. One of them pronounced Harbin "barbaric" and Joe, surprisingly, didn't say a word in response.

Rather than listen to more prejudiced views, we excused ourselves to walk to St. Sofia's Church Museum, which was built 1903, Russian-occupied since the 1880s, and filled with photos. It helped me understand why Harbin's people looked like ruddy, chubby Siberian peasants. After a little shopping for dolls-within-dolls, dusk descended upon us.

We took a bus to "Eighth Ice and Snow World Park." As a wonderland, it was over the top: Trees lighted in garish colors, icy structures in city-sized buildings, sculpted Buddhas, and disco dancers on revolving ice platforms. We climbed slippery Imperial Palace steps, crawled into an igloo, and walked icy gangplanks into ice ships. There were bumper bikes on ice, plus restaurants, tea shops, and even a Korean travel agency. All were made of ice blocks that were stored every year for this purpose. The only things not made of ice were us, stomping feet and clapping hands, and the venders calling us to movable stands. Year of the Rooster pendants were the hottest items of 2005.

When it was time to depart, Joe hailed a taxi. We picked up our luggage and passports at the front desk, peeled off a couple of layers, and headed for the train. At the station, the cabbie told Joe that we were "foreigners, so the price is higher." I tipped him, something Chinese usually refuse with horror-filled expressions. He smiled warmly and closed his fingers over the extra yuan (seven cents).

At Harbin's railroad station, there was a horrendous push to board Car 10. Joe moved like a shield in front of me. Officials roughly pointed us toward the other end of the train, an even worse push. It was near the 11:15 p.m. departure time, so we bulled our way on, wheeling our bags.

It was a pickpocket's paradise. People stood on bags in the aisles below haphazardly overloaded luggage racks. A woman snoozed in my seat. Others departed without apologizing, leaving bags, bottles, and food. My bag partially fit under the shared table, while Joe held his. One of us had no place for our feet; the other had no seat. Train workers yelled, but people remained good-natured. I whispered that I could reorganize the entire car's luggage on top if I were only 6'4" and deep-voiced. Joe smiled, then sat like a clown atop his bag. He whispered to me that he had bribed the worker for an upgrade.

"Just be patient, Regina."

The train pulled out a half-hour late. Then it stopped. A uniformed worker pushed through the bodies, grabbing suitcases and barking orders. We put our bags into the mix, although I felt concerned that mine held my passport in its outer, zippered pocket. Ours soon sat under heavier-looking bags above our heads. Lights stayed on through the night. I counted fifteen people in our space, which seated ten. That same density repeated nine times in our train car, which seated a hundred.

Strong men hammered the window open slightly for air. A teen gave me a tissue to fill the frigid crack after three men leaned across me, trying in vain to close it. Several folks stood until they could squat. Many slept on their feet. One family used floor space under three seats to stretch out in tandem; young people played cards and munched snacks; college kids alternated between sitting and standing with a tourism major holding a platform ticket. She stayed until an official sold her a full ticket. A mother and small boy joined our space. He used a shoe for a pillow, with his backside in Joe's face. No one moved more than a few feet all night.

Joe and I tried propping our heads together, then one head on the table, with the other on a shoulder. We hugged our knees, straightened one leg at a time, and kept at bay the question of whether we could live through the next forty-eight hours. I wouldn't have missed it for the world, but it sorely tested my physical tolerance. At infrequent stops, a few folks got off. Invariably, more boarded.

Next morning, the ticket master parted the bodies again and told Joe, "Come now!" Our sleeping companions smiled happily, passing our bags hands-over-heads the length of two cars, no small trick for sleepy folks. Seemingly by silent consensus, the mother and child were selected to take our seats. Mob rule? This seemed more of a mob blessing.

With our bags' wheels on the aisle floor, I pulled mine eight more cars, saying, *"Diu bu qi"* repeatedly. (Excuse me.) Joe pushed his bag ahead with equal luck. Occasional glimpses past fogged windows revealed icicles on wintry vegetation in the early dawn. The farther we walked, the warmer the inside temperatures became. Arriving at our car, we settled at two hard sleeper bunks across from a young couple. On their third bunk up, a Chinese man in white underwear snored. A magenta-haired punk rocker sat on the third bunk above me. He reached down to lift suitcases while eating noodles at a small, high table across from the doorway.

Joe got me a dry duvet to replace mine, which was wet from window condensation. We fastened the valuables in our fanny packs to posts near our heads.

I won the race to dreamland.

CHINA 65 - SURPRISING MOVES

After thirty hours of bleak, stark, leafless trees and icy fog, our train suddenly barreled downhill, its horn blaring through various tunnels. No more sleep for me. Joe's mussed hair and sleepy eyes peered over the edge of the bunk above me.

My first thought was that my hair was surely a mess, and my comb and lipstick were in my fanny pack, still secure as my pillow. My second thought was, *Who cares! I'm rested, and I've had a wonderful time!"*

Joe shuffled down the second-tier ladder and disappeared, soon coming back with hot tea in disposable cups. It tasted like ambrosia. We sat cross-legged on my bunk and shared a half-dozen *baozi*—pork-filled steamed buns that were as ghostly white as the fog outside the window. I detected Chinese five-spice, oyster sauce, and soy sauce as I broke my fast, telling Joe how my father had taught me to say "breakfast," not "beffa" at age two.

"It meant just that the fast of our long night without food was broken," I added.

Joe listened attentively, then said, "Let's play a game, Regina. Fact or Myth? I am a left-brained person."

He'd been reading some old education textbooks, I surmised. How did I tell the English dean that—no matter how endearing he was becoming—brain technology had revealed that our brains' two hemispheres work together for complex processing?

"I say you use both sides of your brain whenever you do deep thinking. They cooperate. Educators used to label behaviors 'right- or left-brained.' Imagine being hooked up to a machine that lights up synapses while you talk to me. I hope they flash on both sides of the brain."

Joe looked at me like I was some wise guru, and I laughed. "Joe, all I do is read educational-research journals."

"But . . . fact or myth, Regina?"

"I guess I'd say you being 'a left-brained person' is a myth, wouldn't you?"

He nodded thoughtfully. I remembered seeing English crossword puzzles on his desk and continued the game: "Fact or myth, Joe? A crossword puzzle can keep the brain doctor away."

"I see all those students carrying Word Finds and Crossword Puzzles to English class. That's easy. It's a fact: To grow old with a healthy brain, do puzzles."

"My mother would agree with you. She asks for Word Find puzzle books at Christmas and birthdays. And she's eighty-five now."

Joe gave me a quick "gotcha" squeeze. I almost didn't tell him the rest of the story, but my logical brain asserted itself.

"It's one kind of skill, Joe, but it's not the problem-solving brains need to meet life's challenges. Crosswords can't give the variety of thinking skills that brains need to keep functioning well. It's memorization, a pretty low kind of learning."

Joe frowned. No quick squeeze this time. Was that because he didn't like losing twice in a row, or was it that I was opposing his clichéd pronouncements?

"Okay, Regina, fact or myth? Your brain processes all of your five senses!"

What should I do? Bring up proprioception, knowing where body parts are and what they're doing? I thought of nociception then, feeling pain. And chronoception, sensing time's passage, and interoception, recognizing internal needs, like hunger. *Too much information.*

"The way you put it, Joe, yes! The brain processes five senses."

Sometimes, it was better to leave sleeping senses lie. Joe's jubilant "Fact!" enveloped me in a big hug. I put my head on his shoulder and hugged him back. We turned to the frosty window's passing scenes.

There were glimpses of mountain homes set in clay hillsides, canyon cities of adobe brick, power plants, green winter wheat, and occasional shepherds and flocks. We passed mountain monasteries, burial mounds in the fields, and mustard-colored danger signs that I speculated might mark buried cables. At five p.m., Hua Shan, the Flower Mountain I had climbed with Pei Hua students shone in the end-of-day sunlight.

"Joe, I truly feel like I'm coming home," I said, and I meant it.

The train station was the usual push and shove, but Joe soon had us safely in the Pei Hua driver's car. I was in back with the overflow of luggage, and they spoke rapid-fire Chinese in front. I didn't recognize the dialect, nor did I see anything I knew enroute. Joe didn't turn around to reassure me until we pulled over onto a sidewalk and some grass near old XiAn's crenulated walls.

I reached out to tap Joe's shoulder, and he turned to face me. "A personal matter for the driver, Regina. It will be two shakes of a lamb's tail."

Why has he gone back to his old cliché habit?

Joe opened his door and went inside, while I sat, bewildered, in the car.

It seemed a very long time, with traffic whizzing by, spewing exhaust fumes, and me alone in the slanting back seat. *Two wheels must still be on the street, which has at least four lanes.* I wondered if I might be safer if I exited toward the grass on the uphill side. Raindrops dotted the window.

The rain shower passed. I reached for the door handle just as Joe returned with the driver, who got our bags out of the trunk while Joe led me across a sunken grassy area and through a door. I recognized "Gran Melia" in English among the Chinese characters, but this certainly wasn't any grand entryway.

"What's going on, Joe?"

He smiled mysteriously, with one raised eyebrow. "Another surprise, Regina. A gift—a Sofitel Hotel night, your 'home away from home'! You'll dream beautiful dreams on Renmin Square."

"Joe, I need to return to my apartment and get ready to teach tomorrow. I haven't had a shower or proper place to sleep for days. No more gifts!"

"Do not protest, Regina. Pei Hua has honored you. Deal with it."

I couldn't think of anything else to say. My silent mouth hung open as he keyed the elevator, and we rode all the way to the top. It opened to only one door, and he inserted another key. We stepped into what appeared to be the penthouse suite, with a flatscreen TV, white couches, a kitchenette, and a bar sink. Beyond that, I could see a creamy folded duvet across the foot of a king bed through another open door. This was nicer than anything I'd seen in China. *Why not accept their generosity?*

Joe was smiling from ear to ear, pulling me toward the kitchenette bar. "See? It even has an American coffee maker. And the refrigerator is full."

"I must sit down, Joe. It's too much. I don't understand." Overcome by exhaustion, I headed toward the bedroom, kicked off my shoes, and flopped onto the pristine sheets.

Joe simply turned and left. I heard his key turn in the lock as I fell into a deep sleep. Tomorrow would be soon enough to sort out my good fortune.

CHINA 66 - AGAIN UNEXPECTED

It seemed no time at all before I opened my eyes to a darkened room. It took a moment to orient myself. Lying fully clothed on a silken coverlet over a luxurious mattress slowly began to make sense. I switched on a lamp within reach. Pinkish tones reflected off a chrome-and-glass desk and a coffee table, where slick magazine covers bounced light back toward me. I arose and walked past a couch to the kitchenette, remembering Joe's words about a coffeemaker. How long had it been since I'd used one like that? Months? Years? There was a Folgers knock-off packet in a basket om the counter. The directions were in Chinese, but I knew what to do. "You may be Mr. Fake Coffee, but your aroma smells like the real thing."

I soon poured a delicious cup and looked out the window. Renmin Square stretched below me, with the four-tiered Bell Tower alight and majestic. Traffic streamed toward arched entries in and out of the old city below. People the size of ants peered over the first white-layered walls surrounding what appeared to form a solid and square city block of stone or cement. Three darker, reddened layers of tilted roof-corners could be seen below my window level. Their carvings made me think of latticework on a cake.

First light dawned, and even as my eyes picked up movement of more ant-people ascending a graceful stairway alongside the tower, my cellphone rang.

"Dr. Blakely?"

"Oh, Matt, you'll never guess where I am!"

"Please don't play games, Dr. B. Tell me if you're okay."

"Yes, I'm better than okay. You know that I had the opportunity to go to Mongolia, but I'm now enjoying a gift from Pei Hua: a night at the fancy Sofitel Grand Malia. You should see the arches with traffic going under the Bell Tower, Matt! I'm in a dream scene here!" Was I gushing? I realized that I hadn't even told him I'd been to Harbin, and that I should really ask about him and how he was doing.

"Enough about my good fortune. May I ask what's happening in your part of the world?"

"Well," he said, "our neighbors and allies seem to all be in trouble. Canada had a shooting. Our President prioritized kids' education in his State of the Union address. A man flew sixty-seven hours around the world without refueling. The United Nations predicts 90 million AIDS cases in Africa aren't getting help. US soldiers killed an Italian Secret Service Agent in Iraq when they fired on a car carrying a released hostage. Other than that, it's calm here. Two goods. Three bads!"

The poor guy sounded frustrated. My coffee was also getting cold, and I liked it piping hot. "The Secretary must have a lot on her plate right now. You too, Matt."

"And on top of that, I lost touch with you, Dr. B. I assume I'll be able to reach you more predictably in the future?"

"'Anything to make your work easier," I answered with just a tinge of sarcasm. I didn't remind him that he'd been the one to begin our phone conversations.

I ended the call with "Have a pleasant, productive day, Matt." Then I carried my cooled coffee over to the window to gaze, once again, at the Bell Tower. In full daylight, it looked like a huge square groom's cake, with bold tiers of latticework above a white base, surrounded by traffic. Insect-sized people peered over the first story's intricately fenced walls below my window, even as my doorbell sounded.

"I have English *China Daily* and a message for you," announced a high-pitched voice.

I was tempted to return to my spacious bed and ignore any messages from the outside world. On the other hand, I was still dressed in the clothes I'd worn on the train, so I figured that I might as well see what the day might hold. I walked to the door.

The peephole revealed no one. I secured the safety chain and opened the door the few inches it allowed. Still no person appeared. Curious, I undid the chain and stuck my head out. To my left stood Joe, grinning like a naughty child with a *China Daily* under his arm.

He entered and dashed around my apartment, again like a child. His regular voice replaced the high-pitched one that had fooled me into opening the door. "Regina, you are already enjoying coffee!"

"Good morning to you too, Joe." My sarcasm fell on deaf ears, but the flute music wafting up through the window did not. We crossed the room to focus on the dancers, moving in unison. "Oh, Joe. I'm glad you get to see this! That talented woman playing below . . . Isn't it lovely?"

Joe didn't reply right away. Then he lifted a serious face to me. "Remember when I said my wife plays flute?" Something like pride flitted across his face, before vanishing as he turned aside. "Look at the Bell Tower from here! You hardly messed up your bed, I see! Let's explore your amenities!"

He snatched up the coffee-table magazine and pointed to the picture of a gleaming swimming pool with a naughty grin. "Go change into your bathing costume!"

"But, Joe, what about the flute pla—?"

"No 'buts'!" he said sternly, cutting me off with an even naughtier grin turning up both corners of his mouth.

Do Chinese people actually have dimples?

Joe flung open a closet door and produced a one-piece swimsuit in aqua and violet swirls. "See? Just your size! And one for me!" He waved a pair of matching trunks like a crazed magician. "Not another word until we're in the heated pool!"

My head stopped protesting as he put a restraining finger on his lips. I donned the swimsuit in the bathroom, leaving my soiled clothing behind. When I returned, Joe had our matching robes ready. He seemed entirely unconscious of his bare torso with its sculpted ribs displayed plainly above the waistband swimsuit. His legs, too, surprised me, looking strong and muscled. Who'd have thought that slim Dean Zhou would look this boyish in a swimsuit? *I must stop gawking, or I'll end up running back into the bathroom and hide in shame.*

I gave up and slipped into the terrycloth robe's softness. He closed the doors behind us, inserted the elevator key to summon it, selected the proper elevator buttons, and we rode down for a swim. The pool felt hygienic, compared with the few I had visited near old Pei Hua. Those had been filled with people crammed into group showers, men hawking and spitting in the gutters along the edges, and thick, tepid water. Sofitel Hotel offered tile steps and chrome rails that invited us into the turquoise water gently sloping to diving depths. I dove between the reflected light patterns and came up behind Joe. "Boo!"

He jumped! Then began a game of swim-dive-swim tag until we both became breathless. I hadn't had this much fun since I was eleven and at a 4-H swim party in Kansas. Boys had chased and tagged me then too.

Joe whirled fast and enveloped me in a slippery hug. "Breakfast time now!"

I was ravenous, and all-too-ready to follow him robed, barefoot, and dripping down the hall. Instead of a changing room though, we then entered a room with a simple buffet that had been laid out beyond plastic tables and chairs. Several robe-clad people already dined on congee, pickled vegetables, boiled eggs, breads, and watermelon.

As I filled my plate, reality crept slowly back into my head. *What am I doing? What am I supposed to be doing? What would my mother say?*

"Joe," I said between bites, "this has been the most fun I've had in years. Now, I've some questions. What day is it? When am I expected back in my classroom? And how did you manage all this for me?"

"Regina, do not worry." He took another several bites before adding, "You didn't know we are on holiday now? No teaching for a week. Oh, today is Sunday, but it doesn't matter. Have a wonderful time."

Another unannounced holiday? That meant no tutoring with Dong Liu and no lesson plans. I'd sort out what happened to semester's end when I got back to Pei Hua. *Carpe diem!* Seize the moment!

As if on cue, I heard Joe say, "Let's visit XiAn's Stele Museum!"

Like an obedient child, I followed him back to the room and picked up the clothing I'd worn for thirty-six hours during the Harbin train ride.

"Wait!" Joe frantically slid closet doors this way and that. I glimpsed an ironing board and unopened safe before the mirrored door slid away to reveal hanger after hanger of dresses, slacks, and blouses. There was even lacy red underwear. It all appeared to be in my size, rather than the diminutive outfits on display on the shop-window manikins.

"How? When?" I sputtered.

"I have planned well?" Joe asked, obviously pleased at my reaction. "Now, go change back into my Chinese beauty, and we will take you to the Stone Forest." He handed me three hangers and a pair of size-seven shoes.

It didn't take long to rinse off, towel dry, and run a comb through my wet hair. For once, I didn't bother looking for any increase in the number of gray hairs. *Thank heaven it is naturally curly,* I offered up to the god of beauty as I applied lip gloss, then pulled on the red underwear. *How appropriate that it's the Chinese color of good fortune!* The capri pants and matching top fit perfectly. I was ready to go.

Joe looked like a professor again as we caught a bus for the Beilin Museum. Housed in a Confucian temple dating back to 1087, the black marble steles, collected since 1944, were impressively beautiful. Upon first look, they bore similarity to American headstones, set in rows and rising well above my head, engraved with Chinese characters. Joe interpreted a few wise sayings and historical examples. One, attached atop a rounded turtle's shell base, spoke of ancient creation. All gleamed, where light touched the calligraphy, without a single fingerprint. I stood apart and let the ancient wisdom bathe me. I'd had the same experience in cathedrals.

Joe approached, and his tone sounded reverent when he spoke. "Now we visit the XiAn's Nestorian Stone, the oldest in Shaanxi Province, Tang Dynasty, 781."

Soon there, I stood in awe before it. *That predates Christianity! No wonder Joe looks so proud.* I was surprised to feel a quickening I'd usually only experienced during special moments in church. I squeezed his hand, and both his hands clasped mine. It was a sort of holy moment, connecting us: two people born of different continents.

We returned for lunch at the hotel, in a small, quiet room with only a few other diners. Silverware, not chopsticks, lay atop napkins the size of tea towels. They were discretely placed in our laps by competent waiters. I luxuriated in the Western hospitality, let Joe order tender pork chops and potatoes, definitely not Chinese food, and wondered if this was, indeed, a dream. I heard more about XiAn's wonders as we sipped decaf and shared apple pie a la mode.

Surely, this is a dream.

I whispered, "My sister serves this kind of meal in Kansas, and my mother makes the best apple pie in the Midwest. Somehow, you knew to order this meal!"

He gave me a big smile. "Very American. Don't ask. Just enjoy it."

I did.

Returning to my door, he said, "You take a little rest now. Tomorrow, more surprises for you, my lovely one. Wear sturdy shoes and bring your umbrella. You don't want sunburn to mar your flawless skin."

Not really comprehending, I simply floated inside toward my silk-covered bed as Joe clicked the key into the outside door.

As I closed my eyes, I heard his footsteps recede as he headed back to the elevator.

CHINA 67 - SILENT WARRIORS

I was fully alert now and ready to explore my fairytale room. First, though, I took in my penthouse view of the Bell Tower again. Traffic still streamed below me into Old XiAn's bowels, the matchbox cars trailing momentary exhaust. I could imagine China's usual honking din, but all seemed serene and quiet this surreal morning. Sunlight streamed in, and I wondered if the same sunbeams might be touching Joe as he slept. I hoped so, and an almost visceral longing teased at me from somewhere below my ribcage. I told myself that today's promised trip would be soon enough to explore that further.

Turning to the closet then, I saw my apricot-colored, lace-trimmed robe hanging over matching pajamas on a padded hanger. I ran a full tub, poured in complimentary magnolia-scented oil, and lowered myself into the warm water. Minutes (or maybe hours) later, I dried with soft white towels and slipped into silk pajamas, buoyed up by good fortune and the sound of flute music below.

Joe's knock and call startled me: "Regina, are you ready for Terra Cotta Warriors?"

I dashed to the door, pulling on my robe. When I opened the door, there he stood, looking like a t-shirted Chinese tourist in his knee-length shorts, with a camera hung around his neck. His white, perfect knees were in full view, looking like they'd come out of hiding. I stifled a giggle, afraid he'd not feel the affection in my laughter, only a loss of face.

"Oh, Joe, I'm so sorry. I'm not ready."

"It doesn't matter! I'm so glad the robe fits. And the color is perfect for your complexion." The look in his eyes told me it really didn't matter, but that we'd better get on the road soon or else plan to spend the rest of the day on my bed.

"I'll only be a minute." I detoured by the closet to grab the first hanger and dashed into the bathroom. "Terra Cotta Warriors, here we come!"

The jeans and bling-covered tee I'd grabbed felt skintight. *Dare I ask Joe to translate the characters marching across my chest?* It might be very Chinese, but it was unlike anything I'd ever worn. I wriggled into the jeans, gave my face and hair a promise to spend more time later, and turned a gold doorknob to re-enter the main room. Self-consciousness hid behind my silly, "Ta DAA!" Joe's wide grin was reward enough to let me shed my reservations and carry me out the door.

Within minutes, we were elbowing our way onto a bus, sitting as two seats emptied for us. And then we were on our way to Qin Shihuang's Mausoleum and Museum. Joe gave my hand a quick squeeze, then becoming Dr. Zhou and all business once more, he handed me an English brochure. We exited the Old Town area and made surprisingly few stops in the forty-five-minute drive to the LinTong District. In the brochure, I read that a Chinese farmer had dug a well, rotating his half-tube shovel to bring up cylinders of dirt. He'd found, instead, a flowerpot-colored figure that had led to the uncovering of thousands of sculpted soldiers: Emperor Qin's third-century-army lookalikes.

One silent young person trailed behind us like a loyal greyhound, in a flannel shirt and baggy jeans, staying a few steps behind us on the long walk to a mostly barren complex of cement buildings, with few trees and little grass. Joe ignored him or her, but I was curious about the stocky shadow-creature and turned to ask in English, "Would you like to walk with us?"

In a soft female voice, she said, "Yes. I seem to be the only Japanese person here." She looked around. "I have long wished to see the Warriors, but my countrymen don't come here much. I am Charlie."

She stuck out a tentative hand. I wondered if her name had come from an ESL class featuring the old movie named *Charlie,* which had been set in England, or the perfume of the same name. Maybe she didn't know she'd chosen a mostly masculine American name. It didn't really matter. Her English seemed impeccable if somewhat monotone.

Joe kept his eyes elsewhere, but my heart went out to Charlie, along with my western-style handshake. Joe stalked ahead. I had a momentary impulse to comfort him, or at least find out why his mood had turned cold, as the crowd pushed us down the first walkway into a darkened building. Out of the sunlight, the air cooled with a slightly dank smell. Wall-to-wall tourists clustered around flag-holding guides near glass cases. Chinese-speaking tour groups outshouted each other, but I had Charlie, my own scholarly English guide. She told me that Qin had wanted to be buried outside the capital, XiAn, and spent much of his 259-210 BC life replicating an afterlife army to be buried with him.

As he listened, Joe's eyes fixed on a Chinese guide's orange pennant high above our heads. I caught a word here and there that confirmed what Charlie told me.

By that time, the masses had circled past the mausoleum and several displays of horses and carriages behind dimly lit glass. From my vantage point on the outskirts of several groups, I saw practically nothing. I looked around for Joe.

Only Charlie looked familiar. We spilled outside and sought shade under a deciduous tree. I wondered if I should go back inside and look for Joe. Charlie, a stoic paragon of patience, simply sat on a rock. It was at least ten degrees cooler in the shade, so I sat too and listened to birdsong. Joe would surely reappear soon.

Charlie found her voice and began talking about the self-proclaimed First Emperor of Qin, who had taken the throne at age thirteen, with his Dowager Queen mother ruling until he was thirty-eight. Was he a good king? He had unified China's warring states. I'd read that he was brutal and figured you'd have to be to become such a leader. Yet he had changed the practice of being buried with loyal followers by replicating his faithful army in clay to accompany him into the afterlife instead.

I told her how impressed I was with his accomplishments. "He managed to make the settlements along the Yellow and Yangtze Rivers into agricultural civilizations, and he laid the foundations for XiAn's city walls, didn't he?"

Charlie smile was grim. "He might've had vision, but he couldn't have been too smart if he thought he could gain eternal life by drinking arsenic. That's how he died."

As Charlie dropped this last piece of trivia, a frowning Joe rejoined us. I doubted he would have translated this fact for me had it been offered by Chinese guides. He thrust a closed umbrella at me. "The sun is quite hot today," he said, his voice like steel. "Use this."

Joe's old commanding ways had returned with him, and I didn't like it. I purposefully left the umbrella closed. We squinted our way to the largest building, where the Terra Cotta Warriors awaited.

We three uncomfortably silent people entered a long ramp alongside the uncovered section of the twenty-two-square miles of equally silent figures lined up below us. I noticed some smooth-shaven warriors, though most had assorted clay-brush mustaches. Their caps were tilted to right or left, high or low on their clay foreheads, and punctuated by either topknots or two braids elevated to different levels above their heads. Some had their eyes closed, while others were cast slightly downward. Some looked wide awake, and a few seemed either contemplative or bored. All of the still figures showed eerie personalities, with not one giving any suggestion of fearing death.

The farther inside we walked, the more the temperature dropped. The din of Mandarin around us quieted to an almost-hushed awe. We approached the first soldier, who was not as tall as Joe, with another lined up behind him. I was surprised at the absence of any scent in this obvious excavation almost the size of the huge pavilion. The clay faces had features just different enough to suggest distinct individuals and were sometimes streaked with a little red or blue that had faded into yellowed tones like rows of flowerpots left too long in the sun.

I whispered to Charlie, "Can you imagine the thousands of these soldiers lined up underground for thirty-eight square miles?"

She shook her head and continued to study the clay soldiers. I noticed that Joe did the same and wondered if this shrine was affecting him in a similarly profound way. Perhaps I would ask him when the time felt more right.

Other questions came to mind. I couldn't imagine how acres had been excavated without damaging the figures. Clay horses also interrupted the rows of ancient soldiers below me. Maybe the far end of the huge display contained soldiers not yet assembled. I slipped away and moved in that direction, where I could make out tarp-covered mounds marked with yellow tape, like the sort that was used in TV crime scenes.

To my surprise, I noticed that the figures below me seemed no taller than my own 5'2," certainly not the robust sort of bodies I remembered seeing on uniformed family members back home from their military stints. I stood there, my thoughts drifting back over the centuries, until an official with a

Western cheerleader's bullhorn shouted something to the gathered crowd. It started moving. Joe led, and Charlie brought up the rear, as we trailed the others towards the exit through the gift shop.

It was easy to imagine flaring nostrils and flailing hooves on the silvery souvenir horses, nestled like unicorns in red gift boxes. I'd seen at least one of them tarnishing on Midwesterner's bookshelves after people had returned from China trips.

"Purchase a warrior or his steed?" Joe asked me.

Charlie and I both shook our heads. I did get a book of postcards, but the underground tomb of a thousand short Chinese men, all lined up, remained indelibly imprinted behind my eyelids. I wouldn't forget the Qin emperor who'd spared countless men's lives by building this clay entourage to escort him to the afterlife.

The exit was just past a series of street stalls selling different widths of noodles. Joe took command, speaking rapidly in the Shaanxi dialect to an old woman with a few broken teeth punctuating the grin she sent toward him. She ladled out two bowls of wide noodles and broth. As she handed them to Joe, I stepped forward and held up three fingers, then pointed to the three of us. She filled another bowl for Charlie, and I dug into my backpack, ready to pay for her bowl, but Joe rose to the occasion and handed over another yuan.

We silently slurped noodles under a tree. Then we took turns excusing ourselves to visit the restrooms. Men and women washed their faces and hands in communal sinks, but the women's toilets, which spun off to the left, were surprisingly clean. I opened a cubicle to find a toilet that actually flushed, with a proper seat as well! What a luxury! I guessed that the unlatched doors further down were squat toilets with blue tiles on either side of a cement trench, upon which to plant one's feet.

As Charlie slipped away for her turn, Joe and I were left alone. There niggled an almost-painful place where my heart was beating, but I tried to be casual as I looked at him. "You are unusually quiet today, Joe. Can you tell me why?"

He stayed silent a moment longer, then looked crestfallen. "I think I am jealous, Regina. You prefer Japanese company to mine." Then he turned on me, speaking with barely suppressed outrage in his voice: "You know those people are our enemies, don't you? Think of Nanjing!"

I felt my breath catch, not knowing what to make of this revelation. Was that really how he felt after all these years? How could I tell him that this was not part of my understanding of the world, nor something I'd want to hold onto for a half century?

There was no time to protest or smooth things over before Charlie was back at my elbow like an obedient puppy. Without any further words, we got on the bus, with me sitting between the two of them on the long back seat, headed back to XiAn.

As the bus stopped at the city's edge near a youth hostel, Charlie stood up. Joe looked straight ahead, ignoring her departure.

"Nice to meet you, Charlie," I said. "Take care of yourself."

She turned around, slipped me her phone number, and whispered, "Thank you for being a friend."

CHINA 68 - LOCKED DOORS

Coming back inside my fancy apartment, I decided that Joe and I had to brave the risk of facing our cultural expectations. A meeting of the minds was long overdue. We'd played around this meeting of the hearts enough now, and I sensed that I was getting close to a looming heartbreak.

"Please sit down, Joe," I said, indicating the easy chair by the window. "We must talk."

"Then you must bring me tea, Regina." He lowered himself into the chair and sat tall, crossing his arms in front of his chest.

I stood my ground, even as I plugged in the electronic kettle like an obedient attendant. "I will make you tea, but you must promise not to give me the silent treatment again."

He smiled faintly, his voice lowering though without any apparent contrition. "Okay." No longer appearing a stoic Qin warrior, he started to slowly shed the shell he'd kept intact for most of the day as we visited the Terra Cotta Warriors. His expression softened, but only a bit. Had he detected my compromise in acting like one of the tea-serving young lovelies who waited on him hand and foot at Pei Hua?

"Relax, Joe. It's only you and me now."

I saw his shoulders loosen. Then his arms opened toward me. A momentary image of a tired child imploring his mommy to pick him up flickered in my mind as I put green tea leaves into a glass and poured hot water in after it, the way I knew he preferred. My own China cup, a rare treat in this country, got an equal measure of leaves and water.

I sat at the small table and waited in increasingly easier silence. When the last tea leaf settled at the bottom of my cup, I said, "Tell me about Nanjing, though I know it was called Nanking long ago. I also know it was the site of a massacre."

"All Chinese know the Rape of Nanjing, Regina. Yes, it was called Nanking then. At first, it sounded perfect—the Greater East Asia Prosperity Sphere led by the Japanese. China needed re-education in 1937. My young grandparents followed blindly. They hoped to be transformed, along with the rest of the Motherland."

He shifted in the chair, swiping at the renegade lock of hair that I'd come to like a lot when it fell toward his eyes. Then he squared himself toward me. I could almost see that he was thinking bitter thoughts.

"Go on, Joe. I want to know."

"Then the Japanese Imperial Army invaded our capital: Nanking. They raped and killed our women and children. Think of it: eighty thousand women violated; three hundred thousand of our people killed."

"That's horrible, Joe. Are you sure that's accurate?"

"I wasn't born yet, but I believe it. My father's sister told us the story of her family running with Chinese neighbors from the Japanese soldiers. The family could not get across a bridge. There were Japanese guards on the other side. It was raining hard, and the family ran back and went down a steep place toward the water. My aunt saw a Japanese soldier pointing his gun from the bridge where they had just been. She hid behind some tall grass and lay in the mud as bullets flew around her. Much later, when it was quiet, she found her younger brother dead behind a bush. Her mother, my grandmother, lay very still in the open with two children clinging to her. Those children were my father and another sister." He stopped and wiped his eyes.

I was also crying by then. "Those poor children—"

"Regina, this is the first time I have spoken our personal family story." He seemed to nail me to my chair with his dark eyes boring into me like rivets. What came next was like a rush of furious wind: "And you ask me to look on the Japanese with generosity? Paying for their food as if they were friends and not the barbarians they are?"

Joe turned on me then, fire blazing in his eyes. "Their unforgiveable acts will not be forgotten! They should not be allowed to even lay eyes on our historic treasures!"

We just sat there while our tea cooled, both of us breathing heavily. Then finally, I found my voice. "I can see how strongly you feel about this, Joe. Your people suffered a great wrong." My mind was racing, pressing me to ask if the Chinese hadn't also done some horrific deeds in their past, but I knew that this wasn't just a mental exercise. Joe's anger still crackled above the deep hurt somewhere inside him.

I'm grateful that he trusted me enough to tell me his feelings.

It wasn't cultural differences I felt now. It was compassion and love for this dear human being who had suffered, over and over, as history's reminders continually resurfaced. I reached out to comfort him like a baby. He sobbed in my arms, then quieted and abruptly stopped.

"I hope I did not lose face, Regina. You do not seem frightened. You are not angry as I am." With that, he gave me a brief hug and hurried out my door.

I distinctly heard his key turn in the outside lock. I sat and pondered what he'd meant by that. *Does he consider me disloyal because I did not join his anger? Was he saying I'm unfeeling? Why don't I carry similar hurt and anger about Pearl Harbor?*

I did not know what to do with the circling questions in my head. So, I simply finished my tea as the sun set, wild crimsons and flaming yellows and oranges streaking the western sky above the Bell Tower's pagoda-roofed corners.

My indignance at Joe's inability to treat Charlie with courtesy melted into recognition of the dramatic force of hate being kept alive by people we deem important. Hearing his family's stories, the power of textbook messages and lack of interaction with those seen as enemies filled my head.

I felt an ironic smile tug at my lips as I remembered the childhood thrill I'd gotten from reading George Washington's "I cannot tell a lie" speech, about having chopped down a cherry tree. Textbooks had finally dropped that myth, but I admitted to myself that it had left a void in my childhood ties to history. Was suspicion and hatred easier to instill than moral lessons during impressionable times? Especially among family members?

No other questions arose. I felt drained as one last memory surfaced: Luna, a Pei Hua student, had asked me once if I "hated the Japanese" and seemed unable to accept that I hadn't ever even considered that. Her question was now easier to understand after Joe's self-revelation.

The afternoon sky drained vermillion into a cloud near the city skyline. Its rounded edges shone gold as dusk turned navy blue.

I carried my cup and saucer to the coffee table and looked through the hotel materials there, half-searching for my suite key. It didn't turn up among the glossy pictured pages showing fitness treadmills, swimming pools, restaurants, and the lobby in soft light.

There was an envelope, but it was empty too. I assumed it had probably been provided to enclose a tip for the maid. I opened drawers and even looked in the safe. No key. Joe apparently had the only one. I was locked in this luxury prison.

I wandered back to the window, looked down on the Dong Xin street traffic. It might as well have been a thousand miles away. This was beyond curious. Did Joe not want me to leave this room, or was this another cultural practice I didn't understand? I'd insist on keeping the key the next time he came. *If he comes back at all*, I thought. What if he'd felt I'd made him lose too much face yesterday?

I had to think of something else, something productive and within my control. So, I decided to work on a lesson plan, "Passport to Travel," for my last lecture before finals, which would be due in a week. That would put my confused mind to work. Unzipping my bag's outer pocket to retrieve my passport brought another surprise: It wasn't there. I removed bills, lozenges, Kleenex, and extra eyeglasses. No passport. Nor was it anywhere inside the empty bag. My fanny pack yielded nothing but my teaching badge and some used tissues. I sat down to calm myself, then mentally reviewed every time I'd seen or touched it on this trip, from the time I first packed to the last railway ride, with the bag on my bunk, always seeing it in the zippered outer-bag pocket. Abandoning lesson planning, I put my face in my hands and cried.

My cellphone interrupted this outburst with its sonorous bell tone. I sniffed, then accepted the call. *"Wei?"*

"Dr. Blakely—"

Relief of hearing Matt's English brought forth a rush of words: "Oh Matt, I am so glad to hear from you! My passport's missing! It's not where I usually keep it! I'm almost frantic!"

"Chill out, Dr. B! It'll turn up wherever you last put it. Where have you gone since we last talked?"

Good, calm advice, Matt. I gave up my search effort to refocus. "I didn't need it for us to visit the Terra Cotta Warriors. Dr. Zhou taught me surprising pre-WWII history. His mother's family actually went through the Nanjing Massacre!" I knew I was babbling but couldn't stop, "And I met a Japanese girl I liked, but it made Dean Zhou very angry. Did you know that all Chinese seemingly still hate the Japanese? In fact, I just realized why my students asked me if I hated them. It's like Pearl Harbor ten times over!"

"Whoa!" Matt said, and I tried to catch my breath as he continued. "You're quite excited, Dr Blakely. It must've been some day! Let's talk about Japan. Nissan and Toyota are both doing well for our stockholders over there. . ."

He continued, and I felt myself slowly calming down as I listened to his voice and started answering his questions. We discussed the way America had combined forces with the hard-working Japanese for economic gain. Matt, too, marveled at how China kept the old grudges and atrocities alive, fanning flames of hate. I brought up my thoughts about cultural differences and history, but I left out the fact that I'd chosen to comfort Joe when he'd opened up to me about his own thoughts and feelings.

"What's the Chinese sentiment about the Qing dynasty's overthrow of the Ming dynasty in the seventeenth century?" Matt asked then, trying to make some point.

I told him I'd read that twenty-five million had lost their lives at that time. "And what about the Taiping Rebellion?" I added. "That accounted for another twenty million lives lost. It goes back a long way in China, with dynasty after dynasty wiping one another out. But how can I help you prepare the Secretary to understand China's hatred, taught both at home and school, alongside their blind love of the Motherland? She must try to find a common meeting ground for experiences that she cannot yet comprehend—not focus on an agenda for democracy or even forgiveness. That's incomprehensible to the people I've met so far here. Impossible for them to stomach." I was babbling again, steering the subject carefully around something I hadn't yet fully thought out.

A sharp knock sounded on my door, even as Matt asked, "Can we resume this discussion another time?"

I was only too happy for the interruption.

"Of course. Goodbye, Matt. I'll have clearer thoughts next time."

Hanging up, having completely forgotten to tell Matt about the missing key, I hurried toward the door, switching on the light as I went.

CHINA 69 - A PROPOSAL

I stood at the locked door for a moment and heard someone mumbling in Chinese, then footsteps stumbled away. Any other time, I'd probably think it was someone who'd just approached the wrong room. Without my passport, though, I felt paranoid. I propped a chair under the knob, piled on three more, and then set my intention to sleep, tired out by the recent emotional ups and downs.

The next morning, half-awake to the city sounds below my window, I heard a knock on my door and the sound of a key being pressed into the lock. I quickly jumped up. My apricot robe got buttoned crookedly as I stumbled across the room, watching the chairs I'd pressed against the door being pushed easily aside as it opened.

Joe stood at the door with my second roller bag, which I'd left in the closet of my old apartment. Before I could ask how he'd gotten ahold of it, he announced, "I brought your paperwork to turn in grades and prepare for classes after the break." His face was all smiles above a white shirt, navy slacks, and a long black belt. Gone was the frightened man who'd cried in my arms the night before.

What a fool I'd been, letting myself fall for the good times we'd shared. I knew I had to get a grip on more than just the doorknob.

"Come in," I said as I opened the door wider. "And don't put the key away; I want you to leave it with me." With this statement, I had taken command, or at least I thought I had. He moved into the suite, hoisted my suitcase onto my bed, and stepped aside.

I unzipped it to see typed grade lists, with class names written in English on top. I also found *Soong Sisters, Oliver Twist,* and other books that I'd left at my old bedside. Some of the clothing that had hung in my closet, and underwear left to dry on my sunroom racks, was there too.

"How did you get into my apartment? I've had the key to both doors for the past semester."

He ignored my question and turned squarely toward me with an expression that looked quite serious. "We must talk, Regina. I thought you understood some things that must be explained."

"Okay, Joe. And I've a few questions of my own."

"First, do you like this suite?"

"It's lovely, Joe, but—"

"I told a little fib about it," he said, hanging his head. "Just a little white lie." His renegade lock of hair fell across his forehead again, and I had the fleeting memory of it half-curling toward his weeping eyes when I'd last held him. *Why does he have to be so endearing, just when I want to be strong? He's my boss, for heaven's sake!*

Joe took a deep breath that actually puffed out his chest, then announced, "I want you to stay here. I have provided this for you, my special friend, and you may stay as long as you wish."

"I don't understand—"

"In China, it is not unusual for men to provide an apartment for the one they love. I want to visit you here and enjoy this together. I want to make you happy. You surely want to make me happy, Regina. Yes?"

This felt a little like a power play, similar to our old way of negotiating about what I would teach or how many students I would meet. Yet he knew that I cared for him. I just didn't know if it could possibly work out.

"You know that I do, but I still don't see—"

He cut me off with a rush of words: "We can have many swims like the one we had downstairs. We will share this secret hideaway. We can tell secrets like the ones I shared after the Terra Cotta Warriors. We will dine in style in every one of Sofitel's dining rooms. You are my romantic concubine. I am such a lucky man."

"Wait a minute, Joe! *Concubine?!*" That word brought me back to reality fast. *That's not part of any picture I've ever had of myself. Yet here I am, still at the mercy of my boss, who literally holds the keys to my freedom in his hand. What can I say?*

"I need to think, Joe!"

He simply continued, "You would not have gone to Harbin with me if you did not share my feelings. Didn't we have a wonderful time there?" He reached into my bag and pulled out a clear bottle. "Let's drink a toast. To us! To a heavenly future! To a love that lasts forever!"

Joe hurried to the cupboard as I stood there, my mind racing. *This man is full of surprises, no doubt about that.* I'd been more than worried when I realized I was locked inside this suite without a key. Then he'd just appeared with no thought at all to what I'd been through.

"Joe, this is all too much for me. And I've been almost frantic, unable to leave this locked room. Then you came back with my bag, having been in my apartment when I didn't expect anyone could get in there. You even went through my personal clothing. And now you lay this on me? I'm lost in feelings, Joe. My mind won't work rationally. I'm afraid I—"

"Poor Regina, you are as lost in feelings as I am. Trust me, my beauty, and in our future that lies bright and wonderful before us."

"But, Joe, you don't understand. It's not that simple. You can't just wrap it up like that in one of your cliches!"

I felt a rush of anger as I bit off any further words. Tears surfaced, and I bowed my head in an effort to regain control. "Joe, I'm too upset to talk any more now. Please go and let me think."

To my surprise, he turned without another word and left. I barely heard the lock click, as thoughts kept tumbling in my confused head: Maybe he *couldn't* put himself in my shoes for even a second, what with his Chinese upbringing so different than what I had been taught in the Midwest. I had to buy some time in which to get hold of myself. *That's about all I can do. The question is what I should focus on instead.*

To add still more frustration, my tears only increased then. I could feel my shoulders shuddering as I sobbed into my hands. *Why, oh why, did I let myself get involved with this egotist? Why did I get caught up in his schemes? This isn't me . . . or is it?*

These thoughts came quickly as I quieted down and got back into my own head, keeping my face covered more from self-embarrassment than anger.

I have to either become a great actress or face him squarely, standing solidly on my own two feet. The difficulty with acting the concubine role is how darned appealing he becomes when we're having fun. Could I really pull off such a role and not drown in my own feelings? It doesn't smack of integrity, nor how I usually see myself. The problem with standing honestly on my two feet, though, is that Joe still has both my room key and the elevator key. If I openly burst his romantic bubble, he'll probably just leave again with both keys clutched angrily in his suddenly closed hand.

I felt a strong need to talk with Mary; she'd help me get out of my own head and gain some perspective. I tried her Kunming number. No answer. Then I remembered her telling me, *"We work for them here. They can keep us or send us home."* She'd also said something about us not having rights here that brought me to feeling like she wouldn't have been any help anyway. I was truly on my own.

CHINA 70 - SHOW TIME

I held a lesson written in longhand, entitled "Passport to Travel," when I answered Joe's knock the next morning. I even wore a little blush and eye makeup. My brain felt divided though.

"Joe, good morning! Please look at this lesson. I'm excited about it. Students will be able to fly from their nest with confidence after mastering these skills. Most of the world speaks business English, as I'm sure you know."

He glanced at it. "Regina, your English handwriting is lovely, but it is hard to read."

"But I've nothing to type with here in this room. The hotel computers only use Chinese symbols, no help to English-speaking me."

"Oh, I forgot. Let me see the lesson plan." He skimmed over it. I'd drawn crude passports after every few lines. He looked up. "What a perfect idea: a practical lesson. Perhaps I'll sit in on this lecture?"

"You are welcome to, Joe. There's a problem though. I need an actual passport as an example. Mine is missing. Might you have seen it when you brought my suitcase?"

"I'll try to remember." That was all he said. I noticed his eyes stayed level, not moving up and to the left like most eyes involuntarily do when a person is trying to retrieve information. *He knew something more about that passport.*

"Well, I won't have much of a lesson without a passport. You don't have one, do you?" I asked, knowing that this was taking quite a chance. If he had also travelled outside of China, my plan might fail.

"No, Regina, I'm sorry." He cast his eyes downward. "I hope to need one in the future, but—"

"Don't worry, Joe. Although many Americans travel by air, I never flew until my school sent me to another state as part of an evaluation team." I kept prattling on, attempting to cover up my nervousness. "The only time I use my passport is when I fly out of the country or need to show identification to vote."

The charade continued. Joe had tea, while I quickly dressed to return to my old apartment. Soon, we climbed into the back seat of the waiting black sedan below. We were at the old campus in a good half-hour. Then he silently produced a key to enter my musty old apartment.

I rummaged through the closet and announced. "No passport!" I nodded toward the old computer, modem, and printer. "I'll take these to the hotel, along with some clothes."

Dashing to the bathroom, I splashed water on my forehead and eyes, then returned more slowly. "What am I to do, Joe? That perfect lesson will fall short without it."

"Regina, you must not cry. I will bring your passport on the morning you need it, for your classes to succeed. Do not fret."

"Is that a promise?" I asked. Inside, I wanted to demand that he tell me where he was keeping it, then yell at him to give me the key and get out of my life. Outwardly, I lifted a face of innocence towards him.

"I promise," he said, and I knew that he meant it.

I packed up the computer along with three outfits, the scroll painting I'd purchased from a local artist, and a few letters from home. Then I said truthfully, "It's not hard to say goodbye to this apartment, though I've got mostly good memories of this place."

He pressed my left hand between both of his. "We will make better memories in your new place."

I indicated the modem and printer then. "Right now, I need your help to get these to the hotel."

We brought everything down to the car, pushing most of it onto the middle of the back seat. "This will make finals so much easier!" I said as I settled in beside the bulky modem and patted it. Joe sat on the far side of it in the back seat, and at his signal, the driver pulled out into XiAn traffic and headed downtown.

When we arrived at the hotel, Joe handed his keys to the driver and told him to unload the car and take the stuff to my room. Then he pulled me into an empty dining room on the ground floor. "We can order all your favorite dumplings, with Tsing Tao—you'll have a little beer, won't you? We'll celebrate the semester's end and drink to our new life together."

I let myself sink into the faux leather booth, plopped my purse down on one side of me and my sweater on the other, then pointed to the seat across from me. "Sit here. So, I can see you as we talk."

Joe sat and reached for my hand. "It is so wonderful to eat with you, Regina. I've dreamed of when we could hide away from China's constant crowds. Tonight will be perfect."

Tonight? My mind raced, even as I looked deliberately into his eyes. I could feel urgency in the way he was massaging my hand, and despite my best intentions, felt our hearts beating in time with one another.

I withdrew my hand to select two clean and matching chopsticks from the glass of them on the table. "Remember when we first ate dumplings, Joe? Back when I first taught in your department? Does this remind you of old times? That day, you told me that teaching would be 'a piece of cake.' Remember?"

I wasn't sure where I was going with this but hoped to keep him talking. *Then what?* In my mind, the face of a Sichuan Opera figure fluctuated between a coquettish beauty and the fierce face of Taoist Wang—a toad—flashing back and forth.

My frantic mind got a slight reprieve as a lone waiter brought Tsing Tao and two glasses. I looked around, wondering what the rest of the day would bring.

It turned out to be another surprise. After lunch, Joe offered his arm, and said, "I'll show you something. Trust me, sweet rabbit."

Relief and curiosity both tugged me right along with him.

CHINA 71 - TURNED MASK

Joe urged me through the hotel's exit to walk toward old town, the road branching off at an opening that squeezed down a crowded alleyway. The old hutong's narrow twists and turns went off in many directions. We walked on cobblestones and broken bricks between what might have been elegant homes long ago. How many families had lived under these broken-tile roofs? There was no sign of human faces watching through the dirty, cracked windows. A scrawny cat jumped from a jagged-glass opening to a windowsill. Then it dashed away with a snarl.

"Where are we going, Joe?" *Am I repeating myself?*

"You will see, Regina. I want to show you my early home."

He kicked away crumpled plastic bags the wind had plastered against a wall beneath a grime-covered window. Another skinny cat jumped off the crumbling step Joe now stood upon as he knocked on a weathered door.

"Waipo?" he called in an unfamiliar tone that was loud but not arrogant.

I heard *"Wei?"* from inside, then shuffling footsteps. The door creaked opened to reveal a bent and white-headed creature with shining eyes, peering up at us. She wore a blue-dotted shirt and slacks that were threadbare but clean and remind me of the loose uniforms of American childcare-workers.

Joe introduced me to her in a near whisper: "This is my grandmother. My waipo raised me from a young boy."

He started speaking in rapid Chinese to the woman then; I recognized only an occasional Mandarin phrase. As the old woman listened, her face was covered in a network of wrinkles lit by some inner source, or perhaps, simply by Joe's appearance at her door. I recognized the word for foreigner and teacher, plus "Pei Hua," and my name.

She took both my hands in her weathered ones, and I felt like I'd dropped into a strange time where I could be somehow wiser and stronger than I felt that day. I relaxed and let the feeling spread, no longer bracing myself against whatever might happen next.

Joe's waipo bustled us to a worn couch, pinched tea leaves into glasses, and poured hot water from a thermos stashed under a table. She poured another water then and lifted it in both hands like an offering to Joe. She beamed up at him as I heard what seemed like a Mandarin version of gratitude from him. I also caught a word that meant "past" in their exchange.

Feeling a little uncomfortable eavesdropping on so much emotion, I looked around through the shining dust motes in the air. Mao's framed picture reigned supreme, sitting upright among dusty dishes and chipped glassware. I sat and sipped, listening to rapid-fire Chinese and gentle laughter, while I picked up enough words and gestures to know that Joe and his waipo were remembering old days together. As Joe spoke, I eventually recognized the Chinese word for "future," which I'd often heard from the lips of my students.

Abruptly, Waipo stiffened and shook a finger at him. Then she almost shouted at him, her tone strident, and as she stood and straightened stiffly, her back losing its hump, she pointed us out her open door.

I clasped my hands in *shei shei* gesture, feeling shame, even as she lifted her nose and ignored me completely.

CHINA 72 - MASKS TURN

Wordlessly, we walked several long blocks from the ancient housing of the rundown hutong toward Bell Tower Square. Joe, studying the cobblestones, remained lost in thought. No emotion showed on his face when I glanced at him. My thoughts reeled from witnessing the love that had shone from the face of Joe's waipo and the surprising way she'd later turned fierce and nearly pushed her little god out the door. I felt I was somehow connected to her behavior. *But how?*

We paused before a humble Uighur shop not far from the Old City wall. Joe pointed to two stools at a clean, bare-board table. "You must eat, Regina. I must think. This is not typical food of my country, but perhaps you will like it." Joe placed an order with a modestly dressed young woman as she delivered bottled water to our table. My mind started considering stories of suffering among Uighur Muslim minorities during Chinese government crackdowns. It didn't seem an appropriate conversation topic, so I went back to wondering about Joe's waipo's behavior.

He glanced around nervously and kept his thoughts to himself. The aroma of fresh-baked bread hung in the air, and I could see smoke from some kind of meat coming through an open curtain separating diners from a back kitchen. The sound of male laughter could be heard from those cooking there. I tried a smile. Joe didn't respond; he didn't even seem to notice.

We sat in silence for a while until I finally ventured a thought: "I think your waipo is a gentle woman, Joe. I'm wondering how it was to grow up with her."

Once he opened his mouth, Joe began pouring out his childhood for me: "My waipo is very old, born sometime in the 1920s in XiAn. She was sent to the countryside later. She had at least one of her children while working in the fields."

His left leg jiggled, and he put a hand on top of his knee to stop the movement as he kept talking in a low voice. "Farm life was hard, but she never lost belief in the benefits of education. Sending her children to school was impossible. It would mean another mouth to feed that wasn't working to grow food. All day, every day, my mother hoed the fields beside Waipo."

"You were born during that hard time, Joe?"

"I was born as things changed a little, but it was a long while until Waipo and my grandfather moved back to their old hutong house. I was told that my young mother gave me to them and left when I was a baby. We never heard where she went." He only shrugged at this, leaving me to try and process how he must have felt to have that happen to him as a child.

"Waipo sent me to school every year, and neglected schoolwork was the only thing she was ever cross about. I had to excel. I wasn't allowed to attend my grandfather's funeral because I had final exams. You see, my schooling was not on the same standard as those who could afford tutors."

He finally raised his head to look directly at me. "The year after Chairman Mao died, Deng Xiaoping reinstated *gaokao,* and if that had not happened, I would have continued on to the village secondary school, but—"

"Wait," I said. I hated to break his narrative, which was so different from what I'd expected, but I needed clarity: "Excuse my ignorance, but what does *gaokao* mean?"

"It the national higher education exam that was dropped during the Cultural Revolution. I passed it with a high score, Regina, and was given a scholarship." With that came the same look of pride that Joe had shown once before, though only briefly. That was days earlier when I had been admiring the flute player below the hotel window.

Joe continued. "I went to Hangzhou to study education as a way out of a hard life. The scholarship fed me and gave me a dorm room."

Sizzling beef kabobs arrived then. They had been a long time coming but worth the wait. So was the nan bread, which was so rare in my Chinese experience that I dug right in.

Joe's story wasn't finished. "Waipo was very proud when I graduated, but she did not have means to attend. That day was both glad and sad for me. I determined never to be too poor to realize my dreams. When I think of her sacrifice for me, I am deeply touched. Waipo still called me 'Little

Prince' today, after all these years." He lowered his eyes, and I caught a look of sadness. *Or is that shame at his neglect?*

"Joe, she seemed overjoyed to see you. How long had it been since you had seen her last?"

Joe hung his head. "I took my diploma to show Waipo at the time I became Dean of English at Pei Hua. Life was very busy for many years, and I didn't visit her—not even at festival days. I spent holidays with my students at the university. It became my life . . . until today."

"Was your waipo angry that you didn't come home? Was that why she dismissed us today?"

"No, Regina. She did not like what I told her about you."

"Please tell me. Did I do something to offend her? I didn't intend to."

His chin drooped toward the table. "No. No, Regina. It was me. I told her of my plans, and she acted very quickly."

"Your plans?"

"She called me a bad man, a willow easily swayed in the winds of Western influence. She is like a ti plant, never wavering from the boundary where it puts down roots. That is why she lives in that abandoned hutong, when I could easily move her to a modern compound." He shook his head, as if he couldn't believe it.

"But, Joe, you said you told her something about me?"

He ignored this prompting. "I had plans to surprise her today . . . to give her a modern life of comfort and make her proud of my accomplishments. She wanted none of that. To convince her, I told her of how I moved you from . . ."

I stopped listening as I took that in. *So, that's why I suddenly felt such disapproval from her.* And Joe's assumption about his power over both of us hit me then like a flash flood.

"*Your* plans, Joe? Do you *hear* yourself? You saw only through your own eyes and didn't even try to see things from her viewpoint. Or from mine."

I put down my kabob as a bitter taste rose up past my previous swallow. I faced him squarely, almost spitting now in my irritation: "It's the same thing you did to me! Supposing I'd jump at the chance to live in that hotel where you've locked me in like a prisoner!"

Joe blinked. But when he spoke again, his voice remained quiet. "A prisoner? Frankly speaking, Regina, you live like a queen in the hotel."

I pointed my kabob stick at him. "You lock me in each time you leave! Just like a prisoner!"

Outwardly, I felt calm. But inside, I could feel bile heating up, ready to start travelling upward. I clamped my mouth shut.

A look of alarm raised his eyebrows as he opened disbelieving hands towards me, but his voice was still level as he spoke again. "Regina, you were sweet to me in Hong Kong. You took care of me. And after dumplings—"

I reached out quickly and grabbed the collar of his shirt in both hands, then without thinking, I snapped at him, "Whatever made you think I wanted to be your *mistress?* I was hoping for a friendship! But you . . . you. . ." I knew I was sputtering.

"*What*, Regina? Any of those lovely students at Pei Hua would gladly have a part of what I gave you. Lili, Rose, and LiPing all adore me!"

He'd just named the girls I'd seen following him around campus. A flash of past jealousy reared its ugly head, and then ducked low again as I almost shouted at him, "Joe! I don't care if you pen up a whole *harem!* What I resent is your taking me hostage, taking advantage of me, and . . . and I simply won't stand for it anymore! You can put me out on the street, but I won't spend another night as a prisoner!"

"I never meant that you would be a prisoner."

"Then why did you lock me in? I'm going back to my freshman-campus dorm apartment. And I am going home to the US as soon as the semester's over! You can't stop me! Why, in *my* country, you'd be tried and convicted in a court of law for what you've done! You'd be put behind bars!" I knew I was shouting, but the other diners studiously ignored me as just another rude and noisy foreigner.

"Settle down, Regina. Your actions are in very bad taste."

I thought maybe I'd just show him bad taste and opened my mouth to shout some more as tears started stinging my eyes. Then the fight drained out of me, and I slumped back onto my stool, feeling suddenly deflated.

Joe laid a few yuan on the table, and we left. He offered me his arm. I ignored it. I charged ahead, not knowing which way to go. Then I resorted to just trying *not* to walk behind him in the narrow passageways. We maneuvered streets and sidewalks enroute to the hotel. The silent walk gave me time to question whether my angry outburst had blown my chances of escape. If it had, so be it. At least now he knew how I saw him: as a self-centered, pompous fool.

Inside the silent hotel elevator, Joe surprised me by handing me my room key. When we reached the top level, I got off alone, while he stayed behind in the elevator and rode it wordlessly back down.

I wondered what that had meant as I opened my own door and re-locked it from the inside, kicked off my shoes, and fell across my bed. My emotions churned until I could no longer stand. But like Scarlet O'Hara, I determined to think it all through later.

Then I promptly fell asleep.

CHINA 73 - ESCAPE PLANS

Surprisingly rested after the previous night's tirade, I arose early to sit in the sunlight, wearing my favorite Disney character PJs, and try an online search for the phone number to the American Embassy. I found the tourism speech I'd heard some time back on AeroTech's campus, almost verbatim, but no address or phone number. My embassy's contact request brought up a blank page almost immediately, with a heading that read: "This information not found." Was my search topic also taboo, just like Tibet, Taiwan, and Tiananmen?

With preparation needed for finals, I had to focus, not give into frustration, so I sat on my luxury hotel bed to organize my lesson plans for returning to classes. The "parts of speech" lesson reminded me of the note that was almost ready to be slipped to Gao during the upcoming class. Knowing the futility of any scheme that was running through my mind, a kind of grim prepositional humor played at the edge of my consciousness as I imagined him reading it: *"Dear Gao, Please help me to escape. I need to go from a hotel near the Bell Tower to get on an airplane to America, but I may be without a passport.*

This scheme would probably never work; Qian or Joe had arranged all my travel inside China. In the past, I'd trusted the tickets that were delivered by courier to my apartment door, written in Chinese, with only the numbers being recognizable to my ignorant eyes. I knew Qian would never defy Joe or the university to help me leave. And I doubted that any of my students could help either. Most of their families had sacrificed a lot to send them to Pei Hua. Even asking for Gao's help might result in his being kicked out of school, should Joe ever find out. Students who were forced to stand in drafty hallways as punishment for something as minor as being late to class clearly didn't have much in the way of individual rights.

Maybe I'd email my family on the mainland and have them purchase a return ticket for me; Pei Hua had bought my ticket to XiAn, but that could surely be bought from the mainland US as well. Then I remembered the two letters and one package I'd received in XiAn. They had all been opened, re-marked with Chinese characters, and then taped shut. One letter, dated two months earlier than its arrival, had had a corner of Mom's perfect penmanship completely torn away. I had been surprised that the package's contents themselves had gotten to me. Who knew when, or even if, a plane ticket would have any chance of reaching me in the mail?

I went back to my original plan: I could, perhaps, trust Gao if I made up some reason why I needed to go home right away, as I knew that he admired my teaching. A sick family member would suffice. I'd have to come up with a reason to obtain the ticket in secret, though, to protect him. Maybe I could use some half-truth about the university not letting me go.

My passport blocked any hopeful thought about the if's and when's of Gao possibly helping me leave though. Joe surely still had possession of it!

And what if he doesn't?

Frustration hit me like an avalanche then, even stronger than my concern when the police had held my passport, its mysterious reappearance when it was needed for my physical exam, followed by it being returned to them afterwards by Qian. She'd produced the document again for my Hong Kong and subsequent other trips. Since then, I'd kept it safely inside my roller-bag pouch. But now it was gone again.

It was just too much. Tears felt like hot asphalt burning slowly down my cheeks, forming roads that led nowhere but between the hotel room's walls. A salty taste leaked into the corner of my mouth as I howled, not caring who or what might hear me. When I got the noisy reaction out of my system, I punched one of my pillows. Then fully spent, I threw myself down and buried my wet face in the equally wet pillow and fell asleep for a while.

When I was awake again, I called room service for some comforting green-tea ice cream. I avoided checking my red eyes in a nearby mirror and just walked to the window, perhaps to rethink my idea of who might be able to help me. A group of mature women arrived down below my window again. I watched as the one I suspected was Joe's wife took her flute to a shady place. Then a dance began. Delicate fans opened, arcing high, dipping low, and snapping shut. Did these women know how lucky they were to step off a bus and just know exactly what to do in sync with others?

If only I knew more Chinese, looked more Chinese, and sounded more Chinese. . .

I sighed, knowing that I might as well wish to be able to fly out of the window and across the ocean to safety!

The flute's melody lifted my spirits just enough for me to open the window and turn my attention back to expanding my lesson plans. I picked up my pen and started to write:

"The chalk-drawn squirrel near a tree, running around, up, and over limbs, became a bird inside a cage, hitting its wings against bars."

Before I was able to underline any further absurd ideas, a knock at my door caught my attention, and I turned toward it.

"Wei?" I almost screamed this, my brain abruptly shifting away from underscoring prepositions.

"Loom service," replied an unfamiliar voice, even as a key was inserted into the lock and the door started to swing open. I thought fast and quickly started pantomiming my interest in assisting him with his cart. "I will help!" I snatched up a bowl, even as I squeezed past the cart and out into the hallway. "Good ice cream! Thank you!"

At the elevator, he fumbled with a ring of keys, keeping his foot braced against the cart. "Let me help," I said again, giving him my sunniest smile.

To my surprise, he handed me his key ring, ensuring that the elevator key was separate from the others. I inserted it to summon the elevator back up.

"To kitchen?" I asked when it arrived.

He nodded, and we started to descend. When the doors opened again, he wheeled out the cart and pointed to the "L" button. "Robby."

I nodded. "Yes, lobby." He held out his hand for the key ring, and I surrendered it as I got out as well. Holding my breath and trying to appear nonchalant, I strolled out into a group of chattering Chinese travelers and elbowed my way toward the hotel exit. No one seemed to even notice me, although I saw no other foreigners. A few more steps and I was on the wide sidewalk outside the hotel, blinking in the blinding sunlight. Where should I go?

Looking down, I discovered that I had put my feet into two different shoes when I'd dashed out with the young man. One was distinctly brown, and the other was navy. *You can't get arrested here for mismatched shoes, can you?* I also still wore my Disney-character pajama top. I'd put on slacks to eat my snack, having yet to choose a blouse, and then focused on my school planning. It had seemed like a good idea at the time.

Embarrassed, I ducked inside the shadow of the city wall. A group of European tourists listened to a guide speaking fractured French. From their outskirts, I heard *"Chang Kai Shek,"* a smattering of Chinese, and some more French words. No one paid attention to me, a slovenly dressed American.

We swarmed up some steps into a darkened house with high ceilings. Inner doorways were roped off with red rope. I realized that we were in the house where Chang Kai Shek had been held for several days during WWII. When he'd been released, he'd gone to Hong Kong to rule Kuomintang, while Mao had gone on to become China's leader. I'd wanted to visit this place for a long time, but this situation wasn't what I'd envisioned.

The group parted enough for its diminutive leader to charge outside, holding her red flag aloft. I stayed where I was, mostly ignored. The horde exited, but not before another Chinese guide barged in and began his own memorized spiel.

I heard a French *"Quel domage!"* from a man in front of me. *What a mess, indeed.* He evidently disapproved of something. The guide, and what seemed like the entire Chinese contingency, shouted forceful syllables at him. There was no mistaking their strong resentment of his comment. I was afraid fists would fly next. Feeling panicked, I backed into a high wardrobe to avoid the argument. Spotting an inside pull-string on the door, I closed it and hunkered down, my heart thumping in my chest. After several minutes, the noisy French-Chinese conflict lost its momentum.

When all was quiet, I cracked the door. Unfortunately, each time I even ventured a toe beyond the wardrobe, another group entered. It seemed like an eternity passed as I listened to mostly Chinese words beyond the wardrobe's door, punctuated by attempts at French, Spanish, and English. No one opened the door to my hiding place. My legs cramped. I stood for a while, did isometric exercises, and just contemplated what to do next.

It grew quiet again. Hearing no more voices, I stepped out of the wardrobe. I would need to find a toilet soon, but I wasn't keen on going outside the city wall to where the two-story McDonald's had one of XiAn's few sit-toilets. *Why did I ever leave my hotel room? Especially in a pajama top and mismatched shoes?*

I hurried through empty rooms but had no luck finding any plumbing. A sneeze threatened to erupt, and I knew I couldn't hold on much longer. While pinching my nose to stifle the sneeze, I wondered what Chaing Kai Chek had done for facilities. High ceilings and heavy furniture mocked me as I pondered. I'd had no plan beyond getting into the elevator. Had I just figured I'd escape to the street and some Chinese English speaker would get me a plane ticket when I didn't even have my passport? Or had I thought I could just hop a bus to leave this city of twelve-million people? I'd have even fewer English speakers in the countryside.

XiAn had no American embassy; I'd need funds, language, and help to get to the one in Beijing. Even if I were lucky enough to get beyond XiAn, and perhaps even hitch a ride as far as China's far-away borders, I knew that I wouldn't speak those languages either. To the east were ports, but getting passage on a ship would require official papers, plus finding someone who understood English.

"I might never see American soil again." My whisper echoed around the empty room. I stood still while my imagination expanded on these futile possibilities for a whole before returning to my miserable circumstances in the museum. *I might as well have stayed in my comfortable hotel room.* A distant door slam punctuated this thought, even as the room darkened around me.

Dim light slanted from dirt-streaked windows atop dusty walls. The door, entered earlier with the horde of tourists, was now locked from the outside. I was a prisoner once again—this time without a bathroom.

I carefully went from room by room, my bladder twanging with each step. In the roped-off bedroom, a slant of light hit the edge of a brocade-covered bed. A lidded china pot sat underneath it. I ducked beneath the tasseled red rope, carried the pot out of sight of the doorway, and did my business. What a relief!

Sliding the covered pot back under the narrow bed, I felt immense gratitude for having found it, along with a little chagrin. In this part of China, the smells of bodily waste were often found on streets, along paths, and in corners, but I wasn't so sure about its museums.

I pushed on past the dining room to the kitchen where I found a door. I slid the bolt, but it wouldn't budge. Perhaps there was an outside lock. Or worse, maybe someone was pushing on it from the other side. I put my ear against it.

No sound came through the heavy wood, so I threw my weight against it. Nothing happened, though it gave a little when I tried again. Finally, with a heave of my shoulder, it opened, scattering leaves, dirt, and debris in my wake. Outside, the cobblestones smelled musty. I brushed myself off and tried to assume a tourist's look as I headed back toward my hotel.

Under the afternoon sun, I figured I'd simply return to a hot shower and bed. Stepping inside the hotel, though, I saw the man behind the desk was the same one who had been there when Joe and I had first arrived. They'd nodded to each other, something I'd not seen as a problem that day—in fact, I'd probably been a little proud that my escort seemed to know the man. Since then, he'd watched over me while I exercised and swam, and I figured that he might even know that I'd been locked in and be perfectly okay with that.

The elevator was in full view of his desk. So, I knew that I would be seen if I entered it alone, but I was unsure what else to do. I inched toward it through the throng of people in the busy lobby. My thoughts continued to circle like undisciplined children in my mind. I needed to come up with a carefully laid out plan. No more going off half-dressed, waiting for life to just unfold in front of me. I waited near a group until they looked like they might eventually head towards the elevator. So far, no one looked helpful or likely to take my word that I had been trapped here in XiAn.

A woman whispered Mandarin endearments into small poodle's ear as she inserted her elevator key. I stepped in behind her, but she wheeled around and barked at me in Chinese. I lowered my head and stepped back into the lobby, hoping no one had heard her and wondering how to apologize in her language.

I sat down beneath a fake plant then, tucking my mismatched shoes beneath my chair. Then breathing as normally as possible, I waited. The desk worker paid me no mind. An hour or so went by as I pretended to drowse, though my mind was still jumping about. What had I learned from this foolhardy flight? I had gotten out of the room and down to the street, but there had been nowhere to go from there. Joe probably had my passport, which meant he controlled whether I left China. I'd been a fool to let his attention and flattery go as far as it had, but there was no use berating myself. Then realization struck: Joe was the problem. So, he would have to be the solution!

A Chinese man approached the elevator, and with his hands busy with his cellphone, he punched the elevator button with his elbow. I hurried in behind him as the door closed. He continued thumbing his phone until he exited on his floor. Left alone then, I tapped the button for the top floor, ascended, and then stepped out. My door opened, thank goodness. And no one had been in to clean.

I didn't want dinner. I hoped to just stumble through a shower and go straight to bed.

Instead, my cellphone shrilled. It was Matt. "Dr. Blakely? I'm sorry for the way I left our last call. This new job has me snowed under. Can we talk now? Seriously?"

"That's not what I heard when you last called, Matt. But I'm glad to talk, especially if you can help me. I'm stuck in a fancy hotel in downtown XiAn—"

"What? I don't follow you, Dr. Blakely."

I went on. "I managed a one-day escape that brought me right back to this penthouse prison, but even that isn't enough if I don't have my passport." I knew that I was sounding somewhat hysterical, but I couldn't help it.

"What? Where is your passport? Why don't you just ask them for it? Tell them you won't stand for this treatment and come home immediately!"

"That's what I tried to do with my boss! But *he's* the one who locked me in here! I don't know who knows what anymore! Joe hints at having friends in high places, and he's revered at the university. What if China won't let me leave?"

"You have rights, Dr. Blakely. Don't let this situation continue another minute!"

"That's how I used to feel, as an American, but I'm expendable here. I work for China, and I've no doubt that, despite how much they admire my teaching, I've got no allies who would choose to help me if their Motherland was being in any way criticized or confronted. I've even thought I might get to the embassy in Beijing for some help, but that's several day's bus ride, and it's spread out all over Beijing! I think the actual building's slated to be finished by 2008, but that doesn't help me. Hopefully, they'll have more of them in the future. Do you know if that's the case? In a country with only one time zone, it makes about as much sense as having only one American Embassy." I was laughing a bit now, but I knew that my disjointed ramblings weren't making sense to him.

"Wait, Dr. Blakely. Let's back up. Did you say Joe?" He hesitated for a moment, and his voice sounded different when he spoke again. "We don't want to make an international incident out of this. Give me a moment, please." The line was quiet for what seemed like an eternity. I managed to settle down, refocusing and waiting, even as I almost held my breath.

When he finally came back on the line, his voice was low, his words clearly confidential: "The Secretary has a lot on her plate right now. You can surely handle this yourself."

"What?" I asked, my tone rising till it was bordering on hysterical again. "Are you saying that you don't have any way to help or that you're not *willing* to help me?"

His tone was measured and level. "Neither exactly. My job is to determine that you're safe. Are you?"

"Well, that depends on what you call safe. I'm living in a nice hotel and eating good room-service food. But I don't know how or when I'll ever get to leave, let alone go home. I guess I am *physically* safe, Matt, but. . ." I felt my shoulders slump as my voice trailed off.

"That's good, Dr. Blakely. Now, *demand* that passport! Goodnight."

As he hung up the phone, one thing became abundantly clear: I couldn't depend on getting any help from him.

CHINA 74 - PATIENCE LESSONS

I threw my cell phone without even realizing it. Then I gave myself three good yells and picked it back up. It was a good thing that it hadn't broken. I'd surely need it if I was to figure out how to resolve my situation.

Still shaking from anger at Matt's response, which implied that I had been consciously abandoned by my country, I started a pot of water to boil, added twice the amount of green tea I usually used, and set it to steep. My stomach was roiling, and I didn't feel the least bit hungry. One of my mother's phrases from my childhood rang out in memory's ears: *"You have to eat something!"*

I burst into tears. Would I ever see Mom again? I'd sent her letters and cards via Qian when I'd lived on old campus. Mom didn't do email, so that was another blind alley for communication!

I looked out the window, then forced myself to consider Joe and my understanding that the flute player down below it was his wife. Could I somehow blackmail him into sending me home? No, he'd never do that under any threat. And who was I to think I could pull off a stunt like blackmail anyway?

I poured a glass of tea and sat down to consider my options: What if I lived out my days here in this luxury? Would that be so bad? I knew a few couples living in "elephant in the room" situations. Every one of them seemed to live out their roles quite happy. I'd met a few wives and even been to gatherings that the mistress attended as well. I'd even seen two such women conversing like friends. *When in XiAn, do as XiAn does?*

Who was I kidding? That wasn't how I was raised. Mom's parting remark rang in my ears again: *"Don't bring home a Chinaman!"* She had laughed, but I knew she'd been dead serious. I thought she would probably disown me if I stayed here with one.

"I'll think about Joe another time," I told myself in my Scarlet O'Hara voice, which cleared my head a little. I needed to start at the beginning: I had

278

come to China full of idealism about being the best teacher on this side of the globe. I'd gained my student's respect, won over most of Pei Hua's leaders, and raised their teaching standards. And yet here I was, considering selling out in the self-respect department. And for what? Safety?

Helplessness washed over me like a soapy blanket. I remembered that I'd been unable to even formulate a logical argument for why I felt unsafe when Matt had asked. What was wrong with me?

With my tea untouched, I laid down, exhausted, and any further thoughts on this frustrating topic vanished into sleep. Even there, though, the search for a solution continued. A faceless man dressed in dark clothing rowed a boat close to me as I bobbed up and down in the choppy waves, floating on a vast, swelling sea. I raised one hand and screamed to him, "Help!"

My own voice awakened me with a strangely muffled croak. The dream vanished. No ocean sounds remained, but flute arpeggios fluttered up past my closed window, streaming into the room on beams of sunlight. Fully awake, I moved to the window, found my actual voice, and yelled down at the flautist, "Oh, shut up!" The musician and dancers didn't even look up.

I waved them away, then furiously swished the drapes closed on the woman with the flute. How dare she be so talented? Why hadn't she kept her man interested, instead of letting herself get old and unattractive to him? Did she have family money that had boosted him to his position as dean? Why hadn't she put a stop to all those coeds following him around at Pei Hua? Then he wouldn't have presumed to charm me too.

I caught myself up short then, an ironic smile tugging at me. Who was I kidding? I was being ridiculous. If I were teaching psychology, I could probably use that last outburst as an example of classic "projection."

I pulled the drapes back. Down below, she played on. The dancers' fans opened, snapped shut, swooped down, then opened in unison. I closed the drapes again, hoping to shut out the sound as well.

"It's time to get real," I said aloud. I wasn't some lonely teenager, after all. But I knew that I had been lonely in XiAn, with no one speaking anything but very rudimentary English for a long time. And everything had been so strange and new. Then Joe had come along with his goofy grin, that lock of hair that never stayed in place, and the endearing vulnerability that appeared whenever I'd least expected it. If only we could've just remained friends, having fun in Harbin, or the same people who'd shared dreams by the China Sea. Had I somehow led him down this path we'd taken?

It was all too complicated. What had happened to the Zen-like life I'd first lived in XiAn? I'd wandered around my apartment, cooking and cleaning and just waiting for what each day might bring. I'd had no control, yet my life had been a welcome adventure. My awareness had been on high alert then, but I'd hardly ever felt any fear. What had happened to my "this or something better" touchstone, which had long helped me keep my equilibrium?

Maybe the Buddhist idea of acceptance was what was missing. I determined to let go of the arguments that kept cycling and recycling through my head. I'd get back to meditating and focus only on my breathing. I would set aside the anxiety that had worn me out so badly. Maybe that would be just another failed escape, but I crisscrossed my legs, straightened my back, and emptied my mind.

It took a while—and a lot of deep breaths—before some relief floating in on newfound relaxation, descending like a soft cloak all around me. My eyes were dripping again, but these felt like tears of release, rather than frustration. I stayed present in that moment, grateful now for the moisture on my cheeks.

When my tears finally dried, and I opened my eyes, I looked at the clock. It was lunchtime, but I still wasn't hungry. Almost euphoric now, I wandered around the room, enjoying the escape from my previously chaotic state of mind.

An insight occurred to me then: Successful teaching requires the same sort of focus as meditating. I felt a rush of gratitude for my classes then, visualizing each face I'd had the pleasure of teaching.

Quite a contrast to my recent emotional state.

CHINA 75 - ZEN ARGUMENTS

Joe didn't return for the next few days. And I fluctuated between loneliness and boredom. While I could lock and unlocked my door, the penthouse elevator stubbornly stayed closed. I passed the time doing yoga, reliving my recent travels, and reading my used novels.

The euphoria I'd managed to sink into days before had now dipped close to loathing each time my thoughts turned to Joe. Reminders of him were everywhere: a glass he'd used sat on the counter; the outside sound of fans snapping open in time to the trilling of a flute. . . Even the locked elevator seemed to mock me. Joe had promised to give me my passport when he escorted me back to Pei Hua to begin finals. *We'll see!*

I knew that I had to concentrate for the sake of my students. So, I quit gritting my teeth, re-crossed my legs Indian style, focused on my breathing, and relaxed to see what surreal thoughts might come to me next.

Feeling a little foolish, I opened my eyes. I also felt excited about the Zen planning I'd been doing for the upcoming finals. I jotted down three characters: a boss, a teenager, and a parent. Then three places appeared behind my half-closed eyes: a jail, the China Sea, and a hotel. I made note of them on the page before me. Then three activities came to mind to flesh out the assignment: arguing; becoming acquainted; and eating together. I'd give twosomes a half hour to pull from each category and plan a five-minute skit. If the class evaluated those skits, examinees wouldn't be able to memorize what to say ahead of time.

Hey, this is fun!

I'd managed to avoid thoughts of Joe for an entire hour. Finally, I called room service and ordered ox-tail soup and watermelon juice.

Getting back to my preparations for finals, I decided we would review skills and grade on a three-tiered scale. Surely the class could come up with a list of elements to score, like pronunciation, grammar, originality, questioning, tone of voice, and vocabulary.

The afternoon passed quickly, and I ordered up a fish dinner to celebrate my return to equilibrium. Afterwards, as darkness fell outside, I had a fragrant soak in the tub. My earlier anxiety pretty much whirled down the drain, and I felt a new softness as I applied lotion and dressed for bed. Finally, I lay down, turned on my side, folded my hands together beneath my head, and quickly fell asleep.

A vivid dream came to me then: A dusty Han Dynasty opera stage opened up in front of me. I arose from a chair, ducked behind a curtain, and reappeared to crouch atop a tall chest. A brocade costume flowed around me as I sprang down from it, my demon mask glowering at the audience. With a flourish, I turned my back on them and kept turning until I faced them again, now wearing a smiling mask depicting one of China's four beauties. A man sing-song voice reached out, and I whirled again.

My demon mask came back up. And then the man leapt away and beckoned to me from across the stage. I wailed a nonmelodic sound, then ducked my head shyly as the beauty reappeared with my next twirl.

As the next morning dawned, the same wailing notes, played on *pipa* instruments, filled my room. I tried journaling then, hoping to relate meaning to the dream, just as Karl Jung might have done. I thought of the man, the tall chest, and the masks, but no rational insights about them came to me. They'd probably just been some sort of a brain fart!

I called room service for some congee and coffee, which was delivered quickly and cleared away afterwards with the return of the same hotel worker. Seizing the moment, I turned to the man. "Exercise room?"

He beamed at me and nodded, leading me out to the elevator. Inside, after he'd used his key to open it, I felt a panicked need to escape again, but I just breathed deeply till it passed. When we reached the gym, the hotel worker sat down on a bench outside of it, with my dirty dishes beside him, as I started lifting weights and did my best to ignore a captive situation that would never have been tolerated in my own country.

Later, pedaling the stationary bike for all I was worth, I worked out how I might use the school finals and related activities effectively in an imaginary argument with Joe about my passport. He was my boss after all. I got as far as setting it during a meal, steering clear of anything to do with us getting better acquainted.

That's what started this ridiculous romantic farce in the first place!

I reworked the imagined scene until I was ready. I knew what I would do. Signaling to my dozing sentinel, still on the bench outside the gym, I watched as he stood up and moved to the elevator again. Using his key, he brought the elevator to us, accompanied me back upstairs, and then walked me back to my room.

"Zai jian!" he said then, which I believed meant *"See you later,"* and headed back downstairs in the elevator.

Back in my room, I took a deep breath. "Stay calm, Regina," I said out loud. "Focus." I had work to do. I tunneled my attention back toward helping my students to show what they had actually *learned*, not just memorized. That would tell me if I'd taught them well.

The rest of the day passed into dusk outside my window before I even realized it.

I planned my evening carefully, put the teapot on to boil, poured Dove chocolates into a bowl, turned my phone off, and cleared the apartment of the cluttered lesson plans. I promised myself, once more, that I would fully think through my feelings about Joe, at last, and follow through on whatever conclusions I reached.

I unwrapped a Dove logo from the heart-shaped candy and savored the sweet comfort of real milk chocolate, another perk of this fancy hotel. Since coming to China, I'd had only mouthfuls of something that tasted sort of like cocoa powder laced with cardboard. With a deep sigh of appreciation, my sweetened tongue started speaking out loud as I began a dialog with myself, hoping that, perhaps, the spoken words reaching my own ears would reveal things I'd missed when only thinking similar dialogue.

"Well, here goes," I began, my voice loud and firm.

"I'm listening," said my other half, answering the first in what felt like some kind of in-house contract.

"First the facts: You and Joe are from different sides of the earth. That means different cultures, different values, and different expectations. Joe told you early on that he was married, using the old cliche that he and his wife had 'little in common.' To be fair, that was early on when he was still riding along on the backs of such clichés. His English was pretty much only surface stuff. His wife is supposed to be a famous flute player, and he must enjoy elevated status because of that. He's avoided talking about her ever since then, and you've only halfheartedly brought her up. It probably *is* her that plays below your window every morning."

"Fair enough," said my other side. "But I *have* brought her up. A little."

"Okay, you've danced around his other life. You noticed how the young lovelies flocked around him. You felt smug when he dismissed them that day when you met upstairs on the old campus, and when it seemed that he'd cleared out the education office just to talk with you. You're jealous of their youth and beauty, aren't you?"

"Guilty as charged. My students would say 'jealousy keeps me from seeing the sun on water.' Yes, a part of me blames those girls for their hero worship, and the ease with which they look so darned delectable."

"Okay, well, you know that you're nearer to his age than to theirs. You know that's not what the competition is about. You're lonely. Sort that out."

"Again, bingo! If that good-looking artist on the bus had turned up and gotten someone to translate for him, telling me he'd like to take me to dinner, I'd have gone in a New York minute! Excuse me. A MingDong minute! If I'm simply an isolated, lonely American, I have to rid myself completely of any infatuation with Joe."

There. I'd said it: Infatuation!

"But what do I *actually* feel when I'm with him?" I asked aloud. I recalled the tingle I felt whenever he took my hand. And the thrill I got when he looked at me with those warm puppy eyes of his. But whenever he'd started to make a declaration of his feelings, I had cut him off.

My inner voice was beginning to sound like Tevya, from *Fiddler on the Roof,* wondering why I always cut Joe off. No answer came to me though.

"And another thing," I said to myself, "I wasn't raised to interfere with someone's marriage. It's wrong, wrong, wrong. I had a good marriage once, and for several years, I even thought it was deepening and broadening us both. Then after a while, it began feeling more like cracked earth, quickly becoming a chasm as the years went by." I sighed. "I don't see growing old with Joe, even if the other obstacles went away."

"He has been trying," pointed out my other half, "with the whole *Men are From Mars* thing, giving up his insufferable clichés, listening when we discuss things. . ."

The devil on my shoulder came right back with an answer to that: "That's only to impress you. What's in it for him?"

"I could ask him," I replied. "I guess. I know he admires me, has feelings for me, and wants more."

Do I have to decide right now?

I wasn't sure that I was clear enough in my own mind to have a real heart-to-heart should he suggest we move into some next level that might be acceptable to me. Was I strong enough to resist him? Maybe if I focused on his stubborn inability to see beyond his own viewpoint and the way he often jumped to conclusions . . . and ignore the rakish angle of that piece of hair falling towards his eyes.

"Be careful, Regina," I said then. "You're losing perspective. What's really important to you? Maybe you're just feeling a wee bit horny in these menopausal years, and you've mixed up the Chinese adventure with a personal one?"

I sighed again, then nodded firmly. "You might be right. I guess it could simply be a physical reaction. If so, that could be fun—or it could be if it wasn't so likely that the sweet secret would come out eventually. A lot of people would get hurt if it reached their ears: his wife, my mom . . . my kids! Maybe my entire community back in the States. I can't imagine Joe joining me at a lecture at Kansas University, or Montana State, assuming he would even consider getting a passport or leaving China. He'd certainly get an interesting welcome from my Delta Kappa Gamma chapter. Those bombastic statements of his would make those teachers smile for sure."

One side of me chuckled. "Wow, Regina. That was quite a ride, from a secret overseas affair to imagining him in your own American school circles!"

I nodded. "Yes. I think I see things more clearly now. For a while, it was 'through a glass darkly,' to borrow a Christian phrase. Conscience will out though. Both nature and nurture are pointing me to say goodbye to Mr. Joe and keep it professional. And I'm ready to do just that!"

The chocolate dish was empty now, and as I got ready for bed, so was my heart. I had some mango juice sent up to sip while I sat in plum-blossom bubble bath. Warm water enveloped me, washing away any further doubts that the next day would go well.

Another dream slipped into my half-consciousness then. A robotic dinosaur was munching on huge ferns, its movements in perfect sync with others, eating the same flora, stretching as far as the eye could see. A curly-haired puppy scampered up along one of the dinosaur's legs until it reached the mechanical creature's neck and clung to it there, even as the dino's head rotated to check the surrounding landscape. The puppy opened its mouth to bark, but what emerged was a loud "Meow." The puppy grew a long feline tail and whiskers, even as my hand dropped from the tub's edge, smacked the bath water, and awakened me fully.

"What in the world does *that* mean?" I shouted. No answer came. So, I dried off, slipped beneath my duvet, and went properly to sleep.

CHINA 76 - ACT I

As he'd said he would, Joe knocked at my door at seven on the morning school resumed. I lock-stepped in silence as he escorted me to the bus. What was there left to say? He scooted into the seat next to me and held out a manila envelope with a quick, sly look. I touched the stiff rectangle inside and felt heat rise to my cheeks. *It's been a long wait . . . to be reunited with this.* I peeked inside.

Sure enough, my passport was just as I'd last seen it—bad picture, visa stamps, and all. I put enthusiasm into my voice. "Now I can have a top-notch lesson today!"

Joe nearly glowed but looked straight ahead, nodding hello to chattering teachers boarding the bus. He became Dr. Zhou again. I clasped my passport tightly as we zoomed across XiAn to Pei Hua's outer campus. Our bus passed under a new three-story archway of pink and red balloons, framing the education building, probably erected in honor of visiting dignitaries from the Party. It was accreditation time, I remembered, as I walked on newly dried cement sidewalks to the entrance and up to my room. I slipped the passport deep into my pocket. As I moved to drop its envelope into a trashcan, I felt a small remaining heft and fished out a key, pocketing it as well and hurrying to class. *Could this be the elevator key? Was it included intentionally or accidentally on Joe's part? I guess I'll find out later.*

My mini-lecture, with a passport hand-drawn on the chalkboard, took fifteen minutes. My actual passport stayed securely in my pocket. Joe never appeared to watch my lesson, and I slipped Gao my prepositions note sans underscores, adding my phone number, and saying, "This is for you only. Please keep it confidential. Call me."

The students gave extra pre-finals attention. Spoken English classes liked the idea of having choices and presenting with a partner, but most faces showed panic at being given only a half-hour to prepare. Then I gave my speech: "You already have an 'A' for coming to class and practicing English; the only way to lose it is to not show up or to not speak up at finals."

The pre-finals' first duo drew "boss + seaside + argument" and withdrew to plan their skit. I passed out an evaluation form and explained how to assign marks to vocabulary, grammar errors, etc. We had a lively time watching a construction boss berate a laborer, while building a grand villa on a beach. It brought out the natural ham in both students, and they kept a tight rein on verb tense. The laborer finally stood up for himself and quit. Both students knew they'd done well and took a bow to much applause.

As afternoon Written English class concluded, I assigned partners a review dialogue to write together. Inwardly, I thought that partnering would cut my grading in half. "I'll use the same scoring guide you have for evaluation; then I'll adjust individual grades for participation."

Then I double-timed to the teacher's bus, anticipating a solitary dinner and a good night's sleep, with no work needing attention until I turned in grades. Joe ignored me and walked toward a back seat. I exited the bus downtown. Alone.

Once inside my room, I kicked off my shoes, sealed my passport in a plastic bag, and placed it on top of the ice-cube trays in the freezer. I jumped at the sound of my cellphone ringing. I presumed it was either Joe or Matt, and I didn't feel like talking with either of them. The insistent rings wore me down though, so I snatched it up. "Hello. Matt?"

"Yes, it's me. Have you gotten your passport yet? I've been worried."

"No thanks to you, Matt, but I have it." *That was a little hostile, but I'm sick of him.*

"Dr. Blakely, please listen. I'm going to share some things I'm not sure I'm cleared to share, but I feel responsible for you. And I worry about you."

"Go on." *Do I have the time and patience for this? Whatever this is?*

"It's about your Dr. Zhou."

"What about him? And what do you mean by *my* Dr. Zhou?"

"Well, I want to let you know that we've been in touch with him since before you traveled to China. Or rather, he's been in touch with us. He's shared a lot of crackpot schemes with the person who worked in the last Secretary's office before me. Things like suggesting places in Shanghai that could host worldwide banking conferences, or—get this—hinting at gene insertion to control cat populations wherever they interfere with American tourism."

"Was one of those schemes a kind of point system tied to an American neighborhood watch?" I asked, half-joking and half-remembering Joe's seriousness when he'd run that one by me.

"Exactly so! The office laughed about how voters would take to a Big Brother tactic like that." He chuckled. "Oh! Zhou did have one suggestion about non-dairy products that we leaked to manufacturers though, and it seems to have caught hold! Oatica Soy, promoted by a cartoon guy named Oata, may be appearing on grocery shelves soon."

"And I'm guessing Oata wears a pink shirt. Go on, Matt."

"Anyway, Zhou's wild advice appeared harmless enough. So, he seemed the perfect person to keep an eye on the safety of a teacher who had chosen to help the Secretary of State relate to Chinese cultural practices. For a while, I was afraid you were going to blow us off, Dr. B."

Matt's old familiar tone was back, along with his term of endearment for me. I almost smiled.

"And how *was* I picked, Matt?"

He gave a short laugh. "Very scientifically, Dr. B. We had a list of people doing ESL all over China. Somebody put their finger on the list randomly and landed on your name; you turned out to be a lucky find: observant, curious, articulate…"

"Flattery won't convince me. I want answers, Matt. Why did you think you needed Joe to keep an eye on me? Surely you didn't doubt my allegiance to my country when I came to teach?"

"No, it wasn't that. I think Homeland Security and the Secretary's office seriously wanted to make a good impression and avoid offending Chinese diplomats. I told you that truth when I first called. Also, we felt you'd be safe if Joe was keeping an eye on you. Then after you got to travel so much, Zhou's schemes stopped, and so did his sporadic reports about you; he'd just say that you were safe, busy with classes . . . that kind of thing. We got suspicious. Now we suspect he was also feeding his own government anything he could glean from talking with us—or just making up reports for them. What we don't know is why his reports stopped."

Joe as a double agent? Preposterous! Or is it? This is China, after all.

"Matt, can you tell me the date the reports stopped?"

His answer was the exact day Joe had moved me into the penthouse. That confirmed it for me.

Then Matt cleared his throat. "I've tried to give you the entire picture now, Dr. Blakely."

"And?" It all fell into place then. *Joe might've arranged all that travel to give me a broader picture of China, and he must've had my future in his mind a long time before I knew what he was thinking. On our Hong Kong trip. I remember briefly wondering how Matt had called my new cell phone so quickly. But Joe saw the new number and stepped away. Hmmm…*

"Matt, you either have nothing to worry about, or you'll have to send someone to rescue me here. I've nothing more for you now.

With that, I hung up the phone and poured myself some green tea with a steady hand. Conundrums tumbled over each other in my mind until the brew cooled just enough to settle and clear.

CHINA 77 - PLANS PROGRESS

When the bus stopped near the hotel two teaching days later, I scooted out, gave a small wave toward Joe in the back window, and dashed inside to use my two keys—for both the elevator and my door. I pulled on sweatpants and a tee and headed back out, making sure I locked my door behind me. The elevator key worked beautifully, also opening the exercise-room doors. I was pedaling like mad against the electronic "uphill" setting when I saw movement through the glass door. Gao, Lucy, and Willow peered in with wide eyes.

I wiped an arm across my sweaty forehead, as I stepped off the stationary bike. "What a surprise! How did you find me?"

They didn't seem taken aback by my directness. The girls' words tumbled past each other, almost in unison. "Gao said you wrote a note and needed help. Perhaps you are lonely?"

Gao inserted, "I think you could not stand Pei Hua's humble apartment and needed more grand surroundings. This is certainly grand!"

What could I say to them without demeaning their school, their dean, or their country? If I said it was a gift, their insatiable curiosity would want to know who'd given it to me.

"My Pei Hua apartment was quite comfortable. Remember our Christmas party there? I can tell you the story later. Let's go upstairs for some tea, and you can see my temporary room."

We trooped toward the elevator, with me inwardly hoping they could help me to obtain an airline ticket home. Down the upper hallway at my door, a figure in Bermuda shorts and t-shirt leaned away from us, his forehead against the woodwork. It took a moment for them to realize it was Joe. My mind wheeled twice before I decided to relax and see where this went.

The trio stood straighter and chorused, "Good morning, Dr. Zhou."

Joe straightened. "Gao? Lucy? Willow? Good morning." He turned to me. "What is the meaning of this?"

"I had a nice surprise while exercising, Dr. Zhou. Three of my best students came to visit."

Joe's jaw fell several centimeters. "I . . . ah . . . perhaps you had questions of Dr. Blakely about your final exam?"

No, but I have questions about why and how the elevator key got into that envelope. Not that I'm not grateful.

We were all suddenly silent. I busied myself with heating water and putting tea leaves into five glasses. I knew the students would prefer those to Western-style cups. I put on my widest smile. "No questions! I'm sure they are well prepared for Spoken and Written English exams. Dr. Zhou, how surprising to see *you* at this hotel! It is a beautiful, unusual place to visit, isn't it?"

Joe's jaw dropped farther toward the camera around his neck. He drew himself up toward dignity. "It is indeed. There is some Pei Hua business I came to dis—"

"Dr. Zhou," I said, cutting him off, "let us remember that this is the week of finals. Pei Hua students are determining their academic futures. No need for business discussions."

I opened the drapes and windows. "Let's enjoy the flute music while we drink tea. Willow, Lucy, Gao, please watch the fan dancers. They harmonize their actions beautifully with the talented flute player's notes. No need to talk. Let's enjoy it."

Joe sat and watched tea leaves drift toward the bottom of his hot glass, held precisely between two fingers and thumb. I joined the students at the sunlit window.

We sipped. Willow finished first and whispered, "May I use your washroom?"

I pointed her to it, knowing its gleaming fixtures would be a sharp contrast to the dim, smelly WCs on campus. I willed myself to relax, feeling like a director on a movie set without a script. Gao and Lucy, with eyes directed toward the graceful dance below, moved their heads in unison to the music. Joe, with eyes wide, looked like a scared rabbit. A few minutes later, Willow returned with shining eyes.

"Dr. Blakely, this is like heaven!"

"Mmm." I motioned her back toward the window. We sat while Lucy excused herself to use my heaven annex. When she returned, Gao quietly headed in that direction. I knew that he would compare it with the brick-sided outhouse where we'd taken turns in his village. He came back shaking his head. I looked at Joe, tilting my own head to indicate that it was his turn. Horror filled his eyes for a moment; then he grabbed up his jacket.

"You will excuse me, students, Dr. Blakely. I must be going." Then he fled.

If the students had questions about the dean's behavior, they didn't express them. They just walked about, fingering my coffee maker, exclaiming over the small refrigerator's contents, and testing the softness of my bed. "This is how you live in America, Dr. Blakely?"

"Some people do."

My teacher mode completely left me then, and I felt an urgent need to focus on getting home. "May I tell you the reason why I wrote Gao that note? I must go back to my home immediately after finals. Can you help me get an airline reservation?"

Their words competed with one another: "Why do you need to leave? When will you return? We will miss you!" I pressed on, knowing that this next part needed to be handled delicately. I could not cast shadows on the institution their parents saw as their ticket to a happy life. "It is a family matter. Can you help me get a ticket?"

They looked blankly at each other. Then Gao stepped forward. "I have never flown on an airplane. Neither has Lucy or Willow. We can get you a train ticket; we know that procedure well."

The girls began crying. "We don't want you to leave. You are like a granny to us."

Gao stood. His face looked helpless. I found myself reassuring them that I'd keep in touch with emails, that they would see me again, and that I might not even go at all. "I will see you at new campus. If you three can pretend this never happened, I promise to email you each and explain what happens next. But if you upset the other students by talking about it, I will lose my special relationship with each of you. Promise?"

I knew it was a stretch, but I needed their secrecy. I hugged each of them, obtaining their promises, and walked them down the hall to the elevator.

So much for thinking that my brightest students could help with translation; these were inexperienced kids, and now I'd caused them to lose face by revealing their lack of experience, not to mention showing off my expensive bathroom. I felt wretched for a moment, and trapped once again, even with the keys in my possession.

I mapped out a new strategy: three days on buses to the train station, then the train to Beijing. I might be able to maneuver that ticket-buying myself. Perhaps a Beijing English-speaking taxi driver would recognize "United States Embassy," and it would even be open for help. That was lots of "ifs." The Tourism student's account of China's only American Embassy, scattered around and among Beijing's millions of buildings, echoed as clearly as when he'd first given it at AeroTech months ago. Finding the right Embassy office would be like hunting for a needle in a foreign haystack. I recalled that he'd mentioned a four-year building program, as well as plans for embassies in Shanghai and Wuhan. That did me no good.

Some miracle might produce a ticket at XiAn's airport, but who was I kidding? With it written all in Chinese, I'd probably end up in another country altogether. In the US, Missoula sounded and was spelled much like Missouri. Montana was the name for countless mountains. I'd never get home. Finding the embassy, or getting my own ticket, were both longshots that seemed likely to miss completely. I emptied tea glasses, the only productive thing I could think of to do at that point. Then a knock turned me back toward the door.

It was Lucy, almost whispering immediately, "I want to share a secret, Dr. Regina. Willow doesn't know. Neither does Gao. Only you."

She used my first name in the same way that Western students did when they wanted familiarity in English.

"What is it, Lucy?"

"I may get to fly soon." Her face lit up. "I have acceptance at a university in Canada. I am waiting for passport and visa to study there for an advanced degree. If you go to United States, we will be in sister countries!"

"Lucy, that's wonderful news for you! When might you begin in Canada?"

"My parents have approved, and we're saving for a plane ticket. My papers can take up to two years. If you continue to teach here until I get them, I can surely help you obtain a ticket."

I hugged her. "You are generous and thoughtful. I will keep your secret until you are ready to share it. I'm very proud of you, Lucy."

She tiptoed out, saying, "Especially, don't tell Willow or Gao. I could lose my chance for Canada."

I wasn't the only one wanting confidences kept. Communist communities must have as many secrets moving around their circles as Washington. And the reasons were probably the same: wielding power or increasing revenue. I turned back to rinsing the tea glasses. I knew I had exhausted my hope—maybe three hopes—the minute my students had walked out the door.

My cell phone vibrated, and I answered it. *"Wei?"*

"Dr. Blakely, it's Matt. I've tried three times to reach you to see if you were okay."

"Oh? I must have turned my ringer off while exercising, I guess." I might as well take the plunge immediately. "My ticket plan didn't work out. Have you any news of how I might get home?"

"Um, not exactly, but I do want you back here. Are you okay?"

"Then arrange a ticket for me! And I'm okay, just not—"

"That's a relief!" He did sound relieved. "As for the ticket, that's a delicate matter."

"But *why?* You have *nothing* for me?"

"We look forward to your coming home and thank you for the support you provided while in China."

"And I look forward to the next election, Matt, providing I ever get home."

I clicked off then, not caring how much anger he might have heard in my voice.

He called back, but I ignored it.

CHINA 78 - PREMIER PERFORMANCE

It was up to me. There was no rescue in sight. Was I up to it? I prepared carefully for Joe's return. He knocked at dinnertime. "We go for dinner, Regina." I followed him, using my keys, to the dining room. Dumplings arrived. I mixed soy sauce and chopped garlic with vinegar, dipped steaming half-shells into it, and popped them into my mouth. I quickly retrieved the too-hot ones with chopsticks and nibbled on their translucent edges. It was most unladylike, but Joe just laughed. He flourished a pork morsel that was escaping his dumpling. Then his chopsticks lifted to my mouth. "Taste! Delicious! And not too hot."

I swallowed it, although any appetite I'd had was gone. The next several times Joe tried to feed me, I turned toward the picture on the wall just in time to avoid the bite while I chattered away about nothing in particular. He wasn't listening anyway.

"Regina, you are not honoring Chinese custom of showing great respect by offering food that you would like to eat. I honor you." *Is he lecturing me?*

I countered with a mild tone: "I'm still getting comfortable with this, Joe. I grew up with a cup in both my baby hands and setting the family table with silverware. No one eats from another's utensils. My mother told us that caused diseases. My favorite breakfast was scrambled eggs, bacon, and a biscuit on my own plate."

"How curious. You didn't know about the body needing sweet, sour, heat, and coolness to keep in balance?"

No, and this time you won't pull me in simply by crowing wisdom from the Motherland!

He was off on a lecture about Chinese medicine, punctuated by drinks of Tsing Tao. I only had to nod occasionally, while replenishing his glass, and managed to eat one beef-and-onion dumpling.

"Waiter! Bring your best dumplings this time!" I found myself close to shouting. "And another Tsing Tao!"

My glass was still at the three-quarters mark, but Joe's was as empty as the bottle the waiter retrieved and replaced. A half-plan formed in my mind, now that Joe's eyes shone with drink instead of adoration—or so I hoped, at least.

He worked his way through the steaming platter, and a third bottle, from which I'd dutifully poured. Thin sliced triangles of watermelon arrived. I reached across and fed Joe the first bite from my fingers. He beamed and tried to do the same for me. He missed my mouth and smeared juice on my cheek. I laughed, but he roared.

Joe leaned on me as we walked to the elevator. "Sorry . . . can't find the key," he mumbled. I dug into my pocket for mine, then summoned the elevator. Upstairs, we wove our way down the hallway, and I opened my door with my other key.

Joe stumbled to the bed. "Think I'll sleep just a little. . ." And then he was out.

I sat in the big chair, wondering if I might simply escape again. I could lock him in and run, but to where? I had plenty of yuan for cabs and bus rides all the way to Beijing. I might even have enough language to explain myself if I found the US Embassy, if it was open, and if it would help me. *Again, lots of ifs!*

Then again, I didn't even know if the US Ambassador would be there. And who was it anyway? I put my Pei Hua teaching badge and a change of clothing, plus the rest of my yuan, into a shopping bag, quietly retrieved my passport from the freezer, and tiptoed toward the door.

Joe stirred, groaned, and turned in my direction. "Sweet rabbit?"

"I'm here," I whispered.

He opened his eyes. "You are not tired? Come to bed, dear Regina." He flung one arm toward the vacant side of the mattress, still covered with its spread.

"I'll just slip into something else that doesn't smell like soy sauce."

He chuckled with his eyes closed. "I'll wait here."

In the bathroom, I saw only my silk peignoir set, where it had occupied the same hook since my initial visit to the hotel prison-room. My smelly pajama top, soiled from my day in Chang Kai Chek's quarters, lay under the sink.

I ran a bath and climbed in. It would have felt heavenly, except for the dreaded uncertainty of what might come next. I took my time.

"Regina?" Joe's voice came through the bathroom door.

"I'm just putting some bubbles in a bath before bed, Joe."

"Good idea. . ." drifted through the keyhole.

No further sound came. Eventually, I dried my hair with a towel and finally put on the peach gown. I tied it close to cover as much skin as I could. Then I slowly opened the bathroom door. Joe snored in the same arm-out position as he'd been in when I'd left the room.

It looked like I had nothing to fear the rest of the night. I turned off the lights and curled up in the big chair. At around midnight, a thought formed, and I got up and leaned across the empty side of the bed.

"Joe, wake up. I think I heard something outside near the moat!"

"What? Uh. . ." He muttered something I couldn't understand, then opened his eyes.

"Are you awake enough to check on a noise down there?" I pointed toward the window. "It sounds like the place where your wife plays flute."

He sat up. "What time is it? Oh! I must go!" He stumbled upright.

"I will see you tomorrow," I said. "Midmorning, okay?" I kissed his drunken cheek then and helped him out my door and into the elevator, noting that he had one hand pressed against his forehead. As soon as the elevator descended, I hurried to my room, turned back the bedspread and climbed in on my unrumpled side.

CHINA 79 - CONUNDRUM UNRAVELS

Up at first birdsong and carefully dressed for whatever this non-teaching day might bring, I made up my mind while working through past events. There were a few personal givens that I just couldn't abandon, like "Do no harm," which had felt thorny after I'd slept. And yet, I felt ready when Joe arrived.

I held the door firmly open and nodded toward the elevator, calling on my Leo self. "Good morning! May I treat you to breakfast in the room overlooking the hutong roofs?"

His familiar smile lit up his face. "Dining room 8, where we first dined at Sofitel!"

We filled our plates in a crowded buffet room. I picked up a full pot of tea, exited the room, and then led him over to a corner table where we'd dined without interruption a little over a week earlier. We up-righted two chairs while the others kept sentinel on the empty Room 8 with their legs in the air. Joe looked around as though it was the Taj Mahal. *I'll put my questions on hold and move directly to the performance. But can I do this?*

I watched him crack a boiled egg. There was no sign of last night's condition in his appetite.

"May we speak frankly, Joe? I've much on my mind. Much I need to say."

We locked eyes as performance adrenalin ramped its way up my spine. "Joe, I'm thinking of your generosity in all you've done for me in China. I'd never have seen Hong Kong, Tibet, or Harbin without your efforts. You made China fun. I care very much for you, Joe. Because of that, I'm thinking of how my mother might greet you in my country. Also my children, and what they will ask when you come home with me?"

There. Bombshell dropped.

His reply came immediately: "When I come home with you? Do you make a joke?"

I continued on, ignoring his question. "Oh, my family will find your personality so charming! We'll tell them of your becoming dean from very poor beginnings. My people love those stories. It's called 'pulling yourself up by your bootstraps,' something admired by most Americans."

My cliché had turned his sails into the wind. "Uh, Regina, I've heard that it's easy to make a good life in America. Are you saying I could come with you?"

"Dear Joe, of course you could! You know how important traveling home is in your country at your festival times. Well, our national day, Fourth of July, would make for the *perfect* time for you to meet my family!" I was intentionally gushing now.

"What about just staying here as we are now?"

"Oh, dear Joe, I simply must join my family for our national day. You, a capable man, surely can arrange a trip with me. My family ties are about to break without them ever knowing you!"

He hesitated. "I did not know family meant so much to you, Regina."

"Family ties don't break easily, Joe. Where I was born, I heard 'God, then family, then country' quoted often."

I could almost read his thoughts, working out that motto in his CommUnist country of Tao/Dao/Buddhist/Chinese-sanctioned Christianity. I pressed onward.

"I must also tell you this: In the US, most couples make an agreement before they enter a relationship—in fact, my family would insist upon it. It covers what happens to land, property, retirement funds, and keepsakes should the marriage not last. My family expects that I will come home soon, and they suspect I may not come alone. Mother, our family waipo, said something about that before she told me goodbye. She is near your waipo's age. I must see her. I do not wish to disappoint her as you did your waipo."

I let that thought jell in silence for a bit.

Joe abandoned his second cup of tea and bun. "I understand that you must return to see family. I now know the strength of that wish. You need help to achieve that dream?"

The initial performance had been fairly easy, but could I continue it? After taking a big breath, I led Joe on an imagined trip to California, where we'd arrive a calendar day before we left XiAn, thanks to the time difference. We could rent a car and maneuver six-lane traffic to have dinner with my son's family. There was no need for our bicycle skills there. After a two-day drive to Montana, we'd see my brother's barns and ride horses through mountains to make sure bears hadn't broken into my empty cabin. I hoped we wouldn't need the gun we'd take along, as I stressed that bears were a natural part of mountain life.

"We'd fly to Kansas then, where my mother lives. My daughter's family could meet us there. We'd use the family silverware for a reunion meal; you could show them how to use chopsticks, but I doubt they'll learn very well."

"Regina, how far is your nation's capital from Kansas?"

"Washington D.C.?" *Hasn't he been listening?* "Why do you ask?"

"We would have to get permission to go so many places."

"Not at all, Joe. Travel just takes money and reservations, gas or tickets, and preplanning."

He looked at me, speechless. I started gaining momentum, feeling a little breathless as my words tripped along. "My family is not big, Joe, but we have teachers, farmers, morticians, lawyers, doctors, and military folks. Those proud people will ask many questions about your wife, your job, and your plans with me. Are you able to answer them?"

Joe's eyes looked like the scared rabbit I knew myself to be, rather than the crowing rooster of his year sign. He backed up his chair, its legs scraping (loudly) across the floor twice. Then he spoke as he rose to his feet. "Regina, I must consider some things I may not have understood. I must go. Now."

His jacket stayed on his chair like an abandoned feather cloak as he strode purposefully away. I calmly wiped my mouth free of congee, knowing that rabbits, though usually seen as timid, will stand their ground when such was needed. My "Hurry back!" caught up to his retreating back but did not slow him down.

As though at the end of a stage performance, I looked around for someone to give me my standing ovation. My cellphone shrilled instead. It was Matt, and he expressed his usual concern without presenting any solutions.

"I'm working on my return, Matt!" I said, then hung up before he could ask me how.

CHINA 80 - FINAL EXAMINATIONS

Finals—plus a few last-minute cram sessions I offered anxious students who wished additional practice in either speaking or writing English—took up all my attention for the rest of the week. Cram sessions were easy: Students chose fictitious characters and a problem to discuss in either twosomes or threesomes. Among the most memorable were *"Dr. Blakely, wishing to obtain an American catfish from a market vendor, who only knows present-tense English,"* and *"Ya Min, bargaining with a stubborn China Air attendant for more head room above an aisle seat."*

When word got out about these optional oral practice sessions, there was standing room only. I thrust evaluation rubrics into the hands of those who looked on and was able to waive several final exams as exemplary performances were thoughtfully scored and handed back to me.

Written English was even more enjoyable; I gave them the evaluation rubric to apply to various essay starters:

"I find myself *lonely* when____."

"I have responded to *loneliness* by ____."

"Here is what I will tell a friend who expresses *loneliness*_____."

Each new class found a different feeling on the board: *"happy/happiness, fearful/fear"* and *"disappointed/disappointment."* Those who recognized and changed the tenses, and scored above 50 percent on the rubrics, also got to waive their finals. Mostly, I sat back and enjoyed the fruits of my efforts with these creative students.

Finals found me occasionally filling in when an expected Spoken English partner did not appear. Students who had already aced their in-class performances, like Gao and Lucy, came anyway to watch. One boy, who had seldom shared in class, brought me a six-foot silk scroll, saying, "My parents wanted you to have this poem." I thanked him, passed out the rubric, and set the timer for his performance. It was exemplary. Later, I realized that his flawless brushstroke characters rivaled a wall hanging that I had bought from a museum.

Joe, strangely quiet, escorted me on the bus each subsequent day. On the way to the new campus, I chattered about the busy time, filled with turning in grades skewed toward A's and B's that reflected effort by all students, except for one I had only just met. He had showed up for the oral final, sure that he would ace it with his charming English skills. I handed him his 20 percent, plus 0 percent for attendance, plus 0 percent for participation, and suggested that he should've dropped the class if he hadn't had the time to bless us with his presence all semester. Irony seemed lost on his street-language understanding. I didn't care if Joe, listening to all this, "got it" or not. Neither the student nor Dean Joe presented any argument.

At the end of finals week, with the last grades submitted, I finally descended from the teacher's bus and went up to my penthouse to sit in silence for my final hour there. I did not plan to return, and packing didn't take long: my ice-cold passport, the artistic scroll gift, and my Disney PJs and clothing items. I left the apricot robe, fancy swimwear, stylish jeans, and blingy tee for the maid, along with a wad of yuan.

Then I took a bus across to my old campus apartment. It was like rediscovering a familiar stomping ground. Crowding onto the bus, I inserted my coins, and a youngster offered me a seat. We drove through honking traffic, and then I stepped off the bus, receiving a *"Nihau"* from the campus guard.

I went straight to Joe's old office and knocked on the open door. There was no entourage to be seen. Just Joe, sitting at his desk, hunched over some papers.

"Joe, it's Regina. Do you have a minute?"

He straightened like a reverse bolt of lightning, his face lighting up as he hurried toward me. "Come in, Dr. Blakely." He looked up and down the corridor, then closed his door.

I looked at his desk and saw a thick envelope lying there, stamped with China Air's logo (written in Chinese). "Tell me what this means, Joe."

His inner rooster preened just a little. "I have important friends, Regina. It is a gift from Pei Hua. When I asked him, the Education Dean agreed that you need to go to your homeland."

Then his puffed-up feathers collapsed. "On the other hand, it is also bad news. I have no time to accompany you. Here is your ticket. You leave next Saturday. I have learned much from you, dear Regina. I regret that our arrangement can no longer be honored. I hope to meet again when you return to China."

Yes, assuming I make use of the return portion of the ticket, which I don't expect I ever will.

And then that was that!

My next impulse was to ask how long he'd been calling Matt. But almost as quickly, I decided that smart rabbits kept quiet and took grateful advantage whenever and wherever such was given. One curious question niggled at me though.

"Joe, may I ask where my passport was all those times I was frantic without it? And how you obtained this plane ticket without it?"

He preened again. "The Sofitel desk held your passport, Regina, as is often customary in China's more privileged hotels. I instructed the driver to take care of your luggage and present them with your passport on the day you moved in. You didn't know that Pei Hua has had a copy of your passport since you arrived, Regina? They arranged your travels in that way. Do you remember my telling you that China observes, copies, and makes what they see even better?"

Better for whom? I wondered.

As I turned to go, I stifled a quick urge to tell Joe that at least one company in America was coming out with an Oatica Soy product, promoted by a cute little beastie named Oata.

I'll leave that to the politicians to sort out. Joke or not.

"*Shei shei,* Joe," I said sincerely then.

He didn't stop me from leaving, with my precious ticket for the proper Montana airport clutched tightly in my hand. I realized then that, perhaps, I shouldn't have thanked him, since he was probably only doing the best job he could "for the Motherland."

I hurried to the bus stop and crossed XiAn for my last meal with the Dong family. Dong Mai was solemn, then brightened. "Dong Liu will surely be accepted at a university in Canada soon. You will be neighbors! You can visit." I assured her that I would do so, ate one more beef dumpling, and then hurried across town by bus.

The next day's telephoned goodbyes were bittersweet, with Fu Lin, Miss Zhang, Maria, Gao, Lucy, Luna, Bobo, Emily, and Willow presuming I'd soon be back, not even suspecting the finality I felt around leaving Pei Hua. I wrote Qian a heartfelt note of gratitude for her help and enclosed another sealed note to the Dean of Education, full of gratitude for my teaching experience and firmly declaring that I would not be returning there—though without ever stating the real reason. Mary's call was more celebratory, knowing that I could see her stateside once I was back in Kansas.

Using my apartment's blue washer one last time, I left most of my clothing to dry for whomever came next. My suitcase was filled with mementos and gifts. Locking both my doors for the final time, I snatched up my ringing cellphone, and yelled, *"Wei?"*

"Dr. B," Matt said quickly, "I just lost my job."

"I'm sorry," I said, surprised. "I hope it wasn't because of me."

"Oh no. As I told you, you were a great help to the Secretary. I actually resigned, tired of politics and ready to broaden my experience. I'm moving on! I've applied to teach ESL in China! And it's all because of you! I wanted you to know, Dr. B."

The anger I'd felt toward this naive kid, trying to climb the political ladder in DC, all but evaporated at these words. He, too, had just been doing his job, probably never understanding just how abandoned I'd felt.

All I could think of to say was a heartfelt, "Good luck, Matt!" before leaving to catch my airport ride.

Once on the plane, I worked to put together my thoughts as I separated chopsticks for the airline meal that had been placed in front of me. I was leaving China with vivid memories. So many dear faces were indelibly stamped on my consciousness, where they would remain for years to come. Joe's face would stand out clearly above all the rest.

Recognizable Mandarin tones pounded my ears with announcements about passenger safety. I followed the gist of the "in case of emergency" speech this trip. Life in China had taught me patience, broadened my perspectives, and brought deep gratefulness for much that I'd had no idea even existed.

What lay ahead of me once I landed in what I'd once held fast as "my country" was a mystery for now. But what I *did* know, as I headed west, was that I'd find opportunities there for still more new experiences that I'd yet to even dream about.

PARTIAL LIST OF SOURCES, CHINA CONUNDRUM

Baker, Aryn/Mbar Toubab "The Great Green Wall of Africa" Time, September 23, 2019, 44-49.

Ball, Jeffrey "China's Electric Car Showdown" Fortune, April 1, 2019, 24-27.

Barrett, Eamon "Milking Oats for China", Fortune, August, 2019, 37-38.

Campbell, Charlie "Hong Kong's Uprising Rattles the Mainland" Time, July 1, 2019.

"China: Keeping Tabs" The Economist, March 30, 2019, 47-48.

Cipriani, Jason "An Updated Waste Bin" Time December 2-9, 2019, 100.

Dolin, Eric Jay (Liveright) When America First Met China

The Conversation: "Why John Mearsheimer is Right" The Atlantic, April, 2012, 13-14.

"The Fight for Our Faces" Time, December 2-9, 2019.

Interview with Lin and Guan, April, 2008.

Fortner, Virginia. Journal, June 6, 2010.

Google Time Converter, World Wide Web (6 pm in US is 9:00 a.m. the previous day across China)

"Shovel-Ready" Hoey, Peter and Maria, Mike Ives, Sierra 105:1, January/February 2020, 30-31, 49-50.

Kaplan, Robert D "Why John J. Mearsheimer is Right" The Atlantic, January/February 2012.

Kingston, Maxine Hong The Woman Warrior, NY: Vintage International, 1975

Murphy, Cullen "Torturer's Apprentice" The Atlantic, January/February, 2012, 72-77.

"Letter from China: The Love Business, With the country's new freedoms, choosing a mate has become ever more complicated." The New Yorker, May 14, 2012, 76-89.

Luo, Michael. "How the Chinese Changed the Gold Rush" The New Yorker, August 30, 2021, 65-69.

Osnos, Evan. "Letter from China: Green Giant, Beijing's Crash Program for Clean Energy" The New Yorker, December 21 & 28, 2009, 54-63.

Osnos, Evan. "Letter from China: Boss Rail, the Disaster That Exposed the Underside of the Boom", The New Yorker, October 22, 2012, 46-53.

"Prologue: American Icon", Smithsonian May 2020, 7-9.

See, Lisa. Peony in Love (Random House) 2007.

See, Lisa. Snow Flower and the Secret Fan (Random House)

"Special Report: China, Unknown Soldiers" The Economist, November 11, 2023, 3-12.

"Special Report: China, Bogged Down" The Economist, November 11, 2023, 33-36.

"Spirit of the Pits" The Economist, February 2, 2019, 35-36.

Viviano, Frank "China's Great Armada" National Geographic insert

Yardley, Jim (Knopf) 2008. Brave Dragons.

Zhou, Raymond. "My Big Fat BJ Wedding" China Daily, April 9, 2009, 19.

ABOUT THE AUTHOR

Virginia Fortner is the author of *At the Edge* (2012) and, with Mike Eaten, *A Design of His Own* (2018). Her poems and short stories have been published in writers' journals like *Latitudes*, magazines, newspapers like the *Kohala Mountain News*, and several book collections. A lifetime educator and traveler who has spent time on every continent, Virginia taught ESL in China for four years. She is a reader and book club enthusiast, a musician, an outrigger paddler, a plein air painter, a gardener, and a lover of people, with a PhD for which she studied creative thinking. Virginia lives at the northern tip of Hawaii's Big Island.

www.ingramcontent.com/pod-product-compliance
Lightning Source LLC
LaVergne TN
LVHW040431190425
808957LV00003B/11